Deceived

LENA MOORE

Deceived is a work of fiction. Names, characters, and incidents are the products of the author's imagination and are either fictitious or are used fictitiously. Any resemblance to actual events or persons, living or dead, is entirely coincidental.

If you purchased this book without a cover, you should be aware that this book may have been stolen property and reported as "unsold and destroyed" to the publisher. In such case, neither the publisher nor the author has received payment for this "stripped book."

ISBN 13: 978-0-6484876-4-7

Cover art by Art and Edit/Janet Durbin
Editing by Janet Durbin

ACKNOWLEDGEMENTS

Well here we are again. I swear writing the acknowledgements stress me out more than writing the book at times because I don't want to forget anyone! So if I do, just know I have baby mum brain and I'm sorry! Hearts, you all!

First and foremost, I have to thank each and every reader out there who has picked up this book, or any of my books, and taken a chance on me. I'm forever humbled and I have so much gratitude for all. Reading the reviews you guys leave helps me become a better writer/author. Thank you. You are all rock stars.

To my husband... What can I say that I haven't already? You're fucking amazing and your patience and love for me doesn't go unnoticed. You're my rock, my forever after. Thank you for believing in me. I love you.

To my now three boys! Mama loves you all. Without you three I'm only a shadow of who I am. You complete me.

To my Teta Linda. You have been my one constant since I was a child. Your love, support and guidance has helped shape me. If it wasn't for you and Uncle Toohey, I fear where I could have ended up. I love you more!

To my sister Abby and my cousin Jess... You two are absolutely crazy, but I love your beautiful asses. Don't let anyone dim your light or dull your sparkle. You are perfect the way you are.

Teta Helena, thank you for being in my life, reading my dirty words and giving me feedback after it. I love and appreciate you more than you'll ever know.

To my sinful ladies: Sue, Mel and Megan. Thank you all for your continued support, thoughts and ideas. Without the three of you offering me your opinions, I think I'd be rocking back and forth in the corner still procrastinating and laughing manically.

An extra special thanks to Megan for taking the time out and beta reading this book. You are a God damn life saver ! Hearts you xx

To my editor and cover designer, Janet Durbin. I am so thankful our paths collided and that I not only found a kick ass editor but also a friend for life. Your artistic talent and editorial skills never cease to amaze me. Without you, none of this would be possible. You rock!

And last but certainly not least, to the boys from the band Repriever. Thank you so much for allowing me to use your kickass lyrics in my book! It definitely made the scene with Draven more intense! You can find this upcoming metal band over at **https://linktr.ee/repriever**. Show them some love !

To every single person out there on Instagram, Facebook and any other platform who has been following me since the beginning and supporting me throughout this journey of mine. You know who you are and you know I think you're amazing! Thank you from the bottom of my cold, black heart (**insert evil laugh**).

Until next time... Keep it classy with a touch of nasty.

Some of the music I rocked out with while writing this book:

DevilDriver - Keep Away From Me

Bleed from within - End of All We Know

Corey Taylor- Black Eyes Blue

Eva Under Fire - Heroin

Grey Daze - Morei Sky

In This Moment - Beautiful Tragedy

For The Fallen Dreams - Unstoppable

Fire From The Gods - Voiceless

Trivium - What The Dead Man Say

DevilDriver - Dealing With Demons

Make Them Suffer - The Attendant

Repriever - Grim

Other books by Lena Moore

Other books by Lena Moore

Glossary of Terms

Transotic - A form of magic that vampires use to control and manipulate humans and other beings. Similar to compulsion

Irrevensvia - This word spoken will have a mortal do whatever the vampire intends, or simply forget what had transpired between them. It all depends on what the vampire desires at the time.

Revensivia – Reverses the compulsion and state the vampire placed the human under.

Revive – To turn another into a vampire. The person must possess supernatural properties and descend from vampire linage.

Purgatory – Similar to Hell, but worse. Home of the Dark Goddess, Neferity.

The Enchantment – Similar to Heaven. Home of the Light Goddess, Kaltemis.

Nowhere – A realm where the damned and corrupted Otherworlders souls go, usually souls that were pure but have done something irreparable. These souls cannot find their way to The Enchantment or to Purgatory.

Sometimes the darkness is too delicious to resist, and slowly but surely, without really knowing, we submit. All it takes is that little coveted need for us to welcome the darkness inside and fully commit...

– Lena Moore

Chapter One

A black sludge-like substance dripped off the atramentous walls. She scoffed, eyeing the weeping mess from the remnants of the dead. The remaining disposable demons and other beings implored for her mercy as she stepped off the jagged metal throne. She really should have decided on a more comfortable seat, but that was the least of her concerns right now.

Snickering with disgust, she pushed her long, silky, onyx coloured hair over her naked shoulders while her bare feet slapped on the black lava stone floor. She ambled down the narrow vestibule and felt most powerful when she wore nothing but the flesh she lived in; clothes were not required in purgatory. The one thing she refused to remove was the obsidian ring around her finger.

Her consort was leaning on a succubus, causing her jealousy to spike. She had gone through enough shit obtaining the dark angel, not that Kohl would ever remember what transpired. Today was not the day to dwell on that sinister time, though.

Wrenching Kohl off Lilice's shoulder, she pulled him down nearly a foot so her lips clashed with his full pair. How she loved those fucking lips. He pulled back and smirked at her.

"What is it, my love?" he teased.

She peered into his fierce blue hues filled with curiosity and lust as they blinked back at her. *It's both a blessing and a curse that he will never know who he truly is,* she thought to herself. She would do everything in her power to prevent Kohl from finding out because the rift it would cause would be diabolical, not to mention the affliction that

would undeniably come along with it. No, this was not something she was ready to deal with, not today, not ever.

Her thoughts returned to the here and now and trepidation bled through her veins at the thought of Kohl in that harlot's bed entwined and magically bound to the succubus. She wouldn't have it.

Placating her mind, she replied nonchalantly, "Nothing, Seraph." She addressed him by his nickname. "I only despise the way that succubus eyes you. You are mine."

His rough hand reached up, brushing along her jawline whilst he gazed into her dark eyes. "It shall always be you, my love. Always."

If only that were true, she thought sadly. There was a piece of him inside that was void, a piece that she could never reach. That piece of his soul, his heart was with the one person she abhorred with every molecule of her being. *She will never get him back,* Neferity bickered with herself internally.

Snapping her out of her tumultuous ruminations, she felt Kohl's fingers brushing across her peaked nipples. Neferity hissed and leaned into him, unconcerned by the many eyes watching them. It wasn't the first time they'd fucked in front of an audience, and it certainly wouldn't be the last. Kohl was hers and she made sure every single Otherworlder knew that.

"Only you, always you," he whispered before latching his teeth onto her darken nipple.

Neferity threw her head back, moaning, then reached down to stroke his growing erection. All that stood between them was a pair of jeans he chose to wear daily. She hated those fucking things.

Lilice stood behind Neferity and stroked her long hair. The succubus was feeding off hers and Kohl's lechery. She could have that, but she would never have her Dark Angel.

Looking at her through hooded eyes, Kohl lowered himself to the floor. Neferity refused to acknowledge or lay eyes upon the branding that was not of her doing. She averted her eyes and pushed his head down lower.

The hall was filled with every Otherworlder imagined, all flocking to watch the spectacle that was their Goddess being fucked. Demons, succubus's, incubuses, mortals, and every other dark creature that lived in the shadows formed a circle around them so they could leech off of their power and lust.

A cracking sound filed to the left of her, gaining her attention. The breach in the wards was hot and loud as Efah and Gorgon tumbled through the gates of purgatory, flanked with the two mortal demon lackeys. Her eyes landed momentarily on Gorgon's vibrant red irises before shifting away, focusing on anything but him and the magnetism that thrummed recklessly between them.

Neferity shimmied away from Kohl hoping he couldn't sense the exchange. The other beings cleared out of her way as she stormed toward the duo that had undeniably snuffed her moment. Whatever it was that brought this pair back, it probably wasn't good.

No Otherworlder could make their way back to Purgatory once they inhibited a host. They were trapped in whichever realm until their expiration, although Efah and Gorgon were an exception to the rule. Their abilities and sinister edge were welcomed inside the gates of Purgatory. Efah, for once in her forsaken life, had the decency to bow at her feet. Gorgon on the other hand all but ate her up.

She knew what she was getting herself into when she involved him in her little plan without cluing him in on the end game.

Still, he was loyal to her. But Neferity sensed he was anticipating Kohl's demise. She didn't blame him. Hell, she teased him and drew him in with every piece of dark magic she possessed. She needed him, and he knew it.

That was a perk of being a Dark Goddess. Neferity could do whatever she liked and no one dared question her. If anyone did, they bled out of their eye sockets, painfully, or something to that extent.

Kohl wasn't aware of her indiscretions. It was paramount the secret remained exactly that, a secret. Thankfully, Gorgon didn't question her or allow his tongue to flap around in the decrepit breeze in purgatory. Their agreement was theirs, one only the two of them knew.

Breaking away from her deliberation, she stared down at Efah's dark as night hair and demanded, "What did you do? Where is the girl?"

She lifted her face and Neferity saw her red eyes rimmed in amethyst and black were more prominent than when she left Purgatory. Efah stammered, "They – she got away."

Frustration and ire poured off her after hearing those words. The waves emitted were full force, causing the others to slink back into the shadows.

"What do you mean she got away? Do you realise what you've done? How are we to fulfil..." her sentence ran off and her once honeyed voice altered into one only she'd recognise.

Tied to you, tied to me, our essence eternally bound
The dark, the light, Aliyah, must be found!
Slinking in the shadows, Dark Goddess you must be proud
Otherworlders, demons, shifters, Gods alike, bend the knee so we can end this drought...

Neferity closed her eyes and summoned as much magic as possible to push the voice from her mind. When the inflection ceased to exist, she opened her dark, ruby red eyes, only to realise her head was foggy. Neferity peered around the crowded hall and noticed every entity watching on with curiosity.

"LEAVE ME!" she boomed. The hall scattered rapidly, leaving only the company fixed in place she wanted to slowly annihilate. All bar Kohl.

"Tell me everything, and don't miss a single fucking syllable. Unless you wish to be nothing more than ash by the time this conversation is over."

~ Draven ~

"He's not responding!" Draven bellowed out in the back of the car as Dolph took a turn for the worst.

"We need to call on the Warlock, Draven. He is our blood, please!" Laney cried out.

The pain in his side from the diamond dagger was stinging like a bitch and Laney's words slapped him in the face. He'd forgotten all about the mad Warlock, Reikiki. Draven realised it was their only chance at saving his best friend. He only hoped Jadis and Reikiki could forge their magic and heal Dolph quickly.

"Dany, change of plans. Head to Bienville Street. I'll direct you from there," Draven yelled.

Draven turned toward Jadis; he noticed she'd remained quiet since they'd left the fight with Efah and Gorgon. Her hands never wavered from Dolph's body as she attempted to heal him.

The Bel Air was filled to the brim with melancholy and nervous energy. Aliyah looked forward out the windshield, her body rigid and jaded, the pain and deception she'd recently experienced palpable.

His attention turned back to Jadis. She let out a heavy breath, and said, "He's stable. I–I can't reach him though. It's like, fuck, I don't know. Just get me to Reikiki now!" She barked out Reikiki's address in the process.

With a nod of his head, Dany floored the Bel Air. Draven's mind trailed off, thinking, *what has the Mad Warlock been up to lately*? He hoped he'd have his wits about him because they were going to need them.

Terracotta coloured stone walls breached his vision as Dany swung the car into the parking spot allocated for Reikiki's apartment.

Piling out of the 57, Draven wrenched Dolph over his shoulder and took the stairs two at a time, with the rest of the crew following closely behind.

Laney stepped in front of Draven, panting, then opened the door to her uncle's apartment. Draven knew not to attempt it. If Reikiki's magic sensed any ill intent or the person trying to enter didn't bare his blood, the intruder would be set alight, disintegrated at his door step.

Once Laney stepped over the threshold, Draven followed behind her knowing it was safe to do so.

"What is the meaning of this," the Mad Warlock's voice rang out.

"Uncle, we need your help. It's Dolph. He was hit by dark magic and Jadis can't reverse it."

Draven placed Dolph on the multi-coloured lounge as Reikiki rounded the corner with an alcoholic beverage in

toe. He could smell it from where he stood. It was that potent.

He noticed his tiger coloured eyes manically searching
the living room. The beads in his silver tousled hair were
recklessly placed all over his scalp as he pulled on his
equally silver goatee. He wore similar clothes to the last
time Draven saw him: a hippy looking tunic shirt with
matching pants, the white breaking up the colours that
fiercely matched his eyes.

"I see you've brought the whole damn crew, child.
Move, all of you. Except you Jadis, I may need you." He
pulled his tunic sleeves up revealing the ink inscribed on
his body from the Goddess's.

Reikiki wasn't a terrible Otherworlder, although like
Draven, Neferity had sunk her claws in a time or two. He
shook the thought from his mind and watched on, his anxiety thrumming relentlessly through his veins.

Jadis moved with confidence. Her back was straight
and her head held high even though Draven knew she was
depleted beyond measure.

Reikiki placed his hands over Dolph's body and hissed.
"Damnation! What have you all been up to? The darkness
is burrowing itself deep inside his soul." His nose screwed
up, he coughed then continued. "The stench coming off all
of you is deplorable."

The way Reikiki's eyes lingered on Aliyah didn't go unnoticed to Draven. He only hoped it was out of sheer curiosity and not something the Mad Warlock had seen.

He pulled Aliyah under his arm as if to show the man
she was his. He smirked before returning to whatever he
was doing on Dolph. *Asshole.*

Aliyah melted into his arms. Her body relaxed while
they observed the magic Reikiki elicited with his hands.
Beads of sweat trickled down the Warlock's brow, his body
quaking ever so slightly before he reached and grasped
Jadis's hand.

Reikiki's head flew back, revealing the luminous waxen
coloured hue his eyes had taken on. His breathing was
ratcheted as he spoke. "I–I need–damn it–I just need a
little more magic, Jadis, please. It's terribly dark in here."

What was he talking about? Was he inside of Dolph?

Draven wasn't going to question him; he didn't want to disturb any progress the Warlock may have made. Jadis's magic pulsated between her hands to Reikiki's, the once animated bronze now dull and jaded.

Reikiki chanted, his hands flying rapidly over Dolph's body as he siphoned as much of Jadis's magic as he could. Jadis seemed to be in pain as she hunched over holding her hand to her stomach. Draven removed his arm from Aliyah and placed his hand on her shoulder.

"Take what you can from me. I fear you're about to collapse from exhaustion, J."

She tried to smile up at him. Her green eyes clouded from depletion before she moved her hand from her belly and placed it over Draven's. As soon as her hand touched his, he knew it wasn't working.

"Fuck—it's not... I can't, D."

"The boy!" Reikiki's voice rang out. "You need the boy with the dark hair," he heaved.

Dany looked confused. "Me? Why do you need me?"

"Get your ass over here now!" Reikiki called out once more.

Draven stepped away as Dany took his place. Jadis's hand rested on his and then she inhaled deeply. The shock on her face was evident. *What. The. Fuck?*

Jadis's skin was no longer pallid. Instantly, her flesh took on that rich chocolate colour and her eyes shined that brilliant forest green. She stared up at Dany in bewilderment. "How?"

"It does not matter, Witch. Focus, we are nearly done," Reikiki vowed.

Aliyah snatched his hand, and he knew her face mirrored his: shock, curiosity and awe. "What is happening," she hissed, "how is Dany doing that?"

Draven only had one answer for her question. Dany had to be an Otherworlder. He grounded himself before responding and inhaled harshly, attempting to weed out all the scents in the room. He still couldn't smell Aliyah and figured she must be ensconcing her scent because Draven figured Jadis's cloaking spell would have worn off of by now.

His eyebrows pinched together when the dark, earthy

undertone slapped him in the face. He grimaced, then drew back. How had he missed it before? Undeniably, Dany was a supernatural being. Exactly what he was, was yet to be determined.

Aliyah tugged on his shirt, imploring that he explain what was going on. This was not the time or space for this conversation. "Snowflake, enough. I'll tell you later."

She pouted, crossed her arms across her bosom, and then turned away from him. Draven didn't have time for her theatrics. For fuck sakes, his best friend was almost fucking dead!

Reikiki fell backward and landed in a heap on his ass. "He's—how can I say this? He's stuck."

"Stuck?" they all said in unison.

"Dolph is in limbo. He's neither here nor there," Reikiki responded.

"What does that even mean, Uncle?" Laney questioned.

"It means Dolph is stuck between realms. He's not dead. However, there is a shit load of unfinished business he's packing. He's stranded between this plane, Purgatory and The Enchantment. *Something* is anchoring him there, a malignant entity of some sort. For the moment he's safe," Reikiki assured everyone.

Poignancy engulfed the room as everyone looked down at Dolph, with his black and silver hair hanging messily across his face. Gazing down at his best friend, Draven realised Dolph looked tranquil. He wondered how the fuck that could be possible when he was trapped god knows where.

Turning away, he moped around the Mad Warlock's home. Draven was irritable and his veins felt as if razor blades were sluicing him from the inside out.

He scratched his arms and walked away from the crew, attempting to focus on anything but the searing pain screaming through his body.

He felt his eyes dilate and his cock harden when the familiar dark truffle chocolate and whiskey scent assaulted his nostrils. *Snowflake. Aliyah, mine!*

Draven stalked toward her oblivious to the crowd around them. Her lust bloomed and her arousal spilled out.

She was turned on.

He felt maddened, reckless. *How long has it been since I fed?* Wrapping his hand around her wrist, he yanked her toward him and devoured her mouth. She tasted like sin and every damn wet dream you could imagine.

Pulling back from the kiss, he panted, "We must take our leave. Reikiki, I will be in touch. And Jadis, call me if you need anything."

With that statement hanging in the air, he sped back to the Bel Air, threw her in the car, and gunned it down the street.

Draven was famished, starved like he hadn't fed and fucked in days. He eyed her from his peripheral and noticed her thighs rubbing together. Instantly, he knew Aliyah was hankering for him, too. She was turned on, and as the recognition bled through his veins, he knew it was time for them to take their fill.

Chapter Two

~ Aliyah ~

He wasn't driving fast enough and her legs were chafing together, trying to relieve the unrelenting tension that burned within her core. How could she possibly be thinking about sex and blood when her life was in shambles?

Draven parked the car behind Jadis's shop, and before she knew it they were standing in his underground lair. Considering everything they'd experienced tonight, Aliyah was surprised the lair was exactly as they left it. She found it peculiar how so much could happen in a small space of time, yet down here it remained untouched, untainted. Aliyah felt at home.

The plum purple walls seemed as if they were welcoming their arrival, or maybe that was her arousal and blood lust taking front and center.

Draven tossed her over his shoulder and ran through the house until he reached the door with the lock. Immediately, she was giddy.

There was no time for formalities. Draven was hankering for her, his scent palpable as the intoxicating sandalwood, musky chocolate smell obliterated her senses.

He threw her down on the rustic four poster bed, ripped her clothes from her body, and shackled her to the bed. She squirmed and wriggled on the black silk sheets, lusting for him, but all he did was watch her with his long and delicious looking canines on full display.

Aliyah mewled and jutted her hips toward the ceiling,

causing Draven to chuckle low and dark. "Such an avaricious little thing, aren't we Snowflake."

"Then don't fucking tease me!" she exclaimed.

Unbuttoning his pants, he toed out of them at an excruciating slow pace. Aliyah wished she was free so she could lend a hand.

Biting her lip, her eyes found his mismatched pair. The red and amethyst had darkened, yet they still looked as sinful and beautiful as ever.

His mouth kicked up at the sides, forming that panty dropping grin, then he slid down between her thighs and nibbled them.

"What do you want, Snowflake? Tell me," he leered.

Her eyes zoned in on his jugular vein before lowering until she reached his angry looking erection. The head of his cock was red and purple where his piercing sat, and Aliyah knew he was affected more than he was letting on.

"I need you. All of you. Please."

She stared into his hooded eyes while he continued to pepper kisses up her thighs closer and closer to her promised land, but still not giving her what she wanted.

Aliyah groaned loudly in frustration. Her eyes turn into slits as she daggered him, which only caused him to laugh throatily against her sex.

One languid lick from her asshole to her clit was all it took for her ass to leave the bed and her fangs to lengthen.

Aliyah cried out in pleasure, "More, I need more."

"Soon baby, soon." He thrust two fingers inside her, hooking them up toward that squidgy thing inside her pussy, that delicious g-spot.

She keened out as her body left the bed once again while she watched him from under heavy lidded eyes. Aliyah needed to touch him, to feel him under her caress, but those damn restraints were tethered to her wrists.

Draven intentionally avoided her clit. Instead, he indolently plunged his fingers in and out of her now dripping cunt. Aliyah could hear the sloshy sounds her kitty was making, and if she wasn't so turned on she would have been embarrassed. Except now she was irked and desperately searching for that release.

Aliyah's head fell backward and to the side, her body

on fire with the pent up sexual frustration Draven was bestowing on her. She attempted to deviate her mind and focus on the deep red room full of all Draven's sexual contraptions. Alas, it didn't work.

Her body reached octane level as the images of their first time in his shameless fuck room took precedence in her mind, playing on repeat like a broken record.

"Fuck. Your scent, it's inebriating. You have no idea what you do to me, Snowflake," he growled.

Aliyah's head snapped back to focus on her vampire, because he was undeniably hers, and no fucking demon wench would come between them. Damn it, she needed to push that bitch Melantha from her mind. She would get hers.

Draven nibbled on her thigh, applying a little pressure but not enough to break the skin. "What just happened," he questioned as he pulled away from her and slammed his fingers in harder than before.

"Nothing—nothing," she panted.

"Do not lie to me! Are we going to need the safe-word tonight, Aliyah? You do remember it, don't you?"

Ruby, she mused to herself. Aliyah hesitated because she didn't want to confess what was running through her head, especially when Draven's face was painfully close to her pussy. However, she knew if she didn't fess up, Draven would make her a blubbering mess until she did.

"Fine. I was thinking about that slut, Melantha, and how you are mine and not hers."

Something flashed behind his eyes before the blinding smile filled his handsome stubbled face. "You're jealous." He didn't let her reply. Instead, he fingered Aliyah harder, rougher, twisting his digits inside of her, making her wish it was his cock and not his damn fingers.

Aliyah wailed out, her possessive streak front and center as she remembered that vampires were supposed to have intense strength, and for fuck sakes she was a faery, vampire and a demon.

Yanking on her restraints, she groaned in protest until the shackles shattered. Draven smirked up at her, mischief and arousal blooming in his irises while he eyed the tattered shackles.

"I was wondering how long it would take for you to realise you could destroy those."

Aliyah ran her hands through his mane of dreadlocks
and pushed his head down toward her swollen nub, knowing her violet hues were urging him to finish what he started.

"Just for the record, I'm doing this for me and not you."

That dominant streak was forever evident. Aliyah rolled
her eyes at his statement because she knew he was talking out his ass.

Her ruminations were interrupted as her body left the
mattress and it felt like he was performing a fucking exor-
cism on her. Back bent, legs still shackled, she drove her
hips up into his mouth then ground his head into her
snatch. Draven's tongue and fingers were all too eager to
meet her demand.

The talented muscular instrument in his mouth worked
her cunt recklessly and relentlessly, pushing her g-spot
closer to climax.

His cheeks hollowed out as he drew her clit into his
mouth. She was so close, so fucking close, yet not close
enough.

As if sensing her irritation, he abruptly pulled away
from her cunt, wrapped his free hand around his rigid
shaft, pumped his fist up and down, then sank his canines
into the flesh of her thigh, piercing her femoral artery.

The sight of him pleasuring himself as well as her sent
Aliyah's orgasm erupting with fury. Her body contorted
and her vision blurred whilst Draven took all she had to
offer.

The climax seemed to last forever, or perhaps it was
the many orgasms his fingers and mouth pulled from her
as he suckled from her artery.

It was her turn now. Aliyah used her strength to break
the ankle shackles and push Draven underneath her. As
she straddled him, his erection prodded in between her
wet folds before slipping in snugly.

They both moaned in unison. His palms found purchase on her hips, encouraging her to take what she
needed, and she did exactly that.

Aliyah took his mouth first, their tongues tangled deliciously while her hips undulated carelessly, fucking him rough and hard.

She felt him throbbing inside of her and knew he was close. Rocking back and forward erratically, Aliyah drew them closer to orgasm. When she realised how close he was, she sank her canines deep into his jugular, pulling on the crimson liquid.

She lapped at his throat, her tempo never slowing until they both came with a burst. Draven bellowed out then his teeth found her shoulder, spurring another orgasm from her.

The sweet, metallic plasma eradicated her senses. Aliyah hadn't noticed how starved she'd been until her body finally came back down to earth, bringing with it the rest of the issues they were dealing with.

Draven grasped her face with his index finger and thumb, then growled, "Don't. We have all the time in the fucking world to worry about that shit. Don't think about it now. Let us have this moment, please Snowflake."

She nodded once, signalling she understood and agreed. A lone tear slid down her ivory face and Draven swept it up with his tongue.

"Good, because I'm not finished with you yet."

The rest of the night went by in a blur and Aliyah lost count of how many orgasms and times they'd fucked by the end of it. She wasn't complaining though.

Stretching her weary body after waking, she rolled over in Draven's bed to find his side empty. Her stomach dropped. Something wasn't right.

Throwing on one of his shirts, she padded out of the room and down the hallway. There were voices coming from the kitchen, and one of them was from someone whom she despised: Melantha. It seemed the demon found a way to bypass the cloaking spell that Jadis had planted around the lair.

"I fucking told you! No more, Melantha! Our deal is off!"

Aliyah recalled the contract that was formulated all those years ago with Melantha. Draven lost a bet to her, and as a result the demon was able to feed off him, among other things. Her ruminations were disrupted by the demon's ear-piercing screech.

"We have a contract! A fucking contract! Don't you re-member? We sealed it in blood, Vampire."

Concealing her scent so neither of them would notice her presence, Aliyah watched on from the corner of the kitchen.

Draven scoffed, "As if I could forget. It has been some of the worst times in my existence!"

"Just give me a little bit. I–I need it."

That was Aliyah's cue. She barged into the kitchen and stood in front of the demon. Aliyah didn't care the cunt of a thing had at least a foot of height on her.

Her black and red hair flowed magnificently around her face, which only made Aliyah hate her all that much more.

"You. Can't. Have. Him. We are fucking bound. Don't you get it? Why can't you fuck off and leave us alone?"

Her black flecked amber eyes darted toward Draven before fixing on her. "Kid, you have no business here. This is between me and the vampire."

"You are so wrong." Aliyah felt her body heat up and when the demon gasped, she knew she was faery glowing again.

"What are you?" Melantha mused, and moved in closer.

"Do not touch me."

"You smell…" she inhaled the air. "You smell… different. Tasty." She licked her lips.

A guttural growl reverberated around the kitchen, the appliances quaking in place. "You stay the fuck away from her, Melantha. Know your place, demon."

She jeered, "You know there is only one other way you can forfeit the contract besides your demise, Draven. Tread carefully."

Delicately, she opened up her mind and hoped she could summon Draven to talk to her telepathically. The identical branding on her thigh seared beneath and he spoke,

"*Are you ok?*" his voice echoed in her mind.

"*What is she talking about? How can you sever the contract?*"

Aliyah heard his sigh in her head. "*We need to formu-late another contract. This contract is bound by blood, so if*

I kill her before the contract is finalised, I risk corrupting my soul and succumbing to my darkness. I'll also land my ass in Purgatory. Believe me, Aliyah, that's not somewhere I want to be."

"Ok. So what are our options? Can't I just kill her?"

"NO! We are bound; it's not worth the risk. It may see both of our souls damaged and fed to the slums of Purgatory. I need to–I need to trick her into entering another arrangement, somehow."

Aliyah severed the connection and closed the distance between her and Melantha. The demon's head canted to the side. She seemed curious and hungry.

She knew what she was about to do wouldn't bode well with Draven, but she had to try something, anything to rid this parasite from their lives. They had enough drama without her tantrums thrown in the midst.

Aliyah chewed on her lip for theatrics before running her finger down the demon's face. Although Melantha was beautiful to the eye, Aliyah sensed she was putrid to the core.

She repressed the shudder that was burgling up as Melantha's eyes glazed over with arousal. She smelled her lust and it was hideous.

"Make another contract, demon."

Her mellifluous laughed suffocated the room, "And what's in it for me?"

"If you make another contract with a possible out for Draven then I will allow you to feed from me, once."

"Absofuckinglutely not!" Draven's voice darkened with each syllable.

Aliyah turned and placed her index finger over his full lips. His tongue darted out to suck her digit into his mouth and her core contracted with the notion.

She withdrew her finger and pleaded with her eyes in hopes that he'd realise how much this meant to her, to them.

His jaw ticked, a tell she was familiar with now. "What are your terms, Melantha," he relented

"Oooohhh." She clapped her hands together like a giddy child. "Let me think about this for a minute."

The demon paced the kitchen exaggeratedly. It took

every ounce of Aliyah's composure to focus on the silver blade tiles above the black granite benches and appliances instead of ripping her hair out, or tearing Melantha apart.

The demon's face almost split into two when she looked back at her and Draven, her form wavering as Aliyah finally got a glimpse what was beneath the glamour and façade. Melantha was a repulsive and vile looking thing.

Black decaying skin hung from her form. Her amber hollowed out eyes devoured her body and this time Aliyah was unable to hide her disgust.

Melantha teetered, "I will enter into another agreement, but it won't be that easy to dispose of me, vampire. We have fifty years of history to adhere to." She shrugged the fallacy of her slender shoulders. "Five souls, Vampire. They will be corrupted in a sense; however, they can be re-deemed. All of our cards are on the table, Draven. My influence on the soul won't disadvantage you. Although you will need to guide the soul toward purity, so to speak. You are not to explain what you are doing, and your Otherworlder identity must remain covert. If the soul is indeed one of us, then you are still incapable of revealing why you're assisting them. Oh, and I get to taste her like she suggested."

Aliyah stood stoic in front of the demon, her violet hues to Melantha's amber pair. Deep inside, she was pissing her pants.

"The contract and then we will see to this taste," Aliyah spat.

"My, my, my, Draven, I see why you adore this little firecracker. Our previous contract will be severed. Whoever reaches three souls first wins, meaning my feeding days on you are finished. However, for each time you lose a soul, I'm allowed to take sustenance from you. This is not a negotiation. Do we have a deal vampire?" She lifted her too perfect eyebrow in question.

Aliyah wanted to slash that smug look off of Melantha's face, along with a few other things. What option did they have other than to take the deal? They couldn't risk Draven's soul or mind with everything that was going on around them. She had to believe in the Goddess Kaltemis; things would work out. They had to.

Turning toward Draven, Aliyah read the hesitation in

his body language and she knew he wasn't sure, but this was his only out. *Come on, how difficult could it be to save a few souls?* She wondered to herself.

She laced her hand with his and noticed the demon's eyes linger on them momentarily before resuming her façade once more. Something flickered in those eerie amber eyes, something she couldn't put her finger on.

Draven squeezed her hand and spoke, "I have one other stipulation. Any invitation or loophole that allows you access to my domain stops now. After this contract is sealed, if you enter my lair the contract is off, meaning I am free to kill you and maintain my mind as it is."

Can he do that? Does Draven have that much power over this demon?

Melantha sucked in her cheek and chewed on it. She seemed to be contemplating his request. Clapping her hands, she squealed, "Deal!"

Out of nowhere a scroll of some sort appeared, hovering in front of her. The black and red mist pulsated around the piece of paper before Draven plucked it from the air.

Aliyah witnessed his eyes gazing over the contract and she figured he was making sure Melantha hadn't been deceptive in her words.

"Aliyah, bite into my wrist."

Instantly, her canines elongated and the familiar heat in her belly flourished. She should feel embarrassed by the way Melantha eyed her with what she thought was disdain, but she wasn't. It amped her on.

Aliyah grasped Draven's hand and licked his palm. Her eyes moved back to Melantha's as she sunk her teeth into his flesh. Draven's sweet, peppery plasma filled her mouth causing her to moan, and it wasn't theatrics. His blood was like fine wine that had been aged for eons; it tasted divine.

"Enough." Melantha's tone came out in a hiss. That's when Aliyah noticed her forked tongue. *Ew, gross.*

"Sign the contract before I change my terms," she demanded.

Draven lifted his shoulders in a shrugging motion and a mirthless smile graced his sexy face. "Whatever you say, demon."

What was he playing at? Aliyah wondered what was on

the line and where it would leave them if they lost a soul to Melantha. Could she handle the demon feeding from Draven in a bountiful way?

Draven scooped up some of the crimson liquid with his finger and signed the magic ridden contract. Horripilation broke out over Aliyah's body; she could sense the darkness emitting from it.

Aliyah watched as Melantha mirrored Draven's motion and signed her name into the contract, then it disappeared into the nothingness.

"It's done," Melantha advised. "Now let me have a taste of this sweet little blood bag."

Draven tutted. "Stay away from her, demon. You don't have my consent."

"I don't need it; we had a deal."

He chortled loudly. Aliyah's eyebrows hiked up in surprise as she eyed him. "She is bound to me and she is my mate. So yes, you do need my consent. However, that's not the only reason you can't feed from her; it wasn't in the contract."

Melantha shrieked, "You tricked me!"

"No, it was merely an oversight on your behalf. The contract did state that you were no longer allowed in my lair. So if you'd kindly leave and let the door hit you on the way out..."

"This isn't over, Vampire. I'll be in touch." An ominous red mist hissed around her, sounding like snakes, then she disappeared.

Aliyah stood there gawking at the fading red mist until Draven hauled her into his arms and grunted, "That was incredibly stupid, naïve, and oh so insanely fucking hot." He ground his hard length into the back of her, and she moaned.

"Shrek, come on. We have so much to figure out. Dolph, this prophecy..." her speech was cut short as Draven enveloped her mouth with his.

"First, we fuck and feed again. Then we save the world," he mumbled between kisses.

Who was she to object?

Chapter Three

~ Draven ~

Draven emerged from the shower feeling satiated in more ways than one, with a towel draped around his neck and one loosely hanging from his waist.

Aliyah simpered at him while pulling up the faded black ripped jeans she'd chosen for the day, looking stunning as usual. Her long tousled raven hair hung loosely over her shoulders and down her back. Draven had to turn away from her before he decided that saving his best friend and the world wasn't as good an idea.

Distracting himself from Aliyah, he called out, "I'm just going to ring Jadis and find out if they're at Reikiki's."

Draven didn't wait for her response. He extracted his phone from his pocket and dialled Jadis's number.

"Hey baby, you good? You left in a hurry last night." He heard the tease in her tone.

"I'm good, J. Are you still at the Mad Warlock's house with Dolph?"

"Yeah, he's set up a room for the three of us."

"The three of you?"

"Yeah. Dany, Dolph and myself. Long story, I'll explain when you get here. Oh, and did you know about Dany?"

"I should have. I noticed a scent but I guess Aliyah's cockblocked me," he laughed.

"It would seem that way." She joined in on the laughter. "I'll see you soon, and I'll let Reikiki know you're returning." She hesitated. "I think he's been having visions all night."

Draven didn't want to think about his visions. He said his goodbyes and dressed so they could head out. A pair of black jeans, a navy blue trivium shirt, wax in his treads and he was done.

He and Aliyah traversed the short distance to Jadis's shop. When they reached her store front, they stopped abruptly. Bright red paint was sloshed across the window.

The revelation is in motion and none of you can stop us now!

"Fuck," Draven hissed and fished his phone out of his pocket to take a picture, then he called the local cleaning crew. This day was going to be tedious. He sensed it in the air.

Grounding himself, he focused all his energy to see if he could find a lead on who the culprit was. Jada, Gwent, and another dark entity were the scents he picked up.

Instead of hanging around for the cleaner, they hopped in the Bel Air and drove toward Reikiki's. Something told Draven they were about to uncover more than they'd bargained.

They took the flight of stairs to his apartment and waited at the elaborate timber door. The damn thing was beautiful with unique carvings embedded within, but deadly. Draven explained to Aliyah what could happen if his sorceress door believed them to have ill intent.

The door flew open and Reikiki stood there, head canted to the side as his tiger coloured eyes roamed the pair of them.

"Hmmm, your energy, it's intense. And it's all so enamouring." Snapping out of his trance he stepped to the side and continued, "Well, come on in you two. We don't have all day."

Aliyah peered at him from the corner of her eye in question, and he smirked then shrugged, walking over the threshold into the Mad Warlock's lair.

Draven took Aliyah's hand into his and began walking down the corridor, but Reikiki stopped them.

"You do realise what you have is extremely rare, tentative, potentially dangerous and yet somehow so beautiful?"

"Huh?" Aliyah responded.

"You don't know how special you are, do you child? And Draven, I always expected your rising, your magic is astounding."

Draven and Aliyah looked at each other awkwardly. *What the fuck is the Mad Warlock on about now?* He hadn't realised he'd tapped into their telepathic link until Aliyah responded; their branding and bonding must be strengthening their connection.

"Not sure, Shrek, but he's definitely mad." Draven covered his laugh with a cough and walked toward where Jadis and the boys were.

Entering into the bright blood orange room, Aliyah released his hand as soon as she saw Dany and ran to him, her hands opening his mouth to inspect for what he thought were fangs.

"What are you?" Her voice echoed inside of Dany's mouth while he tried to push her away. It was actually hilarious to watch.

Reikiki spoke again, "It's a rather interesting concept, actually. The three of them are entwined so heavily that their magic is fusing together; it's uncanny."

"Magic?" Aliyah questioned and craned her neck to watch Reikiki.

"Yes child. Are your ears painted on? That's what I just said, didn't I?" he scoffed.

"Allegedly, I am part vampire and werewolf," Dany clarified. He screwed his nose up and added,. "I'm a fucking baby vampwolf? Cubvamp? Wait! Cubire!"

Draven grinned while watching Aliyah's body shake with silent laugher before she exploded. "Why do you have to label everything, you dick! Just let it be! Ohhhhh snap! Babe, does that mean he is one of us?"

He sauntered over, snatched Dany's hand in his, and began searching the ink on his arm. Ah there it was, an intricate design on one of his coy fish. "When did you get this?"

Dany hauled his arm back, and sassed, "D-Man, not cool! I've had that for years." His eyes squinted, then bugged wide. "Fuck! That outlining and the water, it's—it's vibrant, it's redder than the queen of hearts. That is new as fuck," he affirmed.

"There you have it, Snowflake, he's one of us," Draven declared.

Aliyah's violet hues lit up the room, glowing slightly before she shrieked, "We're the same! Well, kind of." She sniffed then laughed. "You smell like a dog."

The laughter died down when Jadis stood up to greet them. Draven hadn't even noticed her as he'd been so entranced by Dany and Aliyah's escapade.

He drew her in for a hug before releasing her to take a look at her. "Hey Jadey baby, you look exhausted."

Jadis's eyes were more a moss green than the vibrant forest green they normally were. Her clothes were wrinkled and the purple in her hair was fading out; she needed to rest.

"You need to fucking take care of yourself, J. You are no good to yourself or anyone else if you don't rest and replenish," he chided. "Go and sleep. We will look after Dolph."

When she hesitated, Draven boomed, "Now Jadis! This isn't a request!"

Her eyebrow arched and he sensed she was about to challenge him. Luckily, she decided against it. "You're lucky I'm tired as fuck, vampire. Look after him, please." With that, she was gone.

Draven shook his head, his dreadlocks falling forward to rest on his shoulders as he stepped closer to the bed where Dolph lay.

He pushed his best friend's silver tipped black hair from his face and smiled, knowing if Dolph was awake he'd rip his fangs out for the caring gesture. Draven felt uncomfortable seeing his best friend laying there hopeless.

He shuddered, then turned away from Dolph and walked down the hall to find where the Mad Warlock was. Reikiki was known for being flamboyant and his uncanny and bizarre way of seeing into the future, but what earned him his name was how fucking maniacal he could become.

Some said that he had two personalities, and perhaps he did. Draven believed it was the many concoctions he manicured and then fed into. Not only was Reikiki the leading healer in the Otherworld district, he was also a philter master. He was well known among the Otherworlder community and all types of beings demanded his assistance and his unique elixir's. Draven assumed that's why his front door ate people or incinerated them.

One could not be too careful when they were breaching the bridge of insanity. Although, for all Reikiki's madness, he was a damn good healer, and deep down his heart was in the right place. Allegedly, he spoke with the Goddess Kaltemis often, which made Draven a little envious.

His mismatched eyes finally met the Mad Warlock's tiger-eye pair and Draven noticed that he had a drink in his hand; again, something that was the norm for him.

"Reikiki, can you tell me what's happening to him and what Dany has to do with all of this?" he quipped.

"Down boy," Reikiki teased, "I'll tell you what I know. I haven't even told him yet. Dolph needs his blood to survive and Jadis's love and magic."

"Blood? Since when has Dolph needed blood for sustenance?" Draven asked, curious.

"He needs my blood? Shit! Do I need to drink blood too?" Dany stepped out of the hallway into the room looking a little whiter than usual.

Seeming oblivious to Dany's intrusion, Reikiki replied, "Eventually you will. Once Dolph ingests your blood, I dare say the transition will transpire," Reikiki confirmed.

"I don't understand? How am I one of you? Were my parents? I–I don't remember them much," his voice cracked.

Aliyah was beside him in an instant, wrapping her arm around his shoulder to console him. Draven was no longer jealous of their relationship because he knew it was purely platonic and that Aliyah loved him.

"Continue Reikiki," he motioned.

"Let's move back into where Dolph is and I'll try and explain."

They all filed back into the room where Dolph was laying and once they were settled, Reikiki continued,

"I'm still trying to differentiate through the jargon, Draven. From what I've seen, they've formed a bond of sorts, perhaps when they entered into their ménage type relationship. Actually, Aliyah, child," he turned to face her and said, "You're able to exercise your third eye. Do you think you could find out when it happened?"

Draven eyed her while she chewed her bottom lip as if contemplating his request. "I'm–I'm not sure how it works. It was a fluke with my mother, I mean Jill," she relented.

A crazy smile formed on Reikiki's face, one that made him look a little too insane Draven thought. "Try. The Goddess said you need to nurture it, so nurture."

"How did you know that? Wait, don't tell me," Aliyah replied. "Dany, do you mind?"

He raised and dropped his shoulders in a shrugging motion then replied, "I trust you, and it may actually help me make sense of what I am and what's happening to me, to us." He flicked his hand toward Dolph's lifeless looking body.

She turned to face her best friend and Draven watched on with an intensity he didn't realise he possessed. His Snowflake stood poised. Her determination and strength emitted throughout the room.

Cupping Dany's hands in her own, she brought them higher to rest where his heart was, and then clenched her jaw.

Clamouring out, Aliyah's knees began to buckle while her body vibrated and glowed along with Dany's. She wept loud. Her melancholy sobs reverberated around them. Draven attempted to rush forward, except Reikiki's hand clamp around his wrist and stopped him.

"She needs to do this alone. If you interfere, you'll sever the connection she's latched onto, and this could be our only real hope to find out what's going on."

Draven snarled. He was pissed off that the Mad Warlock had talked sense for a change. Ripping his arm away from Reikiki, he stepped closer to Aliyah, but not so close it would distract her.

He felt her pain as if it was his own. His heart fractured from the grief, the agony, and deception that'd unearthed around her.

As if rehearsed, Aliyah and Dany dropped to their knees in unison, tears steaming rapidly down their faces while they held onto each other like their lives depended on it.

The air was inundated with poignancy, enough to almost bring him to his knees. Dany's affliction was palpable and thrummed through his body as if his own. Draven hadn't even realised he'd been weeping until he swiped the tears off his face.

The magic in the room was ferocious, brimming to the edge and threatening to bottle over. Whatever Dany and Aliyah were experiencing looked beyond painful.

Her body oscillated, while her glowing form flickered in and out until it phased out completely.

Draven scooped her up and placed her on the small lounge in the corner before helping Dany walk. Once they were both seated, Draven sat beside them.

"That was magnificent," Reikiki said admirably.

Draven moved off the couch and crouched between her thighs, throwing him a scowl over his shoulder before wiping Aliyah's face with his hand. "What happened, Snowflake?"

"I–I saw everything that happened to him, Shrek, everything," she sobbed. "He was so young – they were so young. It–it's not fair."

He pushed the stray piece of raven hair behind her ear and spoke quietly, "What do you mean? You're not making any sense, sweetheart."

Draven noticed Dany hadn't spoken a word since the flashback. He wondered if he was in shock. His umber eyes seemed sad and distant. He looked like his mind was no longer with them inside the room.

"Leave him to his thoughts, Draven. He has a lot to decipher through and unpack. Aliyah, can you tell us what you saw, child?" Reikiki queried.

She shook her head from side to side and a whimper escaped those swollen pouty lips. "It was disconcerting how much they suffered. And the blood, oh Draven." She leaned forward and wrapped her arms around his neck.

Draven held her tight and allowed her to cry freely in his arms. He felt absolutely useless while her body quaked with turmoil and her tears soaked through his shirt.

Aliyah drew back. Her violet orbs found his disparate pair before they fluttered closed then open. "They were murdered, babe. Cold blood fucking murdered. Dany..." her sentence faded as she looked toward her best friend before continuing again. "He was so young, maybe three, possibly four, and he was there. The ruthless cunts left him there swamped in his parents' blood. I – shit – he didn't remember what occurred with his parents until I entered his mind and unlocked his memories. We have to figure out who did this!" she shrieked.

"Oh baby," Draven whispered, "I've got you. We will figure this shit out."

"I tried to see who killed them, but every time I felt close to breaking through the dark magic, it rebounded off me."

We will find out who killed his parents, and I promise he will have his vengeance, Snowflake. I..." his sentence was cut short by the loud keening howl beside them.

Draven's head snapped to the side to witness Dany holding his head, screaming. Nothing about the scene was right. "Ahhhhhh, it fucking hurts," he lamented. "Make it stop!" he wailed.

Reikiki clapped his hands frenziedly. "Ooohhh, it's happening. The time has come!"

Glaring at the Mad Warlock, Draven demanded, "Get over here you old fool and help me hold him down. Wait, where is Laney?"

Reikiki dismissed him with his hands. "She left last night. Something urgent she needed to attend to."

That's bizarre, Draven thought to himself. He wasn't able to dwell on the what if's because Dany bellowed out again.

"What's happening to him?" Aliyah's concerned voice filled his ears.

"The grief has triggered the change. I'm uncertain which one though. I didn't believe he was really a hybrid; it's extremely rare that he would be." He paused, ran his fingers over his stubble and continued. "But I think the possibility is high from looking at him."

Draven ground out, "Reikiki, for fucks sakes get your ass over here and help me hold him down or at least use your voodoo to relax him!"

"Are you always this severe?" the Mad Warlock asked nonchalant as he sauntered over to assist Draven. "Keep him still. This may take a while."

Chapter Four

~ Aliyah ~

Aliyah covered her mouth so she wouldn't scream while she watched her best friend in agony. His bones sounded like they were shattering and his scream pierced through her causing her to shrink back in pain.

"Aliyah! Baby! Get Jadis now!" Draven commanded.

She took off out of the room and noticed the dark ash coloured walls decorated in the most eccentric art. All of it blurred past her as she dashed to find Jadis.

Breaking out of her thoughts, she chided herself, *Focus Liah, find Jadis and get back to Dany. This is not a time to get sidetracked!*

Her paced quickened. She sped through the apartment noting how it seemed bigger than she'd first anticipated. She couldn't help but wonder if it was some sort of glamour or magic.

Finally, she rounded the corner and found a door that was closed. Knocking once, she turned the knob to find Jadis sleeping.

Aliyah kneeled down beside the bed and shook her carefully. "Jadis, Jadis, wake up."

Her lids flickered open and her forest greens eyed her with concern. "What is it?" she questioned as she leaped out of the bed.

"It's Dany. They— they think his suppressed memories are triggering the change."

"What memories? What are you talking about?" She

pulled her long cardigan over her shoulders and dashed out the door. "Tell me later. I need to see him."

They ran all the way back to the room and found Draven holding Dany down as Reikiki mumbled some voodoo words with his hands over his abdomen.

"Move," Jadis hissed. "He needs my blood. I feel his hunger and I can taste his trepidation." She straddled his form while Draven held him down.

A knife appeared out of thin air and in an instant Jadis sliced through her palm, bringing it down to Dany's mouth. He growled, then his tongue darted out seeking her blood.

The copper scent assaulted the air, the sweet undertones putting an edge on Jadis's recently sated magic. Although she remembered the taste of Jadis's blood, it was nothing compared to Draven's.

Dany's man bun pulled free and his hair fell away from his face. His hands gripped Jadis's while he lapped at her bloodied palm greedily. His eyes popped wide and Aliyah gasped. His umber hues were a fierce brownish red, the irises now rimmed in amethyst.

She sought Draven's eyes and he grimaced. "He's definitely a hybrid; I can sense it. This will be even more painful than your transition."

"Can I take some of his pain? Can I do anything?"

"It's ok, Aliyah, I'm siphoning away the more afflicting parts of it," Jadis confirmed. "And my blood will help take the brunt of it."

Aliyah's mind felt like a whirlpool threatening to drag her under while she witnessed Dany's vampire change. It seemed as if his body was tethering between his wolf change and vampire as his bones cracked and his body shuddered.

He retracted from Jadis's palm and hollered out in tribulation, "Fuck it hurts! Arrrrggghhh." Then Aliyah heard it; the pop as his canines pierced through his gums.

Dany panted and his head fell back on the couch as his long dark hair fanned out around him. Aliyah had to look away when she noticed the massive erection straining against the placket of his pants.

"He needs to fuck, Snowflake, just as you did. It's just a reaction after the change, especially the first."

Aliyah nodded then stole a glance at Jadis. Her chocolate skin glowed and matched the huge smile on her face. She seemed content.

"So beautiful," she said, and Aliyah heard the awe emanating from her tone.

"I—I need..." Dany groaned.

"I know, baby, I know. I'll fix it."

"Not yet, Jadis," Reikiki interrupted. "Now that he's transitioned, he needs to feed Dolph. It's the only way we can keep him anchored to this realm, to this world."

"What do you mean feed?" Jadis enquired.

Reikiki rolled his eyes theatrically. "What do you think, Jadis. You're a smart witch; you know exactly what I mean."

"But Dolph's never needed blood for sustenance before."

Reikiki shrugged. "Things are changing, High One."

"I'll do it. I don't know what's happening to me, but I can sense and hear his call. He needs me. This connection we share is beyond fucking weird. I'm just putting it out there," Dany grunted as he staggered the short distance to Dolph's bed.

His canines were still elongated and his umber hues were still as vibrant as ever. Aliyah caught him chewing his bottom lip like he was contemplating what he needed to do next.

"How do I do this?" Dany faltered.

Draven offered his expertise, speaking before anyone else could. "Bite into your wrist. Jadis, you hold Dolph's mouth open so Dany can drip his blood into it."

"Bite my wrist? Isn't that going to fucking hurt?" He pointed to his cuspids protruding from his gums.

"You're a hybrid. Stop being an insolent child," Reikiki deadpanned.

Aliyah felt like she was an outsider watching in as the scene unfolded before her violet hues. It was too personal, and the uneasiness blanketed her.

Dolph hadn't moved through the whole ordeal. His body remained in the exact position as when they began. However, Aliyah did note the color return to his face after the blood entered his mouth. It seemed Dany's blood was the precise nourishment he required.

It was unnerving how stationary Dolph seemed, and she wondered if he could still hear them. That was only one of the many questions that plagued her mind.

Aliyah's feet were rooted to the carpeted floor of Reikiki's apartment. Her body there but her mind elsewhere. She remembered how Draven mentioned that her parents, well foster parents, were now Demon Lackeys, whatever that even meant. Was there no justice for them? They were merely human beings caught up in this tangled world of fuckery. *Weren't they?*

Her right shoulder began to burn, the searing pain now familiar and welcoming as she felt the Light Goddess's magic embed into her flesh. There was no malice, only purity in the air around her.

She peered over and noted Draven eyeing her with concern. Although the others were oblivious to what was happening with her, Draven seemed to sense the change. Before she could mutter a word, her eyes rolled back and she was unable to stop the visions forming behind her retinas.

Aliyah's childhood memories flashed through her mind. She felt a smile tug at the corner of her mouth as she relived the reminiscent moment.

An ethereal woman sparked in and out; however all Aliyah could decipher was the long white blonde hair striped with deep ebony locks. Whoever she was, Aliyah knew she was beautiful. The image of the woman wavered until she disappeared and another memory took form.

Aliyah was a little baby with dark little curls and she was cooing at Jill whilst she held her in her arms. She noticed something flicker in those brown eyes of hers, something she didn't remember ever seeing. She didn't linger on the memory as the cognition shifted.

Her smile faded away as she sensed the darkness around Jillian and John. She was sitting with her dad and he was bouncing her on his knee while he played with her hair, whispering in her ear how beautiful she was. Aliyah remembered that moment. It was vague, but the memory was apparent.

Nothing seemed wrong with the image until John placed his hand on her upper thigh. Aliyah's hand went instinctively to where her father had once touched. No, this can't be.

She saw a younger and just as frumpy looking Jill glaring at the duo behind a doorframe in their old house. If she had to describe the look, it was one of jealousy, envy and ire. Jillian despised them.

"What the fuck is going on? Oh my Goddess," she breathed.

The imagery continued on, and suddenly Aliyah's shoulders felt heavy with grief, disbelief, and anger. John viewed her in a way no parent should ever see their child. He was attracted to Aliyah. She smelled the lust and desire that pumped off of him in the memory.

She knew in that moment that Jillian had always loathed her. This was one of the reasons her mother didn't love her, didn't really want her. She'd merely put up with Aliyah to placate John.

She now saw Jill's over protectiveness more to keep her under her wing, to hold her within her vision so she could dictate her every movement.

The fights that seemed lost to her memory developed in her mind and painted a vivid picture. Jill and John's relationship was nothing short of volatile. She recalled how they barely touched each other. They simply tolerated one another, and now Aliyah knew why.

But there were times Jill was cordial, when she'd shown Aliyah love. So why was she only seeing these memories and not the others?

She clenched her jaw tightly. A pain resonated profoundly within her mind as she let go of the cognition she could no longer sustain.

Her knees buckled, but instead of falling to the floor, Aliyah found herself in Draven's arms. Blinking her eyes rapidly, she attempted to focus on everyone around her.

Worry and curiosity shone from all sets of eyes, except Draven's. He looked anxious and pissed. "What the hell happened, Aliyah?"

She began recounting her story. At the mention of her branding, it sparked the recognition that she'd not even seen the etching that Kaltemis had gifted her. Flames encompassed a massive violet eye along with water at the base. It was stunning and outlined in the deepest red she'd ever seen.

Draven's breath hitched and Aliyah gazed up at him to see his mismatched eyes blazing back at her. His lust was obvious, as well as the erection digging into her hip. It was then that she realised she was famished.

She swallowed the lump in her throat and squeaked, "Jill and John... there is so much animosity and immorality that surrounds them, Draven. I—I can't talk about it now because I'm still processing it. I don't mean to sound impertinent, but are we done yet?"

Reikiki's voice resounded around the room. "Go. She needs to feed..." his voice trailed off as a scroll-like piece of paper flickering with flames appeared in the air.

Draven hissed, "Fuck."

"What have you done, D?" Jadis's voice came out sounding jaded and wrung out.

"I did what I had to do. It was the only way, J."

"Again, what have you done? I can sense the sinister edge in the air."

"I entered into another contract with Melantha."

"You did what? What are you thinking, you stupid fucking vampire!" Jadis's voice clipped out.

"Don't you take that tone with me, Jadis! You know what'll happen if I forfeit the contract! My darkness will consume me. I will be relentless, unable to stop. And then after I've left destruction throughout this realm in my wake, my ass will be thrown into Purgatory. So don't you dare question me on this!"

Jadis winced. "You're right. I'm sorry, D. Is there anything else we can do to assist you? To lessen the load?"

"I already did that to an extent. Melantha is no longer allowed to enter my lair, *our* lair." He smiled briefly at Aliyah before continuing. "If she doesn't adhere to the stipulation then I'm able to kill her freely and maintain my sanity. I'm not certain how, but somehow she penetrated and breached your cloaking spell."

"Impossible," Reikiki chimed in, "I know the magic she used, and there is only one way that demon could have slipped through."

Aliyah raised her eyebrow in question while Draven

tensed. "Neferity."

"Yep," Reikiki clarified.

"OK, can someone clue me and Aliyah the fuck in? Her face is mirroring my confusion," Dany deadpanned.

Aliyah smiled at her best friend and noticed how big he looked, how grown up. *Had that just happened because of the change?*

"Neferity has interfered, which isn't permitted. Although the Dark Goddess has never played by the rules." He visibly shuddered before continuing. "We already know these fuckers are after Aliyah. Now I may have stepped into their sinister clutches by accepting the contract. However, if I win, the demon will have no leverage over me and will never be able to contact or bother me again. It's worth the gamble," Draven stated.

"I hope you're right, D. So what are the logistics of this new contract?"

Aliyah held Draven's hand while he rehashed the whole debacle with Melantha and the current stipulations of the contract he'd entered.

"So, let me guess, that floating piece of poison above our heads is the being you're in need of saving?"

"I dare say so," he sighed.

Aliyah nudged him, her eyes moving from his to the eerie scroll. "Open it. You may as well get it over with."

Draven plucked it from the air and read the contents, then growled, "You've got to be fucking kidding me!"

Chapter Five

~ Draven ~

Draven couldn't believe the name inscribed into the paper. Before he had any more time to mule over it, the scroll disintegrated.

"What? What is it? More to the point, who is it?" Jadis demanded.

"You don't look so good, D-Man. Do you need to sit down?" Dany offered.

"Babe. Oi, are you in there?" Aliyah waved her hand in front of his face.

"It's her, isn't it?" Draven hazily heard Reikiki's voice ask.

Draven looked up from his boots and found his tiger coloured eyes. "Yeah, it's her. It's Laney."

"I sensed the darkness around her. I just didn't realise how bad it was. You have to save her, Draven. You have to!" Reikiki pleaded.

"I intend to. She's like a sister to me. The only downfall is that I have no idea what the fuck she's done."

Draven suddenly felt fatigue blanket him, the tiredness tugging at his jaded limbs. No longer was he aroused. Instead, he just wanted to huddle close to Aliyah and forget that the world was literally against them all.

"I need— I need to compartmentalise this shit storm I've landed myself in. I'll be in contact." He scooped Aliyah in his arms and vamp sped to the Bel Air and drove like a bat out of hell toward the lair.

Draven needed to put some space between them all. He needed to figure out what the fuck he was going to do and how he was going to save Laney from herself.

If he failed, shit, he didn't even want to walk down that rickety road. Walking into his lair, he flopped down on the couch. Aliyah followed behind, pulling her hair up into a bun.

Her vibrant violet hues were riddled with concern as her body languidly dropped in front of him. She nudged his knees apart and rubbed her petite hands up and down his thighs.

"Let me look after you. I can feel your confliction, your pain and oppressiveness." Her eyes pleaded with him.

Draven reached forward and cupped her face before drawing his closer to hers to take her mouth. The kiss was slow and timid. He took the time to explore her.

Withdrawing, her nails dug into his flesh as she shook the fog out of her eyes. "No, this is me doing something for you, not the other way around. Sit back, relax, and let me have my wicked way with you."

Her simpering smile stole the beat of his heart. He moaned when he inhaled her lustrous scent, enveloping him, threating to suffocate and draw him under her depraved spell.

Aliyah undid the button on his pants at the pace of a snail: slow, molasses, and oh so teasing. Her eyes never vacillated from his, enticing him, pulling him further into her web so she could eventually devour him. Caressing his length through his pants, he let out another moan while his head fell back, hitting the top of the lounge.

"You're killing me, Snowflake."

She mewled quietly and continued to stroke his length, playing with him from behind the placket of his pants. She was doing him in fiercely, and she'd barely touched him.

Her arousal was heady, delicious. He tried to enjoy what she was doing to him and not leap up and take her the way he wanted: rough.

The cool air from the air conditioner kissed his skin while she slid the zipper down. He knew when she was done because the small patch of hair above his cock was now visible.

Draven lifted his ass up so Aliyah could shimmy his pants down his legs. His cock sprung free, standing to attention. Her hand glided over his thick, veiny shaft and pulled on the apadravya piercing.

He hissed behind clenched teeth and his head fell forward to watch her under heavy lidded eyes. And what a sight it was.

Her pink tongue poked out between her bowlike lips, her pointed cuspids in full bloom. Draven took the opportunity to really look at her. Aliyah's cheeks were flushed with a rosy hue, her violet eyes were darker, and Draven knew she was fully aroused.

Her thick eyelashes fanned her brow while she looked up at him and took him in her mouth. His jaw clutch tightly together. She had the fiercest blowjob eyes he'd ever seen, and he seriously thought he'd cum from watching her.

Up and down; her head bobbed slowly, her canines scraping against his shaft, causing his body to ripple. Fuck, he was close already.

Aliyah smirked up at him then disengaged her mouth from his cock. She was playing with him, the little minx. She was trying to distract him, and it was fucking working.

Aliyah raked her nails down his thighs, drawing blood. Her eyes never wavered from his as her tongue darted out to lap at the pooling crimson liquid.

Draven's thigh muscles bunched, and he pulled at his dreadlocks to keep from throwing her on the couch and fucking her raw.

Her lips were stained with his blood and the red tinge enticed the beast within him to come out and ravage her. But not yet. He would let her believe she was in control a little longer.

Aliyah used her sharp nails to scrape down her wrist. The sweet aroma filled the air. Chocolate, full bodied wine and whiskey, it was enough to render him inebriated.

She brought her fingers up to his mouth and urged his lips apart with her digits. Draven greedily sucked them clean, his erection painfully throbbing between his thighs until she grasped him firmly.

Something passed through her eyes. It wasn't something he'd seen before. Draven couldn't decipher what the emotion or thought was because he was so drunk on the sweet iron-laced scent of her blood that dripped heavily around them.

Aliyah licked up his thigh and in between peppered kiss-es, she spoke in a seductive tone. "What have you done to me, vampire? You've enraptured me, seduced me with your debasement, and I never want to go back to the way I was before you. You've splayed me open. The wounds inside are now less apparent and painful because you showed me what it's like to be loved and oh so fucking wicked."

With that, she sunk her canines into his femoral artery and pumped her hand viciously up and down his shaft. Draven's mind scattered; his eyes rolled back into the back of his skull at the unfamiliar, yet highly stimulating sensa-tion of her suckling from his vein.

In his whole 327 years walking these planes, no one since Delilah had fed from his femoral artery. It was be-yond titillating. Draven found it difficult differentiating any-thing beside the glowing golden light around Aliyah. Her violet hues were enticing, beckoning him to let go. Draven shuddered, calling out her name as his orgasm roared down his spine, making his balls draw tight before spilling his seed all over her hand and his abdomen.

He panted heavily, allowing his hands to stroke her eb-ony locks before pulling it free from the bun on her head. Aliyah's eyes flickered up to his and he was momentarily stunned by how brilliant they truly were.

Her eyes remained on his as she licked the puncture marks to seal the wound and then she slowly stood up. "What? Why are you looking at me like that?"

Draven smirked, then replied, "Nothing. I was just thinking how lucky I am to have you and how you've had your fun now so it's my turn."

He threw her on the couch and she squeaked, "What – what are you doing?"

"Whatever the fuck I want."

The next morning, Draven spent the better part of it pacing around. He felt pasty-faced and hollowed-eyed. He was exhausted. There was too much going on and he didn't even know where to begin.

He'd dropped Aliyah off at the Mad Warlocks place earlier to spend some time with Dany. Having time alone meant he could focus on figuring out this shit with Laney, and possibly this fucking revelation shit.

Fishing his phone from his pocket, he decided to make a couple of calls. The first one was to a friend he still had in the pack.

Draven rarely caught up with anyone from his past. He purposely avoided any history that led him to remember the terrible things he'd done all those years ago.

Shaking himself from his thoughts, he dialled the only other person he could think of: Grunge.

Grunge was the alpha of the Louisiana wolf pack. Not many people knew that Dolph gave up his position ten years ago, but Draven did. Even though they'd been estranged for fifty years, he still kept tabs on his best friend. It's just the way it was. He only hoped Grunge had the answers Draven needed.

He sat down on the leather lounge, kicked his shoes off, and hoped his friend would pick the phone up when he saw his number across the screen.

Seven rings later, a familiar and husky accent spoke through the receiver. "Draven? Is that you, brother?"

"Yeah Grunge, it's me. How the fuck are you?"

"Surprised," he laughed before continuing. "Shit it's mayhem here, otherwise I'm good. There is talk rummaging through the lines of communication around here that you've found yourself in a bit of a clusterfuck. Are the rumours true?"

A whole entire world and still somehow everyone knew his business. Draven groaned, "Yeah, bro, something like that. I wish I could say I called to catch up, but I'd be lying. I need your help. If you think shit is chaos in Louisiana, wait to you hear the shit going on around here."

Draven spent the next fifteen minutes rehashing some of the scenarios he'd found himself in recently. Grunge did the same. Although Draven felt as if he wasn't being honest about everything.

He needed to tell him about Dolph and ask about Laney, but he didn't really want to do that over the phone. Dolph and Grunge were close, hence the reason he was now the Alpha.

Draven hesitated before speaking again. "Is there any way you can get away from the pack for a few days?

"Is it important?"

"Of course. I wouldn't ask otherwise."

"Ok. I'll ask my right hand man Arc to lead the pack for a few days. I can be there this evening; I just have a few things I need to take care of first."

"Sweet. I'll see you later."

After the call, Draven was even more depleted. His bare feet padded across the cold sealed concrete floor to the kitchen. Opening the fridge, he reached down and pulled out a Budweiser then screwed the top off.

The amber, bubbly, liquid was cold and refreshing as he sculled the contents. So much so, he decided he wanted another. With a beer in hand, he leaned against the black shiny granite counter and crossed his feet at the ankles.

One swift sip of the cold liquid and his mind wavered. *What is happening to Dolph, and why is he stuck between our worlds?* he wondered.

There had to be something holding him because there was no other explanation. Draven knew he needed to free his friend from the shackles of limbo and figure out what the hell he was going to do about Laney.

Draven was out of ideas. He knew until he saw Grunge tonight any suggestions he came up with would be futile.

Kicking off the bench, he moseyed over to the lounge, sat down, and opened his laptop that was resting on the coffee table. He pulled up the search engine and typed in Midnight Mayhem. Draven figured if he could work out who the fuck was pulling the strings at the club, then maybe he'd piece together what those demons Malista and Melantha were up to.

Draven hadn't heard boo from the club since his encounter with the demons. That particular experience was ingrained so viciously within, he couldn't bear to think about the adverse repercussions if Aliyah hadn't pulled him out.

Nothing made sense to Draven. He dug deeper and knew he was getting closer to figuring out who owned the club when the air shifted around him, prompting Draven to place the empty beer bottle on the table. He knew that presence, that scent, except now it seemed tainted. He screwed his nose up and waited for his brother to enter.

"Emilio, I can sense you. What do you want?"

The door opened and his brother strut in like he owed the place. He looked... different. Draven couldn't put his fangs on it.

His ash blonde hair had streaks of red through it, and his stance seemed odd. He eyed the ink on his brother's body and noticed it looked unusual, noting that it was on full display, which he rarely did. Draven's quirked an eyebrow and waited for him to reply.

"What? It's a crime to check on my degenerate younger brother now?"

The leather crinkled loudly when Draven stood up, swallowing the retort and anger down. They were never close, his brother and him. Emilio thrived on reminding Draven that he was a mistake, an abomination.

Efah did more than seduce their father; she condemned him. He wouldn't allow himself to be swallowed by that chasm, not when his darkness was already lapping at his heels.

Draven shook the fog from his mind and said, "I'll say it again, what the fuck do you want?"

Emilio's lip curled up at the sides, his pearly white teeth shining almost as much as his amethyst eyes. Those damn irises were a constant reminder of how different the pair of them truly were.

"Oh, you know, I came here to see my *half*-brother's hot new play thing."

Draven's insides swelled tempestuous. The bones in his body felt like they were gnashing together and the familiar feeling of rage permeated the entirety of his being.

The inside of his wrist heated up, burning from the branding that was supposed to help control his darkness. He didn't take the time to observe what the ink was doing. Instead, he bellowed out, wild and unrestrained like a turbulent storm threatening to wipe out this very existence of life.

"You do not fucking talk about her! You do not think of her or even look at her! You, Emilio, are nothing to me.

And your presence is no longer welcome here!"

His ruby eye twitched as wrath swirled within, then he roared viscerally. Everything seemed like it was moving, like the ground beneath was shaking. When he looked up, Emilio was gone.

Draven hadn't seen his brother leave, but sensed Emilio left in a hurry. He heaved in ragged breaths and then fell unceremoniously onto the lounge once more.

He turned his left wrist over to look at the branding. The vermillion ink glowed. Watching in disbelief, the branding slowly returned back to the normal red outline. *What the fuck?*

Draven's head hit the back of the black cherry leather lounge. His eyes honed in on the industrial copper piped lighting harnessed to the antique white coloured ceiling.

He began reflecting on Emilio. Something wasn't right with him. More than usual. What he couldn't shake was his interest in Aliyah? Questions circled, festered within his broken mind as he tried to figure out the riddle.

Draven chewed on the inside of his cheek before sitting forward and reaching for his laptop. His mind felt like one massive destructive hurricane. He didn't know where he began or where this mess ended.

Flicking through more information, something caught his eye. *Sangue,* which was his surname. Following the paper trail that was undeniably left by mistake, he reached the end and wished he'd found the information out thirty minutes ago.

The pieces were starting to come together and make sense, as was the demeanour of his brother. He remembered Emilio's brandings; how they seemed different and unusual.

Draven's mouth turned dry when he came to the realisation that half of his brandings were no longer outlined in red. Instead they were black.

It was extremely rare that one Goddess could or would cancel out the other's brandings, but that's exactly what Neferity had done.

Emilio's name blinked back at him, almost like it was winking at him through the laptop screen. He was the owner of Midnight Mayhem.

Draven groaned, pushing his dreadies back so he could circle his temples. Could they not catch a break in this muddled up and evil infested realm?

His head began to hurt. Tension formed behind his retinas with the comprehension of what this all narrowed down to.

Not only was his brother one sick and twisted son of a bitch, he was also slinking in Purgatory with Neferity. Which meant he wanted Aliyah too. *Shit.*

Chapter Six

~ Draven ~

Draven woke up on the lounge disorientated. The overwhelming headache was still lingering and had smashed his ass for six. Hell, he hadn't even realised he'd passed out.

The heavy sound of knocking ricocheted through the door. Groggily, Draven wiped his eyes then headed toward the noisy knocking.

Opening the steel door, he was graced with the keenest chartreuse eyes he'd ever imagined. Grunge. He looked bigger than Draven remembered. His dark auburn hair sat in a bun on top of his head and his tattooed muscles rippled with laughter.

"You done checking me out, asshole?"

Draven flipped him off and grinned. "Come in fuckface. Wait, shit, what's the time?"

"Just after seven, man."

"Shit. I've got to go and pick up Aliyah."

"Aliyah?"

"Brother, we have so much to talk about. I'll tell you along the way. And Grunge?"

"Yeah brother?"

"Brace yourself."

The drive toward the Mad Warlock's house was filled with despondency as Draven explained everything to his friend.

Grunge shook his head from side to side and Draven could smell the salty tears welling up in his eyes. "Is he going to be ok, man? Dolph? He's like a brother to me."

"Ditto, Grunge. Ditto. I fucking hope so. We are trying everything we can. Right now Dany, Aliyah's best friend, needs to feed him his blood to keep him alive and anchored to this world, or some shit. I'm as confused as you when it comes to this."

"Feed him blood? Since when does Dolph need blood to live?" he asked befuddled. "What about Jadis? Can't she reel him back from lingo?"

"Don't ask me because I have no idea how this shit works. As for Jadis, she's tried to no avail. Jadis is keeping him replenished somewhat with her magic as is Dany with his blood. Reikiki said that their magic is entwined or some bullshit. Whatever that means."

"This is whack, Savage." His street name fell from Grunge's lips easily, and Draven smiled.

"Tell me about it. We're here. We can get into this some more later."

Grunge nodded then exited the car. They walked up the stairs to Reikiki's apartment in silence. He still had so much to ask Grunge, especially when it came to Laney.

When they arrived at the stunning timber door, Draven leaned forward ready to knock. It flew open and Reikiki stood there in his olive green, orange and brown tunic, his tiger coloured eyes staring at the both of them.

"Another werewolf? This place is going to smell like wet dog soon enough." He smirked at Grunge then beckoned him for a hug. "It's been a long time, wolf. Come. We have much to discuss."

Draven stood there flabbergasted, not that he should be. The Mad Warlock always knew more than he let on. Draven only wondered what the man knew that he didn't.

"You coming, vampire?"

He shook himself from his stupor, walked over the threshold, and followed them inside. The door slammed shut as soon as he was in, making Draven jump. *Fucking magic.*

The hallway was lined with the finest Persian rug, complementing the dark ash coloured interior perfectly. He was distracted momentarily by the art along the walls. It was beautifully chaotic if he had to describe it. Draven didn't remember ever seeing such eccentric paintings in all his life.

He paused then gaped at the multi-coloured splashes of paint sprawled across the canvas. The art was enticing to look at, even if he had no idea what he was actually seeing.

A throat cleared and snapped him from his pondering. Draven looked up to see Grunge's chartreuse irises eyeing him sceptically.

"You ok, man?"

Draven nodded his reply and moved past him, heading toward where Dolph lay. Instantly, he was assaulted with the blood orange coloured room and Aliyah's scent. He suppressed the moan lodged in his throat and walked to her side.

Aliyah's long dark hair cascaded down her back framing her slender form. Sensing his arrival, she turned toward him, her luminous violet hues shining back at him.

"Hey Shrek, I thought you might have forgotten about me," she jeered.

"Not possible, Snowflake." He wrapped his arms around her and squeezed. "Any progress?"

Dany interrupted from the other side of the room. "He hasn't moved or batted an eyelid if that's what you were wondering."

"And you are?" enquired Grunge.

Draven spoke first, sensing Dany was about to blow his lid. He knew what the initial transitional stage for a young vampire was like, and Dany was part wolf also so he'd be all shades of fucked up. There was no use these two hot heads battling it out over something as miniscule as not knowing who the other was.

"This is Dany, Grunge. He's Aliyah's best friend, and also one of the only beings keeping Dolph anchored to this realm. This," he paused and smiled down at Aliyah before continuing, "is Aliyah."

"I can see why you've been hard up, Savage," Grunge chuckled, eyeing Aliyah.

"Savage?" Aliyah's eyebrow hiked up in question.

"I'll explain later. Where's Jadis?" he deflected.

"She's in the other room, recaning her magic or something. That's what she said anyway."

"She's cleansing, child," Reikiki piped up, dismissing the comment. "Now Grunge, tell us about Laney."

"Wait? You know about what's happened?"

"Not completely. I drank one of my philters last night and had a vision. She's in danger, that much I know.

"How accurate is this vision," Jadis questioned as she waltzed in.

Reikiki shrugged his shoulders. "As accurate as a drunken warlock can be." He took a sip of the alcoholic concoction in his hand.

"Continue then," Draven demanded. He needed all the information he could find if he was going to beat Melantha at her own game.

"Grunge, tell us about you and Laney first, then I will re-enact my vision."

Draven turned toward Grunge and noticed the red blush creep up his neck to his cheeks. "Oh shit, you and Laney were bumping uglies?"

"Fuck you, man. Why you have to be so vulgar all the time. You haven't changed, D." Grunge shook his head in what looked like disbelief.

"Laney and I were *together* at one point. Something changed though. She changed."

He paused, and Draven noted the sadness in his eyes. Grunge reeked of melancholy. *The poor fuck. What the hell had she done to him?*

Jadis ambled over to Grunge and placed her hand on his shoulder, then squeezed it. "Start from the beginning, honey."

A small poignant laugh bubbled up out of his throat. "I wish I could go back to the beginning, at least shit made sense then."

Draven was about to query his statement, but Grunge resumed speaking.

"About eight months ago, I was engaged to a wolf named Margarite. We'd been together for about two years and were set to marry in the fall. Things seemed to make sense with her, you know? I figured I was as happy as I could be. Hell, there were worse people to wed. As Alpha, marrying and having cubs is a part of the role." He shrugged. "Margarite was nice enough. I wasn't in love with her, but she was ok with it. I suspect she thought over time I would fall in love with her. All that backfired when Laney returned to the pack."

"What do you mean retuned?" Draven asked.

"Just let him talk. Damn it, vampire," Reikiki scolded. *Sheesh.*

"After Dolph handed the reins to me and made me Alpha, Laney disappeared. I suppose you could say she went rogue; I didn't know that at the time." He sighed before recommencing his story. "When she arrived back, I was absolutely enthralled to have her close again. I've always had a soft spot for Laney, ever since I was a cub. There was something about those lime green rimmed, coal eyes that captivated me."

"Did Dolph know?" Jadis questioned.

"I think he suspected as much. He never said anything though. Anyway, as most of you know, we stay close together. The pack had a few free cabins in the forest that we lived in so I offered her one. She seemed to find it difficult to fit in, seeing she'd been gone for so long. The fact the other wolves were suspicious of her didn't help matters. So for the first couple of months, I started spending more time with her, figuring I was helping her adjust to being back in the pack. Obviously Margarite wasn't crazy about the idea. We kept drifting apart, me and Margarite. One night, Laney asked me to come over, said she needed to talk to someone she could trust. Let's say when I entered her cabin we didn't talk much. I think that was her plan all along. Hell, to be wearing nothing more than G-string said as much."

"She seduced you?" Aliyah said sounding shocked.

"Is it seduction if you wanted it just as much?" he answered her with a question of his own.

"What happened to Margarite? Did you tell her?"

Draven noted the curiosity in Aliyah's voice. This was starting to sound like a soap opera to him.

"We snuck around for a week or so. Then I told her. I couldn't deceive her anymore, and I felt terrible for being unfaithful. It really didn't matter in the grand scheme of things anyway. I found out Margarite was cheating on me long before Laney even arrived."

"I'm sorry, Grunge," Jadis said. "She didn't deserve you."

"How can you say that, you didn't even know her."

"I know enough, G. Now continue," Jadis replied.

"Okay, okay, sheesh woman. Well, naturally Margarite was exiled from the pack. I found out she was doing some sketchy shit behind my back for longer than I realised. Me and Laney seemed to be heading in the right direction. She moved into my cabin and lived with me for three months. I'd fallen for her and she'd fallen for me. She'd told me as much. But then she disappeared, along with something that is irreplaceable and means the world to me. I haven't seen her in about five weeks. The last month before she left, I noticed something really different about her. She was acting rather peculiar and I even thought she was on drugs. When I confronted her, she lost her absolute shit. I—I just wanted to help her..."

Reikiki cut in, stopping Grunge from walking down guilt ridden lane. "What did she take from you, Grunge? Please tell me it isn't what I envisioned."

Draven watched between the two of them, his head going back and forth like a ping pong ball as he waited for them to cease the silent communication.

"Spit it out, Grunge. Cause believe me, Laney is in more shit than whatever the fuck she's stolen from you," he demanded.

Grunge's demeanour shifted and he tensed. "You don't know what the fuck you're talking about, Draven! Don't start this macho bullshit with me." His shoulders slouched and he looked defeated. "I don't expect you to understand."

Draven had enough of his poor pity me charade. Grunge was an old friend, but he was also pissing on his last nerve.

He moved Aliyah from out under his arm then stalked to his friend and poked him in the chest with his index finger. "I have one fucking week to save her sorry ass from landing in Purgatory. One fucking week, Grunge! If you don't help me then we may as well send her a farewell card now!"

"What are you talking about? Purgatory? Are you fucking high, Savage?"

Jadis stepped between the two of them and pushed them apart. Draven noticed her hands were glowing that eerie amber tinge. He stepped aside, sensing she was about at her limits.

"Both of you shut the fuck up. Dolph is lying here in Limbo while the two of you have a pissing match. Let me dumb it down for the both of you. Laney has deceived us all, and more than likely betrayed us. This is bigger than everyone in this room. Grunge, Draven made a blood oath with Melantha to save five souls to end his current debt with her. Laney is the first on the list. That's why hot head over there is losing his cool. Now, please tell us what she took."

He watched the tears well up in Grunge's eyes and felt like a complete prick. "She took my mother's totem. It's all I had left and the only way I could contact her in the spirit world. It's sentimental and priceless to me, but in the wrong hands it could be destructive."

"In other words, if some evil demon or Neferity gets their hands on that totem, then all of us are in a world of hurt," Jadis relented.

"What's so special about it, I mean other than your connection to your mother," Dany questioned with caution.

"It's laced with ancient, powerful magic. I once heard my mother talking about my grandmother's totem. She said they can be used to barter with the Gods; that our totems are compelling. The Gods despise them because they make them weak."

"Gods? I thought we only had Goddesses," queried Aliyah.

"Snowflake, the Gods... there is no good and evil when it comes to them. They don't have rules or codes to follow. They simply work off their own agendas. They're twisted, malicious, and relentless."

"So they're evil?"

"They thrive on drama, pain, and anything that wounds or renders any being defenseless, baby."

"So why did Laney take it?" asked Dany.

Reikiki sculled the last of his drink and slammed it down on the table, causing the group to jolt. "Because she's going to make a deal with Neferity."

Chapter Seven

~ Aliyah ~

Shortly after Reikiki's bombshell, Aliyah, Draven and Grunge made the commute back to the lair. She was completely spent. It seemed Laney had been up to no good for some time, and saving her soul sounded almost futile to her.

Aliyah didn't want to bring Draven down with her observation. She could sense the oppression weighing heavily on his shoulders.

The steel door creaked upon opening, as if objecting to their arrival. Aliyah stood in the entry way, observing Draven and Grunge walk in and plop down on the cherry black lounge.

Draven's dreadlocks were dishevelled as was Grunge's man bun. They both looked crushed, their hopes barely holding on by a thread.

Moving away from the door, Aliyah closed it quietly and traversed to the kitchen to grab the boys a drink. This whole Otherworlder's shit was new to her. Hell, being a walking faery, angel, vampire, demon was new to her.

Grabbing two beers from the fridge, she set them on the counter then poured herself a wine, stopping to ruminate and appreciate the interior of the kitchen. It was one of her favourite places in the lair, and one spot she usually found herself thinking lately when things were overwhelming her. The copper pots and pans hung beautiful over the black old style oven, complementing the black granite benches, silver blade tiles and grey walls perfectly.

She stood there longer than necessary, deliberating over what and where her life was now. At eighteen, the last thing she imagined was precisely what was happening now.

What does Neferity want from me? Why am I so special? And how the hell do I maneuver through this chaos without burning myself or someone I love?

Aliyah's darkness was ever prominent lately. Something that she'd yet to share with Draven. It was a conversation she'd shied away from at all costs. Unfortunately, she knew it was one they needed to have.

She was interrupted from her musings by Draven. "Snowflake, you ok?" his loud voice echoed through the lair.

She kicked off from the bench, refilled her wine glass, and walked back to the lounge with the beer for the boys.

Handing Draven and Grunge a beer, Aliyah sat in the single lounge seat sipping her wine. She was uncharacteristically quiet while she listened to the boys relive old memories together.

Draven was once close to Grunge. Not as close as Dolph, but none the less they all shared a bond. Her thoughts left the conversation they were having and she wondered if vampires and wolves were actually supposed to be companions.

Figuring that it really didn't matter, and all the supernatural kind of shows she'd ever watched were a bunch of bull, she tuned back in only to hear Draven calling her name.

"Snowflake? Earth to Aliyah? Oi?"

Shaking the fog from her head, she smiled then replied, "Yeah, sorry, I was just thinking is all."

Aliyah was met with mismatched concerned eyes and a pair of chartreuse irises assessing her. "Hey D, I'm shattered. How's about you take care of your girl and I'll hit the hay." He paused, then smirked before continuing. "These walls are sound proof, right?"

Draven's chuckle reverberated around the space while Aliyah felt her face heat up with embarrassment. "Go to sleep, you horn bag. We'll see you in the morning," Draven replied.

Grunge grinned and winked then turned on his heel and walked toward the room that used to be Aliyah's. She focused on him leaving until Draven cleared his throat. "Should I be worried?"

"Huh?"

"You're checking Grunge out," he jeered.

"No I wasn't. I was... just lost in thought."

"Come to bed, baby. Something is on your mind, and once I've rocked your world, you're going to tell me exactly what that something is."

Damn this vampire and his words. Watching Draven traverse toward the bedroom was a sight in itself. His tight jeans magically hugged that taut sexy ass of his.

As if sensing her checking him out, his dreads flicked over his shoulder when he turned and smirked. "See something you like, princess?"

Aliyah rolled her eyes and flipped him the bird. "Nah, been there, done that."

He rushed toward her, threw her over his shoulder, and slapped her ass, causing her to cry out. "And you're about to go there again."

After the intense fuck session, Aliyah was completely sated. Draven was snoring quietly, which she was thankful for because it meant they didn't need to discuss what was happening for her.

His little snores compelled her to watch him while he slept. He was her vampire and she was his; there was not a doubt in her mind.

Her eyes wandered down to the black satin sheets wrapped around his leg, leaving the rest of his body exposed. Carefully, Aliyah perched up on her elbow to ogle him.

She watched as the colours waltzed along his inked stomach, right down to the Holy Grail. A manscaped small patch of hair housed that monster of a package with the piercing poking out.

Secretly, she loved these moments. The world was quiet and it was just the two of them. If only it was that simple.

"What are you thinking about? You're hurting my head,

Snowflake," Draven said sleepily.

Aliyah jumped, startled by his words because she thought he was still asleep, then sat up on her knees. "Shit, Shrek, was that necessary?"

"Don't change the subject. You're not getting out of it again. Talk. What's been eating you...? Except for me," he teased.

Smiling because of his comment, she shook her head and wondered where to start. Chewing on her lower lip, she relented. "I—I haven't been feeling myself lately."

"You're going through a lot right now. The change, being wanted by your maniacal father, the Dark Goddess, dealing with me, and this fucking revelation prophecy bullshit. It's natural to feel that way."

Aliyah knew he was right, but why was the darkness closing in on her? Deciding to bite the bullet and tell him her real concern, she blurted, "I feel my darkness more. More than before."

She observed Draven tense momentarily before schooling his expression. "Liah, baby, unfortunately that darkness will always be inside of us. We just need to learn to control it. 327 years on these planes and I'm still learning."

Aliyah felt her face heat up; hot tears threatened to escape her eyes. "What...what if I can't control it?" she whispered.

Draven dragged her down to him and nestled her into the crook of his arm. "You will learn to control it. You know why I'm certain of it?"

"No," she replied with a sniff.

"Because you are strong, determine, and one hell of a beautiful hard ass. You won't subjugate to the darkness, but you'll learn to draw from it when required and make it your bitch."

"You sound so sure."

"I am. I believe in you, Snowflake. You just need to believe in yourself, as well. Now let's get some sleep. Who knows what tomorrow will bring."

Draven kissed the crown of her head and she snuggled close into his chest. He was right. She needed to believe in herself.

As Aliyah began to drift off to sleep, she tried to convince herself she wasn't going to let these assholes get what they needed from her. She only hoped that convincing herself was enough.

Aliyah's face screwed up while she looked around. Everything was murky, grey, and smelled horrendous. Long dead vines draped down off the trees and the ground was muddy and wet. She had no idea where she was or what was happening. She walked cautiously through the dirty muck, watching as it slowly morphed into what appeared to be black lava stone. Aliyah stilled, taking in the bituminous jagged walls. Suddenly, the chill set in and embedded itself right to her marrow. Something wasn't right. She'd never seen this place before, but the debasement and sinister edge told her she wasn't in New Orleans anymore.

She knew she should go back, that she shouldn't go any further, but the magnetic pull urged her on. Aliyah looked down and noticed she was naked. What the fuck. Searching frantically, she found a torn piece of material. She fixed it around her waist and wrapped one hand across her boobs to shield them. Honing in on the walls, she noted there was some sort of bluish sludge dripping from them. She'd seen that somewhere before, but she couldn't put her finger on where. Aliyah felt the goosebumps encompass her whole body. Stopping abruptly, her eyes darted around the space, searching. Violet irises found a pair of bright red eyes in the distance, drawing her in, compelling her to step closer, all while her mind screamed NOOO.

Draven's face flickered behind her irises. Drawing strength from the image, Aliyah remembered what was important in her life and that she needed to be strong. It took all her might but she rooted herself in place as she felt the familiar darkness suckling on her soul. She didn't want to unveil her weakness, but a part of her liked it. A sleazy chuckle bounced around the space and the dread set in. She knew that voice.

"Stop fighting it, child. You will succumb sooner or later to the darkness, to me. Although, I must admit I am surprised how difficult it was to slip into your unconscious

mind. You're getting stronger, Aliyah, and soon you won't be able to hold that anger, resent, and darkness back. Remember – my blood viciously pumps through your veins like old wine..."

"Nooooooo!" Aliyah jumped up from the bed, disorientated. Hot tears tracked down her face as she slowly came out of the dream state.

She hadn't realise Draven was standing in front of her until he placed his hands on each side of her face. The connection immediately sparked, calming her nerves.

"Talk to me, baby. What happened? You scared the fuck out of me."

"No, no, no, it can't be. It can't be!" Aliyah peered up into Draven's mismatched irises and found him looking at her with what she knew was concern.

"What can't..." Draven's sentence was interrupted by a knock on their bedroom door.

"I heard screaming. Are you good, D?" Grunge questioned.

"Yeah, brother. Aliyah had a nightmare. I'll be out shortly."

Draven's body looked wired and she could smell his heady scent mixed with his fear. Once she was satisfied Grunge was gone, she took a deep breath and spoke.

"It–it was Gorgon. He managed to get inside my head, Draven. It felt so real."

"What do you mean he was in your head?" He grabbed her hand and led her back to the bed to sit down.

"It felt too real to be a dream. I swear it wasn't," she pleaded. Aliyah thought she must sound like a damn nutcase.

"What happened?"

She rehashed everything that had occurred to Draven. She was certain she was losing her fucking mind. "He told me that I will succumb, subjugate to the darkness. That I won't be able to fight it forever."

Draven's hand disengaged from hers as he stood up. His brow furrowed and his face seemed etched with uncertainty. "I'm surprised he was able to contact you from Purgatory and show you that hell hole."

"That was really hell? Are you serious?" she asked in

disbelief.

"Yeah, that was definitely it. Don't worry, Snowflake, we will find a way to block him from entering your mind again. Shit, it's five am. Come on, I'll make us some breakfast and then we will head over to Reikiki's. I'm sure the Mad Warlock will have a concoction that'll help."

Numbly, she heard Draven dressing. She threw on a pair of ripped black denim shorts and a red sweater that had a black skull on.

She'd actually seen hell, well part of it. The images and smells were still raw in her mind while she made her way to the kitchen, her feet scuffing along the floor.

Gorgon had something over her. Maybe it was his blood, or perhaps it was something else. Unfortunately, she couldn't deny the pull toward him. And she daren't say it aloud or admit it to anyone, but Purgatory intrigued her.

Through her reflection, she hadn't realised earlier a part of her had welcomed that darkness, to let it nestle in and slowly consume her in Purgatory. Luckily, the lighter side of her, the good side of her, reminded her of who she was and what was important.

The stools scraped across the concrete floor, drawing her away from her thoughts. She vaguely listened to Draven and Grunge's voices infiltrating the kitchen.

She had to be stronger. She needed to be. However, all she could think as she heard Draven ask her what she wanted for breakfast was: *what if I like the dark side of myself too much?*

Chapter Eight

~ Draven ~

Draven zoned out from whatever Grunge was saying and watched Aliyah move her food around on her plate. She'd barely eaten a bite or said a word since they all sat down for breakfast.

The dream seemed to have really spooked her and he had no idea how to placate her. Meanwhile, he felt the heaviness weighing down on him with everything that was happening around them.

Draven was finding it difficult to keep himself grounded. Questions circled around his frenzied mind. How was he going to rein in the darkness, find a way to wake his best friend up from limbo, protect Aliyah and everyone he loved, along with saving Laney from Melantha's vindictive claws?

Was that demon really going to play fair or would she somehow twist the contents of the agreement to her own advantage? Draven didn't trust her as far as he could throw her decaying ass.

His head was pounding and he'd only just woken up. How the fuck was he going to get them out of this bullshit? His ruminations were disrupted by Grunge's voice.

"Oi? Asswipe, you in there?" He tapped the top of Draven's skull. "Between you and Aliyah this morning, I'm not convinced you two have got your shit handled. We *all* have a lot going on and we need our heads in the game if we are going to beat these sadistic motherfuckers at their own game. You feel?"

Aliyah's head snapped up, her violet irises burning ferociously. She looked at Grunge first, then him, and replied, "It's not that fucking easy. I wish it was. Draven, can
we go to Reikiki's now? The sooner I get this philter or
whatever you called it, the better."

Draven didn't have time to respond. Grunge spoke
first, his tone laced with worry as he questioned Aliyah.
"What happened? Why do you need one of his concoctions? Are you ok?"

Her eyes fluttered closed and she took in a heavy
breath then released it. She opened her eyes and explained her dream for the second time that morning. She
looked tired and troubled. Draven sensed another emotion
there that surprised him. Curiosity.

Deciding not to bring it up in front of Grunge, he suggested they all finish up their breakfast and head out. Draven had a feeling this day was going to get hairy.

The door to Reikiki's flew open again without any of
them knocking. Draven wondered if the man had cast a
spell to allow them entrance whenever, seeing the Mad
Warlock was nowhere to be seen.

Stepping over the threshold cautiously, he waved Aliyah and Grunge to follow. The apartment was eerily quiet
and the pictures along the wall once again compelled him
to peer into their colours.

Shaking his head, he looked forward and ignored the
pictures. A clink sounded to the right and Draven followed
it.

Walking into the room with Aliyah and Grunge in tow,
Draven noticed the dark panelled glass French doors that
opened up to Reikiki's balcony were open. Apprehension
filled his bones; it was never wise to sneak up on a Warlock.

"Reikiki? Are you here?"

"Out here," he called out.

"I think I'll wait here," Aliyah stated.

Draven's highbrow rose in question. He shrugged his
shoulders and walked over to the balcony with Grunge following suit.

He was not prepared at all for what his precious eyes

endured. "What the fuck, Reikiki!" Both Grunge and Draven cursed at the same time.

Reikiki laughed deep and throaty at them. It was like a car crash. Draven couldn't turn away. He watched on, befuddled as the Mad Warlock took another swig of his drink and pushed the man's head down so he gagged on his cock.

Collecting himself, he turned around and walked back into the room where he found a giggling Aliyah. She was sitting at a round high timber table. The kind you sometimes see at a bar with people standing around.

"Something funny, Snowflake?" he said, trying to hide the smile that was threatening to breach his face.

"How did you not sense it? Smell it?"

"I wasn't even thinking to be honest. Mind you, you are still transitioning, so your senses are still elevated."

Aliyah rolled her eyes and shook her head. "Uh huh. Keep telling yourself that."

The small grin widened on those lustrous bow lips. She was baiting him. Later he would tend to that mouth of hers. Now, they had bigger fish to fry, and Reikiki's blowjob wasn't one of them.

Draven held Aliyah's hand and sat down on the mustard coloured leather lounges in one of Reikiki's rooms. The room was decorated with fancy embellished silver and black wallpaper with a few framed photographs and paintings of himself with other beings that Draven assumed he met in his long life. While he was admiring the room and pictures, Reikiki came inside. Thankfully, all his clothes were in place. He sat down and started talking with Aliyah.

Tuning into the conversation, he listened as Aliyah retold her dream to Reikiki. Leaning back into the lounge, the Mad Warlock's tiger eyes seemed intrigued with Aliyah's story. Draven observed how he fiddled with the beads in his silver hair and occasionally stroked his goatee.

"So can you help me?"

Reikiki stood suddenly and the alcoholic drink in his hand sloshed all over the floor as he stretched his arms wide. "Well of course, child! They don't call me the Mad Warlock for no reason now," he said dramatically and winked at Draven. *Shit.*

His eyes had taken on that manic edge they did when he was sinking slowly into madness. Although he always found a way to bring himself back.

He whizzed his hands around in the air, uttered a few words quietly, and purple/blue light emanated from his palm. Aliyah gasped and Draven watched on in awe at how those brilliant violet hues sparkled brightly.

"Here you are. Take this one now. Later, I'll make another for you to take home. The other one will be more potent so you'll only need a drop every other day if you sense the philter fading."

"Ok. Thank you so much, Reikiki, I truly appreciate it."

He waved her off, then smirked. "Now if you two wouldn't mind, I have some business to attend to."

Aliyah stifled a giggle and Draven ran his hand through his dreads, not wanting to envision this "business" he was insinuating. "Go on, you horn dog. We need to check in with the others anyway."

With those words, Reikiki was gone.

Aliyah brought the small vile up to her mouth, readying herself to drink it. Draven hid the wicked grin from his expression and observed. He knew from experience they always tasted rank.

On cue, Aliyah scrunched her eyes closed tight. Her face turned bright red and she fanned it rapidly.

Draven knew he shouldn't, but he couldn't stop the laugh crawling up his throat. He busted out with a full bellied chuckle. Tears ran down his face because he was laughing so much.

Aliyah stood up and gawked at him, her foot tapping furiously and her hands on her hips. "Why the fuck didn't you tell me it was going to taste like ass!"

"Let's just say it's payback for your little stunt earlier." He winked at her then got up and walked off in the direction of Jadis, Dolph, and Dany's room.

Pulling his phone from his pocket, he saw it was only seven thirty in the morning and figured he should be quiet in case they were still sleeping. Draven slowly opened the door, not learning a lesson from before and tuning into his senses like he should have. He saw Dolph in the same position as normal, then his eyes adjusted to the dim room.

He saw more than he'd cared to see.

"For fuck sakes. Twice in the matter of an hour," he groaned and closed the door. Seeing Dany's white ass in the air as he and Jadis bumped uglies was not something he'd needed to see.

Draven looked up and saw Aliyah leaning on the door frame across the hall with a grin pasted on her face. "Yeah, yeah, I get it. Pay back."

Leaving the pair to their business, Draven sat in the sitting room across from Dolph's room with Aliyah. He looked around the decorated space and began to wonder how the fuck Reikiki fit so many rooms into one apartment. Magic of course.

Dark timber bookshelves lined one wall, and in each corner there was a long red velvet reading lounge. They looked comfortable. His mind went to the gutter as he visualized Aliyah sprawled out, naked, ready, and waiting for him.

Repositioning his semi erection, Draven rolled his head around and cracked his neck while waiting for the pair to grace him with their sexed up presence.

Through the entryway, he saw Jadis step out first. Her purple fringe was dishevelled and she had a smile fixed on that pretty face of hers. Dany stepped out next. His hair didn't look much better. His man bun was mussed like Jadis had run her hands through it, which she probably had.

"We didn't expect you so early," Jadis stated.

"Gathered," Draven grunted. "How's Dolph? Any progress?"

"Nothing. Actually, Dany you should probably feed him."

"I'll come with you," Aliyah offered.

Once they were out of earshot, Jadis pulled him further into the room. "I don't know how much longer we can keep this up," she whispered. "He's unresponsive and I'm fucking depleted. I know this is probably TMI but I feel somewhat replenished when Dany and I fuck. It's not enough though. Maybe those fuck knuckles did something to me, or perhaps it's because I'm missing Dolph. I feel so helpless."

He wrapped an arm around her because he could relate to how she was feeling. There was so much going on around them and they could barely catch a breath.

"We will get through this, J. I promise you."

"Don't..." she was interrupted by Dany and Aliyah screaming out to them.

Draven was in the room in an instant. "What? What happened?"

"He moved. He fucking moved!" Dany exclaimed.

"How? What? When?" Jadis demanded.

"Just now. Aliyah was holding his mouth open so I could drip my blood inside. His eyes flew open, he twitched, and then he was gone again. Back to how he's been."

"Fuck! If I was here, I could have tried to bring him back! Dammit."

"You don't know that, Jadis." Aliyah attempted to assuage her.

"You're right, and now I'll never know." She dragged her feet toward his bed, looking shattered. Aliyah and Dany moved out of her way so she could plop down on the bed. Once she laid her head on his chest, she wept uncontrollably. Dany moved toward her and sat down beside her. Languidly, he stroked his fingers up and down her back trying to soothe her.

Draven wished he could say something, anything to ease her pain. Alas, he knew it was futile when the guilt was deep seated.

Something sparked within Draven as a lightbulb set off in a tangent in his mind. It definitely wasn't the perfect time, but he figured it could help alleviate some stress from them all if they could pretend for a little while they weren't being swallowed by the chasm beneath their feet, even if they were.

"Have you fed, Dany?"

Dany's umber orbs bored into his mismatch pair and his nostrils flared. "Not today."

"That's a weird question, Shrek."

Draven ran his hand over his stubble and eyed each of them. Of all the times, he picked this one. Draven decided he was going to introduce these newly transitioned vampires to feeding.

Hell, it would certainly take his mind off of the bullshit for five minutes. He wanted, no *needed* to know the pair of them would be ok if shit went pear shaped. Especially Aliyah.

The abrupt urge to teach them was unexpected and vicious. Regardless, they both needed to know how to feed surreptitiously if they were to survive in this realm.

"I'm taking you both on an excursion tonight."

"Oh?" came from both Aliyah and Dany.

"Tonight I'm going to show you both how to feed and stay under the radar from the humans. I need to know if something happens to me, you'll both be ok."

"Why do you have to talk that way for, D-man? Can't you see Liah is about to blow a damn gasket over that statement?"

Draven looked into those violet hues and saw the unshed tears forming. He softened his stance and said, "I'm not saying anything is going to happen. If it does, I need you both to be prepared and to survive if there are any issues along the way. At least this way you'll both have a means to an end if shit goes haywire. I was always going to teach you, Snowflake. I just chose now to do so."

She nodded, swiped her hand across her nose, then sniffed. Dany rubbed his hands together, showing that Cheshire smile of his. He ran his tongue ring over his pearly whites.

"Tonight we feast!"

Jadis moved her head from Dolph's chest and pursed her lips briefly before speaking. "I will be servicing that ass before you leave, spunky. No funny business out there."

"No need to eat out when I can eat at home," he replied smoothly.

"Eeewww... TMI, you two," Aliyah grimaced. She added, "Hmm, maybe I can find a nice hunky man to sink my fangs into."

She was trying to entice the beast inside of Draven to come out and play. She forgot two could play at that game.

Draven grinned, knowing he was going to make those pretty cheeks on her face red. "Well while you're doing that, I'll be fucking that pretty white ass from behind."

Aliyah gaped and he watched the flush travel up her neck to her face. Oh, the things he imagined that mouth of hers could be doing...

Already the blood was rushing to his cock. He wanted to get her sinful body home so he could have his way with her.

Unfortunately, Draven couldn't shake the feeling something wasn't right. That's when he realised one of their party was missing, that he hadn't seen him since the encounter with the Mad Warlock and he had excused himself to go to the bathroom.

"Have any of you seen Grunge recently?" Everyone shook their head no.

Out of nowhere, Reikiki appeared and answered, "He left with Laney about thirty minutes ago."

Shit.

Chapter Nine

~ Draven ~

What the fuck was he thinking? He knew I was looking for Laney. Now I'm going to have search for the pair of them. Fuck.

Draven had known since he woke up that today was going to be a bitch. He hadn't foreseen any of what transpired so far this morning, though.

His veins itched like hell and his skin was prickly with need. It been close to forty-eight hours since he'd fed, and at this rate he didn't know when they were going to catch a fucking break.

Aliyah sidled up beside him, one hand on his lower back while the other rested on his right bare bicep. Some of his agitation bled from his form, but not completely. It'd been a couple of days since the blood debt and he was still no closer to bringing Laney back to the less evil side.

He groaned, placed his left hand over Aliyah's right and looked to Reikiki. "You didn't try to stop him?"

Reikiki tutted, then sassed, "I was kind of in the middle of something, vampire. By the time I realized what was happening, I decided to allow it to play out. I haven't had a vision, but something told me that letting them leave was the right thing."

Draven's head fell back, his eyes finding the elaborate, adorned ceiling as he released a sigh. "While you're doing that, I'm going to take Aliyah home and figure out what the fuck I am going to do with this shit storm that is currently my life. Oh, I forgot to mention that my half-brother is the owner of Midnight Mayhem. He stopped by yesterday. I need to figure out what his play is in all of this. He's turned dark, rouge. His brandings are no longer Kaltemis's. Neferity has overruled them all."

Reikiki gasped. "Impossible."

Draven ignored him, feeling Aliyah tense up beside him.

Aliyah stilled. "You didn't tell me he came over. What did he want?"

"Come on, baby, what do they all want?" Jadis relented. "It's got to be you."

"Ding, ding. I'll tell you about it later, Snowflake. If any of you see Grunge or Laney, call me ASAP." With his last comment hanging in the air, he grabbed Aliyah's hand and headed back home.

On the drive to the lair, Draven explained his relationship with Emilio and his sister, Nevine. He hadn't seen his half-sister for some time so he had no idea where she was. His brother on the other hand was like one of those bugs you wanted to squash. He was always buzzing around, even though he wasn't welcome.

Draven and Emilio had always had a volatile relationship, ever since they were little. He figured his half-brother held him culpable for what happened to their father later on in their lives.

Draven didn't go into the details about his dad to Aliyah. The pain was still raw when it came to that subject.

As he parked the fifty at Jadis's shop, Aliyah spoke, "One day, when you're ready of course, I want to know about your father. Your pain is palpable, babe. It's excruciating if I'm honest."

Draven offered her a sad smile; she knew him so well. "I promise baby, I will. Just... just not yet. We have so much going on around us right now. I can't afford to possibly lose myself if I was to rip open that wound."

"I know. I'm not going anywhere anyway. You'll tell me when you're ready. Hey, let's go get something to eat. I'm not ready to go back home yet. My head is all over the place."

His face kicked up at the sides upon hearing her say

home. He would never tire of that. Motioning toward Decatur Street, he took hold of her hand and suggested she chose where she wanted to eat.

The street was bustling with people. They pushed through the crowd and zigzagged through the traffic until she found what she was looking for.

Aliyah picked a small, cozy café. Draven observed the place while they waited for someone to take their order. It was modern with and industrial touch. Old style shed lamp lights hung from the ceiling, while the walls of the café were white timber cladding. A few pot plants were placed around the shop, giving it a fresh feeling. It was pleasant.

A young male waiter dressed in black slacks and white crisp shirt came over to greet them. After placing a cold bottle of water down, he asked for their order.

Draven ordered two lemon lime bitters and a tasting plate to share then sent him on his way. It didn't go unnoticed the way the waiter was eye-fucking what was his. Alas, they had more important things to worry about than a human ogling his woman.

His shoulders were tense, his body wired. He felt all of Aliyah's emotions. They were that damn palpable. They sat in silence, clearly battling their own issues while they waited for their order.

The waiter returned, smiled at Aliyah and lingered longer than necessary. Draven cleared his throat and the young man scampered off.

"You didn't have to scare him, Shrek."

He examined his nails before looking up at her with a smirk in place. "You're right, I didn't. But it was fun."

Shaking her head, Draven noticed her trying to hide a smile, which only made him smirk wider. Aliyah hadn't been herself since that damn dream. He knew he was about to kill the mood, but he needed her to talk about her feelings instead of bottling them up.

"You've been awfully quiet this morning. That dream really shook you up, didn't it?" The small smile that was on her face immediately fell and she turned away from his sight.

"I don't want to talk about it right now. Please."

"You can't keep suppressing it, baby. It will eat you

from the inside out."

"I said I don't want to talk about it right now."

Draven noticed they'd gained some spectators and he definitely didn't miss the tick in her jaw. He knew he should drop it, but his mouth had other ideas.

"I understand that, but I've been there before and keeping it inside was my undoing."

It happened so quick. Aliyah jolted upright, spilling their drinks everywhere. Draven noted her brilliant violet hues were clouded by red specks. Her darkness was setting in.

He knew from experience it was too late to placate her. Now he had to endure her anger.

"Oh right. Because you're a three-hundred-year-old vampire or some shit, right? Because you've been there, seen that, done that, right? Because I am insignificant, young and have fuck all life experiences, right? How could I possibly know more about my own mind than you? Fuck you! You don't know what I'm going through. You have no fucking idea!"

Her body was vibrating and he noted the slight golden hue emerging around her. *Shit.*

Draven's eyes moved around, casually counting how many patrons were in the café. He didn't want Aliyah to get the wrong impression because his eyes did not stay on hers. There were roughly thirty patrons and five staff ogling them.

Standing up slowly, he focused again on Aliyah. "You're right. I don't know what you're going through. It was wrong of me to assume or tell you what you should and shouldn't do. I'm sorry baby."

She relaxed slightly, although the red in her eyes hadn't dissipated. It'd been a long damn time since he attempted transotic on more than one human at a time. He knew because it was a compelling glamour magic. It was the very reason why vampires had gone undetected for so many years. A vampire could manipulate the humans mind to do many things. In this case, Draven was going to make them forget they'd ever seen them.

Focusing all his energy, he summoned as much magic as possible to perform the transotic. Aliyah gasped, and he noticed her eyes had returned back to their luminous hue.

The civilians looked frightened and he realised he hadn't completed the transotic yet. Peering down, he noticed he was shaking. He needed to do this and quick.

"Irrevensvia." Every human's eyes in the place took on a glazed look. This word was how a vampire set the transotic into place. "We were never here. You will not remember us and you will not recall ever seeing either of us. There is no such thing as vampires."

Reaching over, he offered his hand to Aliyah. She placed hers within his. Something passed through her eyes, something that he believed resembled awe. Right now he felt anything but. His body was growing weak from summoning that amount of energy and magic.

Walking out of the café, Draven uttered one last word, "Revensivia." The sound of dishes clanging and people talking reached them.

By saying the word Revensivia, he knew every being was under the compulsion was no longer stuck in the trance he had put them under. To their benefit, they wouldn't remember a single damn thing.

There were only a couple of humans who could repel the transotic. Those humans had what the Otherworlder's call the sight. Draven didn't sense anyone with that ability in the café.

"How did you do that?"

He couldn't answer that question. "I—I don't know. I've never done that with so many people at once."

Aliyah didn't ask him anymore questions while they staggered down the alleyway. Suddenly, Draven's body turned rigid. His senses kicked up a few notches and his possessive and protective streak took front and center. He pushed Aliyah weakly behind him, sensing a malignant entity close by. One he'd sensed before.

"Show yourself, Malister. I really don't have time for these fucking games."

Orange mist formed around them and then she appeared. Her fiery orange hair was pulled up in tight bun with a couple of strands framing her face. Those eerie, red speckled sapphire eyes assessed them as her voluptuous host body circled them.

"I could end you right now, vampire."

Aliyah moved from behind him. "I'd like to see you try," she sneered.

Malister only smiled, her eyes briefly flickering toward Aliyah then back to him. "I would watch your back, Draven. You seem to be getting stronger, but your mother won't rest until you're thrown to the fiery depths of Purgatory."

"Why are you even here? To warn us? Why?" Draven retorted.

"Let's just say that I have my eyes set on a different prize." With that statement, she disappeared.

"What the hell was that, Shrek?"

"I have no idea, baby. I—I need to get back to the lair and recharge. Come on."

They stumbled through the large steel door hand in hand. Fatigue and depletion had set in deep down to his marrow. He needed blood. But first he needed to rest.

Disengaging, he released her hand and said, "I'm just going to rest a little. Make sure you wake me up so I can take you and Dany out later." He kissed her lips faintly and staggered toward the bedroom.

Draven hit the mattress with a thud. His eyes felt like sandpaper was sliding across them, and the grogginess was overwhelming.

There was a niggling feeling in the back of his skull when he began to drift off to sleep. That part of him was urging him to stay awake and comfort Aliyah, but he was so damn tired.

And to top it off, he wasn't sure how the fuck he'd done what he did in the café. Or what the fuck Malister wanted. Something told him he was going to find out real soon.

~ Aliyah ~

What in Perdition just happened? Aliyah's mind was restless and active as hell. She paced up and down the lounge area barefoot, ripping her clothes off and throwing them all over the shiny grey floor.

She was hot. Her clothes felt like they were strangling her, chafing her from the inside out and she needed them off. Standing in her black lace bra and panties, she pulled her hair from her messy bun, stilled and watched the raven tendrils fall around her face.

Blood hissed through her ears and she closed her eyes, trying to slow her breathing. Those embers were igniting in her belly; the acrid animosity slowly coming to the surface. How was she going to control this anger? Was Gorgon right? Would she eventually subjugate to the darkness? To him?

Running her hands through her knotty locks, Aliyah sauntered over to Draven's room, cracked the door and noticed he was passed the fuck out. His jean clad legs hung over the edge of bed and his dreadlocks over his face, providing a curtain from the world.

Aliyah envied him in that moment. He looked peaceful while she was ready to rip her damn hair out. Tiptoeing toward their bathroom, she closed the door and stepped up to the tub.

Turning the copper faucets on, she watched the water stream out and the steam billow up above the black and copper claw foot spa. She pushed the plug in and watched the water start to fill. Reaching over toward the dark timber vanity, she pulled the cupboard door open and hoped she'd find some salts or something to put in the bath.

Her muscles ached and her jaw clenched and unclenched continuously. Shaking herself, she forced herself to relax and count her breathes. One, two, three, four, five...

Finally, her body eased a little. Reaching to the far end of the cupboard, she found what she was looking for. A bag of scented salts was bundled up. They looked like they hadn't been used in eons. Shrugging her shoulders, she palmed the bag and poured a heap into the bath.

She observed the splash and ripples in the steamy water as the tub filled. For a second she felt it looked a lot like her world lately: disturbed and constantly choppy. Would they ever catch a break?

Peering up, Aliyah caught her reflection in the mirror and wandered over. She wiped the condensation off and stared at herself. The same ebony hair fell down the length of her back. Her heart shaped face and dark pink lips opened slightly as she stared into her eyes. They were that shade of violet she'd always loved.

Aliyah leaned closer to the mirror, forcing herself to look into those same eyes she'd been looking into for eighteen years. For the first time in god knows how long, she noticed how the creases marred the sides and how they didn't look as big and vivacious as they had before. She looked tired.

Focusing on her irises, she leaned even closer and noticed the red speckles glaring back at her, taunting her, reminding her that she was not only vampire, faery and angel, but also part demon.

The realization hit her in the gut like a god damn bowling ball had smashed into it. Growling, Aliyah slammed her palm into the mirror and shattered it. Her eyes grew wide at the blood oozing from her palm.

She breathed heavily and waited for Draven to barge in and demand what happened. Aliyah stood there for what felt like a couple of minutes, but nothing happened. She guessed the magic he used had drained him more than he'd realised.

Letting out a sigh of relief, she was thankful she wouldn't need to listen to him prattle on in a condescending tone for not controlling her anger. She reached over, turned off the copper faucets, stripped out of her undergarments and hopped into the bath.

Aliyah welcomed the searing hot water nipping at her body, taking away some of the doubt and pain that had burrowed itself deep inside of her flesh.

She needed to get her head in the game. Gorgon was playing with her. He was the cat and she was the meek little mouse that he wanted to condition and devour.

Leaning back, she rested her head on the tub and closed her eyes. Aliyah needed to find a way to be one step ahead of her so called father. She needed to figure out what his game was and why he needed her. But how was she to do that when she had no idea whether she was coming or going?

The darkness was more demanding, vicious and lustrous. She couldn't allow that part of herself to consume the lighter side of her, the unsullied part.

Kaltemis had said that she and Draven were stronger together, that they needed each other. However, since they'd met, their lives had been nothing short of mayhem.

The violent hiss bucketed through her veins and she seethed. What was this damn prophecy and what was her role? What fucking part did she play? And what about Dolph? Would he be in that state forever? What would happen to Jadis and Dany? More to the point, what would happen to each and every one of them if they didn't figure out what these damn fiends wanted from them.

Aliyah knew one thing for certain; none of them would go down without a fight. The warrior in each of them was furious and fierce and none of them would relent.

Her fingers trailed over the celesite crystal around her neck then she wrapped her bloodied palm around it and noticed it was already healing.

The stone suddenly felt really hot and her left thigh where her third eye branding was, the one Goddess Kaltemis gifted her with, tingled. Aliyah's brows creased. She pinched the bridge of her nose and sat up in the tub.

Gazing down, she noticed the red outline glowing. *What now?* she wondered, irritated. All of a sudden her eyes rolled back and she was somewhere she didn't know. Thankfully, she didn't feel like she was in danger.

The air around Aliyah felt warm. The colour of deep lavender stretched out before her eyes as pink and yellow honeysuckle flowers dangled from what looked like weeping willow trees. Turning her body in a small circle, she noticed she was wearing a white silk sheaf. Slowly, she took in the stunning blue lotus flowers bobbing up and down in the water and a long red brick path weaved through the field of grass, flowers, and water. It was breathtaking. *Where am I and why do I feel so calm here?*

Aliyah wandered up the path, taking in the atmosphere. Glancing up, she noticed the crystal blue waterfall cascading down some rocky outcroppings. It was enticing and she stepped off the path, veering toward the water.

Running her fingers through the ripplets, she breathed a contented sigh. She felt grounded here. However, she'd noticed the darkness was still niggling deep down.

The hair on the back of her neck stood on edge and she rounded quickly, standing up and facing the field. White and black mist poured out around her. She squinted, trying to gage what or who was forming in front of her.

Finally, the mist dissipated and a slender woman stood before her in a similar sheaf to her own, except hers was lilac. Her eyes were a brilliant violet and her hair was as white as snow, with what looked like black foils through it. The lady, or whatever being she was, stepped forward. A smile was planted on her face and her brilliant lily white skin was adorned with brandings as she moved closer to Aliyah.

Aliyah put up her hand in a stop gesture. The smile on the woman's face faltered and something passed through her eyes, something that resembled what Aliyah thought was pain.

The woman didn't stop, though. She continued slowly toward her. Aliyah could smell salt in the air when the woman approached. She realised it was caused not only by the woman's unshed tears, but her own as well.

"You know who I am, don't you?" her voice broke and Aliyah watched the tears fall down her heart shaped face.

Swiping the tears that felt like torrential rain falling from her face and clouding her vision, Aliyah cleared her throat. It felt like a golf ball was lodged in her larynx. She whispered,

"Mum, is that you?"

Chapter Ten

~ Aliyah ~

Aliyah watched with both curiosity and caution as the woman's steps faltered before she moved toward her once more. *Could this really be my mother?*

The woman stood in front of her. She hesitated before placing her hands on each side of Aliyah's face. A sad smile appeared. Aliyah wasn't sure how to feel about her yet.

Peering into her violet eyes, Aliyah watched as more tears slid down the woman's high cheekbones, and she shuddered.

"I'm— I'm so sorry Aliyah. It wasn't meant to be like this," the woman sobbed. "I am your mother. My name is Serene."

Aliyah removed Serene's hands from her face and staggered back. So many emotions flooded her senses now that she was in fact standing in front of the woman who birthed her.

Sadness, intrigue, grief and anger were only a few of the emotions percolating within her body. *How could this woman just leave me? She knew what type of man Gorgon was and she still screwed him. She knew!*

More tears flooded down her mother's face while her body racked with silent sobs. The smell of the salt in the air was stronger and her eyes darted around this phantasmal place. *Is this a trap?*

"Why now?" Aliyah demanded. "You never reached out for eighteen fucking years! Eighteen years! I thought the people who raised me were my parents. But they've turned out to be just as sick as you and Gorgon! How could you procreate with that monster? How! You knew what you were getting into when you spread your legs for him!"

Serene held her hand up to silence Aliyah. "Don't you dare talk to me like that! You think I stayed away from you because I wanted to? I was always there, even when you didn't know. Now don't make me shut that potty mouth up. You will listen to me, and you will listen to me good," she ground out. Her tears had stopped.

Aliyah stood stock still, her eyes bugged wide. She did not expect that outburst from her estranged mother, and a part of her wasn't sure how to swallow that word vomit.

Shaking her head, she waved her hand for Serene to continue. "Well? Go on. Tell me why you left your daughter in the hands of strangers."

Serene flinched at her words. She motioned for Aliyah to follow her toward an old tree that was carved into a bench seat situated in front of the waterfall. She followed, sat down and faced her mother. *This is going to be good,* she huffed.

Serene pushed her hair behind her ears, released a heavy breath, and spoke. "For one, I didn't procreate with that demon willingly, although I can't regret the action because I have you. He raped me."

Aliyah reared back. Her heart thundered through her ears and she thought the damn thing was going to perforate her chest cavity. Her blood clamoured through her arteries as that ubiquitous deep heat claimed her body.

"I. Am. Going. To. Kill. Him!" Aliyah enunciated each word with venom. Her vision began to blur with shades of red. How was it that five minutes ago she didn't want a bar of this woman, and now, now she was ready to kill for her?

Aliyah didn't registered Serene's voice or the touch of her skin until she let out a high pitch scream. Her neck snapped toward her mother, the red fog dissipating as she saw Serene glowing. *Is that what I look like? She looks magnificent,* she wondered in awe.

"Enough! Listen to me, Aliyah. That darkness, that anger inside of you, you need to learn to control it. If you don't then you will walk straight into their welcoming arms. They want your light, but they *need* your dark."

Aliyah's eyebrows pinched together. "What does that even mean?"

"This revelation, this prophecy that they're trying to fulfil is much grander than we initially thought."

"We?"

"Yes, we. The Goddess, Kaltemis and few other magical beings here."

Aliyah made a show of looking around the massive field. "There are more of you here?" Actually, where exactly is here?"

The smile reached Serene's eyes as she gracefully stood and circled around. The bottom of her sheaf flared out then she stopped and sat back down on the log seat. "This my beautiful girl is The Enchantment."

"Uh?"

"The Enchantment is a realm, a plane for the light. You cannot see anyone but they were all around you earlier. There is a glamour in place and once you tap into your faery and angel magic, you shall see everything that is blind to any naked eye. We are getting off track, Aliyah, and we haven't got much time. You can't stay rooted to the realm for too long. It's dangerous."

She was so fucking confused. The Enchantment had other magical beings and that damn revelation would not piss off. What was she supposed to do? Why couldn't anyone give her a clear cut answer?

Closing her eyes, Aliyah breathed in then out and opened her eyes to focus on her mother. She still hadn't told her the full story about Gorgon.

"What do I need to do? Tell me, please. I don't have any idea how I'm to deal with Gorgon."

Aliyah noticed Serene's jaw grind together and her eye twitch. "The time will come, beautiful girl. But right now, time isn't on our side. I'm not sure how you were able to find yourself here. Your magic must be enhancing." Aliyah thought she was saying that more to herself than her.

"If you're able to replicate the magic you summoned then you could return at some point. Although you won't be able to frequent here often. Once you return to earth, to that realm, you will be extremely weary. An abundance of energy, determination and magic would have been required for you to bring yourself here." She scratched her chin and stared hard at Aliyah.

"Why are you looking at me like that?"

"In all my years, I've not seen anyone find The Enchantment without the Goddess's assistance. You, my beautiful girl, are even more special than you think. Harness your magic, reign your darkness in and stay close to Draven. I will see you again shortly, daughter."

Aliyah gasped, her legs and arms flaying and splashing water all over the bathroom floor. She was back in Draven's bathroom. Her eyes darted around and then she felt the prickle behind her irises. A tear escaped.

She had so much to ask her, so many questions still unanswered. How did she know about Draven? What happened with Gorgon and Serene? She knew he raped her, but how was that possible? Could her mother leave The Enchantment?

Aliyah drew her legs up to her chest and wept silently. She was exhausted, both mentally and physically. Forcing herself to stand, she exited the tub and dried herself off before entering the room.

Draven was still out cold, and all she wanted was to be in the comfort of his arms. She dropped the towel to the floor and stood naked gazing down at him. He was magnificent. His long dark eyelashes rested on his high cheekbones. His full lips were slightly parted and his dreads covered the right side of his face. She smiled, then crawled quietly onto the bed and wrapped his arms around her torso

Her mother was right. Aliyah felt the heavy blanket of fatigue weighing down on her. She needed to rest... if only for a minute.

She was roused from her sleep, the familiar bundle of nerves heating her entire body. It was like a live wire going off inside of her.

Aliyah moaned and opened her eyes up. Peering down, she saw Draven between her legs biting her inner thigh and then he suckled her swollen lips into his mouth. Wetness trickled down toward her asshole and pooled on the silk sheet.

His mismatched eyes met hers, the glimmer of every-thing sinful staring back at her as he bit down on her clit.

"Ooooohhh fuck," she whimpered.

Aliyah propped herself up on her elbows so she could watch him as he devoured her. His tongue penetrated her pussy and then he dragged his adept tongue up the center and sucked on her clit. Aliyah cried out and threaded her hands through his dreads.

"Yes, fuck, right there, please!" she implored. The im-pending orgasm was barrelling up; she just needed a little more pressure to set those fireworks off.

Draven chuckled darkly, pulled away from her and stood up, rearranging his hardness. "Come on Snowflake, it's time to go. We have to pick Dany up for our little ex-cursion." He winked.

"You are fucking kidding me, right? You can't leave me like this!" Aliyah waved her hands up and down her body and noticed the flushed tinge on her flesh. She needed to cum.

He leaned down, his nose to hers, and whispered, "Oh yes I can... Just think how hot it will be when we finish the night off. How horny you will be for my cock after you've learned to feed. Believe me, baby, you will be dying for it." He trailed his tongue across her lips and pushed off of the bed.

Aliyah was hot. Her whole body was vibrating with the need to shatter around him. She was severely pissed, but she was also intrigued at his statement.

She watched him yank up a pair of ripped denim jeans and put on a black shirt that hugged his inked biceps. If she opened her mouth now, Aliyah knew she would drool over the place.

He smirked at her as he leaned against the door frame. Begrudgingly, she sat up and flipped him the bird before storming over to the wardrobe where Draven had moved her clothes.

Aliyah threw on a small, tight black dress, pairing it with a short leather jacket and her Dr Martins. She swung her hips in dramatic fashion, causing him to chortle behind her.

All she could think was *two can play at that game, baby.*

They arrived at Reikiki's to pick Dany up. He'd mentioned to her along the way that he wanted to check on Dolph and she and Dany could wait in the car if they'd like. Dany wore tight black denim jeans with a burgundy oxford that had the sleeves rolled up, exposing his inked arms.

He was uncharacteristically quiet as they walked to the exit.

Aliyah stepped down the stairwell with Dany in toe. "You alright, D-bag? You don't seem yourself."

"I'm not sure how I should feel or what to expect. This whole vamp-wolf shit is uncanny. I feel like we're still missing something."

Aliyah ruminated over his statement. Once they reached the end of the stairwell, Aliyah stepped out and assessed the street. Deeming it safe, they walked to Draven's Bel Air and climbed in. "What do you mean *we are missing something?*"

"You remember how you entered my mind recently?" Melancholy tinged his words. "Did I really suppress that memory or was it taken from me? You know, like Jill's was?"

Aliyah's brow crinkled and she chewed the inside of her cheek. He did have a point. Why now? Then she remembered Serene and that she'd forgotten to tell Draven. *Shit.*

"That is a valid observation. It hadn't crossed my mind until you mentioned it. I just figured that you'd repressed the memory being so young."

"Can you do me a favour bitchface?"

"When you ask so nicely, how can I deny you." She rolled her eyes dramatically.

"Will you try and enter my mind again? Not now of course," he rushed, "but sometime soon. Things don't add up. If I was truly there, I would have seen the person or people responsible for their deaths."

"That makes a lot of sense. Are you sure though? The last time was excruciating for you?"

"Yeah, I'm sure," he lamented. "It needs to be done. I need some fucking closure."

The door swung wide and Draven hopped in. She nodded her answer to Dany and faced Draven. He quirked and eyebrow at her and then Dany.

"You two ok? It feels heavy as fuck in here."

"Yep. We're good, D-Man. I'm sure Aliyah will fill you in later. Nothing to worry about."

Draven's eyebrows pinched together then relaxed. He nodded his head in acquiesce and turned the key in the ignition. The fifty roared to life as they sped toward The Quarter. *Get your head in the game, Liah. There's time to ponder later.*

Lights lined the dark streets as the three of them traversed down the chaotic path of The Quarter after parking the car. The nightlife was something else and Aliyah's veins frizzled with energy, the blood pumping wildly through her arteries.

Draven's hand was hot in her own and she loved the feeling of having him close. Aliyah knew she would be poking the bear with Draven tonight, and she was no doubt going to get punished for her little escapades by the end of the night. Serves him right for waking her up with his tongue in her snatch, then leaving her high and dry. Aliyah smiled to herself and pushed the dark strands of her hair behind her ear with her free hand.

Dany shouldered her from the side and she cursed, "What the fuck, asshole?"

"I know that face. D-Man, you're in for one hell of a ride tonight," he chuckled.

"Oh is that so? You think I should watch my back, Dany? That this little minx has something in mind, huh?"

Aliyah shot daggers up at her best friend and noticed his crooked grin peeking out from what looked like three day growth stubble.

Dany closed his fist while leaving his thumb out and pointed it toward her. He jeered, "Told you."

Both Draven and Dany were chuckling now, which pissed her off. She straightened her back, opened her leather jacket up and sashayed away from them. *Wankers.*

It was nearing ten at night when they pulled out a few stools at a local club. The bar was like one of those old school ones but with a modern flare. Old timber tops lined the bar, stools were pushed underneath and loads of alcohol lined the wall behind the bar. Tables and lounges were scattered around the dark space, lights flashing on and off in the distance.

Aliyah took a sip of her drink that Draven had ordered and breathed in the atmosphere, all the while watching the people around her. Sitting next to Dany, she noticed him gazing around also. He looked lost in thought.

Aliyah didn't want to intrude so she turned away from him and watched as the majority of the humans were yelling over the music and spilling their drinks all over the damn place.

Shaking her head, she reached over and gulped down the rest of the whiskey in her glass. Draven's eyebrows quirked. He looked at her, then the empty glass before signalling the waitress and ordering another.

Four drinks in and Aliyah's body was humming with need. Her head felt as if it was swimming and her blood charged viciously through her veins. She was certain she could smell every single little thing.

Bringing her left hand down, she rubbed small circles around her abdomen, feeling the heat pool between her thighs as she sipped her whiskey.

The bar smelled like sex. Pure, adulterated, filthy sex. How many of these humans were living two lives. Pretending they were single so they could mingle here, so they could feel like they once did: wanted and desired.

Aliyah watched a young woman with bleached blonde hair and a tight little body grind on a young man that was covered in tattoos and piercings. She cocked her head to the side and observed them, her insides liquefying while they basically fucked on the dance floor.

Aliyah knew Draven was loitering close. She could feel his presence and smell his lust. A part of her was curious if it was the club or if he'd been watching her reactions.

He hadn't mentioned whether they would find someone in the club to feed off or what any of it would entail. Aliyah sensed the tiger inside her sharpen her claws. She threw her long hair over her shoulder, finding Draven's eyes. She winked then stood up and sauntered toward the couple.

Aliyah was certain she heard Draven growl and she wondered just how far she could push him. Arriving in front of the couple she beckoned them closer and yelled, "Do you mind if I join you both?"

The blonde's eyes widen and Aliyah thought she saw a flicker of jealousy as her dark eyes roamed her body. The ink junkie slid the woman in between himself and Aliyah and the three of them began grinding and thrusting together.

The woman's knee was wedged between Aliyah's legs and her knee was between the blonde's legs. The friction was almost too much and she could smell how sweet the woman smelled.

"You two are fucking driving me insane," the tatted guy yelled between them. "Fuck, I'd give my left nut to see you two come undone between each other's legs."

"That can be arranged."

Aliyah looked over her shoulder to see a red faced Draven. Dany stood with his arm around a brunette.

"Who, who's this?" the inked junkie stuttered.

"I'm her boyfriend. But you're welcome to watch." He winked.

Aliyah was drawn away from the pissing match by something wet on her leg. Turning around, she faced the blonde. The woman's head was thrown back and she was humping her leg.

The blonde's arousal slammed into her nostrils and Aliyah moaned. She focused on her jugular artery jumping up and down in her neck. She needed to taste her.

Draven moved her inky hair away from her neck. He placed his hand on her hip and whispered in her ear, "You want her, baby? Do you want to feel her blood spurt all over your tongue as you suckle down her sustenance?"

Aliyah wrapped her hand around Draven's neck and brought his lips down to hers. The kiss was hard and hot as their tongues tangled while he squeezed her nipples.

She could still feel the woman riding her leg. When she pulled away from the kiss and looked down, she realized it was the woman's hands kneading her tits and not Draven's.

Eyeing the club, she realised everyone was oblivious to the make out session on the floor. Canting her head to the right, she saw Dany was standing at the table with his legs spread. Underneath it, the woman was between his legs blowing him.

Dany and Aliyah's eyes met and she felt her cheeks heat. He had his hands on each side of her head as he fucked her mouth. His eyes remained locked on Aliyah's with a cheeky grin on his face.

Her senses were overwhelmed as were her emotions. She continued watching Dany while Draven kissed her shoulders and the woman ground up on her leg and played with her tits. It was too much.

Dany's face tightened. When he stilled, Aliyah averted her eyes to the woman between his legs and noticed her swallowing. Aliyah's insides clenched as she watched her best friend climax in public. Ripping her eyes away from him, she looked around to see if anyone had noticed. They all seemed ignorant to what just unfolded. However, Aliyah was anything but. She was turned on beyond measures with everything that was occurring.

"Come with us, pretty girl. I think my Snowflake has something for you." The woman moved away from Aliyah's leg and blushed. Dany moved toward them with an asymmetrical smile on his face and the brunette back under his arm. Aliyah took one last look around the club, realising the inked man that was dancing with them was nowhere to be seen. She figured Draven must have scared him off.

Draven motioned for the four of them to follow him outside. The fresh air smashed into her face and she inhaled dramatically. Her body felt like a fireball. She was hungry, horny and she needed... more.

Walking down the busy streets of New Orleans, they stayed close to Draven while the two women giggled profusely. Entering a dimly lit alleyway, Draven moseyed to the darkest corner and stopped abruptly to face everyone.

"Ready? I can tell you're both wired," he smirked.

Dany spoke first, "Fuck yes."

Aliyah nodded her agreement.

"Ok. Irrevensvia." The two mortals' eyes glazed over. "When I release the compulsion you both need to focus and harness all your energy. It will feel overwhelming to begin with, seeing that you're both only recently transitioned vampires. Can you scent them?

"Yeah," they both answered in unison.

"If they're from vampire linage, you'd be able to smell a hint of chocolate, possibly coffee or wine. Not everyone with vampire linage can or will ever turn. However, if they have vampire blood then they can produce vampire off-springs. Can you smell anything?"

Aliyah inhaled. She watched as Dany did the same. "Nothing. I smell alcohol, perfume and lust," she said.

"I smell the same, but also something dark, almost sinister," Dany wondered, pointing to the woman he had brought.

"Good. Her soul is tainted. She isn't an Otherworlder, but she can easily be manipulated. Dany, if you ever smell those traits make sure you wrap your dick before you fuck them, just in case they're shedding.

"Shedding?" Dany's face screwed up in question.

"Yes, shedding. Shedding is when a female vampire or mortal woman who has vampire blood in her system is fer-tile. Until you're aware of the scent, please wear protec-tion. Unless you want a little Dany boy running around?"

Dany groaned, "I always wrap it up, but fuck me that doesn't sound appealing at all."

Aliyah snorted and Draven smiled down at her and winked. "OK, enough of that. You will be fine as long as you protect your meat." Looking at them both, he asked, "Can either of you feel the heat of your caninesyet?"

Dany and Aliyah nodded yes.

"Ok, good. Repeat after me, Irrevensvia."

They practiced the word a few times, and when Draven was convinced, he reversed the transotic, the compulsion the women were under.

"Revensivia."

The two girls giggled again, like nothing had even hap-pened. Like they hadn't been standing in the land of stu-por.

Aliyah stepped toward the blonde and Dany moved to face the brunette. They locked eyes for a brief moment before she focused on the task at hand.

"Irrevensvia," she said loudly. The woman's eyes glazed over once more and Aliyah wanted to do a happy dance. Looking over to Dany, she'd noticed the woman he was with was in the land of stupor once more.

"Now focus all your energy and magic to direct the mortal what to do," Draven explained.

Aliyah heard a zipper and her head whipped toward Dany. She watched as he rolled the condom onto his dick.

"Focus, Snowflake," Draven threatened.

Her eyes snapped back to the blonde and she placed her hands on her face. "You are going to enjoy yourself, pretty girl," Aliyah muttered. Then she slid her hand up the woman's skirt and pulled her knickers to the side.

"What are you doing, Aliyah?" Draven demanded.

"I want her to feel good. After all I am about to take her blood."

"She will feel good. Your canines release endorphins into any mortal that you bite. Some of them become addicted to our venom, per se. But fuck me, baby, you're turning me on something fierce, even if I'm a little pissed and jealous that you're touching someone that's not me. Now bend over, you dirty little minx. I want to feel you clench around me while you feed from her."

Aliyah mewled and did as instructed. She started to circle the woman's clit, causing the blonde to moan and buck into her hand. Aliyah could here Dany and the other woman's skin slapping as he fucked the brunette only meters away from them.

Bringing herself back, she glided her tongue up the woman's jugular vein and sucked on her neck. Aliyah was inundated by all the senses, sounds and smells around her. When Draven sunk into her abruptly, it caused her canines to elongate and embed into the woman's neck.

Splashes of color went off like fireworks behind her eyes as she suckled the blood into her mouth. The woman tasted sweet like honey, but nowhere near as enticing or concentrated as Draven's blood.

He slammed into her over and over again, her climax nearing as she felt the woman shudder and coat her fingers with her climax.

"Dany, Aliyah, listen to me," Draven ground out while his hips continued to thrust back and forth. "Feel the pulse. When it begins to slow down, you need to stop. If you continue, you could potentially kill the human. When you're done, lick the bite mark to seal the wound."

Aliyah pulled away from the woman's neck and did as he'd instructed. She felt Draven's grip intensify and she knew there would be bruises on her hips.

"Fuck that's hot," Dany whispered.

Aliyah's face flushed as she circled the woman's nub again, forcing her to cum once more. "Don't get any ideas, Dany. I'm just warming to you," Draven growled.

Her best friend chuckled, "Duly noted and no need to worry, D-Man. Purely platonic."

Aliyah felt her body climb higher and higher as Dany's voice droned out. She was so fucking close. Draven bit into her shoulder and she clutched around his cock, crying out in pleasure as starburst ricocheted behind her irises while he emptied out inside of her.

She removed her hand from the woman's knickers and panted. That was one of the most intense orgasm's she'd ever had.

Draven pulled out of her and cupped her pussy with some tissues. Fuck knows where he got them from, but she wasn't complaining as he cleaned her up.

"You two remember the word to reverse the Transotic?" Draven breathed.

"Yep," Dany replied, and Aliyah nodded.

"Once you reverse the compulsion, we will vamp speed out of here. The pair of them will be none the wiser."

Aliyah watched her best friend nod and she followed suit. Standing in front of the woman, she ran her fingers down her face and mirrored something similar that she'd heard Draven say.

"Thank you for that, pretty girl. You won't remember anything that happened here. You never saw me and you won't remember my friends."

Looking to Dany, he nodded his head.

"Revensivia," they both uttered together. Then Aliyah, Draven and Dany vamp sped out of the alleyway, leaving the two women none the wiser of what had occurred.

Dany decided to stay at the lair instead of going back to Reikiki's to be with Jadis and Dolph. Although Aliyah was a little dazed, she saw the conflict in her best friend's eyes as he threw himself on the couch and brought his hand up to his face, covering it.

Her heart broke a little as she watched him slowly drift to sleep. Dany had slept with someone else. Aliyah sensed he didn't want to face the music and tell Jadis what he'd done.

Aliyah reflected on the night she'd had as the hot water hit her flesh in the shower. Not once since her and Dany had been friends had they done the dirty in front of each other. Her face turned hot again at the memory.

Their friendship had definitely taken a different turn. Although it was insanely hot to watch him and he watch her, that's all it was. Nothing more and nothing less. She didn't feel any lust coming off of him when they spoke after the debacle. He seemed, pensive and unaffected by what he'd witnessed earlier.

Hopping into bed, Aliyah hadn't realised how incredibly tired she was as she cuddled up to Draven. The thought of her mother entered her mind briefly, and she reminded herself that tomorrow she would confess to Draven everything her mother had said. And how she'd been to The Enchantment.

Aliyah only hoped that when Dany told Jadis about what transpired tonight, she would be forgiving. After all, she wasn't one to talk. She was in love with Dolph, and Dany was somehow linked to them. She really did feel for her best friend. It was like he was the third wheel in that relationship.

As she started drifting off to sleep, she prayed that Dany would be ok, and that the love that Jadis allegedly had for him would be enough.

Chapter Eleven

~ Draven ~

Stretching his long arms, Draven looked over and watched Aliyah snore quietly. Her raven hair was sloshed all over the bed and her face. She looked peaceful.

He moved the long tendrils from her flesh and placed a small kiss on her forehead. She stirred but didn't wake up.

Draven slid out of the bed and fixed the black duvet over Aliyah then walked out the room. When he entered the sitting room, Dany was sitting on the lounge with his elbows on his knees and his hand pulling at his hair.

"You ok, man?"

Dany jumped then turned to face him. "Shit, Draven, you scared me."

He ignored his protest and instead repeated, "You ok?"

Dany sighed and stood up. He had lost the shirt from the night before and was just in his jeans. "I honestly don't know."

"Is there anything I can do?"

He smirked, "Can you find the cunt that murdered my parents? Find out if Jadis really loves me, or if I am just here to appease the Gods and be the third wheel in that relationship?" He held up his hand to prevent Draven from interrupting, and said, "Hold on, there's more. Can you tell me how the fuck I am going to come to terms with who I am now and then tell the woman that I love I cheated on her last night, even though I feel she cheats on me every single fucking day?"

Fuck. This was some heavy shit. He'd wondered how long it would take Dany to feel like he does now. Draven hadn't thought he was someone who liked to share his girl.

"Come in the kitchen. I can cook while we talk."

Dany followed behind and sat at the black speckled granite breakfast bench. Draven went to the fridge and pulled out some fresh avocadoes and free-range eggs.

"You want bacon or smoked salmon?"

Dany's umber eyes met Draven's before he shrugged his shoulders. "Whatever man, surprise me."

Draven opted for salmon. Filling up a pot with water, he threw in some salt, a splash of vinegar and then cut up slices of Italian bread while he waited for the water to boil so he could poach the eggs.

"Talk to me, Dany."

Draven stopped what he was doing and leaned back on the granite bench, crossing his feet at the ankles and waited for him to respond. The kid was a mess. Under his eyes were massive bags and his black hair wasn't in his usual man bun. Instead, it hung messily down his back as he threaded his fingers through the tendrils and pulled.

"How do you do it? How do you stand there stoic and composed? Like you have your shit together when everyone around you is falling apart?" he exclaimed. "I'm–I'm not strong like you, Draven. And I'm certainly not built for all of this crap."

He was so not expecting that. *He thinks I have my shit together? That I'm not losing my damn mind every second of every day? That I barely fucking sleep because I feel suffocated from it? Damn, the most sleep I've had lately was when I used too much magic to transotic those humans after Aliyah's outburst. And the only reason I slept was because I was depleted.*

Draven remained silent, ruminating and compartmentalising how he was going to respond to Dany's accusation, because let's face it, that's what it was.

He picked up the egg and cracked it into a small cup then swirled the boiling water with a wooden spoon to make a whirlpool. Once he was happy with the circling water, he dropped the egg in slowly and repeated the process with the others before turning around and putting the bread on to toast.

Looking up to the ceiling, he released a long breath and said, "I don't have anything together, Dany. Far from it. I may seem complacent, content even on the outside. However, in my mind I've murdered every asshole I hate in the vicinity over and over. I don't sleep. I force myself to eat. And at night when Aliyah finally drifts off to sleep, when she thinks I'm snoring quietly beside her, I'm staring at the roof of this fucking lair wondering how the hell I'm going to save everyone I love around me. How I'm going to bring Dolph back, save Laney, keep you, Jadis and Aliyah safe. The list goes on..." He sighed. "I'm not strong, Dany. I'm anything but."

Draven's confession came out strained. He hadn't expected to word vomit like he did. His body was thrumming with pent up emotions, namely anger, because he found himself once again in a fucked up situation.

The toast popped and snapped him from his thoughts. Draven peered down at his phone and realised the eggs had been cooking for a few minutes.

Grabbing the slotted ladle, he scooped up the eggs one by one and placed them on a plate. He buttered the toast in silence, waiting for Dany to speak.

Draven sliced some avocado for the toast then layered the salmon and eggs on top. He put one plate aside for Aliyah and handed Dany's to him, along with the salt and pepper shaker.

The way Dany was staring at him made him feel awkward. Breaking the silence, he cleared his throat and said, "Want some hollandaise sauce?"

Dany nodded and Draven walked to the fridge, grabbed the sauce, squeezed some on his then handed it to him.

He heard the hollandaise bottle wheeze as Dany smothered his eggs in it. "I'm sorry, D-Man, I didn't think. I'm such a selfish shithead. I don't know what I'm doing anymore. I feel like I'm drowning," he admitted, then picked up his cutlery and began eating.

Draven knew that feeling all too well. That niggling, annoying, throat grazing, gut churning asshole of an emotion was one he would never forget. It lived inside of him every single fucking day.

"Don't be sorry. You're entitled to your feelings, man. And to be honest, you've got a shit load of things happening in your life. The majority of them you didn't know about until recently. As for Jadis, I don't know what you want me to say about her, or the relationship between her and Dolph. Has she opened up about any of it?"

"Not really. She's vague. Saying shit like they shared a history. That was it. She tells me she loves me all the time, D, but it doesn't feel authentic. I don't think she loves me like I love her," he finished with a whisper. "And maybe, just maybe that's why I'm subconsciously sabotaging this relationship, like what I did last night with the brunette. I know when Dolph wakes up I'll be pushed to the side. Whether or not he'll need my blood when he returns to the living, I know if push comes to shove Jadis will always pick him. She loves him more."

Ouch. The saddest thing about his statement was Draven believed Dany hit the nail on the head. Jadis and Dolph's history would have been an epic love story had it survived. Alas, this was not his place to tell him, even if he wanted to ameliorate the kid's feelings.

"Whatever happens, know that we are here for you. Aliyah is here for you. That girl would die for you, but don't you dare let it come to that, shithead," Draven retorted, trying to lighten the conversation.

He shovelled his eggs in his mouth and Draven observed how the smile reached his eyes when he'd mentioned Aliyah. "Thanks, D-Man. I appreciate it. I won't let her die for me, as long as you don't shag her to death."

Draven choked on his breakfast, almost spitting it all over the counter. After he swallowed down his eggs, he reached forward to take a sip of his drink. The pair of them busted out laughing. Just for that moment, they both seemed a little lighter and Draven felt the forming brotherhood with him.

Even after Dany had watched them fuck and feed, Draven knew he would never jeopardize his friendship with Aliyah. No matter how intimate that moment had been, they were friends and nothing more.

Aliyah took that moment to stagger into the kitchen.

She wore a pair of short shorts, a white cami that did nothing to hide her nipples poking out, and her hair looked like something out of the movie Hairspray. She padded over to the breakfast counter and yawned. Draven's cock swelled immediately. That would have to wait. He had a niggling feeling lately she was holding something back from him and hoped today would be the day she told him what was on her mind.

"You wanker's woke me up," she grumbled.

Dany forked the rest of his eggs into his gob then spoke with a full mouth. "Riiiighht, like you haven't woken me up before," he grinned after swallowing. "I'm gonna do the three S's – shit, shower and shave, just in case you didn't know, Bitchface. Can I grab a ride back when I'm done, Draven?"

Draven waved him off. "No probs. I want to check on Dolph before I continue this shit show with Laney. Come get us when you're done."

With a wave, Dany turned on his feet and left the kitchen. Aliyah came up behind him a laced her arms around him. She whispered, "Morning, handsome." He heard the seductive lilt in her voice. *The minx.*

"Hmmm... What can I do for you, my love?"

"Love? Not sure I like that nickname. It sounds... old." Draven noticed something flash through her eyes. It was there and then it was gone.

He pushed the observation to the side and chuckled under his breath. Turning around with her arms still laced around his neck, he replied, "I am old, did you forget?"

Aliyah's eyebrows rose and then she smoothed them back out as Draven pushed a lock of raven hair behind her ears. "No. No. But you know what they say?"

"And that is?"

A mischievous look formed on that heart shaped face and her lips kicked up at the side. "You're only as young as the woman your feeling."

She moved in like she was going to kiss him but bit his lip instead and darted away laughing.

Draven growled then bellowed out after her, "You're about to feel how fucking young I really am, wench!"

After a quick fuck session with Aliyah pushed up

against the glass wall in the shower, they emerged from the room dressed and ready for the day.

They walked toward Jadis's shop to pick up his fifty. Draven took a minute to study the building. The same energy pulsated around it; the glamour was still in place.

Any mortal who walked past it wouldn't see what he was seeing: an abandoned store, rickety boards covering the windows and a security guard standing at the front.

Jadis had told Draven she didn't want any young hooligans breaking in and ruining her stuff. As for the Otherworlder's, they knew not to fuck with the High Witch of New Orleans. Jadis was feared by many. There wasn't any Otherworlder Draven knew who would want to endure her wrath, no matter what they could gain. It simply wasn't worth it.

He observed Aliyah and Dany laughing and hopping into the fifty. Her ass was on full display from her ripped black jean shorts. Draven suppressed a groan. He repositioned his growing erection and opened the driver's door.

His eyebrows knit tightly together. "What are you doing, Aliyah?"

"I'm driving, what else?" she smiled up at him with a glint in her eye.

"No. Move."

Her smile faded and frustration replaced it. He could tell by the pull in her eyebrows and the slight tick in her jaw she was trying not to lose her shit.

"Why."

"Because I said so. Now move, please," he acquiesced.

"You let Dany drive. Why can't I?"

"Burn!" Dany blurted out.

"Shut it, asshole!" Draven retorted.

Shit. She had a point and Dany hadn't helped the situation. "That was different and you know it."

Aliyah jutted her chin out. A small smirk threatening to peak out from that perfect mouth of hers. She had his balls in a vice and she knew it.

He tucked his hands into his pocket, tilted his head to the sky and grumbled. Once he felt composed, he fished out the keys and suspended them above her head.

"I swear to the Goddess if you hurt my car, I will make

your ass fucking red."

Aliyah squealed and snatched the keys out of his hands. Slowly, he walked to the passenger side, sidled into the seat then clicked the seatbelt in place. Draven heard Dany in the back, chuckling. He turned around and glowered at him, which only caused the man to laugh harder.

Tears leaked from Dany's eyes when he placed his hands up in front of his chest in mock surrender. "It's not me you should be worried about. Have you seen her drive?"

That was the last thing he heard as the fifty roared to life and Aliyah took off down the street like a fucking grand prix driver.

As soon as the car was parked at the front of Reikiki's, Draven unbuckled and flew from the car. "What the fuck, Aliyah!"

A storm brewed inside Draven as he watched the pair of them step out of the car. Aliyah didn't seem fazed by his outburst. Instead, she and Dany were holding their stomachs while they doubled over laughing in the middle of Bienville Street.

"What. Is. So. Fucking. Funny," Draven growled, emphasizing each word.

"Man! You should have seen your face!" Dany replied, wiping the snot coming from his nose. "She really did a number on you!"

Draven was not impressed, not in the least. Aliyah swiped at the tears running down her face and Draven sensed she was trying to calm herself down.

"I didn't tell you I was a revhead, huh?" She looked to the sky and then her violet orbs found his once more. "Sorry about that."

Draven was aware she was goading him because Aliyah knew he loved his car. "You're not driving my car again. I'll fucking buy you one," he grumbled. "Now let's get this over with. We have a busy fucking day."

Draven checked on Dolph; there hadn't been any change in his situation. He was really starting to worry if his best friend would come out of this...alive.

Heaving a deep sigh, he laced his hands through Aliyah's. He was still pissed at her for her little stunt, but he didn't want to stay around to feel Jadis's wrath when Dany told her what occurred last night.

Before leaving, he slipped Dany a piece of paper. He scrunched his face up, his eyebrows pinching tightly as he unfolded it. Draven watched him read the contacts and pocket the note. He nodded once, hugged Aliyah and walked into the room to confront Jadis.

"What did you give him?"

"I'll tell you once we get out of here. Believe me when I say this is our cue to leave. Come on."

Draven drove toward the Mississippi River. He found a car park and ushered for Aliyah to get out. Rounding the fifty, he popped the boot and pulled out his laptop.

"What are we doing here?"

Draven closed the boot and started walking toward the Riverwalk Gazebo. Hearing Aliyah's feet hitting the pavement behind him, she yelled, "Oi!"

It was still early hours of the morning and thankfully there weren't many people around. He sat down at a table, opened up his laptop then switched it on. Turning to Aliyah, he felt his eyebrow arch up. "Do you have something to tell me?"

Her face morphed into what he thought was disbelief, and he knew in that moment what he'd been sensing was correct.

"I've been meaning to tell you. I—I haven't found the right time, and then I keep forgetting."

Aliyah was still standing so Draven waved his hand for her to sit beside him. "Go on."

"I met my real mum."

"Come again?"

"Her name is Serene. I don't know how. Shit, she didn't even know how. But somehow I transported myself to The Enchantment."

Draven scratched his stubble and canted his head to the right. In his 327 years alive, he hadn't heard of any Otherworlder being able to enter The Enchantment without the Goddess, Kaltemis.

"Hmmm, interesting."

"Huh? What is?"

"Oh, nothing really. Except, I am surprised you entered

that realm, especially without the Goddess. However, I have noticed you haven't been yourself lately. I figured it was due to everything going on around us."

Draven leaned in toward Aliyah and inhaled. His eyes closed as her scent slammed into his nares, causing him to shudder. Yes, there was something different about her. How had he missed it?

"Ummm, Shrek? Are you ok? You're kind of freaking me out right now."

Draven's eyes snapped open. He sat up and moved backward. "You smell different."

Aliyah interrupted, "What? Is that a bad thing?"

"Far from it. Although, you need to remember to mask your scent."

"I have."

"I can smell you, Snowflake."

"Well... Well maybe it's our bond? Maybe it's stronger," she stuttered.

"Hmmm, you could be right."

"Tell me what's changed with my scent?"

"I can smell the divinity around you. You're even more alluring, Aliyah. How did I miss it?" he said more to himself than her. "Perhaps I used too much of my magic for the transotic the other day, I didn't realise how depleted I truly was? Bazaar."

"Okaaaaay. Babe, you're weirding me out. Your eyes have taken on this glow and it's kind of eerie."

It took a moment for what she said to sink in and when it did he understood what she meant. He felt it. Shaking himself from the madness or whatever the fuck was going on for him, he reached over, squeezed her leg and started typing.

"Not sure what just happened, but I'm good. I need to do a little more research and try and find out what the hell Laney has been up to." He attempted to use all his strength to focus on his task at hand and not the fact that Aliyah had been to The Enchantment.

Draven knew he should ask her more questions about her mother but he was finding it difficult to keep his dick in his pants and his mind on the task in front of him. She smelled fucking delicious.

He was disrupted from his thoughts by Aliyah replying, "Mhhmm, you do that and I'll do some reading."

"Let me guess, you're reading some dirty smut?" Draven caught her grin from the corner of his eyes.

"Get to work, slacker. Maybe I can show you later."

Draven chuckled, put his head down and began re-searching. It was almost noon by the time he leaned back on the bench seat. It was hard and uncomfortable.

He stretched his neck from side to side and back to front. So far, he wasn't able to find out anything about Laney from the net. It was as if she didn't exist.

Draven used his encrypted software, the one he used for his business, Obscured Visions, and still found nothing. Feeling agitated, he exited the screen and began research-ing more on Midnight Mayhem.

How is it that I didn't know my half-brother was the owner of that twisted club and that he's gone rogue? What does Neferity want with him? It has to be something big. Otherwise he wouldn't have flaunted it in front of my face. He thinks he's untouchable now the Dark Goddess has him under her wing. Little does my brother know, once Neferity is finished with him, she will spit him out and feed him to her mangy fucking fiends.

Draven's phone began to ring. He pulled it out of his pocket and looked at the number. He didn't recognise it.

"Hello?" he answered dubiously.

"Thank fuck! It's Arc, Draven. You need to get your ass here to Louisiana now! Grunge has been hurt."

Chapter Twelve

~ Draven ~

As soon as he finished his call with Grunge's right hand man, Arc, he threw his laptop in the bag and raced toward his car.

"What's going on, babe?" Aliyah asked, worried.

"It's Grunge; he's hurt. Get in the car, we need to start driving. I told him I'd call him back when we are on our way."

Draven threw the laptop in the back of the fifty and was thankful he always had a bag of clothes in the boot in case of emergencies. Aliyah wasn't aware, but he'd made her bag a couple weeks ago to go with his.

Once they were in the car and buckled up, he maneuvered out of the city and down I-10 W toward Louisiana.

Draven noticed Aliyah was uncharacteristically quiet in the passenger seat. He squeezed her thigh and sent her a reassuring smile. "It'll be ok baby, I promise."

She smiled back at him and then he put the phone on speaker and dialled Arc. Two rings later, he picked up.

"Are you on your way?"

"Yeah, just got onto I-10. Jadis put a spell on my car a few weeks ago so the cops won't stop me. I'll drive like a safe maniac and will be there in ninety minutes. What happened, man?" Draven didn't know Arc as well as Grunge and Dolph. He'd only met him a handful of times when Dolph was the Alpha. And that was a long time ago.

"I'm not 100% sure. He has bite marks in his neck.

He's not bleeding out but the wound isn't healing quickly like it should be. I asked him what happened and he told me to call you then said Laney."

"Fucking hell! I am going to save her sorry ass then kill her myself!" Draven raged.

"What?"

"Nevermind. Long story."

"Yeah, well, let's just say your girl Laney isn't exactly loved around here. So if she's still around, shit could get messy."

Fuck. "I'll be there as soon as I can. If you see Laney, find a way to tranquilize her ass with some wolfsbane. It won't stop her but it'll slow her down." With that, he hung up and put the pedal to the metal.

In just under the allotted time, Draven drove down the hidden track toward the forest land where the pack housed their little colony. Like his lair, it had a protection spell around it. No one would find this place if they hadn't been here before.

Pulling up, he heard Aliyah gasp. He turned toward her and her violet hues were almost popping out of her head. "It's–it's stunning.

They both stepped out of the car and he watched on as Aliyah circled around, eyeing the area. She looked mesmerised.

Draven observed the surroundings as well. It was a whole different universe here, and if he had to describe what it looked like, he would say a beautiful, quaint village.

Timber log cabins were scattered around. Vegetable gardens, flower beds and fruit trees had popped up everywhere since Draven was last here.

In the center of the village was a huge bonfire setting that he adored. Draven remembered sitting there many times, listening to the elders speak of their traditions and legends as they all feasted around the fire. It seemed like a lifetime ago. He supposed it was for a normal human being.

Snapping out of his revelry, he heard Arc calling to him. "Draven. Thank the Goddess you're here. Come with me. He's in the hospital cabin."

Draven sought Aliyah's hand and jogged over to the cabin where Grunge was located. "Have you found Laney?"

Arc looked over his shoulder and hollered back, "We saw her but we couldn't catch her. She looks feral, Draven. Something is off about her."

Ice crept all over him and dread found itself into every molecule in his body. Laney was becoming darker than light. Draven hadn't banked on that. He figured he'd have more time. Shit.

Walking through the timber logged door, he saw Grunge lying on his back. His hand was cupped around his neck and his face seemed etched in pain. Grunge's brows were pulled together tight and his jaw was clenched.

"What the fuck," Aliyah breathed.

Draven released her hand and stomped toward Grunge. First Dolph, now this. He flicked his eyes down and thought, *what next?*

"Grunge, brother. Can you hear me?" "Dra—

Draven," his voice faded out. "Is that chu?"

"Yeah man, it's me. What happened?"

Grunge let out a keening cry, "Ahh fuck it hurts! Make it stop!"

"What do we do? I have no fucking idea man," Arc relented.

"I dunno. Fuck!" Draven raked his hands through his dreadies. *Think, Savage, think!*

He was pushed aside abruptly. Draven looked to his left and focused on Aliyah. She was glowing again.

"What—what in The Enchantment is happening?" Grunge groaned.

"Aliyah, baby, can you hear me? What are you doing?"

She silenced him with her palm. Draven peered down at his friend and noticed how wide his chartreuse eyes were. They darted between him and Aliyah.

"Draven, what's going on?" Grunge stuttered.

He shrugged because he had no fucking idea what was going on with Aliyah. Draven sensed something... different about her and he wondered if it had something to do with her visit to The Enchantment.

Aliyah moved Grunge's hand from his wound. Her golden glowing hands hovered over the puncture marks.

Draven couldn't believe he was witnessing this. Aliyah's brows were drawn in and her jaw clenched. He assumed whatever she was doing it was taking a toll on her.

Grunge sighed in what Draven deemed as relief. "It–it still hurts but not as much. What are you doing to me?"

Aliyah leaned down and before Draven could stop her or know what she was doing, her mouth wrapped around the bite marks on Grunge's neck and she sucked.

Draven hardly registered the growl that left his throat. He canted his neck and leaned in lower. She wasn't feeding from Grunge, that much he could tell. *Thank the Goddess*, he mused. He wouldn't want to have to kill his friend after all this was said and done.

Aliyah reared back coughing. Draven patted her back, attempting to sooth her. She turned her head away from the bed Grunge was laying and spat. Blue black sludge slithered away. *What in Purgatory was that?*

"Fuck," she coughed. "That was vile. Don't ever do that again, Grunge. Shit."

He sat up gingerly and clamped his hand to his neck. The wound was gone. "How did you do that?" he asked, his tone filled with curiosity.

She huffed, "Again, I have no fucking clue. I was working on impulse and instinct."

"Wait... What is your bloodline?"

Aliyah's eyes flashed toward Draven. She looked jaded and hesitant. He nodded once, signalling she could trust Grunge with this piece of information.

"Allegedly, I am from a royal bloodline. I have vampire, angel, faery and demon blood running through my veins." Draven noted her cringe when she mentioned the demon lineage.

Grunge pushed his dark auburn hair out of his face and smirked, "So that's why Dravey over here has it bad for you?" he coughed.

"Fuck you, asshole," Draven groaned.

Aliyah simpered and lifted her shoulders in a shrugging motion. "I'd say he's only human... but you know."

They all laughed. Draven had heard that phrase amongst the mortals and never truly understood it, until now. She was blowing smoke up her own ass and that made him smile wider.

Aliyah swayed on her feet and Draven gripped her elbow to steady her. "Are you alright, Snowflake?"

Her eyes rolled upward then focused on him. "I—I think I need to lie down. Is there somewhere I can..." Aliyah didn't finish her sentence. Instead she fainted and Draven caught her.

"Shit, is she going to be alright?" Arc piped up.

For a moment, Draven forgot he was even there until he's voice filter through the room.

"She's probably exhausted from using her magic and energy. Is there somewhere safe I can lay her down so we can talk about what to do with Laney?"

Arc signalled for Draven to follow him. Aliyah lay limp in his arms once again. He was beginning to really despise how they always seemed to find themselves in these precarious situations.

Arc opened the door and waited at the threshold for them to enter a log cabin next to the hospital. Aliyah was still nestled in close to his chest as he stepped into the space.

The cabin was simple, yet clean. Two windows sat flush against the log cabin walls with yellow faded curtains. Draven walked further in and noticed a small kitchen to the left. An old lounge sat in the middle of the room in front of a TV and a double bed with two bedside tables was at the back on the space. There was a door off to the right and Draven assumed that was the bathroom.

He laid her down on the white linen sheets before inspecting the cabin further, checking to make sure the windows were locked. He returned and gazed down at her, smoothing her raven hair back. Aliyah looked paler than usual. She was spent.

Draven scribbled down a note and left it on the nightstand then pulled the white blanket up, tucked her in and placed a chaste kiss on her forehead.

Quietly, he approached the front door and once outside asked Arc to lock it in case Laney was still hightailing it around. He wouldn't risk his Snowflake for anyone.

Arc turned the key and twisted the door knob to make certain it was locked. Once they were both satisfied, they moseyed over to the hospital cabin.

Walking in, Draven was slammed with salacious scents.

Looking over toward Grunge, he saw him shovelling food in his mouth. "Where did he get the food from?" Draven wondered.

"One of the women probs brought it over to him. It smells good, doesn't it?"

"Mmhmm," was all Draven replied. "So... Sir eats a lot. You finished yet?"

"In a minuuuuutte," Grunge said with a mouth full.

Draven shook his head, grabbed a chair from the corner of the room and sat down beside his friend's bedside. He watched him as he inhaled chicken drumsticks.

Ten minutes later, he was done. Draven waited impatiently for him to hurry up and tell him what was going on. "Well?"

Grunge picked up the tea towel, wiped the grease from his mouth, skulled some water and said, "She's in trouble, D. Like deep shit."

"Why did you go with her alone? I thought we were on the same page, man. Reikiki mentioned you left his apartment with her and I knew you wouldn't risk putting her in harms way by notifying anyone she was with you."

"You're right, I didn't tell anyone. As for the same page, we were. We are," he groaned. "Fool me once, shame on you. Fool me twice, shame on me."

"What are you jabbering on about?" Arc replied, sounding frustrated.

"What he said," Draven countered.

"Do you really need me to spell it out? Laney told me she'd give me the totem back. That she didn't want to hurt any more people. She told me we could finally be together again, but I had to come with her now because she was in trouble."

"And you believed her? Draven snickered.

"I'm in love with her, asshole!" he boomed. "I—I didn't believe her but I wanted to more than anything in this realm. I figured if I helped her out of this situation she'd landed herself in, then maybe we could rectify everything. That you could save her," he whispered. "I feel she's too far gone."

"Elaborate," Draven insisted.

Grunge closed his eyes, ran his hands through his

messy dark auburn hair and his voice cracked when he spoke. "Her eyes, those insanely beautiful, lime green rimmed coal eyes," he vacillated, "are beginning to turn red."

Draven stood abruptly, the chair sliding across the timber floorboards. His head went from side to side as he tugged on his dreadlocks. "Fuck! She's turning too quick. Did you get the totem back or at least figure out if she has given it to Neferity?"

"She still has it; I saw it peeking out of her bag. When she realised what I was up to, she lost her shit. I've never seen her like that, Draven. Laney is almost–she's almost unrecognisable."

Draven gnashed his teeth together; this was not good. His hands pulled at his face while he paced the small room. *What am I going to do now? What is this stupid deal she wants to make with Neferity? Does she realise the danger she's putting herself in? That she's putting everyone in?* Draven wasn't sure how he was going to tolerate all these spanners being thrown into the chaos that he was already neck deep in.

A piercing scream filled the air. Aliyah. Draven responded before he even recognised what he was doing. Why hadn't he sensed the danger?

Stopping abruptly, he saw Laney clawing at the door in her wolf form. As if sensing him, she turned to face him and growled. Grunge was right. The lime green around her eyes was fading into red.

Placing his hands in front of his chest so as to not frighten her, he hushed, "Laney, honey. It's me. It's Draven. Please come back to us."

"The wolf stepped forward, canines on full display, the growling continuing. *Shit, think!*

"Do you remember that time we were wrestling and you shifted mid-air, breaking your ankle when you landed? Remember how I helped heal you? Or that time when Dolph was badly injured and we thought he was going to die? He's still with us. He's still alive, Laney. Come back and let me help you."

Laney stopped prowling and Draven observed how her irises were oscillating between red and her natural color. In that moment, he knew there was still time left to save her.

But just as he thought he was making a breakthrough with Laney, she howled and darted off into the woods. Draven was about to vamp speed after her until he heard Aliyah scream his name.

Running toward the log cabin, he ripped open the door. Fuck the lock. She launched herself at him and wrapped her legs around his waist.

His hand searched her face as his eyes raked over her to see if there were any injuries. "You ok? I'm sorry I left you but after you fainted... You needed to rest."

She shimmied down his hard body and shushed him. "I'm ok. A little tired but otherwise I'm fine. I was woken by her clawing at the door and when I walked toward the window, I knew something wasn't right when I looked out." She shuddered. "When I saw her eyes, I didn't recognise her. All that stared back at me were red eyes. I thought Gorgon finally found me."

Draven drew her into his chest, smoothing her hair down and trying to placate her while at the same time attempting to calm the clamour of his own frantically beating heart.

Ice coated his veins. Draven couldn't allow Melantha to win this round and claim Laney's soul. Deep down in this ruined canvas of his, he was certain if she was successful, he would never forgive himself, that he would lose a piece of himself to the darkness.

No, he forbade it. Aliyah disrupted him from his ruminations when she cleared her throat and said, "She didn't look like the Laney we know, Shrek. I don't want to say this, but is it too late? Has Melantha won?"

Draven sensed and witnessed the trepidation circling Aliyah. She had every right to be concerned. The sand was splintering through that hourglass rapidly. Time wasn't on their side.

Instead of voicing his earlier worries, he attempted to assuage her doubt and said, "She's still in there. I just don't know for how much longer."

Those violet hues popped wide and her lips quivered.

He'd failed.

Chapter Thirteen

~ Aliyah ~

Aliyah pushed off of Draven's chest. She stood back, eyes gaping as the tears threatened to break through the stony wall she was trying to hide behind. Draven was really beginning to frighten her. And let's not get started on how she fucking healed someone.

She closed her eyes, inhaled sharply, then let out a long breath. Aliyah repeated the action a few more times before she opened her lids.

Draven was observing her, eyebrows pinched tightly together as he played with the bead in one of his dreadlocks. He looked contemplative.

Tearing her eyes away from him, she grabbed the lackey around her wrist and tied her hair up in a loose ponytail because she needed to do something with her hands.

"Talk to me, Snowflake. Something is up. I can sense it."

"I—I..." She paused then changed the subject. "Is Grunge ok?"

"Hmm, yep."

"Is he coming back with us?"

"Is who coming back with you?"

Aliyah's head snapped to the deep voice. She smiled when she saw Grunge limping over toward them.

"You," she replied.

"We aren't going anywhere until we figure out this shit with Laney. I feel there is more to the story and I can defi-

nitely sense her trying to fight whatever possession is going on within her."

"Why do you say that?" Draven questioned.

"She's changing and I don't think she understood what
kind of grave she was digging for herself. Now, now I think
she's petrified. But she can't stop. It's like she feels she's
gone this far so why stop?"

"It's contradictive. Her actions to what you're suggest-
ing," Aliyah speculated.

"It is, but Grunge could be onto something. Laney was
never indecisive. She knew what she wanted and she went
for it. Maybe she's feeling guilty," Draven wondered. "I just
wish we knew exactly why she was doing all of this. What
deal is she wanting to make with Neferity?"

"Whatever the reason, we need to rectify it, and soon,"
Grunge said. "Laney is slipping. I've been racking my brain
since I saw the totem, and I don't understand how she is
turning dark if she hasn't made the deal yet."

Aliyah chewed on his statement for a moment. Stepping
outside, she began pacing the front of the cabin. Peering
inside, she noted Draven and Grunge watching her with
what looked like perplexity painted all over their faces.

"What?" she demanded.

"What is going on in that pretty head of yours, baby?"

Aliyah canted her neck towards Grunge and proposed,
"What if your ancestors or whatever are doing something
to her? Is it possible your mother could be reaching out
and punishing her for stealing her totem from you?"

Grunge leaned his head back and released a breath.
Then his eyes found hers. "Now that you've said that, it
could be possible. The spirits don't have much sway, but it
is their magic encompassed inside the totem. That totem
is my mother, her quintessence."

"Okaaaaay," Draven drew the word out. "So do you
think it's her?"

Grunge seemed to consider Draven's question. "No.
It's not her. My mother was a kind woman and she would
never dip her paws into dark waters. This has to be Neferity."

Aliyah didn't even deliberate what she was about to do.
She stepped back inside and said, "Hand."

"Wh–what?" Grunge stumbled over the word.

"Give me your hand, please."

Begrudgingly, he placed his hand in hers. She placed his palm against her chest where her heart was and watched his eyes dart from her to Draven. "This will hurt a little."

"What are you..."

Aliyah's eyes found the back of her skull. Her left thigh burned and she knew her third eye branding was activated. Images began flashing inside her mind, playing around like a damn carousel. Something was unique about this experience with Grunge. It wasn't the same as the times she'd done this in the past.

Clenching her jaw, Aliyah attempted to control the pain that was bucketing through her temples. Whatever she was about to find out, she knew it was important.

Her knees were weakening but she forced herself to ground with the earth underneath her and asked silently for strength.

As if her quiet prayers were answered, a hot palm squeezed her shoulder and she knew without looking that Draven was offering his strength and energy.

Honing in on their link, she inhaled as much of his magic and energy as she could. Pictures swirled around like a hurricane. Grunge and Laney were smitten with each other and in his memories they looked happy. But something changed. Aliyah anticipated a dark entity and immediately horripilation consumed her body. *Just a little longer. Come on.*

"Fuck, Draven. What the fuck is happening," Grunge's voice plunged into her control and she wavered. He was scared. *Almost there, stay with me Grunge,* she pleaded.

Aliyah felt something shift. The vision was taking a different direction, one she hadn't experienced before.

A slender figure began to take form in the black, murky mist transcending around Laney's figure. She was lying on what looked like a hard surface. Everything was black. There was nothingness to this image as Laney shivered. So did Aliyah.

"You're failing, Laney. You have a debt to repay, remember!"

Laney stayed silent, shivering and weeping on the

ground. Aliyah felt herself squint at the figure. Long legs were draped in a see-through sheer, she was naked underneath.

Creeping around in the image, Aliyah snuck in, trying to see the woman standing over Laney better. Long, dark, onyx hair flowed down her back effortlessly. She was a stunning creature. *Creature? Why would I think that?*

Shaking out of the thought, she listened intently as the woman began to speak again. "You promised me. I need that fucking totem now," she bellowed.

The woman's face snapped upward and darted around the area. Aliyah's veins turned arctic and the earth around her began to fracture. *No, no, no! Please don't let her see me.*

Aliyah was rooted in place, waiting for the Dark Goddess to find her, because that's who it was. Eyes the color of crimson gripped Aliyah and she was certain she was about to perish from fear and suffocation.

Those eyes were the color of blood and they screamed death. She was done for; she knew it. Then another voice entered her mind. *"Focus, ground yourself and blend in with the elements. Use your light."*

"What the fuck, mum?" she replied internally.

There was no answer. Aliyah centred herself and tethered herself to the elements, praying it worked.

Neferity's eyes crinkled at the corners then she snapped her neck back toward Laney. "You have one more chance. Don't make me do this, because I will."

A few more words were shared, ones that Aliyah could barely decipher. However, the ones she could hear rocked her world and made her knees slam to the floor.

Aliyah was yanked upward and her eyes flew open. She nestled in close and inhaled Draven's earthy, musky scent and allowed it to envelop her. He grounded her, and right now that's what she needed.

"What happened, Snowflake?"

Wiping the wet mess from her face, she turned her eyes away from his chest to find Grunge. He looked defeated.

"What did you find? One minute we were holding hands and the next... the next you were standing there glowing again, solo."

Aliyah screwed her face up. "We weren't bound?"

"We disconnected."

"Oh."

"Oh what, Aliyah. What happened?" Draven set her down on her feet but kept a firm grip on her. He asked in a concerning tone, "Can you stand?"

Aliyah nodded her head, signalling she could in fact stand. He let her go. "Images upon images of the two of you circled around. Did you see that, Grunge?"

He nodded yes.

"And then I saw Laney on the floor in the fetal position. She was crying. There was a woman yelling out her. I soon learned it was Neferity."

"What?" Draven growled.

"It was Neferity. I'm assuming Grunge's connection to Laney is what led me to her." Aliyah paused and swiped at a stray tear that had escaped. "Grunge, when was the last time you two were together?"

"Around two months ago. I hadn't seen her for five weeks until recently. And like I said previously, the last month before she disappeared was when I noticed the change in her demeanour."

"How so?"

"How so what?"

"How was she different?"

"Laney wouldn't hunt with me or really eat much." He smirked, "I know it's TMI, but she was a fucking fox in the sheets. Couldn't get enough of me. That last month she wouldn't touch me. She seemed angry and her moods were erratic."

"Fuck."

"What?" Grunge eyed her cautiously.

"You need to sit down. I know why she stole the totem. It wasn't to make a deal with Neferity like Reikiki thought. She's indebted to her somehow."

"That doesn't make sense," Draven interrupted.

"Well I'm telling you both right now, that's what I heard. I don't understand why she's turning dark. My only thought is that it's Neferity's damage."

"What aren't you telling us," Grunge speculated.

"Laney didn't steal from you because she's turned rogue or because she's a drug addict searching for her next hit. She stole the totem because she's protecting something extremely precious to her—to you: your unborn child."

The next few hours went by in a blur. After Aliyah spilled the beans, Grunge shifted then sprinted off into the forest. She knew he was trying to find Laney. Somehow, she knew that wasn't going to happen.

Draven spoke in hush tones to Arc about Grunge. Aliyah couldn't help overhearing what was said with her enhanced sense of hearing as she sat on the bed. Once Arc left the cabin they were staying in, Draven walked over and smiled down at her.

"I think we should stay the night. If Grunge isn't back soon, a few of the pack will head out and track him. How did you do it, Snowflake?"

"Hmm?" She was too consumed with her own thoughts that she missed the question.

"How did you witness the exchange with Laney and Neferity? More to the point, how did she not sense you?"

It had totally slipped Aliyah's mind until Draven brought it up. "My mum. She reached out somehow. Told me to focus and to blend in with the elements. To use my light."

"Ah, so that's why you were glowing then." He scratched his stubble. "I'm becoming more and more confused with everything that is happening as time moves. Our bond, magic, Goddesses, the fucking revelation," he laughed then continued, "just everything."

Aliyah stood up from the bed and walked the couple of steps toward Draven to wrap her arms around his waist then looked up into those mesmerizing mismatched eyes. His lips twitched at the sides while her fingers trailed up the ridges of his defined back.

She exhaled, then said, "Whatever road we have to stumble down, I'm happy that I have you to stagger with me. We will get through this."

Aliyah leaned up on tippy toes and her Dr Martins squeaked just before she found Draven's mouth. The kiss was slow, tentative, unrushed as their tongues danced with one another.

Her body hummed with need and she knew Draven was feeling it, also. Especially as the rigid column of his erection pressed into her abdomen.

It wasn't long until the kiss turned feverish, both tongues tangoing in a world of who could dominate the other more.

Draven shoved her down on the bed and ripped her clothes off her body in one quick succession. The sound of her shirt ripping echoed through the cabin and the buttons from her jeans flew across the timber floor, landing like a coin circling before it stopped.

They were both panting, their hands all over each other with their lips still enmeshed with another. Aliyah unbuttoned Draven's jeans and let out a growl of frustration through the kiss when she couldn't yank them down.

He laughed, breaking off the kiss so he could shuck out of his clothes. Aliyah watched in awe as his muscles bunched while taking off the items. She would never get over how fucking good he looked.

Those damn brandings and rippled muscles did her in every single time, and she knew better than to even start on his sexy ass. Aliyah bit her lip and moaned just thinking about it.

The heat was travelling throughout her body rapidly and she knew without a doubt that she would be saturated to her core.

Draven ungracefully fell to his knees. Pulling her to the edge of the bed, he hooked her legs over his shoulders so he was eye level with her weeping pussy.

He grinned up at her then slid his index finger from her ass up to her snatch before slipping in the tip of his finger.

"Fuck. Your cunt is so wet, Snowflake. I'll never get enough of this, or you." With that statement, he inserted another finger, slamming them into her tight cavern at the same time he lapped out her core.

Aliyah mewled and withered on the bed, trying to reach for Draven. She was already on the precipice of an orgasm.

"Wait, no, shit. Not yet," she pleaded while attempting to push his face away from her pussy. "I need to taste you, please."

Draven stopped licking, sucking and nipping at her as Aliyah looked down at him. His fingers were still embedded inside her, but that look on his face was pure sex.

He had the most endearing and lecherous glow to him, his smirk reaching his eyes. "You want a sixty-nine, baby?" he cooed.

Aliyah blushed. She didn't understand why because they'd done dirtier things. "Um, yes," she stammered.

Draven removed his digits and she yearned for his touch immediately. He ushered for her to move up in the bed. Their eyes never wavered from each other as she watched him stalk his prey: her.

"Over the top of me," Aliyah rushed. He quirked an eyebrow. "You'll be able to control the pace," she said meekly.

"You mean I can fuck your throat and make you gag?"

She nodded. Her whole body was ready to combust. Draven stepped over then slowly kneeled so his cock was pretty much sitting on her face.

"Open up, Snowflake."

She did as she was told and welcomed the salty musk-iness of his skin as his cock entered her mouth. He groaned then leaned down so he could reach her pussy.

Aliyah took him deeper into her mouth, needing to feel him pulsating inside of her throat. She could already taste the pre-cum as he moaned and devoured her kitty.

His fingers worked her cunt like a well-oiled machine and she felt herself climbing higher and higher, but she didn't want to cum yet.

Clawing into his buttocks, she began sucking him vig-orously, making sure to pay attention to his balls as well. Aliyah's eyes rolled to the back of her head as the sounds of their licking and slurping ricocheted around the room. Her senses were elevated and she wanted more, just more!

Draven pumped his hips down into her mouth simulta-neously with his fingers inside her pussy. The wet sound of her sex made her core clench. She wasn't sure if she'd been so turned on before.

Aliyah gagged when Draven amped up the speed of his

cock fucking her mouth. Both of them were pleading, moaning messes.

"Fuck yes. You feel and taste so good, Aliyah. Your mouth is the fucking devil reincarnated," he growled.

Aliyah mewled, feeling her insides clutch on his fingers as his tongue flicked over that tight bundle of nerves. She was so fucking close.

Draven sucked her nub into his mouth and pistoned his fingers into her cunt and his cock into her mouth. Aliyah felt the warm tears cascade down her face while her body was reaching that pinnacle of climax.

The orgasm was right there, so close. Draven sucked on her, nibbled and licked, but it wasn't enough. She reared her head back, forcing his dick to fall out of her mouth then wrapped her hand around his cock and starting stroking him. The canines inside her mouth elongated and bit into his femoral artery. Suckling harshly, she inserted a finger into his ass.

Draven bucked manically above her. "Fuuuuuucccckkk!" he cried out as he bit into her femoral artery.

Aliyah's moans were muffled and her vision blurred as the orgasmic waves came smashing down like a tsunami, threatening to drown her in bliss. Draven tensed and stilled above her as he ejaculated all over her face and chest. She didn't even give a fuck that he'd just given her her first facial.

Their suckling slowed on each other as they started coming down from the high they'd just ridden. Aliyah removed her finger from his asshole then disengaged from his artery and licked the bite marks. She felt Draven do the same.

Gingerly, she wriggled beneath Draven and he moved off to the side of her. Her body was like jelly as she looked up into those mischievous eyes.

"I did not expect the finger in the ass, Snowflake. A little warning next time?"

Aliyah busted out laughing. "It wouldn't have been a surprise if I'd told you, would it?"

He shook his dreadlocks from side to side, his hard body rippled from the silent laughter he was trying to hide from her.

"Come on, let's have a shower. You know things have gotten harder since you've been around," he grinned.

"That's what she said." Aliyah smirked and stood up, feeling like her legs were going to buckle. Luckily they didn't.

"I should get a dozen sandwiches for that orgasm," Draven chuckled.

Shaking her own head from side to side, she staggered to the bathroom. Draven followed her. Just as they were about to enter, his phone started ringing.

His brows drew together when he stalked toward his phone and read the screen. "It's Jadis."

Shit.

Aliyah watched Draven's features change. His shoulders relaxed before tensing again and she wondered what the hell was going on.

He hung up, darted around the cabin picking up his clothes and dressing. She placed a hand on her hip, waiting for him to clue her the fuck in.

"Get dressed, Snowflake. Dolph's awake."

Chapter Fourteen

~ Draven ~

He is finally awake! Draven hurried Aliyah toward the car. Once she was seated, he launched himself into the driver's side.

Draven wasn't comfortable with leaving Grunge in his current state, but Arc reassured him that he would update him if anything happened or they needed his help. Right now, he needed to see his best friend.

Dolph waking up was more than he'd expected. He truly thought he would need to say goodbye to his best friend, that this was their ending. Thank the Goddess it wasn't.

Multiple scenarios flashed behind Draven's eyes regarding Dolph's time in Limbo. He only hoped that none of the craziness his mind was thinking would come to surface when Dolph told them what had happened.

He saw Aliyah in his peripheral. She was toying with the hem of her shirt while looking outside the window. Lights blurred as they drove down the highway, providing a shadow of a halo around her head.

Both of them were quiet, seeming to be in their own world lost in thought. Draven thought back to how she healed Grunge and the uncanny way that she was able to transport herself into The Enchantment. Not to mention her seeing Neferity and Laney. What was going on with her?

Draven didn't want to pry but there was a piece of him

that wanted to test the boundaries and strength of their telepathic bond. Could they read each other's minds? He scalded himself for even thinking of invading her privacy and focused on the road.

Dolph is awake!

It was close to ten at night when they finally arrived in Bienville Street. Draven parked the fifty in the car park at the front of Reikiki's and switched the engine off.

Turning to Aliyah, he reached out and took her hand. She turned to look at him and that's when he saw how truly fractured she looked.

"Talk to me."

She groaned and shook her head. "Let's work out what's happening with Dolph. We have heaps of time to talk."

Aliyah didn't wait for a response. She removed her hand from his, opened the door and stepped out of the car. The door wheezed in protest as she slammed it and began the trek up to the Mad Warlock's apartment.

Draven had no idea what was happening with Aliyah, but a part of him wished he'd invaded her privacy and tried to tap into her mind. Heaving a massive breath, he exited the car and jogged after her.

Aliyah was already inside when Draven reached the ominous door. It swung wide as if sensing his presence. That was never going to jive with him, he thought to himself.

Averting his eyes from the paintings on the wall, he stalked down the hallway and headed straight for Dolph's room.

He sensed Aliyah before he saw her and looked to the left. She and Dany were sitting on the lounge inside the library type room across from Dolph's. They didn't seem to notice Draven's presence as they talked. His head cocked to the side and he was about to snoop into their conversation when the bedroom door opened.

"There you are! Hurry, hurry!" Jadis exclaimed.

Draven looked around the room. The walls were still brighter than shit but the atmosphere definitely had shifted. Reikiki was sitting on a seat with his legs crossed sporting one of his tunics. This one was blue and gold. His tiger eyes found Draven's and he raised an eyebrow in what Draven thought looked like a challenge. He smirked, his eyes darting away from Reikiki's before landing on his best friend's jade-rimmed, coal irises. Draven closed the distance between them.

"Don't you ever fucking do that again, Terror," he growled, using Dolph's street name.

Dolph tried to laugh but it came out more of a wheeze. "Yeah, I missed you too, brother."

"What happened?"

"I was waiting for you to arrive before telling everyone, much to these ballbusters disgust. I didn't want to repeat it. Fuck, my throat feels like fire when I talk." He ran his hand up the column of his neck and Draven watched his Adam apple bob as he swallowed.

Reikiki cleared his throat and waved his hand around, urging Dolph to continue.

"I was stuck in Limbo, as you probably all gathered." He stopped and cleared his throat. "The ancestors are angry with me," he finished on a whisper.

Draven was about to question him but Dolph pushed on.

"I have a few things to explain to you, the first being the reason why I landed myself in the shit with the Ancestors." A lone tear escaped. He swiped at it and continued. "After Delilah died, you pretty much died too, D," he stated, finding Draven's eyes before moving to Jadis's. "And you, fuck, you were the love of my life. I was sure our love was written in the stars or some shit. But then you ended shit. You left me, followed Draven around like a lost puppy and I was left missing two pieces of my heart and soul."

Dolph's confession rocked his world and he knew everyone sensed the shift in the room. Angst bled through every inch of the small space the four of them occupied. *Did he hate me for finding comfort in the sheets with Jadis? Surely he knew that we never loved each other, not like the two of them?*

Dolph continued, answering his question as if Draven had spoken them aloud and not in his head. "I don't blame either of you. Nor did I hate you for it. I was jealous albeit, I admit," his tone wavered then he spoke with more confidence. "All I felt was loneliness and abandonment. My heart lay shattered and beating in front of me because I no longer had the love of my life or my best friend. I couldn't understand your agony, Draven, and for that I am sorry." Dolph stopped, took a deep breath and then released his confession quietly on a whisper, "I met someone."

Draven's eye's snapped to Jadis. The palm that was lovingly rubbing circles around Dolph's bare chest had ceased and he could see the tears building and threatening to escape.

Dolph lay his hand on top of Jadis's, and said, "It wasn't a love like ours, Jadis. She just took away the pain and I didn't feel as hollow when she was with me. I missed you so fucking much and I know now what I didn't know then. We didn't have a choice. Our ancestors had different ideas for us. Our love and our hearts meant nothing to them. We were collateral damage when it all boils down to it. And if I'm being honest, for a long time I felt as if our relationship would prove futile."

Draven's eyes were still on Jadis. Her shoulders were shaking and he knew she was quietly weeping. The puzzle pieces of their too short love story was about to come to head.

"My ancestors wanted me to lead the Louisiana pack. And yours, well it seems they just wanted to use you as a puppet. I'm sorry, baby." He wiped the tears from her face and smiled sadly at her.

"Rayleigh, that was her name. She and I spent our days running through the forests and our nights tangled under the stars. But she still wasn't you, Jadis." He swallowed harshly and Draven noted the tears pooling at the side of his eyes.

"We'd come back to the pack after a night on the town and somehow I still remember how cold it was, even though I was drunker than a foul mouth sailor. As you all know, my body runs hot, except this night. I was shivering underneath my coat. Naturally, Rayleigh noticed and suggested we shift and head out for a run to warm ourselves and shed off some of the alcohol. I obliged."

Draven noted how Dolph's hand stilled on Jadis's back as he looked up to the ceiling. He looked lost, tortured, and Draven had no idea what to say because he wasn't sure what blow his best friend was about to deliver.

"I—I mean we were dashing through the forest. The wind was like ice slashing across my fur. Somehow I'd lost Rayleigh and couldn't smell her anymore. I didn't bother looking for her because I knew she'd find me after our run. I remember feeling carefree as I dodged trees and bushes. I felt like nothing could touch me. Fuck was I wrong."

"I ran and ran until the scent of fresh copper tinged the air. When the smell assaulted my nares, I slid across the grass to stop. I trotted toward the blood and noticed it was fresh. I didn't question at the time of how reckless it seemed to be or how it got there. Instead I devoured the corpse." Dolph stopped and shuddered.

"After I feasted on the flesh, I remember feeling invigorated but also intoxicated. I should have known then that something was wrong. I should have fucking known!"

Tears were now tracking down Dolph's face and Draven had a feeling he knew where this was going. He only hoped he was wrong. Draven watched, listening to Jadis trying to sooth him and realised she'd joined the dots as well.

"I didn't stop, and I didn't want to because in that moment it was as if the pain was gone. There wasn't a huge gaping chasm in my heart. I revelled in it, basked in the inebriating feeling. So much so, that I didn't even realise the warning signs. Black spots danced behind my eyes. I was completely drunk on what I'd just consumed. I heard some growls coming from the left of the forest so I changed direction and sprinted toward the noise. I saw two figures enmeshed, and at that point I was too far gone. The blood had well and truly entered my stream and I—I wasn't me..."

"Of course it was you, baby, who else would it be?" Jadis questioned.

Dolph's breath picked up and Draven watched as his body rattled from the breathing. Whatever he was about to divulge still had his best friend in knots. He peered out of his peripheral and noticed that Reikiki was still in the same position, looking more curious than anything. Returning his attention toward Dolph, he waited for him to continue.

Dolph turned to face Jadis. A flurry of emotions flashed through his eyes, ones that Draven hadn't recalled seeing in a long fucking time. His best friend was going to break again if he didn't settle the hell down.

Dolph shattered his thoughts as he spoke. "You don't understand, Jadis, because you haven't seen this side of me." His voice came out as a growl. Draven recognised what he was feeling in that moment because he'd been cursed with those emotions since he could remember. Dolph was riddled with guilt and shame.

"It's all a haze. One I don't want to remember but I have to. I have to tell you all of this wretched shame that I carry. I refused to see the signs after I consumed the body. It wasn't an animal, my love," he said sadly. "It was a human."

Jadis froze at those words then asked him to continue. Draven noticed how shaken she seemed. Dolph's eyes deviated from Jadis's and found his.

"I understood then, brother. The hankering desire for one's blood, except for me it was a side of myself that I had kept contained, hidden. But, fuck, the rush. Desire coursed through my veins, unbidden, and I accepted it with welcome arms as I pounced through the air toward the pair fighting. I slashed one through the abdomen. The noise that came from the animal was distorted and I couldn't differentiate what animal I'd just hurt. By this stage the black spots dancing in my eyes were vicious and I remember feeling so fucking hungry. But then I was knocked from behind by the other animal. It pinned me to the ground as we wrestled. The hold on me slipped and I took the opportunity to reach up and rip its throat out," Dolph finished on a whisper. He brought his hands up to cover his face and break eye contact with Draven.

"I—I woke the next morning in my human form, covered in blood and with the worst hangover known to any being. I stood up disorientated and my whole body ached. I looked around the clearing and screamed when my eyes landed on the bloody, mangled corpses on the ground. I didn't want to believe it, but when I saw the necklace in the woman's hand, there was no disguising the fact that I'd killed Raleigh."

Dolph began to sob uncontrollably, chanting the words sorry, Raliegh, I'm so fucking sorry over and over again. His angst was palpable and Draven realised his knees were buckling from the agony bleeding through the room.

He sat down on the bed and removed his friend's hands from his face. Dolph's face was red and splotchy from crying and the blanket was wet where his tears had fallen.

Those jade rimmed, coal eyes found his and Draven saw the shame, guilt and so much fucking pain reflecting back at him. He figured his friend had a secret. He hadn't anticipated this.

"It wasn't your fault, brother. The bloodlust is a fucking cunt. If I had of known, I could have helped you control it. I'm so fucking sorry, Dolph."

Dolph brushed the stray tears away, closed his eyes and sighed. When he opened them, he said, "I lie to myself you know? I tell myself that I don't kill often, and when I kill an animal it's because I have to. But D, even the blood of animals intoxicates me. Humans," he huffed, "that blood turns me into a completely different being. I can't control it. Perhaps I have suppressed that side of me because I don't want to hurt anyone."

Draven held his best friend's eyes and an unspoken dialect filtered through Dolph. He realised he didn't want to voice his fears about feeding or the fact that he actually enjoyed it. Those voiceless emotions slammed into Draven like a freight train and he knew instantly the guilt and shame was feasting on Dolph from the inside. That's what he didn't want Jadis to hear. And Draven understood that feeling all too well.

He nodded once, signalling he understood Dolph's precarious situation. "It's ok, wolf, you needn't be ashamed of who you are," Reikiki said as he finally entered the conversation. "I sense there is more to this story, though, so please proceed."

Dolph propped the pillows up behind him then repositioned himself and sat up. Draven thought he was stalling more than anything.

"My ancestors are livid with me. I didn't honour Raleigh like I should have and provide her body, well the remaining pieces of her, the ceremony she deserved. I saw her when I was in Limbo." His eyes glazed over and he sought the ceiling once more. He whispered," She told me she forgave me. That she didn't blame me and that I need to forgive myself before I could leave that dark, ice-ridden land. The ancestors, yeah, they're not as forgiving."

"Is that how you woke up? You finally forgave yourself?" Jadis wondered.

Dolph tilted his head away from looking at the ceiling and side eyed Draven. *Oh shit. Whatever he's about to say is going to rock our world, I can feel it.*

Reaching for Jadis's hand, Dolph squeezed it and his coal eyes met her forest greens. "No, Honey Bear. Well, not exactly."

Draven noticed Jadis soften at the use of her nickname, and he couldn't remember the last time Dolph had called her that. It'd been many years though. Dolph used to call her that because he said Jadis was as sweet as honey and as ferocious as a bear. One you shouldn't ever cross.

"I woke because of my own will. I had to come back to you all. The ancestors haven't completely forgiven me since Rayleigh was of royal bloodline and she could have done a lot for our kind, but they needed me back in this realm." He hesitated. "Jadis, baby, what I'm about to tell you is going to alter the way you no doubt think about your mother."

Jadis opened her mouth and Dolph placed his index finger over her pouty lips to quiet her. "I know your mother died when she gave birth to you. What we didn't know was that you were actually a twin."

Jadis's chocolate skin turned pallid and Draven noted the tremble running through her body. "That's—that's not possible, is it?"

Dolph ran his free hand down the side of her face then cupped it and offered her a sad smile. "It is, baby. His name is Jayden."

"Jayden..." Jadis spoke his name aloud and seemed far away in thought in that moment.

Dolph continued, "But this is where it gets messy. Shit, Jadis, I'm sorry to have to be the one to tell you this." He hesitated again, "Jaylian, your mother, had an affair with a wolf. Somehow, even though you both shared a womb, you don't share the same father. Your father was a Warlock and Jayden's is a wolf."

"Wait, what? How is that even possible?" Jadis returned, shocked.

"Tis possible. Highly improbable, but none the less possible." Reikiki stated. His tiger eyes took on that mad look as he rolled the beads in his hair within his thumb and index finger. "Fascinating..." he trailed off.

"Ok, so what happened to Jayden?"

"Jada."

"Jada?" the three of them said in unison.

"She would have only been a teen. What does she have to do with this?" Jadis retorted.

"Honey Bear, Jada was dark even at such a tender age. She has been using black magic on and off her entire life. Jada had Jayden whisked away at birth."

"What the fuck?" Jadis seethed, "Where the fuck was my father?"

"Julian," Dolph scoffed. "After finding out that your mother cheated on him, he advised Jada to do whatever she had to do to make Jayden disappear. He knew she was dark like him and would get the job done. According to the ancestors, he handed you to one of the witches then went down the hall to toy with the help."

Draven thought about Julian and how he had died some time ago. All that was found of his body was a pile of ash with a tooth among them. It was confirmed by Jadis to belong to Julian. Draven hated him and he was happy the man was dead because he was an evil son of a bitch. He put Jadis through hell.

"What did she do!"

Dolph winced. "Julian figured Jada would kill him, but she didn't. She left with the baby and found his father. Jada cast a spell on both Jayden and the father Jacoby so they wouldn't ever remember her."

"They're alive?" Jadis asked hopeful.

"Yeah, yeah they are." Dolph stated.

"If their minds are strong, it's possible that they've started to connect the dots and could be remembering stuff," mused Reikiki.

"So I have a twin brother. What the fuck is wrong with my sister? Why would she do something so nasty?" Jadis fumed.

Draven noticed Dolph's jade rimmed eyes assessing Jadis. He ran his hand through his unruly hair and chewed on the inside of his cheek. He was nervous.

Draven canted his head to the side and pushed his dreadlocks behind his ears before prodding, "Brother?" Dolph's eyes immediately focused on him. "What aren't you telling us?

Dolph released a heavy breath and looked to Jadis once more. "It's Samson. He's not dead."

Chapter Fifteen

~ Draven ~

"What the fuck are you talking about, Dolph? I held him in my hands as he made his way to The Enchantment," Jadis exclaimed.

Draven was flabbergasted. *Samson is alive?* Samson was Jadis's cousin and he died many moons ago. He was part of the reason that Draven and Jadis became so close.

His late fiancé Delilah was murdered two centuries ago by his mother, Efah. Efah stabbed Delilah through the heart with a gold-laced diamond dagger. It's the only weapon that can kill a royal or pure-blooded vampire, and Delilah was pure blooded.

Samson perished not long after her. He was poisoned by another warlock. Those were some of his last words to Jadis, although he hadn't given her a name. Still to this day Jadis hadn't learned who the warlock was and why he killed her cousin. And the Goddess knows she's tried to figure out the unruly puzzle behind Samson's death.

Draven and Jadis could relate to each other's pain and loss. It was partial to how they found themselves tangled within the sheets.

He was catapulted back into the present by Jadis's uncontrollable wails.

"No, no, it's not possible! If it were Samson would have come back to me! He wouldn't do this to me." Jadis sobbed loudly, her head nestled into Dolph's chest as she found purchase in his forearms.

Draven cocked an eyebrow in question. "Brother, if this is the case and Samson is in fact alive, then where is he?"

"Perhaps I can answer that question for you all," Reikiki elaborated. "Samson is—how do I say this—he's trapped. He has been ever since that dreadful day when you held him in your arms, High Witch."

Jadis untucked herself from Dolph's chest and when she looked at the Mad Warlock her forest green eyes were ablaze. Draven was grateful they weren't directed at him.

"You knew, Reikiki! You fucking saw how destructible I was back then. How tattered and in pieces I was, and yet you didn't tell me? Why?" Jadis finished on a whisper, her eyes fading back to deep pools of green melancholy.

Reikiki rolled his eyes then shook his head, uncrossed his legs and leaned forward to look Jadis in the eye. "Do you really think if I had of known I would not have told you? Come on, Witch, we have been friends for a very long time. Don't humiliate yourself."

"How long have you known?"

"I wasn't sure if my vision was correct. I received the first insight a couple of weeks ago and I have been chasing up leads to figure out if it is in fact true. I did not want to come to you with this information if it proved fruitless. Satisfied?" Reikiki taunted.

Jadis sniffled and wiped her nose with her forearm. "You're fucking lucky that I'm debilitated, you old fool. You should have come to me as soon as you visioned Samson," Jadis oscillated. "Is he at least safe?"

It was Reikiki's turn to balk. "He... he looks lost."

"What do you mean lost?"

"I believe he doesn't realise that he isn't here. I feel strongly that he is in another realm and that is why he hasn't sought you out."

Draven watched the encounter between Jadis and Reikiki like a damn table tennis match. And looking at Jadis, he knew she was as confused as he was. Dolph on the other hand looked exhausted.

Jadis started to speak but was interrupted by a keening cry. Aliyah. Draven bolted out of the room and found Aliyah and Dany embraced like before.

His hand was cradled in hers and rested where her

heart was. Draven saw red. How dare they try her third eye shit when no one was around! He stepped forward, fuming.

Jadis pulled him back. "Don't interfere, D. It must be important if the pair of them waited until no one was around to perform this ritual."

"Ritual? What the fuck, Jadis? She doesn't even know how to control whatever the fuck she's doing." Draven's irises shot to Dolph as he staggered out the room and found his place beside her. *Figures he'd be on her side.*

Jadis shot daggers at him while Reikiki spoke, "Aliyah is trying to find out who killed his parents."

Draven tuned everyone out and ogled Aliyah and Dany encapsulated in her brilliant golden hue. His fingers twitched to reach out and steady her when he recognised the agony etched in each of their faces, along with feeling every single one of her emotions bursting through him. Her poignancy and anger palpable.

Tears cascaded down their faces like a raging river threatening to burst through the gates that originally held them in place.

Aliyah began to chant, something he hadn't seen her do in the times she'd perform this—this ritual in front of him. He wasn't convinced it was in fact a ritual, but he had nothing else to go on. Perhaps Jadis was on the money.

Aliyah's body convulsed as she held onto Dany's hand with a white-knuckle grip. Draven was antsy. He sensed she was on the precipice of being thrown from Dany once more. Whoever killed his parents was trying exceptionally hard to keep Aliyah from figuring out the riddle.

Dany roared, his knees collapsing to the floor as he hung onto Aliyah's hand with all his might. Draven reached out again, this time Dolph grabbed his arm.

"Savage, I know it's difficult to see your woman in pain, but something tells me this is important. If you touch her or she senses your presence, it could sever the connection between Dany and herself. Can't you sense it? Just a little longer."

Draven was about to question his lunacy until he felt it. The air was riddled with fervour, angst, fury, and Draven could taste how close they were. Aliyah's determination was prominent. *Just a little bit longer. Come on Snowflake. You've got this, baby."*

The four of them stood by for another minute or so until Aliyah bellowed out.

"NO!"

Her knees finally gave way and she landed with a humph in front of Dany. She let go of his hand and wrapped her arms around her best friend.

No one said a word while Aliyah and Dany wept in each other's arms. Their bodies shook and the pain was evident within the room.

Draven desperately wanted to approach and take Aliyah in his arms, but somehow the moment seemed intimate. They needed each other more than anyone else right now.

He wasn't jealous; however, he did feel hopeless. Draven tore his eyes away from Aliyah to see what everyone else was doing.

Dolph and Jadis were sitting on one of the red velvet lounges snuggling, the one he'd recently envisioned seeing Aliyah on naked. Reikiki was leaning on the timber bookshelves with his legs crossed at the ankles looking bored, playing with the beads in his silver tousled hair. It seemed seeing it once was enough for the Mad Warlock to no longer be in awe of her gift.

Meanwhile, Draven felt jittery because he had no idea what had just occurred in Aliyah's head. He cursed himself once again for not trying to see if he could get inside of her mind when she was performing this... this thing she did.

Finally they pulled apart. Draven cautiously walked the short distance toward the pair. His kneecaps cracked as he knelt down beside her. Her brow was drawn together with sweat dotting her lily-white skin. Her eyes were downcast.

Draven glanced at Dany and saw he was no better for wear. His jet-black man bun was hanging in wet strands around his face, and his once vibrant umber orbs were now marred with lugubrious sorrow.

He wanted to take away their pain, but of course that was futile, or at least that's what he believed. The ubiquitous burn travelled down his left shin and this one stung like a thousand thorns piercing his skin.

"Fuck," he hissed.

Aliyah's violet hues found Draven's. Concern etched her face as she studied him. He ripped up the left leg of his jeans and thank the Goddess, it was outlined in red.

Draven canted his head to the side so he could visualise his new branding better. The heart in the ink looked as if it was still beating. It was eerie as fuck. A bloodied hand was wrapped around the heart and it seemed to be squeezing.

He admired the branding and sent a silent thank you up to the Goddess. This time she responded.

You're welcome, child. Now you can absorb pain. Such a selfless vampire, but be careful not to take it for granted. There is only so much one being can handle.

At first he was flummoxed, then he smiled to himself. *You've forgiven me. Thank you for this gift and for believing in me, Kaltemis. I won't disappoint you.*

Bringing himself back to the moment, he gazed around and noticed everyone gawking at him.

"What does it do, brother?" Dolph interjected.

Draven placed his left hand on Dany's heart and his right hand on Aliyah's. He figured that's where the pain was likely coming from.

"Terror." He used Dolph's street name. "I can absorb pain now, and something tells me this is going to hurt more than getting fucked up the ass by a cactus with no lube to soften the blow." He glared at Dolph. "Don't say it."

His best friend snickered, "That's what she said."

He turned away to focus on Aliyah and Dany. Draven closed his eyes, inhaled in through his nose then exhaled through his mouth. Pain shot up through his hands and radiated throughout his body at light speed.

He squeezed his eyes tighter in hopes to soften the agony bursting through every single inch of his internal and external being, to no avail.

Draven grimaced. His teeth gnashed as the onslaught of pain thrusted itself inside of him, embedding itself to his core.

Licks of flames within grew like wildfire. Draven felt like he was going to vomit from the anguish and sadness the pair was divulging.

Draven removed his hands from Aliyah and Dany, bracing himself on the hard wood floor and gasped. The pain was relentless, bucketing through his mind. Acrimony, with a touch of heat, washed down with saltiness filled his mouth. He knew that whatever pain he absorbed was riddled with bitterness, anger and sorrow.

His dreadlocks fell forward draping around his face as he heard Aliyah and Dany breathe what he thought was a sigh of relief.

"Thank you," they both said in unison.

Draven head was suddenly heavy as he lifted it up to look at them. "Please tell me that was worth all this fucking agony." He winced, placing one hand on his forehead to massage his temples.

"This woman," Aliyah paused and her breath stuttered before she continued. "The woman that killed Dany's parents was merciless. Celeste and Janson didn't stand a chance. They hid Dany in the bushes as soon as they sniffed danger. We—we saw it all, Shrek. It was horrific. No one should have to deal with that kind of death. And somehow I feel that she's someone one of you know. I'm not sure how but I could sense it. Can you all show me photos or paintings or whatever? It may spark something for Dany and me. We couldn't see her well but we did notice that she had long dark hair."

"Oh honey child that could be anyone. If you haven't noticed, the majority of vampires and wolves have black hair, and even a lot of demons choose to darken their hair. Let's say it was a witch. She could have used a glamour," Reikiki scoffed.

"It wasn't a witch," Dany remarked. His eyes wandered to where Dolph and Jadis were before pulling away and focusing on Draven.

Draven noted Jadis's eyes soften before the hurt flickered through them. He finally believed what Aliyah had been saying all along: the three of them weren't going to bode well.

Reikiki was the first to push off the wall. His voice rang off loudly into the room as he chanted. Although Draven could hear him clearly, he still couldn't understand a fucking word he was saying.

The Mad Warlock's arms waved around until a projector-like image sat before them. "This is my photo album, I tend to keep things in my mind now days, you know just in case. Anyway, a lot of the beings that the others know or knew, I did also. So let's see if we can kill two birds with one stone and flick through my pictures."

Draven made himself as comfortable as he could after absorbing all that pain from earlier. He sat cross-legged next to Aliyah and Dany and grimaced from the movement. Aliyah rested her head on his shoulder while Dany crossed his arms across his chest. Draven felt for the kid.

Images danced across Reikiki's makeshift projector like a slide show you'd have on a computer or TV. It was uncanny to watch. Even after all these years alive, Draven still was surprised by little things like this.

Reikiki took a seat on the other love seat and watched on as the memories of his life passed. At times, Draven recognised affliction flash through the old man's features but he quickly smoothed them away like it was nothing.

Draven directed his attention back to the images. There were so many Otherworlders he'd known along the way. A lot he'd no clue what happened to them, and others he couldn't even remember their names. He winced thinking about how fucked up his life had been in this realm.

The clock second hand ticked in the distance. Draven looked up and noticed it was approaching thirty minutes since Reikiki had started the stroll down memory lane. He felt a little jittery watching the images flash by because he knew sooner or later his once beloved would show up on the screen.

Sparing a glance toward Dolph and Jadis, he saw Dolph strumming his fingers up and down the length of her back.

Jadis had tear tracks on her face and Draven knew it was due to seeing all the perished Otherworlders on the screen.

Draven was so busy looking at the couple that he didn't registered when Aliyah spoke.

"That's her. Stop! That's her! She's the one that killed Dany's parents, Celeste and Janson!"

Draven turned his eyes toward the screen and his veins turned to ice. *No, no, no!* He was momentarily stunned. He felt three pairs of eyes on him: Dolph, Jadis and Reikiki.

"Are you sure, Snowflake?" he hesitated.

"I am. Dany?"

"Yeah, that's the bitch," he growled.

Draven's world began to capsized. *How the... No way, it's not possible.*

"Babe? What's wrong? You're paler than normal? Do—do you know her?"

Draven didn't respond. His heart was lodged in his throat, threatening to rip a hole through his trachea. He couldn't take his eyes off the image of the woman as his body trembled.

She was wearing a red and black lace tea length burlesque corset with her dark curly hair resting on her shoulder blades. Those vibrant purple eyes were staring back at him, mocking him as he tried to catch his breath

Aliyah's hands found each side of his face as she turned him to look at her. Her violet hues were brimming with concern and question.

Dolph's voice was laced with agony as he spoke the last two words Draven wanted to hear. The words that would shatter his resolve.

"It's Delilah."

Chapter Sixteen

~ Aliyah ~

"How is that even possible? She's dead. Draven told me she was murdered. Is there something we are missing here?" Aliyah pleaded, looking into Draven's mismatched eyes. He said nothing, looking stunned.

"I have no idea how it's possible. Delilah was murdered. She should be bound to The Enchantment. Could it be a glamour, Reikiki?" Jadis asked.

Reikiki's tiger coloured eyes had taken on that hint of madness at Jadis's question. Although Aliyah wasn't sure what would tip him over and send him spiralling into insanity, she felt it was only a sliver away at any given time.

He stroked his silver goatee and tilted his head to the left, absorbing her query. "I don't believe so, High One. Only one way to find out. Aliyah, would you allow me to enter your mind and extract the image you saw when you were in Dany's head?"

Aliyah chewed on her lip. "If it's the only way, then I'll do it. Just that image. Don't go prodding into my mind, Reikiki. Alright?"

He waved her away. "Oh stop it. We have more pressing issues at hand than me dillydallying around in your head. Now come, we haven't got all day."

Dany squeezed her leg, reassuring her as she pushed off the floor and walked toward Reikiki. She glanced back and realised that Draven still hadn't moved. Sighing, she waited for him to begin his magic.

Reikiki grabbed her hand, withdrew a small Celtic look-ing dagger and pierced her palm. "What the fuck, Reikiki?" she hissed.

He raised an eyebrow. "I thought you did this once with Jadis? I will need a few drops of your blood and you will need a few of mine to bind us. Damn it child, your palm has healed already. Less talk, more action." He stabbed her hand again.

A part of Aliyah wanted to smack him upside the head for being a dick, but she needed to figure out if this was re-ally Delilah. Afterward they could work out their next step.

Reikiki clenched her hand together and squeezed it over his mouth. Drops of her blood hit his tongue. He licked his lips and then slashed an incision into his palm and told her to stick her tongue out.

Aliyah did as she was told. Her eyes focused on his fist clenched over her tongue. Rich vermilion plasma dripped onto her palate and a burst of electricity shot through her.

Reikiki smirked at her, knowing the effect his blood was having on her. It was... different. Sweet, a little bitter and she swore she could taste the madness if that was even possible.

Placing his hand on each side of her temples, he com-manded, "Let me in child."

Aliyah felt her eyes roll back as pain took front and center. Fuck it hurt. Images of Dany and his parents sped by until they reached Delilah. Reikiki muttered something and then the connection was severed.

She hadn't even felt Draven's presence until his arms wrapped around her waist. He kissed her shoulder and held her weight. It was a good thing too because she felt like her legs were going to give way.

Aliyah let out a heavy sigh and turned to face him. Draven's eyes looked hazy and bloodshot, but she was grateful to see that he'd snapped out of his daze. Alt-hough, from the deep crease in his brow and the clench in his jaw, it seemed he was still in pain. Aliyah wondered if it was because he sensed her agony through the ritual that brought him back into the present, or if it was the after effects from taking hers and Dany's agony.

Jadis spoke up first. "Was it her?"

Reikiki vacillated before replying, "Without a doubt. It was definitely Delilah."

"But how?" Draven asked quietly.

Aliyah studied his face, for what she was uncertain. A part of her wondered if he found out Delilah was alive, would he drop her ass to the curb and reunite with her instead. *Does he still love her?*

She shook herself from her ruminations and waited for Reikiki to answer. He seemed contemplative and cautious with how he would vocalise his observations.

His eyes rolled upward a couple times and Aliyah was curious what that was all about. That was a question for another day, though. First, they had to figure out how the fuck Delilah was alive. *Wait, is she actually alive?*

"I am not convinced with my finding, vampire. I need to tap into a few other avenues before I expose my thoughts on the matter. None of this makes sense. Delilah was murdered two centuries ago, with a gold lace diamond dagger to be precise. One does not simply come back from that. These jigsaw pieces aren't slotting together like they should, and I have no idea as to why." He seemed to be talking more to himself than to everyone around him.

Nothing was making sense to Aliyah in this moment. Dany's parents were brutally murdered by her boyfriend's ex-fiancé fifteen or so years ago?

Was that what they were? Boyfriend and girlfriend? It seemed too juvenile for the shit storm they'd encountered since meeting one and other.

Jealousy swirled within and Aliyah sensed her darkness fuelling it. She slammed those thoughts down and looked up to find Draven gazing down at her.

"Are you aright, baby?" he asked.

Aliyah pushed away from him and faked a smile. "Yeah, I'm good, babe. I have a headache from the tumultuous tsunami I just rode. Otherwise I'm peachy."

Draven cocked an eyebrow and assessed her studiously. He didn't believe her.

Drawing her from Draven's scrutinizing eyes, Dolph spoke, "Ok. So as of now we know Delilah isn't actually in this realm. If she was, I'm assuming one of us would have known by now. We all have a lot to fucking unpack right now. Samson, Jayden, and Dany's parents being murdered by Delilah just to name a few. Draven, how about you take Aliyah home. You both need to rest. Dany, you can stay with us. We should talk anyway," Dolph suggested.

Dany scoffed. "Yeah, nah man, I'm good. You don't seem like you need my blood anymore. Something tells me you're gonna need someone's though." He left his sentence hanging as he stormed out of the room.

Aliyah was about to chase after him until she heard the front door slam. She knew he needed space. A piece of her was more worried about his wellbeing and mental health than giving him space.

She took a step around Draven but he pulled her back. "Dolph's right, Snowflake. We need to revitalise our magic and energy. I can see by your pallor and body language that you're straining to stand upright." He tilted her chin up so she was forced to peer into his beautiful mismatched eyes. "It's late out. He probably just needs a whiskey to cool off. If he's not back by morning, we will look for him. You have my word."

Aliyah reluctantly agreed to head back to their lair, only because she was ready to topple over. She knew she'd be no good to anyone if she couldn't even summon enough magic to protect herself.

They were heading to the door hand in hand when Draven stopped abruptly and turned around. "Shit, Dolph. I forgot to tell you about Laney, Grunge and Arc. Fuck," Draven cursed.

He informed Dolph of everything that had happened since he'd been trapped in Limbo, minus the part about his sister being pregnant. She assumed he was leaving that piece of information for Grunge, given it was his news and not Draven's.

Aliyah noticed on a few occasions Dolph's jaw gnashed together and his fists clenched and unclenched. She had to hand it to him; he was taking it like a fucking champ for someone who almost died then woke up to this clusterfuck. She wasn't sure how she would have responded if the shoe was on the other foot.

Finally, after Draven finished, they said their goodbyes once again and left. Draven parked the Fifty in the garage, locked it up and then staggered with Aliyah down the streets of The Quarter. She was spent and didn't think anything could ameliorate the exhaustion she was feeling.

They were approaching the lair when horripilation bled through her body. Darkness consumed them in the atramentous alley. Aliyah gripped Draven's hand tighter.

"Show yourself, demon," Draven said, his voice sounding tired.

"You're running out of time, vampire. My, my, my. Doesn't she smell divine," came the mellifluent voice.

Aliyah searched where the voice was coming from but saw nothing. She kicked herself internally for not masking her scent and wondered if she even had the strength to summon that kind of magic after everything that'd occurred in the last twenty-four hours.

"Demon, my patience is riding thin. Show yourself or fuck off."

"Temper, temper," came the same voice. This time Aliyah recognised it.

Orange mist draped around them as long shapely legs took form, accompanied by a body that any model would kill for. Aliyah's eyes travelled up until she saw auburn hair piled messily on top of the demons' head. What sucked the air from her lungs were her eyes. Red speckled sapphire orbs shot glaciers at her.

Aliyah momentarily entertained Malister's animosity toward her before squashing it.

"We meet again, Malister," Aliyah yawned feigning nonchalance.

"The pleasure is certainly all mine, young one. Although, you aren't exactly doing what you should be doing." She circled her razor pointed finger around Aliyah before dismissing her and focusing on Draven.

"You're running out of time, vampire," she stated sternly. "If you don't pull your head out of your ass, or hers," she motioned toward Aliyah, "then Melantha will win this round and Laney will be lost. I'm sure that's something you don't want on that poison infested mind of yours, now do you?"

"What do you fucking care? We are not friends, Malister. You said as much the last time you summoned yourself here. I'm not playing into this sick twisted vendetta you're on. Either you make your move and tell me what the hell is going on instead of speaking in riddles or fuck off. I don't have time for your shit."

Malister smirked but said nothing. Then she was gone. Too exhausted to analyse what the fuck happened, Aliyah pulled Draven the rest of the way toward their place. Once inside, she closed the steel door and breathed a sigh of relief.

Shucking off her jeans and throwing her shirt on the cold sealed concrete floor like she did when she was a child, she headed toward the bathroom.

Draven cleared his throat, causing Aliyah to stop midway and turn around to face him. Even though she knew he was absolutely spent, hunger and desire still burned like a raging fire in his ruby and amethyst eyes.

Aliyah stood there in her bra and panties. She cocked her hip out then rested her hand on it and waited for him to continue. He shook his head from side to side and she noticed the grin peeking out the corner of his mouth.

"Always so sassy. I'll fix that mouth of yours later," he leered. "Right now we need to talk."

"Can we do it in the shower?" Aliyah teased, figuring she could distract him with sex. The last thing on her mind right now was having a deep and meaningful conversation. Everything was still red raw and unattainable in her mind.

"We can shower after this. Sit down, Snowflake."

She huffed, "No. I'm going for a shower."

"Sit the fuck down Aliyah!"

Horripilation broke out all over her body and she felt her nipples pebble at the sound of his demanding tone. As if her body was moving on its own accord, she found herself shimming closer to him, taking a seat on the couch.

Draven sat down beside her. His massive hand massaged small circles around on her thigh before he finally looked up at her.

There was something swirling around in his eyes, something she couldn't recall really ever seeing. It looked like fear.

Reaching up with his free hand, he trailed his fingers from her eyes down to her chin before cupping it. "Tell me what you're feeling, baby."

Aliyah chewed on the inside of her cheek and swallowed the lump in her throat. She didn't want to have this conversation with him right now.

So instead of being honest with him, she mustered up the fakest smile she could, and said, "There's nothing wrong, babe. I'm good."

Draven's eyes took on an edge. Gone was the fear in his beautiful unique irises. Now all she could see was anger. *Fuck.*

"One last chance, Aliyah. Tell me, otherwise I'll find other ways to extract that information from you," he stated, arching his eyebrow in challenge.

Fuck him! "Like I said, there is nothing wrong. I'm fine."

Draven stood up and lifted his shoulders in a shrugging motion as he threw her over his shoulders.

"Let me down right fucking now, Draven!"

He slapped her ass. "I told you I'd find other ways to get you to open up. Instead you chose to be stubborn. Let's see how long that lasts."

Aliyah banged on the back of his dorsal, hoping he would release her, but he didn't. He just continued walking to his destination. Silently she wondered how he had the strength after everything that'd transpired tonight.

Aliyah didn't have long to ponder that thought. She heard the key slide into the key hole and she stilled. He was taking her to his shameless licentious fuck chamber. She'd remembered him calling it that once.

Usually she'd be thrilled to be entering this domain. Tonight, not so much. He was angry with her for withholding how she was truly feeling, so ascending into this room probably wasn't going to be for pleasure. She shivered.

The smell of leather assaulted her nostrils as Draven kicked the door closed behind them. His shoes clicked loudly, echoing around the room full of all his sexual contraptions.

Another shiver racked through her whole body as her core heated. Aliyah was turned on and knew she'd be wet if Draven decided to look.

Laying her down, she was welcomed by the feel of cold leather under her body. Aliyah looked down and realised she was laying on the spanking bench. Draven reached above her and pulled back some cuffs.

Aliyah's eyebrows arched. "Didn't we do this last time? I'm sure we both established I'm strong enough to break the cuffs."

He smirked and reached behind his back. Curiosity strummed through her body and she wondered what he was doing.

When he pulled back, he had his diamond dagger in his hand. Aliyah blanched and the arousal she felt earlier dissipated.

"You're seriously not going to stab me because I didn't tell you what was on my mind," she squeaked.

Draven's smirk widened. "So there is something on your mind. Interesting. But no, I'm not going to stab you," he said contemplatively. "I am however going to give you a little incentive to open up and be honest with me."

Before Aliyah could protest, Draven snatched her wrists and drew a light circle with the dagger around her wrists then cuffed them.

She hissed as blood trickled down her forearm. Draven's nostrils flared; lust flickered through his eyes before it was gone.

"There. This will weaken you just that little bit. By the look on your face, I'm not sure it fazes you." He canted his neck to the side, assessing her.

Draven lifted her arms above her head and clicked them onto something so she couldn't move. The cuts were painful but not as bad as she thought it would be.

Cupping his chin with his index finger and thumb he took a step back. Aliyah chanced a look at him and noticed the sadistic, yet sexy smile on his face.

The air crepitated around them like always, and Draven was looking at her like he was about to devour her whole. "You look stunning, Snowflake. I'll never tire of you."

Although she was pissed off with him, her heart warmed at his declaration. "So what now? We just stay here until I tell you what's up?"

His laughter rang out loudly around the room. "Oh baby, you have no idea. Moving toward her, he leaned down close to her face and said, "Are you going to tell me what's on your mind?"

Aliyah shook her head no. He tutted and placed the dagger against her chest bone and stared down at her. Although the dagger was cold on her skin, it didn't stop the volcano blooming through her loins. She desperately attempted to mask her scent before Draven could smell her desire.

The right side of his face kicked up at the side. It was too late. He already knew. Draven flicked the dagger up and her bra flayed out exposing her tits to him.

Aliyah squirmed, mewling.

Draven traced the dagger lightly down her torso, her abs contracted with each movement. She watched in awe as the vermilion liquid pooled to the surface of her flesh.

The diamond was sharp and elicited enough of a sting to make her gasp, but also enough agony to make her insides clench. She was turned on beyond belief and she despised the empty feeling she was experiencing.

Aliyah's neck began to ache as she extended it more so she could watch what Draven was going to do. The blade stopped at the junction of her thighs. Draven's eyes stayed downcast as his tongue darted out, circling around his full lips before he drew his bottom lip into his mouth. It was one of the sexiest things she'd seen him do.

His head snapped up, those mesmerizing irises ablaze. He was ready for more than teasing, and Aliyah wondered where he'd discovered this new found energy when he struggled to walk down the street just moments ago.

"You ready to tell me what's going on in that pretty head of yours?"

"I already told you, nothing."

"Very well."

The dagger sliced into her skin a little as Draven severed each side of her panties. She cried out as the mixture of agony and bliss swirled deep inside of her.

Draven dragged the blunt handle of the dagger down to tease her folds and began to slowly open her up. Aliyah panted and wriggled her hips up to apply more pressure on the place she wanted it most.

Draven chuckled low and deep inserting the handle inside of her a little then he stilled. It was probably no more than an inch, but it was quite thick and she felt it every-where.

Aliyah's body was on the edge, her nerve endings feeling like electricity was thrumming ferociously through them. She wanted nothing more than for him to stick his big, gorgeous cock inside of her and help her find a release. Alas, Aliyah knew he wouldn't give her what she wanted until he got what he chasing... her mind.

Dropping her head back to the bench, she listened to her ragged breaths echoing around them. He pushed the handle in a little more and her hips jutted upward to meet the hilt.

Draven placed his free hand on her belly and pushed her down to the bench. The sexual frustration was pent up inside of her but she didn't want to give into him. She only wanted one night off from her mind, from talking. Was that so much to ask?

Aliyah could feel Draven's digits traced a figure eight on her belly. Lifting her head again, she watched as he smudged her blood all over her tummy. The small wounds looked like scratches now because she was healing.

Draven's eyes focused on hers as he stopped what he was doing and brought his digits to his lips. He inserted them inside his mouth, sucking on them until he groaned.

Aliyah tore her eyes away to look down at his pants. Her mouth watered at how hard he was behind the placket of his jeans.

Noticing where her eyes had drifted, he looked down, grinned and pumped the handle inside of her a bit faster.

"Fuck, Draven. Please!" she pleaded as her hips lifted up to fuck the handle. The familiar heated tingle was billowing within and she knew she was close to toppling over the edge. *Just a little bit more...*

"What's on your mind, Snowflake?" his voice came out like gravel.

She shook her head slowly from side to side as tears began brimming behind her eyes. Draven slowed his pace to one of molasses.

"No! Please!"

"Tell me what's wrong and I will make you cum. It's that simple."

Her stubborn streak was fierce. She shook her head no once more.

Draven withdraw the dagger and pressed a little harder as he traced the pointed diamond up her stomach toward her tits.

Aliyah's teeth clenched and she cursed under her breath. Although it stung, she couldn't deny how utterly turned on she was by it.

Remembering she was cuffed, she yanked down on them, hoping they'd snap like before. They didn't. *Fuck sakes!*

Draven whirled the diamond dagger around her nipples. Blood rose to the surface as she cinched her legs together. The heat of the incision was fucking with her resolve something cruel.

Leaning forward, Draven's dreadlocks fell forward, providing a curtain around his face while he took one of her hard nipples into his mouth.

He growled while sucking on her nipple, sending the vibration straight down to her cunt. Aliyah became dizzy. She was that turned on that her vision started to blur.

Pulling away from her nipple with a pop, Draven licked his lips and asked again, "Ready to tell me. Believe me when I say I can do this all night, because I can. Test me, I dare you. I enjoy torturing this body and mind of yours, especially after absorbing all that pain earlier. You're my perfect distraction, Snowflake."

His canines elongated and she mewled.   Draven dragged the dagger down her torso and inserted the handle deeper inside of her. He pumped the object of her present desire in and out her faster.

Aliyah's body shuddered. She was so fucking close. He pulled out the dagger and she whimpered. "Tell me, Aliyah."

"Fuck you," she hissed.

Draven chuckled and slammed the handle of the dagger harshly insider of her. It would have hurt like a bitch if she wasn't turned on. But she couldn't deny it due to the wet sounds of her pussy ricocheting around the room.

Just as she was about to cum, he stopped and arched his brow in question. Sweat dotted her forehead and tears were threatening to bottle over.

Instead of giving in, Aliyah growled, "Go fuck yourself, Draven!"

He thrusted the handle in again while he undid his jeans with his left hand. Aliyah's eyes gravitated to his swollen cock. Even when it looked purple and angry it was beautiful.

Draven pumped his length at the same speed as the handle inside of her. He knew how much she loved watching him fuck his hand. *Asshole.*

Aliyah tried to slow her breathing down and stop her moans from toppling out, figuring he may not be able to tell when she was about to cum.

Her canines elongated, she sucked her lip into her mouth and bit down. The sweet metallic taste of her blood filled her mouth.

Draven moaned and she knew he was as close as she was. An electric current began to travel down her spine and into her core. She was ready to combust.

The handle of the dagger stilled and his hand slowed on his cock. Tears streamed down her face and she screeched at him, "Let me fucking cum! It hurts so much, please Draven."

"Tell me," he ground out, "then I will."

"It's fucking Delilah! You nursed a broken heart for two hundred years thinking she was dead, but now there is a possibility she's alive and maybe you still love her. If she's alive maybe you won't need me."

Draven withdrew the dagger, pulled her roughly down the bench, snapping her arms within the handcuffs tight against her head, then plowed into her. Starbursts formed behind her irises while her eyes rolled to the back of her head.

She felt the coldness then the stinging of the diamond dagger when Draven slashed it into her flesh. The pain was more prominent than earlier and she cried out.

Aliyah heard a clinking sound and realized he'd thrown the dagger to the floor. He spread her legs as wide as they could go and continued to piston into her. She was about to cum but he slowed his pace.

"Why?" she wept.

"Because you don't trust in me or in what we have. I

love you, Aliyah. Only you. I told you before that our love is different to what I had with Delilah. We are bound. You, Aliyah Serene are my forever after." He pummelled into her faster and harder than before.

Aliyah's body was on fire. Her eyes didn't stray from his as he slapped her clit and bellowed, "Cum for me now!"

She scrunched her eyes shut and cried out, her orgasm washing over her like a damn tsunami as she toppled over the edge, freefalling into heavenly bliss.

Opening her eyes, she watched him thrust into her relentlessly. Perspiration spread across his brow and his dreadlocks swung to and fro while he slammed into her over and over again.

"I love you, Draven Sangue."

Just as the words left her mouth, he roared. She felt his cock jerk inside of her as the heat travelled up her body. But he didn't stop there. He leaned down and sank his fangs into her clavicle and suckled.

Her body was wired. She felt another orgasm creeping up and the feel of Draven sucking on her clavicle spurred her on. She took that opportunity to sink her canines into his neck. They both moaned and shuddered when their second orgasms slammed through them at the same time.

Draven was draped over Aliyah panting while she tried desperately to catch her own breath. Her eyes felt heavy; they slid down to close. She inhaled, smelling Draven's intoxicating scent.

She was damn tired. Slowly, she began to fade out of consciousness, but not before she heard Draven whisper something above her ear.

Aliyah fought to open her eyes so she could look at him and decipher what he was saying. The sandman had spoken and was making is difficult for her to focus. Fighting hard, the last thing she heard before fading completely was, "Delilah, I don't love you anymore."

Chapter Seventeen

~ Aliyah ~

It was dark when Aliyah gingerly opened her eyes. Her hand automatically sought Draven. Instead, she found his side cold.

She sat up, looking around the room. The bathroom door was wide open. She could see the granite winking back at her but Draven wasn't inside.

Aliyah's head was pulsating and she felt as if a migraine was coming on. Lifting her hands from the bed, she placed a couple of digits on each side of her temples to massage them.

Massaging in a circular motion, an odd sensation fizzled through her body. She didn't have time to examine the feeling, though. Her eyes slammed shut once more and her head fell back onto the pillow just before the world disappeared.

Mummy! Mummy! It hurts. Please mummy, help me. Aliyah had tears streaming down her face as she cried for her mother to come and help her. She peered down at her scrape. Blood trickled from her knee then slid down her shin. It looked icky.

The flyscreen door flew wide and hit the side of the old weatherboard house where they were living. Aliyah immediately cowered when she'd seen her mum heading toward her. She looked angry. Her sandy hair was laying on her shoulders when she stormed toward her. Her shirt was skewed and her pants were unbuttoned.

"What have you done now, Aliyah! For fuck sakes, can I not have five minutes peace without having to deal with your stupid ass?"

The tears flowed freely from her eyes, gliding down her cheeks. She tried to tell her mother what had happened but she wouldn't listen to her. Her mummy was never this nasty. Why was she being so mean now, Aliyah wondered.

Brushing her knees off, she stood up and looked into her mum's eyes, trying to convince her that she was strong and that she didn't need her. But looking into her mother's eyes petrified her. They weren't the normal blue that she remembered. These eyes were scary.

Aliyah squinted up just as she noticed her mother smirk at her. Jill's eyes had a blood orange rim around them. Her arm darted out and gripped Aliyah's throat.

"I am so fucking glad I am rid of you. You meant nothing to me. You are nothing, you promiscuous little slut!"

The tears pooled in the corner of her eyes once more as she clawed and scratched, trying to break free. Peering down, she kicked her legs trying to hit Jill and realised she'd grown. She was no longer a little girl. Now she was a big girl.

Aliyah didn't have time to ponder how she was bigger because her head felt dizzy. She knew Jill was about to kill her.

A voice reverberated around her. "ENOUGH! Let her go this instance, you despicable demon lackey!"

Aliyah dropped to the floor like a discarded bag of potatoes. She coughed and spluttered, holding her hand around her throat in the same area where she'd been strangled.

Her long raven hair was draped around her face when Aliyah saw an extended hand appear before her. Hesitating, she decided to take the stranger's aid to help her stand up.

Aliyah was greeted with hair as white as snow with black foils weaved throughout. The woman stood there in a lilac sheaf, similar to the last time she'd seen her. Butterflies filled her belly as her eyes met her mother's violet pair.

"Mum? How are you here?"

Serene smiled. "I sensed you were in trouble, Aliyah. Where else would I be? But come quickly now. I don't have much time."

Serene squeezed her hand a little tighter and Aliyah winced. "You're hurting me."

She didn't respond. Instead, she weaved through the large, tall trees that were behind her childhood house. Poison ivy draped around the thick tree trunks. Poison Ivy? There is usually no poison ivy here, Aliyah thought.

Serene was dragging her now and the grip on her palm had intensified. Something wasn't right but Aliyah didn't think her mother would put her in harm's way. She was clearly worried about her and that's why she seemed frantic. That's how she attempted to convince herself.

The trees began to darken and the ground turned squishy and muddy. Before Aliyah knew what was happening, she noticed the bluish/black sludge hanging from the tree branches. Aliyah tried to pull her hand back from her mother's, but to no avail. She wanted to say something, anything. Her voice felt lodged in her throat.

The floor morphed from mud to what she knew was black lava stone. Her blood froze in her veins as the trees dissipated and turned into jagged looking bitumen.

She tried again to yank her hand back and that's when she realised how cold her mother's hand was. Why was she bringing me here? she wondered anxiously.

Peering down, Aliyah saw she was naked. This was all wrong. What was Serene doing here? Her head snapped up and Aliyah noted how her mother's hair was turning the colour of onyx. Gone was the luminous snow-white hue. Now it was all black.

Horripilation scattered all over her body when she realised this woman couldn't be her mother. The woman's back was still facing Aliyah while she dragged her down the narrow vestibule.

She squinted, trying to decipher what or who this woman was. Something told her she wasn't going to like the outcome. With all her might, she dug her heels in and the woman stopped abruptly.

"Move," she hissed.

"Look at me," Aliyah demanded.

The woman's laughter came out in a burst, causing the hairs on the back of Aliyah's neck to stand to attention.

"You do not get to tell me what to do. I am your mother!"

"Then look at me," Aliyah's voice cracked on the last word.

"You're coming with me. Now move."

This was not Serene. Aliyah knew it with every fiber in her being. It wasn't only her hair changing colour, or the rapidity of how she pulled Aliyah along behind her. What caught her second guessing this woman was the fact that not once had she called her daughter like Serene had when she'd visited The Enchantment.

"Neferity?"

The woman's feet stammered and the lilac sheaf disappeared, leaving the slender woman nude. Dropping her hand, the woman turned around. Aliyah was met with one of the most stunning creatures she'd ever encountered. Her lips were red and full, almost as if they were beseeching to be kissed. She had a strong jawline that was soften by her high cheekbones that rested just below her large eyes.

Those eyes, yeah, they still scared the fuck out of her. She'd only seen them once before when she'd somehow managed to find herself looking in on Laney and the Dark Goddess. Neferity hadn't sensed her, thank fuck, but Aliyah recalled those penetrating crimson coloured irises. It was definitely her.

Her lips curled up at the sides. "You definitely didn't get your intelligence from Gorgon. Well maybe a little bit." She pinched her thumb and finger almost together, enunciating little.

Aliyah wasn't sure where the strength came from, but she lifted her shoulders and stared at the Goddess. "What am I doing here? More to the point, how the fuck did you enter my subconscious again."

She giggled, which sounded eerie and not right. "You think the Mad Warlock's philter can keep me away from you? You will capitulate sooner or later. After all, it's already written, young demon."

Anger bubbled to the surface. Trying to keep her dark-

ness in check, Aliyah forced down the insult searing the tip of her tongue.

Instead of succumbing to Neferity's heckle, she smiled and replied, "I might be part demon but there is more light than dark in me. My light taints my dark, which you will find out sooner or later." She threw Neferity's claim at her with nonchalance, even if part of her didn't believe herself.

Aliyah observed the small tick in the Dark Goddess's jaw and the way her nostrils flared. She'd hit a nerve.

"You stupid, insolent child! How dare you talk to me with disrespect! I am your Goddess whether you like it or not."

"No you're not. Kaltemis is my only Goddess."

"My sister is not worthy of that title!" she screeched. "And you, you should have kept your mouth shut. Now I'm going to make this painful."

The strength Aliyah feigned earlier dissipated and was replaced with trepidation. The Dark Goddess was in front of her before she'd even had the time to blink.

Neferity's smile seem to have a ruthless edge as she speared her arm forward, her hand sinking it to Aliyah's chest cavity.

"I only need a slither of your soul to alter your perception and to have you subjugating your pathetic self to my whims," she singsonged. "Now hold still, this will only hurt a fuck load."

Aliyah's eyes popped wide as she gawked at Neferity while pain radiated throughout her body; so much she thought she was going to vomit all over the Dark Goddess. She screamed out brutally loud, and summoned all of her magic and energy in hopes she could stop Neferity from stealing a part of her soul so she could control her.

Aliyah's teeth felt like they were about to splinter inside her mouth with how tight she clenched her jaw. She had to remain stoic otherwise the worlds could be doomed. That was something Aliyah wouldn't have on her conscious.

"Stop fighting it, Aliyah! I always get what I want!" Neferity's teeth chattered at the end of her sentence. She was struggling.

Her mind was foggy and her vigour was waning. Aliyah

wasn't sure how much longer she could hold on.

"Snowflake!" *Draven's voice vibrated around in her skull.*

Aliyah couldn't even breathe a sigh of relief because she feared if she let down her guard then Neferity would get her hand on her soul.

She thought she was hallucinating when she saw Draven's form appear behind Neferity. No, it was a trick. The Dark Goddess was playing with her.

She pleaded within her mind in case Draven was in fact communicating telepathically with her. She implored for his help and hoped he'd hear her cries and fears.

Aliyah's legs were beginning to crumble, her fortitude failing before her eyes. Her orbs hadn't faltered from Neferity's pair once and she witnessed the triumph slashing through those crimson blood eyes.

"You're about to submit. I can feel you shattering and it's a marvellous sight to behold."

No, no, no! *This could not be happening. Aliyah knew she'd need to figure a way out of this before it was too late.*

"Hold on, Aliyah, I'm coming for you," *Draven pleaded.*

Three, two, one... Everything went black, Aliyah's body convulsed as she bellowed out. Fear washed through her. She couldn't see a thing.

The last thing she heard before jolting upright was Neferity's vow. "Next time I won't underestimate your bond with that vampire. Mark my words. I will get what I am owed, what is rightfully mine...your soul."

"Wake up, Aliyah. Baby wake up!"

Aliyah tried to open her eyes. They felt like sand was wedged underneath them. *How did she get inside my head again?*

"Snowflake, you're scaring me. Tell me what happened?"

She was finally able to open her eyes, to find Draven's intense mismatched pair eyeing her with what looked like concern.

Aliyah lifted her hand and rubbed it against her forehead. It felt like a herd of motorcycles were roaring inside her mind as she slowly caressed the creases in her brow.

Taking a deep breath, she confessed, "It was Neferity. She was inside my mind again."

Something flickered in those magnificent amethyst and ruby hues, something that she knew resembled anger with a hint of despondency and guilt. Aliyah was confused with the conflict of emotions seen flooding through those irises.

"I keep fucking failing you. I should have been here for you. I should have protected you."

Aliyah attempted to assuage Draven, but it proved fruitless.

His eyes blazed down at her. "Have you been ingesting the philter Reikiki concocted for you?"

"Of course. I haven't missed a single dose since he gave it to me."

"Get dressed. We need to head to the Mad Warlock."

"Wait. Where were you? I woke and you were gone."

Draven averted his gaze. He not only looked uncomfortable but guilty as well when he spoke, "Nowhere. Now get dressed," he replied dismissively.

Aliyah scrunched up her brow. She wanted to question him more about his whereabouts, but she chose not to run into the battle with Draven blind. Although she actively decided against questioning him, it did little to mitigate her anxiety because she knew he was hiding something form her.

She walked to the cupboard without saying a word. Her nerves were frizzling within her body and her mind was high strung like a junkie needing its next hit. Nothing seemed fucking simple in the Otherworlder's world. And a part of her missed when she was only Aliyah Parker. Not a vampire, faery, angel and demon with royal blood, but Aliyah fucking Parker. *But I'm not a Parker, am I? So what is my true birth name?*

Thoughts tumbled around in her mind. Those small, inadequate feelings flaying around on not knowing who she really was. A piece of her felt like her identity was lost—stolen in fact, given the circumstances in which she grew up. Not knowing that Jill and John weren't her biological parents had really fucked with her, and she couldn't help wondering what could have been if she had known who she was and what she was meant to be all these years? Would this have come easier to her if she'd had the knowledge early on?

And then there were the feelings of Draven lying to her. Those seem to pain the most. Aliyah pulled on a pair of black, ripped skinny jeans as she rummaged through her shirts until she found a maroon one that had 'Thorns are pricks too' scrawled across it. Aliyah thought the shirt was fitting given her feelings toward Draven at this moment. He was beautiful, yet dangerous to touch and most definitely a prick for hiding whatever he was from her.

Aliyah spared a glance at Draven as they headed toward the steel door to exit the lair. His dark denim jeans hugged his thighs like a second skin and the white shirt he wore did little to hide his bulging inked biceps.

She pulled her eyes away and stepped the last couple of paces until they arrived at the door. Their fingers brushed slightly and the electricity shot up her fingertips and throughout her body. The familiar crackle crepitated around them, but sex wasn't going to fix this. He was hiding something from her and she knew she wasn't going to like it.

Stealing her hand back, Aliyah crossed her arms across her chest and waited for Draven to open the door. He placed his hand on her shoulder but she shucked him off.

He sighed and opened the door so they could make their way toward The Quarter. They walked in silence toward Jadis's shop to pick up his Bel Air. He pulled the car out and Aliyah hopped into the passenger seat.

Instead of paying Draven any attention, she plucked her phone from her pocket and texted Dany. Aliyah still hadn't heard from him and after the bullshit that happened with her dream this morning, she'd forgotten all about him storming off. She felt like a bad friend as she began typing a message to him.

D-bag... Are you alright? I'm worried about you.

Three dots appeared immediately.

Yeah. I'm ok. I'm sorry for putting you through that shit yesterday.

Aliyah heaved a sigh and noticed Draven eyeing her from her peripheral. She ignored him. It annoyed her that Dany would think he was a burden on her. She would do anything for her best friend.

Don't be a douche. I wanted to figure out who murdered your parents as much as you. I didn't anticipate Draven's ex-fiancé though.

The three dots appeared then disappeared for a couple minutes. It was almost like he was writing but then deleting his message. Finally his reply came through.

I'm torn, Liah. I'm so fucking angry, yet bleached in melancholy with what happened. She mangulated them beyond recognition. She looked so angry. Why? What did my parents do to her? I can't get the smell of their blood out of my nostrils. It's as if I'm reliving it all over again. Then I wonder how did Delilah even do it, wasn't she dead? And a small piece of me is pissed off with Draven. Did he know? Of course he didn't, right? I can't stop thinking about you and how all of this would be affecting you as well. His message seemed rambunctious.

Aliyah stole a glance at Draven. He was focusing on the road, his white-knuckle grip on the steering well prominent. Good, let him be pissed off.

She ached for Dany. If only there was something that she could do to ameliorate his angst. Looking away from Draven, she typed her reply.

I can't begin to imagine how you feel. After seeing the memory with you, I'm a little shook up as well. I don't believe Draven knew Delilah had done it or was still alive. I'm almost certain there would have been no me and him if that was the case. Don't worry about me, D-bag, I'm a big girl. We're almost at Reikiki's. We can talk more then.

She hit send and the three little bubbles surface once more.

I'm not there. I have to go, Liah. I'll catch you later.

What? He's not there? Speed typing, she replied,
Where are you?

No three dots emerged signalling he was replying; however, the little read notification was above her message.

Groaning, she sent her phone to sleep and looked at the window.

"Anything you'd like to talk about?"

Aliyah ignored Draven's question, instead focusing on

the light posts they passed. *What is he hiding from me,* she questioned.

They didn't talk the rest of the drive or even when they entered Reikiki's domain. She centred herself, leaving Draven behind and strode toward where she knew the Mad Warlock would be.

True to her senses, Reikiki sat perched on what looked like an antique day bed. The material shimmered in bright orange and pink, clashing with his mustard yellow walls. She always wondered what the go was with his eccentricity and vibrant colours.

He was lying down in his usual tunic style clothes nursing a tea cup, but that wasn't fooling Aliyah because she could smell the whiskey permeating throughout the room.

His tiger eyed gaze flickered up to her. Something flashed in those intense yellow orange eyes and the realisation of her question earlier came staggering in.

The Mad Warlock surrounded himself in bright colours and idiosyncrasy because in his mind he lived in atramentous bleakness.

Reikiki averted his eyes from hers. Aliyah sensed it was because she caught a glimpse of his tired and tattered soul.

He cleared his throat, took a languid sip of his *tea,* *then* his orbs found hers once more. "The Dark Goddess penetrated the philter I see."

"What? How did you know? Did you have another vision?" she stuttered through her questioning.

"No."

Aliyah felt the furrow in her brow deepen. "No? Then how did you know?"

Sighing dramatically, Reikiki sat up. His hands flayed around in the air toward her. "Your aura is all mucked up."

She kicked her right leg out then pulled her arms out to the front of her to see if she could see what he was talking about. Alas, she saw nothing.

"What do you mean? I can't see anything," Aliyah replied exasperated.

"Seriously, child." Reikiki rolled his eyes. "You have an abundant amount of magic that you don't know how to use. It sincerely pisses me off."

Aliyah's eyes bugged.

"When any human or Otherworlder comes in contact with Neferity, their aura is skewed," he paused, then continued. "Kind of like tainted. Your aura used to be golden and vivacious with a tinge of violet scurrying through. Now? Now there is a murky darkness encompassing it."

"There the fuck you two are," came Draven's baritone voice. Even though she was pissed at him, his voice still made her insides quiver.

"Did you know, Vampire?"

"Did I know what?"

"Don't fucking tell me you can't see it either?" came Reikiki's aggravated tone. "Not all of us are so lucky to have the gift of reading aura's, but I know for a fact that you have that ability. Look at her!"

Draven's eyes bulged momentarily and that flicker of guilt resurfaced. Again she wondered what he was hiding.

He ground his jaw and she heard his teeth gnash. "Neferity's trademark. I didn't see it before. I didn't even remember the gift to be honest."

"You of all people should remember, Vampire. You know what it feels like for Neferity to have her claws embedded into your flesh, into your soul."

Draven winced while Aliyah watched the tennis match between the duo. *What am I missing here?*

"Can someone please tell me what the fuck is going on here?" she spat.

Her frown increased as Draven's eyes shot to Reikiki.

"Your darkness will be vicious for a little while, Snowflake. Neferity's malicious tendrils of darkness have rooted to your soul. Fuck. How could I let this happen!"

"Where were you?" Aliyah whispered as the trepidation set into her veins.

His eyes flashed toward Reikiki once more.

"She'll find out eventually, Vampire. Mark my words."

"Find out what?" Aliyah questioned vehemently.

Draven remained silent. His mismatched eyes all but pleading with her.

"Tell me, Draven! Right fucking now."

He shook his head. "I was nowhere."

"You're lying to me again! You expect me to bow to

your every whim, capitulate to you, to our binding, yet you can't even be honest with me? Fuck you, Shrek. I'm out."

Storming out of the room, she went the next mile and slammed the door. Aliyah knew she wouldn't have long until Draven stalked her and threw her over his shoulder like a cave man.

Using as much of her energy and magic she could muster, Aliyah connected with the earth to mask her scent and tethered to the fire element to temporally block Draven from her mind. She wasn't sure how she knew how to do it but was thankful she could. Right now he didn't deserve to be bound to her. With that lingering thought floating around, she vamp sped out of Reikiki's and straight into the lion's den.

Bursting out of the Mad Warlock's apartment building and into the scorching heat, Aliyah's eyes darted in all directions. She needed to pick a route and fast.

Her ears pricked up and she heard a door slam inside the building. She knew it was Reikiki's and that Draven was in pursuit. "Shit," she cursed.

Something told her to go right, so on a whim she raced down the street and darted down another to stay out of view. She crouched down behind a bush before she saw Draven exit the building, looking frantic.

A sliver of guilt coiled around her gut, but then she remembered why she'd fled and it dissipated. Honing in on his face, Aliyah noticed his nostrils flaring at the same time he began screaming her name.

Aliyah sat back and really looked at Reikiki's apartment building. She hadn't noticed how out of sorts it appeared until now. A light bulb went off in her mind and she figured it was a glamour.

Draven was pulling at his dreadlocks now, his eyes searching furiously for her. Guilt seeped in once more but she pushed it away and stood quietly. He turned left and she took the opportunity to flee in the opposite direction.

Aliyah wasn't sure how long she had been running. She just knew that she needed to get out of there and fast. Peering over her shoulder to make sure Draven hadn't changed routes, she breathed a sigh of relief and then collided with something... something hard.

She stumbled back, looking into red eyes. Trepidation prickled all over her body. Aliyah turned to run but her arm was snagged.

"Where do you think you're going, princess? Daddy needs a word with you."

Gorgon's voice was the last thing she heard before she saw black.

Chapter Eighteen

~ Draven ~

Where the fuck could she be? Draven silently cursed himself. He'd been searching for a little over an hour and still hadn't found Aliyah.

His muscles were burning and he was beginning to feel a little dizzy with how much he'd exerted on himself. Not to mention he hadn't fed from Aliyah in what felt like forever to him made his body scream.

Draven stopped dead in his tracks as his veins turned arctic. Something wasn't right. He tried to tanker into her mind and froze when he realised there was a barrier of some sort blocking him. *Fuck! When did she learn to do that?*

He didn't have time to think about that. Aliyah was in trouble and he'd bet his left nut on it. He sped back to Reikiki's.

Barging through the front door, he stopped abruptly when he was met with blazing tiger eyes. "You fucking imbecile! You lost her! And you want to know who has her, hmm? Gorgon fucking Vascillie."

"No. That can't be. He should be in Purgatory."

"Do you truly know nothing, you fool?"

Dark tendrils of anger wound themselves tightly within his ancient frame. "How the fuck do you know so much, Reikiki? Another one of your visions, or is it from past experiences." He winced at the venom lacing his voice and immediately felt like a cunt.

The Mad Warlock's eyes flamed a burning brilliant yellow orange in those tiger like irises.

"How dare you speak to me like that! Don't you ever bring up my history with the Dark Goddess again. Believe me, next time I won't be so lenient." Reikiki stared Draven down, and he knew he'd fucked up.

He placed his hands out in front of him, and said, "I apologise. I shouldn't have taken my shit out on you. I'm so fucking scared of what's going to happen to her if I don't find her soon."

Reikiki nodded once, and Draven figured he'd accepted his apology. "You should be scared. Gorgon is a sadistic son of a bitch. And yes, I do know that from past experience." He shifted uncomfortably. "Did you try accessing her mind through your link?"

Draven flinched at his accusing tone. "Somehow Aliyah has blocked communication."

Reikiki raised a perfectly manicured silver eyebrow. "She can do that?"

"So it seems," Draven scoffed.

Reikiki's face kicked up at the sides. "She's a sassy little minx, our Aliyah."

"Not ours, mine."

"Oh hush, vampire. I didn't mean it in a derogatory sexual sense like you. She is her own Otherworlder. You have to see that. Being bound to you is not an easy task."

"What does that mean?" Draven growled.

"Stop it, Draven. I've known you for centuries and I've seen your demons at play."

Fuck, what was it with him tonight and busting my balls while knocking me down a few pegs? Asshole.

"Point taken. Now how about we stop talking about how undeserving I am of Aliyah and try and find her for fuck sakes."

"Come. I'll need Jadis's assistance."

~ Aliyah ~

Aliyah's eyes were heavy as she slowly opened them. Where ever she was, it didn't feel like home. Groaning, she sat up on what felt like a bed and immediately her hands flew to her skull. The pain ricocheting within was intense. *What the fuck.*

Looking around the small room, Aliyah attempted to regain her bearings. Once her eyes adjusted and the pain eased off some she realised where she was.

The bedroom was exactly the way she and Draven had left it all those weeks ago. Back when this life was new to her, back when she didn't believe in things like vampires, demons, and god damn faeries.

Debris littered the ugly pink floor that was the madness of her bedroom. Aliyah didn't think she would ever be back here.

Memories invaded her senses like a fucking freight train and she groaned, holding onto her head tighter. Dropping to her knees, she hissed and looked down to see glass had punctured into her knee.

"Aaaahhhhh, fuck!"

"That's no way to greet your father is it?"

Aliyah pulled her heavy head up and stared into the hauntingly red eyes that were shaped so much like her own. She hated it.

Gorgon stood there, hands in his suit pant pockets smirking down at her. Her wayward thought was wondering why the fuck her demon dad was wearing a fucking suit.

"Your mother, fuck she was insatiable. She was breathtaking, much like yourself. You more so now with Neferity's magic freshly encompassing your aura. How I love knowing how susceptible you are now, so easy for me to bend."

Aliyah felt the vomit coat her esophagus at his statements, all while trying to ease the excruciating pain that has returned hardcore to her skull.

"What the fuck do you want," she ground out.

He made a show of running his index finger down the line in his scarred right cheek. "There's a lot I want, *Aliyah*. But for this moment I need to bring you to my Goddess."

"Why did you bring me here if you're to deliver me to your fucked-up Goddess?"

Gorgon tutted. "Are those memories still circling? Of

course they are. I just wanted to help you remember this one memory before I'm rid of you. Hold on tight, honey, this is going to hurt!"

Harrowing pain sliced through Aliyah's mind, shredding the fog and images that were playing havoc within. She clawed at her skull in hope that she could stop the affliction.

The pain was tightening around her like a python as the bile rose upward, making her feel nauseous. Aliyah knew she was going to vomit everywhere if it didn't subside.

Hearing dark laughter, she remembered where she was and who she was with. She didn't want to become subservient to Gorgon's twisted magic and games.

Smog began to clear and the pain lessened a little as she felt her eyes fill with tears. The image before her crippled her. Draven was looking into the eyes of woman with dark curly hair, pale skin and lips as red as sin. She was gorgeous, which made her despise her even more.

Delilah hung on every word Draven was whispering in her ear and her red lipped smile grew with each second. They looked... they looked happy. That gutted Aliyah down to the marrow.

Jealousy ripped through her like the green-eyed monster itself while she watched the image flicker. Delilah was reaching for Draven's belt buckle.

"Noooooo!" Aliyah keened out and pushed the image from her mind.

Placing her left palm to the ground, she pushed up on shaking legs until she was standing. It was only a sliver of time, a fraction of a second, but Aliyah saw the worry filter through Gorgon's crimson eyes.

Collecting himself, he crooned, "Not what you want to see, princess? Don't want to see how happy his *fiancé* made him?" He didn't give Aliyah time to respond. "That's ok. It wasn't the memory I wanted to show you."

Aliyah's knees crumbled once more and her cuspids elongated when the searing white pain slammed into her again. Her jaw was clenched so tightly from the agony that she thought she was going to snap her canines off.

Pictures swirled around and this time she couldn't stop

the vomit exiting her mouth. She spewed all over the ugly pink carpet, retching then gasping for air.

Colours broke out then swarmed together like a kaleidoscope before fixing on an image, an image she daren't think she'd ever see.

Aliyah folded over on herself. The foremost image was of Gorgon and Serene standing hand in hand holding a swaddling bunch of blankets. Realisation crashed into her as she watched them knock on the door. The very same door with the white paint peeling from it that she'd walked though for the first half of her life.

It swung wide and a younger, less frumpier Jill stood next to John at the entrance. Both of them looking bored at Gorgon and Serene.

"What can I do you for?" Jill said through chews of gum.

That was all she heard throughout the image. The four of them laughed no doubt at some insidious joke on Aliyah's behalf then Serene handed her to Jill and turned away.

Serene clutched Gorgon's hand tightly and he drew her in closer while they walked down the drive like they hadn't just given up their daughter.

Everything was spinning. Aliyah desperately tried to regain some composure, some focus as she played over the memory again in her head.

"Your mother loved me once, can't you see that?" came Gorgons smug voice.

No this wasn't right, something was wrong because none of this made sense. Aliyah purged through her memories, attempting to remember what Serene had said to her.

Red, hot anger seared her entire body when recognition of her encounter with Serene came to the forefront of her mind. Gorgon had raped her. This whole thing was a lie. Aliyah wasn't sure how he did it but he'd planted those falsified memories into her mind. This charade was a bunch of chicanery, and Aliyah wasn't going to have it.

With everything she had within, she anchored herself to the earth, to ground her while her anger brought on the fire. She tethered to those flames, drawing in strength and bellowed.

Aliyah knew from the flabbergasting look on Gorgon's face that she was glowing. It only made her madder.

"You fucking raped her! You took from her what wasn't yours! You had no fucking right you piece of demon scum!"

Gorgon's red eyes bulged wide, pulling on his scar. Aliyah knew in that moment that he hadn't expected her to know that information.

Venom spluttered through her veins as she felt the darkness taking over. Trepidation crossed Gorgon's face briefly before he smiled smugly.

"Yes. It is happening! This isn't over, Aliyah. I vow to you right now that you will see me again. I will always find you. Remember, my blood pumps viciously through your veins like old wine." With that parting speech, blackish green murky mist formed and he was gone.

Aliyah breathed heavily. She was so fucking angry, angry and so fucking hungry. Before she knew what she was doing, she vamp sped out of her childhood home to find her next fix.

The streets of the French Quarter were crawling with tourists. The street lights shone dimly, casting an eerie vibe. Aliyah didn't think she could run that fast but she knew it now.

Scratching at her skin, she looked around the streets, surveying the Quarter. Women and men were staggering drunkenly in every direction.

Her thighs drew together involuntarily, clenching as if they could suppress the rising tension blooming in her core. Not only was she angry and hungry, she was downright sexed up and ravenous.

She stalked the streets and inhaled the air. It smelled of every bad decision: sex, alcohol, debauchery and more trouble. It was exactly what she was and what her body was craving.

There was a voice deep within, a muffled voice trying to warn Aliyah off. Her lip curled up in disgust as she silenced the echo inside. All she wanted to do was feed, fuck and have fun. Was that too much to ask?

A little voice whispered, *You deserve this after every-*

*thing you've been through. Do not subdue your true na-
ture. You are a predator, an Otherworlder. You need to
feed and fucking is a part of that.*

Aliyah nodded her head in agreeance to the unknown
voice. She deserved this. This was her right.

Drawing her finger into her mouth, Aliyah rubbed at
her itchy gums. Her canines were out on display, ready to
sink into some fresh flesh.

She was jittery. Her ears pricked up, hearing every little thing and her vision seemed more enhanced. Every
sense of hers was heightened.

Pulling her finger from her mouth, Aliyah rubbed up
and down her arms as if that would stop the heat emitting
from her veins and the itchiness of her skin.

Aliyah's head jerked from side to side. She felt too hot,
too high-strung. *You need to release. Find a willing being
to sink your teeth into. Someone willing to please you.*

She nodded   again,   her neck   jerking   anxiously.
Smoothing down her top and jeans, Aliyah walked toward
a young attractive woman smoking. As she drew closer,
Aliyah realised it was pot and not tobacco. *Fuck she is
stunning,* mused Aliyah.

Screwing her nose up slightly, she inhaled once more.
The woman's scent was beguiling. It smelled like strawberries and cream mixed with whiskey and the sweet smell of
marijuana.

As Aliyah approached, she noticed the woman had
beautiful pale skin and long natural red hair cascading
down her back to her waist. She wore a tight polka dot red
dress that finished above her knees and her lips were
pouty and full as she sucked on her blunt. Aliyah wished
they were sucking on something else.

If she thought she was on fire earlier, she was blazing
now. Aliyah stopped next to the woman, popped her hip
out and leaned on the red brick of the club or whatever it
was.

The redhead quirked her eyebrow, watching Aliyah.
She kicked off of the green post she was leaning on and
stood next to her.

"You want a drag, pretty head."

The flourishing heat travelled up her body and she

knew her face would be red from the compliment.

"Sure," she replied, feigning nonchalance.

Redhead handed her the blunt and Aliyah took a small hit. Fire burned her throat but she kept the cough at bay. Occasionally she'd smoke with Dany, and although he always said you gotta cough to get off, she warded it off right now.

Miss redhead crooked her finger a couple of times. Her vivacious malachite eyes sparkled with mischief as Aliyah dipped her head closer.

Redhead's lips descended on Aliyah's and she groaned. Winding her fingers around the woman's hair, she released herself from the kiss and licked down her neck. Her jugular vein jumped fiercely beneath her pallid, lightly freckled skin.

Aliyah needed her blood. She could smell the intensity of it in the air and she was famished. Her cuspids grazed the woman's neck, causing her to moan and reach down to Aliyah's crotch to rub it.

Aliyah felt hotter than she'd ever been and heady as fuck. She flicked her button of her jeans to give the woman access. Just as she was about to puncture her neck, Aliyah heard the cat calls and whistles.

Snapping out of her sex fogged brain, she pulled back to see a crowd forming around them. Pulling the woman's hand from her jeans, she yanked her down the closest alleyway.

Once Aliyah was satisfied no one had followed them, she pushed a strand of red hair from the woman's face and purred, "Where were we?"

The woman bit her lip, then dropped to her knees and started to pull Aliyah's jeans down. Her head rolled back, hitting the dirty brick wall when she realised her wish about the woman sucking on something other than that blunt was about to happen.

In the past, Aliyah had fantasised about being with other women but the experience never presented itself, until now.

Long ebony hair flanked her face when her head fell forward. Peering down, she noticed the woman smiling coyly. She then ripped her panties to the side and her tongue delved between Aliyah's folds.

Redhead licked and sucked at her pussy ferociously. The wet sounds echoed around the dank alleyway. It wasn't romantic, but that's not what Aliyah wanted right now. She wanted it dirty. Filthy. Depraved.

Grounding her cunt into redhead's mouth, she pushed her head against her mound, moaning, "More. Fuck. Yes! Just like that! Don't you fucking stop!"

The woman giggled through her tongue assault before inserting a finger. Aliyah spread her legs wider and lifted up on her feet until they were on tippytoes.

Her core tightened, the intense electric feeling coiling around her cunt as she exploded in the woman's mouth.

"Fuck. Yes!" she screamed.

Puffing and panting, Aliyah felt the mixture of her arousal and the woman's saliva dripping down her legs as she bent down to yank up her jeans

Aliyah pulled her up off her knees and their mouth's collided. Everything was foggy. Hell, it'd been that way the entire day, and all she could feel was how the sloppiness of the kiss was making her pussy weep again in anticipation.

Reaching down, she lifted redhead's dress and found no panties and a bare pussy with a strip of hair. She groaned into the kiss. Aliyah had no idea what she was doing because she'd never done this before, but figured how hard could it be?

Dipping her finger inside the woman's snatch, she found her saturated. The smog intensified. Her pussy contracted around nothing, feeling empty, and all she saw was red.

I am a predator and I deserve this. I am going to take what is rightfully mine. Fuck. She feels so tight around my finger, and her blood, fuck, I can smell how sweet it'll taste on my palate.

Redhead was putty in Aliyah's hands as she circled the woman's clit with her thumb and thrust in and out of her cunt with her fingers.

Aliyah broke away from the kiss. Eyes were shining up at her in adoration as Aliyah whispered, "This may hurt a little but the pleasure will be so much better, beautiful."

The woman's eyes were hooded with lust and a hint of

confusion. With that Aliyah uttered, "Irrevensvia."

She watched as the woman's eyes glazed over then sank her fangs into the woman's neck while she still worked her pussy with her hand.

Red and white spots danced behind her retinas while she drank from the redhead. Her blood was not like what she'd ever tasted before. It was sweet but not as good as... she couldn't remember whose blood she was comparing it to. A small niggling feeling nestled in her gut. She quashed it and continued feeding from the bombshell in front of her.

The plasma flowed easily down her throat, coating her esophagus with life force. The woman bucked on Aliyah's hand and screamed out her orgasm.

Removing her hand from the woman's pussy, she placed it on her chin and pushed it further out of her way so she could suckle faster.

Haze, that's all she saw as she pulled and pulled at the woman's neck. Aliyah knew she should stop but she couldn't rise away from the blood pulsating in her mouth. She tasted so sweet and Aliyah was rapacious.

Pushing the woman harder against the dirty brick wall she sucked with determination, avarice, drinking in all she could take.

Something cracked in the distance and Aliyah drew back from the woman's neck, out of her trance. Eyes darted around the grimy alleyway, but she saw nothing, heard nothing.

Aliyah's heart beat frantically as she turned reluctantly to look at the woman. Her pale skin was now ashen, her malachite eyes grey, and she was limp.

Aliyah dropped her body and scurried away.

"No, no, no. What have I done?" she chanted over and over again, recognition settling in as she remembered someone vital to her. "Draven. No, no, no! How did I forget about him, what is happening to me?"

Crawling over to the woman, Aliyah reached for her carotid pulse and noticed how shaky her hands were. Placing her fingers on the woman's neck she reared back in horror when she felt nothing.

Loud footfalls drew her out of her dismay.

"Aliyah! Aliyah! Fuck. Where are you baby?"

Draven.

She began sobbing uncontrollably. Black shit-kicking boots appeared in front of her and she peeked up under wet lashes, feeling ashamed at herself. Draven was looking at the woman slumped on the dirty bitumen floor.

When his eyes found hers, she expected to see disappointed and disgust pooling in those amethyst and ruby depths. All she saw was sorrow and understanding. There was no judgement on his face and a fleeting thought presented itself in her mind, *Has Draven done this before?*

Draven offered his hand to Aliyah. Her eyes found the floor instead of looking into his when she crashed into his chest.

"It's ok, baby. I got you."

Aliyah hiccupped, spilling more tears over what she'd done. Draven nudged her chin up with his finger so she was forced to look into his mesmerising orbs.

"Tell me what happened and don't for one second think that I see you in a different light given what just happen. Believe me when I say I've done a shit load worse than this." He pointed to the woman lying too still against the wall.

Aliyah rehashed everything but the sexual side of the encounter with the woman. She didn't feel comfortable talking with him about it right now, given what'd transpired over the hours they were apart. A lot was unattainable or foggy in her mind and she hoped that she hadn't done anything worse than this.

"We will talk about this Gorgon shit when we get home. I'm mighty pissed with you right now, Snowflake."

Horripilation broke out all over her body as Draven kept her close to his chest. Sniffling, Aliyah noticed he'd tensed and she lifted her neck to look up at him.

She followed his gaze and noticed how wide his eyes were while looking at the woman she'd just killed. Humiliation and guilt washed through her like a tidal wave and her throat closed up as she let out a wail.

Draven's eyes snapped back to her. "Did you inhale her scent, Snowflake?"

Aliyah's eyebrows drew together. "Of course I smelled

her. It was another reason I pursued her. The redhead smelled delectable," she said and immediately felt ashamed of herself.

"It has to be Neferity fucking with you. She's tainted you with her fucking dark magic. It is the only reason I can muster up," Draven ranted before moving to the side of the woman.

She felt her face screw up. "What are you talking about?" she asked, confused.

"Hurry up, we haven't got much time."

"You're scaring me, Shrek."

"Get your ass over here. You need to make a decision now before it's too late."

Aliyah interrupted him. "What the fuck are you talking about?"

He raked a beefy hand full of his skull rings down his face. "Smell her, Aliyah. It has to be Neferity's magic fuck-ing with you. Otherwise you would have smelled the vam-pire blood in her veins."

Aliyah felt herself pale as she wobbled on her knees. *Vampire?*

"This is your chance to save her. You may have taken her human life but you can gift her with being an Other-worlder." Draven placed his fingers at her carotid artery. "It's slowing down. Make your mind up now!"

Aliyah heard the desperation in his voice as her knees hit the cold bitumen. "What do I need to do?" she whis-pered.

"Your blood, she needs your blood. Thankfully you didn't drain her completely so the transition should work."

"Should?"

"The longer you leave it, the less chance she has, Snowflake."

Drawing her canines down, Aliyah bit into her palm and hissed at the stinging pain. Crimson pooled instantly to the surface. She leaned over and dripped her blood into the mouth that Draven held open.

She watched the woman intently for a few seconds, and. When nothing happened, tears filled her eyes again. "I killed her didn't I? She's not coming back is she?"

He hushed her. "It takes time, Snowflake. Let's take

her back to our lair. Use your vamp speed and head home. I'll be right behind you. Now go!"

Draven didn't have to ask twice. Convoking as   much magic as she could, she ran toward the lair as fast as she could. Barely registering her feet hitting the pavement, Aliyah sent a prayer to the Light Goddess. *Please let herbe ok, Kaltemis, please.*

Chapter Nineteen

~ Draven ~

Picking up the redhead's body carefully, Draven did a quick inspection of the alleyway to make certain no I.D was left behind or anything to tie Aliyah to being here.

He was about to leave the dank smelling vestibule when a familiar chuckle filled the air.

"Fuck sakes. Can't I catch a fucking break?" he cursed. "Show yourself you piece of shit."

Tutting, "Now, now... Is that anyway to greet your brother?"

"What the fuck do you want, Emilio? I don't have time to talk to you right now."

Even as the words left his mouth, he wished he didn't have this woman in his hands so he could rip his half-brother to pieces. He wanted possession of his Snowflake. *Over my dead body,* he ruminated.

Emilio's tall frame stepped out of the shadows. A cold smirk was on his lips when his eyes flickered down to the woman in his hands then back to meet his.

"Just give me the little bitch and you can go back to what you do best." His chin nudged toward the woman.

Draven saw red. His grip on the woman increased and he had to calm himself before the darkness invaded every one of his senses. "And what the in Purgatory is that, *brother,*" he growled.

Taking his eyes off Emilio briefly, he peered down at the woman. He could sense that she didn't have much time left. He needed to make this fucking quick if she'd have a chance.

"Fucking shit up, of course," Emilio laughed and canted his head to the side.

Draven ignored his snide comment. "I will never give her up. The sooner you and the rest of your Perdition worshipping cunts get the memo the better."

Emilio stepped forward, his cold smirk now an agitated one. That's when Draven noticed that his irises were more crimson than amethyst. *What the fuck is Neferity doing to him?*

He shrugged his shoulders. "Let's do this the hard way."

His stance shifted and Draven knew he was going to rush him. One of Kaltemis's gifts to Emilio was additional strength.

Emilio advanced on him, his right fist coming toward Draven's face. Dodging it, he ducked and averted his brother's punch and vamp sped out of the alleyway. Thank the Goddess that he was faster than Emilio.

He used that to his advantage. Once he stumbled through his ominous steel door, he found Aliyah pacing and chewing her nails.

She jumped as he barged in. Kicking the door closed with his shit kickers, he looked to her. "Are you alright?"

"Where the hell have you been? You said you'd be right behind me. Fuck Draven, I was worried sick."

Her eyes found the redhead and shame flooded those gorgeous violet hues. It almost broke him there and then.

"Stop it. She will be ok," he said, attempting to assuage her fears. "I ran into my brother. That's why I was late."

Her eyes popped wide and he shushed her. "Don't fret. He won't risk coming here again. He's on uneven ground when he's in my domain, and I think he realised that last time he appeared."

Aliyah worried her lip. "Are you sure?"

"I am. And even if I wasn't, I would protect you with my life none the less."

Walking the short distance to the lounge, Draven delicately laid the woman down on his leather couch. He propped some cushions behind her head and placed a throw rug from the back of the couch on her.

Closing the distance between him and Aliyah, he wrapped his arms around her and she looked up at him. Resting his forehead on hers, she shuddered. Draven felt the blood race straight to his cock as she circled his waist with her hands.

"What the fuck is wrong with me, Draven? What if she didn't have vampire blood in her lineage? I could have killed her," she whispered.

He trailed his hand up her back and wrapped his hand in her long black hair. Aliyah's head moved away from his so she could gaze into his eyes. She chewed her lip and he knew she remembered what he'd said in the alleyway.

Hell, he wanted to know what had happened with Gorgon, but right now he wanted to punish her for leaving him. Again.

When Draven couldn't find Aliyah, panic wasn't even the word he would have used to describe his emotions. He was straight out fucking psychotic. Thoughts and images circled around his mind like a damn cracked out carousel.

Draven growled as the images surfaced once more. Silencing them, his mouth descended onto Aliyah's red bow-like lips. She opened up for him immediately, tongue lashing his as she moaned into the kiss.

His hand tightened in her locks and he ground himself against her tummy. She gasped into the kiss. Draven's released her mouth with a pop and forced her down to her knees, with his hand still thread around her tresses. She hissed when her flesh hit the cold sealed concrete floor.

Aliyah's eyes darted nervously toward the couch they were standing behind. She wouldn't be able to see the redhead from down on the ground.

"What if she wakes up?" she stuttered.

"She won't, and if she does, too fucking bad. You've earned this fucking punishment for your reckless, fatuous behaviour today," he drawled. "Now open that pretty mouth of yours and get ready to take this cock."

With his free hand, Draven undid his belt and demanded with his eyes she unzip him.

Aliyah nodded meekly, but Draven could see the lechery fogging that emotion almost instantly. Licking those fat lips, she pulled the zipper down and shimmied his jeans down a little.

His cock sprang free painfully erect. The apravadaya piercing winked back at her. Aliyah mewled and looked up at him for instruction. "Take me to the back of your throat. Work me, fucking worship my cock, Liah."

Opening her mouth, her tongue lay over her lips as he felt the roughness slide over his length. Draven hissed, his eyes rolling back at the contact.

Gazing down at her, he saw Aliyah's violet hues peeking up at him. She reared her head back, averting her eyes from his to look at his cock. She spat on it then her eyes were back on his as she took him to the back of her throat.

Aliyah swirled one hand around his shaft while she cupped his balls, rolling them in her skilled hand. The girl knew how to suck cock like a fucking champion.

Up, down, up, down, her head and hand bobbed. Draven's thigh muscles bunched and he knew he wasn't going to last much longer.

Ripping her mouth away from his dick, he ground out, "Take your fucking shirt off now."

Aliyah irises never strayed from his as she ripped down the centre of her shirt. The weak ass cunt that he was, he nearly blew his load as her tits fell heavily. Leaning down, he pulled on her nipple ring and she cried out.

Draven straightened and guided her back to his cock. Aliyah's mouth nosedived onto his length. The suction was almost too much as she recommenced her mouth fucking.

He looked down and saw the devilish twinkle in her eyes while her tongue rolled around the tip and tugged at his piercing.

"Fuck," he hissed, "I love that filthy fucking mouth of yours and the fact it's all fucking mine."

Weaving his other hand in Aliyah's hair, he instructed her to open her mouth wide. She complied. Draven jutted his hips forward, his cock hitting her uvula, causing her to gag.

Aliyah's eyes glistened with unshed tears as he worked her mouth like a fine-tuned machine. Her gagging only fuelled him on. His thighs bunched again as the current travelled straight to his balls.

Pulling back from her mouth, he tensed, his vision slightly blurred. He watched the thick streams of semen painting her face and tits.

Panting, he offered her his hand and she took it. His lips collided with hers and he could taste the saltiness of him cum on her lips.

Aliyah whimpered when he drew back. "You're not cumming. Maybe you'll think twice before running away from me and landing yourself in this shit."

Draven witnessed the anger flash through her eyes and she tried to pull away from him. His grip tightened. "Not so fast, Snowflake. I love you but you fucked up. You promised you wouldn't run away. Then the going gets tough and you sprint."

Guilt coiled itself around his intestines. He knew he wasn't taking any culpability for what happened or being completely honest with her.

Aliyah's face turned bright red and Draven placed his hand out to stop her. She huffed and he realised that probably wasn't the wisest thing to do in this circumstance.

"ME? Are you fucking serious? You're putting this all on me?" she said exasperated.

Draven cast the redhead a look and then his irises landed back onto Aliyah.

"Let me lock the door and then we will go in the kitchen. I will tell you everything but first I need a drink."

Confusion and worry clouded those violet orbs. Draven hoped when he revealed where he was that it wouldn't further weave a wedge between them.

Checking the door was locked, he then turned around to find Aliyah gone. He strolled slowly to the kitchen and then to the stainless-steel fridge to grab a premixed jack and coke.

Aliyah was propped against the granite breakfast bar with her arms crossed. Draven sighed and offered her a drink. She shook her head no and waited for him to continue.

Tipping back the whiskey, he skulled it then reached

into the fridge for another before admitting, "I didn't lie to you when I said I was Nowhere."

Aliyah rolled her eyes and kicked off the black granite bench and readied herself to leave.

"Wait," he growled. "Let me finish for fuck sakes." He pinched the bridge of his nose with his thumb and index finger and sighed.

"Nowhere is a place. It's where all the damned go."

Aliyah froze, her irises pinning him with a glare. "What do you mean *damned?*"

Draven's jaw clenched and unclenched. He knew Aliyah was going to rip him a new one when she he revealed the truth.

"Nowhere is a different realm. The damned are corrupted souls of the Otherworlders that cannot find their way to The Enchantment or to Purgatory."

"I don't understand. I figured that all the bad souls would return to hell. Isn't that what you said to me once?"

"Yeah. But these particular souls are usually pure," he paused. "However, these souls have usually done something irreparable, something so terrible that's turned them dark."

Draven looked to Aliyah and saw the awareness and sliver of pain flooding through her. She knew where this was going and he hated himself for it.

Raking his hands through his dreadies, he continued. "These Otherworlders can't handle the darkness, or the guilt penetrating and encompassing their souls. It's almost like they have flaw in their judgement. Something snaps and they spiral and do something untoward."

Watching Aliyah grasp the bench he chewed the inside of his cheek. She looked both intrigued and pissed with this story but he knew she was soaking up every drop of information.

"So why do they go to this Nowhere realm?" she queried.

"Because the waters of Lethe flow within."

"Huh? Like the Greek mythology Lethe?"

"It's not a myth, but it also isn't in Purgatory."

"You're not making sense, asshole."

He smiled at her lack of endearment. "The waters of

Lethe flow through the realm of Nowhere but it's not attached to Purgatory. By the sounds of it, you have some grasp of the concept of Lethe?

"Yeah a little."

"Ok. Well it sends the Otherworlder into a sense of Oblivion. They no longer remember their past or what they've done, and although that may sound desirable, the Nowhere is anything but."

"Cut to the fucking chase, Draven."

"After we found out that Delilah killed Dany's parents, I had to find out whether she'd taken herself to the Nowhere. You have to understand, the Delilah that I knew wouldn't have hurt a black tendril of darkness if it slapped her across the face."

Aliyah's whole body was vibrating, the faint golden glow coming to life. Anger was written all over her face until her lip quivered and melancholy replaced the animosity.

"You still love her?" A lone tear raced down her ivory cheek.

Draven rushed toward her, although he didn't wrap her in his arms because he knew she didn't want his comfort right now.

"Then what? If you don't love her why would you go to the Nowhere and lie to me about it? You must see how this fucking looks, Draven," she fumed.

Aliyah was right, it did look bad. Contempt wound itself around his guts, corkscrewing his guilt to his fucking damned soul.

"I really fucked this up, didn't I," he halted. "I figured if I'd told you where I was going and what I was doing, you'd think that I was still pining after Delilah. I'm not. And before you say anything else, I'm not making excuses up for my actions. I need you to hear me, Snowflake, I'm not. I know I fucked up, but I needed to know. I needed to see for myself."

"What did you have to know and see, Draven? How the hell did you even find this place? Because right now you're not making a butt load of sense."

Draven let out a long breath. "I didn't want to believe that Delilah could do something so hellacious. That's not the woman that I remember, Snowflake."

He saw Aliyah flinch and he immediately felt like a prick.

"Keep going," she insisted.

"Because I have demon blood in my lineage, I'm able to find the Nowhere. Hell, I've considered taking a one-way ticket there myself in the past."

"You wouldn't," Aliyah gasped.

A small smile played at the corner of his lips. "No, not now that I have you. Aliyah, you have to believe me, I only have eyes for you. Delilah didn't even hold a torch to the way I feel about you."

Aliyah's shoulders slumped slightly and he noticed her stance and eyes soften some. "You should have told me. I would have understood. This..." She waved her hand between him and herself before saying, "This can't happen again. You can't shut me out, Shrek. Even Kaltemis stated that we are stronger together. We are bound, babe, and I need to know that you're in this for the long haul. Otherwise all this shit is worth naught. You hiding shit from me will only push me away."

Although Draven was relieved to hear Aliyah using her pet names for him, his heart fractured a little at what she'd said. If he lost Aliyah he would lose himself to the darkness or worse.

"Same goes for you as well, Snowflake," he reprimanded. "No shutting off our link because you're pissed at me. Those kinds of stunts drive me out of my damn mind."

Aliyah nodded once, signalling she understood. Draven skulled the rest of his whiskey and then urged, "So what happened with Gorgon?"

She opened her mouth then closed it, her nostrils flaring right before they heard a raspy voice. "Hello? Is anyone there? Fuck my head hurts, where am I?"

Aliyah's face paled considerably, her eyes bugging wide at redhead's voice. "We will talk about this later. We have more pressing things to tend to right now."

Putting the glass stubby on the counter, he turned on his heel and headed for the sitting area. Craning his neck over his shoulder he watched Aliyah following behind at snail's pace.

The woman came into view and shrieked when she saw Draven. Even scared, she was beautiful. Not as stunning as Aliyah in his eyes, though. No one held a torch to his Snowflake.

Drawing his attention back to the moment, he watched her worried stare quickly morph into one of appreciation as her bright malachite eyes roamed avariciously over his inked frame. She rolled her red lips between her teeth, then her eyes grew wide and deviated to look over his shoulder.

Canting his neck to the side, he noticed Aliyah was standing behind him. She was wringing her hands together and averting her eyes from the redhead. Draven realised she seemed nervous and he wondered what had happened before he showed up.

"Yo—You?" the redhead stammered, "did I pass out after we..."

Aliyah paled then sent her what seemed like an apologetic look before whispering, "I'm so sorry."

The woman jumped up from the lounge. Her malachite irises darkened and her eyes widened. "What did you do to me? I—I feel really weird. I'm so fucking hungry and horny and my head feels like I had a head on collision with a freight train. I need to smoke," she rambled

She patted down her dress frantically before dipping her hands inside her bra to pull out a bent blunt. She sighed in what sounded like relief.

Draven cocked his eyebrow and folded his arms across his chest. Craning his neck to the side, he watched Aliyah's reaction to the woman. Her violet hues snapped to his and something passed through them that he couldn't decipher. He watched the flush creep up her neck as she looked away. It was that moment that he knew something had happened between the pair.

"Need to tell me something, Snowflake?"

Aliyah was disrupted by the woman cussing. "What the fuck? Where is my damn lighter!" Finding it, she lit up and then turned her attention to him and Aliyah.

Part of him wanted to snatch the damn thing from her thick lips and snap it in half as the pot infiltrated his nostrils. Instead, he focused on her jittery movements, the sweat beading her forehead and knew she'd need to feed real soon.

Choosing to ignore the niggling feeling travelling to his gut, he asked, "What's your name, sweetheart?"

His lips tilted up as he heard Aliyah growl beside him after he said sweetheart. Someone was jealous. Redhead's eyes darted between him and Aliyah and she placed her hand on the crook of her waist.

Omitting his question, she began waving her red fingernail between the pair of them., "Are you two like a couple?" she mumbled around the blunt hanging from her mouth.

Draven nodded yes. Those malachite irises focused on Aliyah. "You fooled around with me when you have that?" She pointed at Draven then added, "What the fuck were you thinking?" She licked her lips, laughed, then began scratching at her skin.

"Fuck why do I feel like my veins are on fire!"

Draven ignored the woman's whining and quirked an eyebrow at Aliyah. "Explain."

Aliyah stuttered, "I—I... I mean we kind of fooled around. I couldn't help it."

The redhead laughed. "That's what they all say, sugar."

Draven shook his head and honed back in on Aliyah, casting her an impatient look. He watched as Aliyah swallowed the lump in her throat.

"The darkness," she whispered. "I was in a haze and I only had one thing on my mind." Her eyes found the floor once more as her ebony hair fanned around her face.

Even though Draven was mad at Aliyah, he couldn't fault her. He knew firsthand what it was like when the darkness sunk its claws within. And if he was honest, thinking of Aliyah with another woman was pretty fucking hot.

"We will talk about this later." Turning away from a defeated looking Aliyah, he faced the redhead who was stretching her jaw in all sorts of directions.

He tried again. "What's your name, sweetheart?"

"Lorelei. My name is Lorelei. Now can someone tell me what the fuck is going on because I feel strange as fuck and my body feels like someone lit a fire inside my stomach. Shit, why are my gums aching? Maybe my wisdom teeth are coming through or something."

Grabbing Aliyah's hand, he stepped closer to Lorelei and watched as she stepped back from them.

"What are you going to do to me? Because if you're going to kill me then get it over with, alright?"

Draven burst out in fits of laughter. Once he calmed himself down, he said, "Believe me, if I wanted you dead I would have done it before you woke up transitioning, sweetheart."

Aliyah squeezed his hand as if scolding him for saying what he did as Lorelei screwed up her pallid face and questioned, "Transitioning?"

"You'll have to excuse my apathetic boyfriend." Aliyah made a show of rolling her eyes. "Would you sit down please, Lorelei," Aliyah urged. "I give you my word we won't hurt you."

Lorelei rolled her lips between her teeth before huffing and sitting down on the lounge. Draven pulled Aliyah's hand, coaxing her around the couch with him so they could sit down the other end of the long leather lounge.

"So, whoever is wearing the pants tonight in this little twosome better hurry up and tell me what the hell is going on because I need to eat and fuck. Not necessarily in that order." She grinned." Or maybe you both can help me out." Lorelei lifted her eyebrows in an expecting manner as she all but ate him and Aliyah up.

Draven inhaled and smelled both women's scent's, capitalising the space around him. Squirming, he realized that beside Lorelei's arousal thronging in the air, there was something different about her. He just couldn't put his finger on it.

Inhaling again, he was rewarded with the faint scent of Aliyah's lust. It was permeating, encompassing him in her siren call. Her arousal was like some voodoo witchcraft shit, summoning him like a damn beacon. And even though his dick was hard, again, he couldn't help thinking to himself that this whole situation was beyond intriguing and hot as Purgatory.

Bringing his mind back to the present, Draven cleared

his throat and announced, "You're transitioning into a vampire."

Aliyah slapped him on the shoulder, hard. "For fuck sakes Draven, do you have to be so callous?"

Lorelei giggled. "You two are cute. But if you're only going to fuck me around, then I'm out. Aliyah? That's your name, right? Doesn't matter does it, pretty head? Let me let you in on a little secret. Your cunt tasted divine, but I'm not about to be the butt in your joke. So you either tell me what the hell is really going on otherwise find someone else to mess with."

She stood up glaring at both him and Aliyah as she re-positioned her dress. *Aliyah let her taste that perfect little pussy. She is definitely getting spanked for that! But fuck would I pay to see that shit.*

With his mind in the gutter, he faced Aliyah and asked, "Did you enjoy it?"

Aliyah's cheeks flamed and Lorelei laughed. "Of course she did, I do this thing with my tongue..."

Both Aliyah and Lorelei's eyes snapped down to his crotch as Draven's eyes darted between them before he rearranged his granite like cock.

He shouldn't have been turned on in this situation, not at all, but fuck was he ever. A lightbulb went off in his mind and he began hatching his plan.

"I am not lying to you. You do have vampire in your blood. Now before you pipe up, I need you to listen before you go all crazy on us. Maybe afterward we can reward you with a little something." He quirked his eyebrow at Lorelei before turning to Aliyah.

She didn't look impressed, and right now he wasn't fazed with her pouty, angry look. After all she was the one who landed them in this pile of horseshit. Although, Dra-ven was seeing a bright light at the end of all of this. Hell, finding out what he did tonight, he believed Aliyah would be ok with it at the end.

"How?" Lorelei disrupted his kinky fuckery rotating in his mind.

"Only a human with vampire lineage running through their veins can be revived. Aliyah revived you. She thought she killed you. But then I smelled your scent, your blood in the air and knew you were one of us."

"Us?" Lorelei's eyes bugged wide, frantically dancing between him and Aliyah.

"Yes, us," he sighed. "Don't worry we aren't going to kill you. Like I was saying, someone in your family at some point was a vampire. They could actually still be alive. Who knows. Anyway, I'm rambling. What I'm saying is that because your body embraced the vampirism in your blood, you are now in the transitioning state.

"Your senses will no doubt be on high alert. You'll feel jittery, hungry and *horny*," he dragged the word off his tongue and watched Lorelei's malachite eyes flame.

"You need to feed, and soon. If you choose not to then you'll live out the rest of your days in excruciating pain until your body finally has enough."

"What the fuck are you talking about?" Lorelei yelled. "I'm not a vampire! There is no such thing! Why are you both lying to me?"

Aliyah withdrew her hand from Draven's and moved closer to Lorelei. "I know this is hard to understand or accept, but believe me when I say I know what you're going through and how you feel right now. I was you only a couple months ago and all of this scared the fuck out of me."

Draven moved so he could see the look on the woman's face. Tears had begun falling down her face like a steady stream of water.

"Why are you both lying to me? Did my abusive parents put you up to this, huh?" Lorelei stood up and started pacing whilst chewing on her nail. "If vampires are true, then prove it. I want to see both of your fangs, now."

Aliyah squirmed in front of him, probably remembering how this demand went for both her and Dany recently.

"I think we should talk a little more, help you understand. I didn't take it too well when I first found out either."

"Newsflash, pretty head, I'm not you. Now show me your fangs before I hightail it out of this..." she paused and looked around the lair before adding, "bunker. Or is this some sort of ruse? Hmm?"

Draven heard the pop before he saw Aliyah's cuspids elongate. Lorelei's gasp drew him away from watching Aliyah to find her pushed up hard against the dark purple wall.

Lorelei's eyes were squeezed shut. Her fear laced chanting bounced off the walls, the stench of trepidation heavy in the air. *"No, no, no,"* she repeated whilst pulling at her hair on either side of her head.

He had no connection to this woman like he did with Aliyah, so gawking at her as she fell apart had him feeling awkward as fuck.

His Snowflake stepped forward and Draven's jaw clenched and unclenched, anticipating what would happen next.

Aliyah held her hands up in a surrender gesture as she stepped closer to Lorelei. She opened those malachite hues and fixated them firmly on Aliyah's fangs.

A burst of arousal filled the room. Lorelei was still scared as fuck but she was turned on also. That scent, there was something different about it and it was driving him mental. Draven needed to get his head in the game so he could figure out what else was hiding in her veins.

Lorelei moved closer. Her hand was shaking as it came up slowly toward Aliyah's face. Snowflake didn't even flinch as her fingers touched her skin, although, Draven found it difficult to not intervene. Instead, she indulged Lorelei.

"Did it help?" Aliyah smirked.

"Not really," Lorelei sniffed.

This time when Lorelei raised her hand she touched Aliyah's canine, causing her to whimper at the sensation. Aliyah was also turned on by all of this, he could tell.

Lorelei withdrew her hand and started prodding her gums.

"You need to focus to elongate them. It can take some time." Aliyah was interrupted as Lorelei's lips descended on hers.

Both women moaned into the kiss while Draven hissed between clenched teeth, watching what was unfolding before his eyes.

His cock was as hard as concrete, punching at the zipper of his jeans trying to escape. Releasing the button and zip on his jeans, Draven let out a ragged breath.

Upon hearing his breath, Aliyah disengaged from Lorelei. Her snow-white skin was flushed. She looked fucking delicious.

Lorelei stood behind her, malachite eyes heavy lidded as she looked between the pair of them. Draven knew he should finish explaining the transitioning process; however, his dick had different ideas. He figured they'd probably never see her again after this.

Stalking toward Aliyah, his hands threaded into her long ebony hair and he growled, "You want this? You want to fuck her?"

Aliyah mewled but didn't say anything. He looked over her shoulder to Lorelei and recited, "You want this? You want to fuck *my Snowflake?*"

Lorelei's head bobbed slightly up and down, signalling she indeed wanted to taste Aliyah once more. He on the other hand had other ideas.

"Lie down on the couch, Lorelei, and take off you panties, now," Draven commanded.

Lorelei scurried over to the couch and lifted her dress. That's when Draven noticed she wasn't wearing anything underneath. His eyes collided with hers briefly before taking a quick glimpse at her pussy and he noted the small strip of red hair leading down to her clit. He could already see the moisture pooling from where he was standing.

Focusing back on Aliyah, he advised, "Snowflake, you're going to repay the favour and lick her cunt until she's screaming in bliss. And me," he grinned, "I'm going to fuck you while you do it."

Aliyah's eyes widen in disbelief before she schooled her features to stipulate, "You're not fucking her. I can't, I can't stomach the thought of you being with someone else."

Draven's lips crashed against hers. The passion infused tango was cut short as he ripped away and brought his head to rest on her forehead. He whispered so only she would hear, "I only have eyes for you and the only cunt I need is yours. I'm doing this more for you than me. Now get your perfect round ass over there."

Aliyah gave what Draven deemed to be a pleading look at him before turning away and making her way to the lounge. She stripped off her clothes without being asked and Lorelei moaned at the sight of her naked flesh.

A possessive growl threatened to emerge from his too gravelly throat, but he suppressed it and noticed the slight tremble of Aliyah's body as she assumed the position that he'd ordered.

The leather crinkled and wheezed under their weight and Draven took this time to admire the scene before him. Violet and malachite eyes trained on him, anticipating his next move.

But his feet were rooted to the floor and the insistent little voice heckled within. Quashing that piffling thought, he sauntered toward the pair and appreciated the sinful view of Aliyah's phat ass and wet slit. She was saturated.

Draven's cock jackhammered against his undone jeans. The fucking thing threatened to bust through the denim if he didn't release it completely.

Tipping his head back Draven felt his dreads slide down his back as he inhaled dramatically. Pheromones pilfered the air. Their scents hung thick in the air laced together, almost making his knees buckle. And again, Draven knew there was something different about Lorelei but right now was not the time to dwell on that.

Chocolate, whiskey, strawberries and wine, infused with his earthy scent slammed into his nares and his eyes rolled back.

When he opened them, he saw Aliyah's long black hair was falling down the side of her as she ogled him from over her shoulder, biting her lip. She was breathtaking. Draven stole a quick glance at Lorelei to find her red hair sprawled out all around her with a similar look to Aliyah's.

Shedding his shirt both women whimpered at the sight of him. He felt his face kick up at the sides knowing they were both checking out his ripped and inked torso. Draven was going to miss the feel of Aliyah's fingernails raking and carving the indentations of his muscles as he fucked her raw.

Pushing his dreads over his shoulders, he let his hand travel slowly down his abs until he palmed his heavy cock. Aliyah bit down on her lip harder and the sweet copper laced whiskey, chocolate scent permeated around him. She'd pierced her lip and he was rewarded with the slight trickle sliding down her full bottom lip.

He heard Lorelei's deep intake. When Draven reluctantly tore his eyes from Aliyah he saw lust filter through those malachite eyes, but also embarrassment and shame. She was confused.

Grudgingly he asked, "Are you two sure about this? Maybe we should hold off..." He was disrupted by both Aliyah and Lorelei stating they wanted this and that they'd talk after.

Draven didn't need to be told twice and hoped Aliyah's eagerness was due to the darkness more than anything else. Looking down, he ripped his dick free from his open pants and heard their audible gasps and moans, which only further harden his already granite like cock.

His head up and his eyes locked on Aliyah's, he brought his knee to the leather lounge. The leather hissed under his weight as he placed the head of his cock at her sodden entrance.

It took all of his strength and energy not to pummel inside her and feel the welcoming heat and cream sliding over his length.

Between gritted teeth, he commanded, "You will eat that pussy like it's the blood flowing from my veins while I fuck you until you scream into her little cunt. Do. You. Understand. Me?" he enunciated each last syllable.

"Yes, I understand."

Flicking his eyes to Lorelei, he asked, "You good with that?"

The feisty little bitch had the audacity to roll her eyes at him, which only made his grin widen. "Of course I'm ok with it. Now, can we silence the chit chat and get down to fucking?"

Draven chuckled. "As you wish." With that he slammed into Aliyah's hot body pushing her head down to Lorelei's awaiting pussy.

It was like he was on fire as he rocked into her body at a steady pace. The slurping of Aliyah sucking and licking the redhead's clit spurred him on.

Lorelei was a moaner and a screamer. Each time Aliyah tugged on her nub, she'd scream out and push Aliyah's head down harder. It was truly a sight that he wouldn't forget in a hurry.

Draven knew Aliyah was close by the way her cunt strangled his cock. He slowed down and she growled into Lorelei's snatch. Draven smirked. She didn't realise how painful this was for him, as well.

Aliyah moved one of her hands from bracing her and dipped her digits into Lorelei's core. Both of them moaned loudly at the connection.

He'd avoided Lorelei's eyes throughout the fucking, but just for a split second his irises locked on hers and he could tell she was in pain. She needed to cum then she needed to feed.

Averting his eyes he instructed, "Pump your fingers into her tight cunt faster and lick and suck on her clit with everything you have. She needs to cum, Snowflake, and as soon as she does you will too."

That was all the encouragement she needed. Aliyah set her mind to the salacious task at hand and had Lorelei writhing and crying out in pleasure in no time. Her screams bounced off the walls in the lair.

That was his cue. Draven increased the speed of his cock, rutting into her like some fucking crazed being that he didn't know. Aliyah continued to lick at Lorelei, causing the redhead to keen out another release.

The air was thick and intense with the mixture of their arousal hanging heavily in such a small space. It was inebriating and suffocating at the same time, and he knew what he and Aliyah needed.

Paying no mind to Lorelei's gawking eyes as his fangs elongated, he leaned over and still keeping his pounding pace into Aliyah's constricting cunt, sunk his cuspids into her right shoulder.

Draven felt Aliyah jerk back and observed under heavy lidded eyes Lorelei's drench cunt as Aliyah's mouth was no longer between her thighs. Averting his eyes from between Lorelei's legs, he instead focused on the sound of Aliyah's scream as she cried out in agony and bliss from his bite, her walls clutching around his length.

Lorelei's presence faded away and only Aliyah and Draven were left in their lechery brimming bubble. She keened out her climax, threatening to take him over the edge with her as her pussy clamped down on his shaft

Draven concentrated and kept his orgasm at bay. He relished in how the white stars danced behind his retinas as her life force jetted into his mouth, and surged throughout his body giving him sustenance and the familiar heady feeling that was completely Aliyah.

Draven continued to pull from her while his fingernails dug into her waist. He pistoned into her unrestrained and rough, seeking his release.

He knew she was watching him before he allowed himself to focus on her again for the smallest of moments. Remembering they weren't alone, he looked down and saw Lorelei's red hair in a tangled mess. Sweat beaded her ivory face as her malachite irises watched him feed from Aliyah with intrigue.

Turning away from her stare, Draven removed his hand from Aliyah's hip and tugged on her nipple ring before moving lower to the Holy Grail.

Her clit was distended and ready for another orgasm while the electric current began circling his lower back and drawing into his balls.

Circling her clit, he moaned around the blood in his mouth as Aliyah shattered around him, this time sending him over the edge with her.

A kaleidoscope of colours ricocheted in his mind as he grew rigid and felt himself empty out his seed into Aliyah's glorious little hole.

When the fog had cleared a little, Draven removed his fangs from her shoulder and licked the puncture marks. Gingerly he disengaged himself from Aliyah's core, feeling a little lighter, but wondering if allowing Lorelei intimately into their sexcapades was the best idea he'd had.

Deviating from that thought, he yanked up his jeans and sat back on his knees watching as both Aliyah and Lorelei disentangled from each other. Both their faces were flushed and he sensed a little embarrassment from the two of them.

After fixing their clothes, Aliyah moved closer to Draven and pulled the throw rug over her and Lorelei. Lorelei offered her a small smile and then began scratching again. Sex was never enough for a fledgling vampire. She still needed to feed.

As if reading his mind, Aliyah turned to face him. She placed both hands on each side of his cheek and chewed on her bottom lip.

"She needs to feed. I held out and I swear I was going to go insane with the bloodlust." Draven was about to object when she added, "Please. Let me do this. It's the least I can do for her after what I put her through and forced upon her."

Every hair follicle, every cell and every piece of his fucked up possessive mind was screaming no. However, Aliyah was right. And he didn't have it in him to show her how to feed. Fatigue and exhaustion were bleeding through his veins after the day he'd had. He reluctantly nodded his head once, signalling it was ok. Even if it was anything but.

Draven observed and hearkened every word that Aliyah relayed to Lorelei. The tension in the air had lessened and he realised how relaxed Lorelei seemed in Aliyah's company.

He couldn't take his eyes off the pair of them. When Aliyah lifted her hair to one side readying for Lorelei's bite, Draven jumped up and growled, "No! Not your neck. Your wrist, baby." Her neck was too intimate of a place to feed. Considering what they'd done, it didn't really make much sense.

An emotion flickered through those malachite eyes and if Draven had to pick one he would have deemed it disappointment. That's when he knew his instincts were correct, and maybe this little tryst wasn't such a good idea. He had completely forgotten how a transitioning vampire could become obsessed and reliant on the vampire that revived them. He sent a silent prayer to the Goddess, hoping Lorelei wouldn't be one of them.

Honing back in on the scene, he noticed Aliyah relax at his command and stick her wrist out. She explained how Lorelei could help her cuspids elongate, and when they didn't, he noted how frustrated Lorelei became.

"Baby." Aliyah's head whipped over her shoulder, her violet hues finding his mismatched pair as she waited for him to continue. "Bite into your wrist. The scent of your blood may trigger her first elongation."

When she turned away from him, Draven found himself moving so he could face her and witness what was about to occur.

Aliyah's lip rolled between her teeth before she lifted her wrist and bit into her radial artery. Draven's canines lengthen further and he found himself hissing at the pain of it.

Chocolate tainted with whiskey and a touch of old wine filtered through his nostrils, all while he watched the crimson plasma drip onto the sealed concrete floor. His dick punched the zipper of his jeans once more. He was fucking rock hard again.

Lorelei yammered out in pain, stealing his attention from the sweet nectar of Aliyah's blood that he wanted to devour.

The deafening pop shattered through the air amidst her screams as her fangs broke through her gums. She looked up and Draven couldn't believe his eyes. Lorelei's malachite irises were muddied with violet specks. They were insanely intense and that's when he realised he was staring. Turning away from her, he heard Aliyah's gasp.

"Fuck me, Lorelei. Your eyes... they're gorgeous," Aliyah reiterated his thoughts. Although in his mind there was only one other pair that shone a light on hers, and they were Aliyah's.

"What's wrong with them? Have they changed? Fuck it, why do I feel so weird? Shit I actually have fangs" She lifted her finger to prod the tip and squeaked, pulling away.

"My body is on fire. Is it meant to feel this way? What's happening to me?"

"Your body is urging you to feed. Remember when I said you would live in pain if you didn't feed? Well multiply that feeling by a million and you have your answer," Draven stated.

Straightening her stance, Lorelei nodded and looked to Aliyah's eyes then to her wrist. The puncture marks were already healing and the blood and ceased seeping through.

"So I just, like, bite into her wrist? And suck?"

"Yeah. I'll stop you when you've had enough. As a new vampire you won't know when to and Aliyah's blood won't sustain you for a lengthen period of time like she does mine. You'll need human blood."

Lorelei cocked her head to the side, seeming to mull over what he'd just said. "How can she sustain you but not me?"

Aliyah butt in before he could answer. "Because we are bonded."

"Bonded?"

"It's a long story and not one for tonight. Feed. Afterward you can stay in the spare room for the night. We will discuss the schematics tomorrow," Draven insisted. He was feeling antsy as fuck and just needed his woman in his arms.

"Ok," Lorelei answered then lowered her head to Aliyah's wrist and bit into it.

Jealousy surged through Draven, thundering like a menace and ricocheting through every cell in his 327-year-old body. The emotion was unrelenting and the intensity of it was foreign.

His eyes were glued to the scene before him. He drank it in like it was him suckling from her vein and he despised the green-eyed monster circling within.

The front steel door of the lair burst open and in the blink of an eye, Draven rounded quickly, fangs out, ready to annihilate whoever chose to fuck with him.

He was met with blazing forest greens and jade rimmed coal irises. "Fuck," Jadis hissed." Stop!"

Lorelei pulled away, looking between the four sets of eyes watching her, trepidation clearly written across her features.

Jadis released a sigh and tore her orbs from Lorelei to look to Draven. "She's not only a vampire, Drae, she's a fucking witch."

"Huh?" Lorelei muttered. Her eyes glazed over and Aliyah caught her as she passed the fuck out.

Chapter Twenty

~ Aliyah ~

After Jadis burst in, Aliyah dressed quickly and covered Lorelei's body with a blanket, pulling her dress down to conceal her crotch first. Dolph walked in not long after and she tried to ignore the cacophony of voices booming throughout the lair. Instead, she peered down at Lorelei. She figured she'd smelled a little different but in no way would Aliyah have believed that she had vampire and witch blood running through her veins.

Thinking back, she was certain she had heard Draven and Jadis remark on vampire and witches mating. It was almost never done.

Brushing the strands of red hair from her face, she laid Lorelei down on the lounge. Heat shot up into her core at the reminiscent moments they'd shared on this very couch only moments ago.

Aliyah felt her cheeks flame as she looked down one last time before participating in the conversation with Draven, Dolph and Jadis.

Sensing her arrival, Draven snaked his hand out and wrapped it around her waist to pull her flush up against him. She threaded her arms around him and inhaled. Her nostrils flared at his intoxicating scent.

Aliyah ducked her head into the crook of his neck to hide her blush. The smell of sex and blood was evident in Draven's woodsy, whisky earthy scent. She figured Dolph and Jadis would suspect what had occurred between the three of them.

Her thoughts were disrupted by the rumble of Draven's chest as he spoke. "How do you know she's a witch as well, J?"

Aliyah turned from his neck to face Jadis and Dolph and witnessed her roll her eyes. "I am the High Witch, Draven. I can sense when there are new witches and warlocks close by." She screwed her face up. "But this one... There was something different about her and I now know it's the vampire blood in her lineage."

Draven seemed to mull over her statement while she watched Dolph scratch the stubble on his chin before he countered, "So what does this mean?"

"It's extremely rare that a vampire and witch would mate, especially as far back as her lineage goes," Jadis said, curious.

"It is," Draven concurred. "So what now?"

"I'll take her back with me and Dolph."

"You're still staying at the Mad Warlocks?" Draven questioned.

"We were planning on coming home. However, she will need guidance and Reikiki can assist me."

"Her name is Lorelei," Aliyah huffed. "Not she. She is the cat's mother, Jadis."

Jadis raised her eyebrows in confusion, then smirked. "Okaaaaaaay. Lorelei will come with us. I'll make enough room in my little bunker down here for all of us when I return. Being out and about as a fledgling vampire and witch is not a good idea."

"I know she needed to... well be revived to become a vampire, but would she have any witch properties before now?" Aliyah asked.

Jadis tapped her chocolate fingers against her thigh. She looked as if she was musing over her question. "I believe she probably would have had some properties, but nothing like you've seen with me or anything else in this realm. I feel that Lorelei's magic was suppressed and when you revived her, you kick started her magic from lying stagnant."

"How do you know it was me that revived her?"

Jadis smirked and lifted her chin toward Draven. "Be-

cause there is no way he would stick his fangs near anyone else unless it proved futile. You've got him wrapped
around your little fingers, Liah."

"Oi," Draven countered. "I'm right here."

Jadis shrugged her shoulders and ignored him. "Once
she's awake, I'll see if she's comfortable enough for me to
read and channel her magic to figure out why I haven't felt
her in The Quarter before tonight." Jadis grinned. "I can
tell the three of you felt something tonight though."

Dolph chuckled and his eyebrows danced as he looked
to Draven. Aliyah knew without a doubt that her face
would be bright fucking red with the intensity of the heat
firing to her cheeks.

Draven reached out and slapped Dolph upside the
head, which only aided in Dolph completely losing his shit.
His loud, baritone laughter reverberated around the lair
along with Jadis's chuckle .

Between fits of laughter, Dolph wheezed, "And you
gave us shit for our little fucking trio. You are a hypocrite,
Savage."

Aliyah pulled back from Draven's embrace and noted
the shit eating grin plastered over his face. She shook her
head and looked to the floor, hoping her dark ebony hair
cascading around her face would hide her flushed face.

Groaning from the couch stopped the playful banter
between the four of them, or in Aliyah's case embarrassment.

"What—what happened," came Lorelei's groggy voice.

The couch crinkled under her weight as she sat up
holding her head and looked over to find four sets of eyes
watching her.

Lorelei's eyes snapped wide. Her highbrows seemingly
hit her hairline as her mouth opened in the shape of an O.

"Fuck. I'm a vampire and witch," she whispered, her
face crumbling before Aliyah's eyes. She looked lost.
"What does that even mean? How is this happening?" she
asked no one in particular.

Jadis stepped forward tentatively and Aliyah observed
her face soften as she spoke. "Hi sweetie, my name is Jadis. I know this is overwhelming for you but you need to
know that none of us are here to hurt you. If anything

we're here to help?"

"My fucked up parents set this up, didn't they? I know they hate me, but for fuck sakes." She waved her arms around frantically. "This is a new low."

That was the second time Lorelei had mentioned her parents negatively and Aliyah had to wonder what the fuck they'd done to her in the past. A sense of dread conjured up within herself. Whatever happened, Aliyah knew it wasn't good.

Tears began falling down her ivory face. She pulled her knees to her chest and mumbled something under her breath.

A crushing, protective feeling overwhelmed Aliyah. Stepping away from Draven, she sauntered to the couch and wrapped her arms around Lorelei's shoulders. She began whispering in her ear, assuring her everything would be ok. The tension dissipated.

The melancholy poured off of Lorelei all while the darkness thrashed around inside of her. Muddied images circled in her mind, and Aliyah could sense the damnable things her parents had done. She couldn't interpret them unfortunately, but she knew it was despicable.

Lorelei pushed off Aliyah lightly and smiled at her, but the smile didn't reach those malachite hues. Clenching her jaw and using her eyes, she looked to Jadis and told her to continue.

Jadis nodded. "If you're comfortable, I'd like you to come with us so I can help you understand what is happening with your body."

Lorelei stiffened. "What—what about you, Aliyah? Will you be with me?"

Aliyah heard a small sigh behind her and instead of answering Lorelei she canted her neck to the side. Her irises collided with Draven's mesmerising mismatched pair and something passed through them.

Feeling her eyebrows pull together, she studied Draven's stance. He seemed stoic, tense, yet somehow worried. He shook his head and Aliyah knew this wasn't the time to question him.

Deviating her eyes from his, she faced Lorelei once again. She noted the hopeful look in those malachite orbs as she pulled her long hair to one side, trying to figure out how to answer the question without upsetting her.

Aliyah sensed how frightened and fragile she was and hoped she wouldn't push her over the edge. "Lorelei, I need to stay here with Draven. I can accompany you with Jadis and Dolph if you'd prefer. I really feel that Jadis and Reikiki are the ones who can help you the most right now."

"You can't just ship me off and out of your life after everything that's happened!" her voice hiked, reaching higher octaves.

Her anxiety and turmoil was palpable. Aliyah took a long breath and said, "That's not what I'm doing here. I barely know shit about any of this stuff. I've only been a vampire for a couple of months. I still struggle knowing what little I do. You are half witch as well as vampire. Jadis and Reikiki are the most powerful and eldest witch and warlock I know. I trust them, and I'm urging you to trust them also."

Lorelei brought her fingers up to her mouth and began chewing on her nails whilst her eyes darted from her to Jadis and Dolph. "How long until I see you again?"

Draven groaned behind her and Aliyah could sense his patience waning. Before Aliyah could say anything Jadis spoke up,

"I have an idea." She brushed her purple fringe from her face and smiled brightly. "What about you, me and Dolph head over to meet Reikiki. I swear to you, Lorelei, he is the one being I would trust with my life. He has seen a lot in his time of this earth. After we check in with Reikiki, I will bring you back to my little lair down here."

She turned away and focused on Draven. "I'll make it larger. Or perhaps I'll make a section down here for both Dany and Lorelei so they will have their privacy."

"Who's Dany?" Lorelei queried.

Aliyah smiled. "Dany is my best friend. He's recently shifted as well. He's half vampire, half werewolf."

Lorelei's eyes grew wide. "There is such a thing as werewolves? Really?"

"There sure is," Dolph stated in a matter of fact tone. "I'm part vampire, mainly werewolf though."

Lorelei's head canted and her eyes leisurely roamed

from Dolph's feet up to his face. Aliyah smirked, watching Dolph fidget under Lorelei's eye fucking. Jadis on the other hand didn't seem fazed, and Aliyah knew there wasn't much that would frighten the witch. Especially given she was the most powerful being in the vicinity.

Jadis clapped her hands together. "Good, it's settled. Let's head over to Reikiki's."

"How did you get here?" Draven countered.

Dolph's face lit up, his eyes twinkling. "D, wait until you see my baby!"

Aliyah saw the shift in Draven's face. He looked like a damn kid in a candy store.

"Fuck off. What did you get?"

"She's fucking beautiful. 1962 Plymouth Fury Max Wedge. Black with red and black interior. She's so fucking sexy."

Aliyah looked to Jadis, asking what the fuck with her eyes. Jadis rolled her eyes and shrugged. "Alright you two, you can talk cars later. We need to get to Reikiki's," Jadis stated.

Draven's shoulders sagged a little before he gave Dolph a fist bump as he left. Aliyah was confused. These two were acting like they just had all the dreams coated in glitter and rolled into one.

She was interrupted from her thoughts by Lorelei nudging her shoulder with hers. "I'll see you a little later," she said confidently, "Thanks for everything. And just for the record, I'm only going because you told me to." she winked and walked off swaying her hips, and something told Aliyah that wasn't good.

Once the door closed, Draven sidled up to her. He wrapped his beefy arms around her back and rested his chin on her head. Aliyah inhaled and sighed. He smelled like home.

"What's on your mind, Shrek?"

Running small circles over her lower back, he relented, "I think she's obsessed with you."

Aliyah pulled back to search his eyes and the only thing shining in those brilliant mismatched hues was honesty.

"Why do you say that? She's only met me a few hours ago."

Draven pushed aside a black tendril that had fallen into her face and sighed. "Sometimes when we revive a human they can become somewhat infatuated with whoever awoke the vampire gene within. Not always, but sometimes they form a bond, even if it's not reciprocated," he groaned." And Lorelei is showing all the signs, baby."

Aliyah ducked and tucked herself into his chest. She had to admit Lorelei was acting a little peculiar. Come to think of it, her comment as she left kind of insinuated as much. Her head was beginning to bang.

"Will it wane if... if she is obsessed with me?"

"It depends on the Otherworlder. Lorelei seems to have a shit load of emotional baggage so she might hold on for a while. Anyway, let's get some sleep. Its early hours of the morning and I want to sink my dick into your hungry hole one more time before I pass the fuck out."

Aliyah pulled out of his embrace and saw the shit eating grin on his face. Her core tightened as she stepped to the side to pass him, then she ran to the room.

"Catch me if you can, big boy."

Draven chuckled darkly. "I'll always catch you, Snowflake."

And that's all he had to say to have her shedding her clothes and lying in wake for him to enter not only her body, but her heart, mind and soul too.

Aliyah was jolted from her sleep by loud thundering on the front door. Hopping out of bed she realised Draven wasn't beside her and figured he must have woken from the banging on the door.

She slipped on a pair of skinny black ripped jeans and a hoody then looked at her reflection in the mirror. She looked like a hot mess.

Shrugging her shoulders, she rubbed at her sore thighs before padding into the front room barefoot. Draven was standing topless with his low-slung jeans hanging off his waist talking to Grunge.

Hearing her arrival, Grunge's head snapped up and his chartreuse eyes found hers. He nodded stiffly at her then turned his attention back to Draven.

"You need to come with me, D. I think I know where she is."

"Have you told Dolph yet?" Draven asked.

"No," Grunge groaned and raked his hand through his unkempt auburn hair. "I haven't told him that I knocked his sister up."

Draven groaned in return. "You need to tell him. I deliberately skipped over that when I informed him what had been happening while he was in Limbo. It wasn't my place to tell him."

"Gee, thanks, Savage. Tighten the noose while I'm already hanging why don't you? I haven't even seen him since he woke up, and I know the cunt is going to fucking neck me when I confess that I not only screwed his sister but knocked her up, too. I love her but something tells me that Dolph isn't going to care about that."

Aliyah stepped forward and said, "I don't think he'll hurt you. Although the longer you keep this from him, the more he will feel betrayed. That's how I would feel if one of my best friends hid the fact that I was going to have a little niece or nephew."

"Fuck. That had totally gone over my head. You know the fact that Dolph is going to be an uncle to my unborn child. I've only been thinking about myself and Laney. I'm such a selfish piece of shit," Grunge grumbled

Draven pushed his dreadlocks behind his ears and scratched at his head. "I've got an idea. How about we go and check in with Dolph and then we can head to this destination you think she's at."

Grunge's eyes scanned around the area briefly before landing back on Draven's. "Ok. But seeing this is your idea and I'm being a pussy, if he tries to kill me you need to talk some sense into him. Like the fact that his niece or nephew would like to know their dad."

Draven chuckled. "Yeah, I can do that for you. Let me put boots and a shirt on then we can take off." He turned to Aliyah. "You ready Snowflake?"

"Born ready, Shrek."

Grunge laughed under his breath. "She's gonna rip your balls apart, brother."

Draven smirked, then said, "Don't I know it."

Fifteen minutes later they were in Draven's car and on the way to Reikiki's. Butterflies and apprehension settled in her stomach at having to see Lorelei so soon. The woman was beautiful but Aliyah only saw her as a friend. A super hot one she was in no way going to fuck again.

The images of her, Draven and Lorelei entwined flooded her mind and her pussy clamped down around nothing. It was debauched, unexpected, however none the less sinfully sexy.

But that's all it was and would ever be. At the end of the day Aliyah only had eyes for Draven. She'd sensed the dependency flowing off of Lorelei last night and was starting to believe Draven could be right about her possible obsession.

Shaking herself from her thoughts, she looked outside the window to realise they were approaching Reikiki's clandestine apartment.

Draven pulled over to the sidewalk, switched off the car and turned in his leather seat to face her. "You good?"

"Yeah. Just this whole Lorelei thing is kind of awkward." She felt her face heat with the admission.

Grunge pulled himself between their seats, his head looking from Draven to her with a puzzling look on his face.

"Who's Lorelei?"

If Aliyah's face was hot, it now felt like an inferno blazing underneath her skin at Grunge's question. She risked a quick peek and saw his hands fly to his mouth.

"Oh shit! No way!" He turned to face Draven. "You lucky fucking bastard!"

Draven smacked the back of his head. "It's not exactly how your perverted mind thinks it happened, asshole."

"No?" Grunge's eyebrows danced and his chartreuse irises darted between both her and Draven.

"Well... Not completely," he smirked before adding, "I'll give you the short story and not ass around it. I fucked up and Aliyah lost her shit and took off. Neferity has been able to infiltrate her dreams and sunk her claws into Aliyah's aura and tainted it some. Given my girl over here has demon blood and darkness as well as light in her, she became more susceptible to the dark side of herself because of Neferity. In her little rampage..." he paused and offered her an apologetic look before he spoke again.

"In her little rampage, she had an episode. The darkness was unrelenting. You remember what I was like back in those days, Grunge." Draven hesitated before adding, "She was famished and found a young woman to feed off. She went too far and almost drained her. What Aliyah hadn't suspected in her fog was that the woman was from vampire lineage, so Aliyah decided to revive her. We kind of had a little fun, then Jadis barged in to inform us that Lorelei was also part witch. She's here with them now."

Aliyah refused to look up and see Grunge's expression. She was beyond embarrassed.

She heard the leather crumpled under Grunge's weight and assumed he was sitting back. "What the actual fuck have you crazy fucking nymphs been up to since I've been out of action. You know... I thought I had my whole world up in arms, but I've got nothing on the pair of you."

Aliyah risked a glance up and saw Draven's eyes twinkling with devilry and his mouth kicked up at the sides. He was loving this.

He craned his neck behind to look at Grunge and replied, "Some like it easy. Me? I'll take what I have with Aliyah and multiple that by a million as long as this little one is right here beside me."

Tears gathered in her eyes at his sweet words. She smiled at him, hoping he knew exactly how much he meant to her as well.

"You are so fucking pussy whipped, D," Grunge laughed, then sobered. "But remember your promise, save me if Dolph tries to kill me. Now get your pansy ass out of this car and let's get this over with so I can check these coordinates for Laney."

Aliyah unlocked her eyes from Draven's, swiping the stray tears that had fallen and reached for the door handle.

A strong hand pulled her back right before Draven's lips smashed against hers. Aliyah moaned into the kiss then pushed away when she remembered Grunge was still in the car.

She felt giddy and knew her skin was flushed. Draven smirked at her and Grunge whistled loudly in the back seat. All of a sudden the car seemed hot and stuffy. She needed to get the fuck out of there.

Beyond embarrassed, Aliyah reached for the door handle and wretched it open to welcome the cool breezed against her face. Breathing in, she smelled spring in the air. The scents of flowers and grass slammed into her.

Aliyah scuffed her Dr Martens along the concrete as she walked toward the door to the apartment building. Opening it, she heard Draven and Grunge talking behind her. Right now, she needed to be far away from the pair.

Ascending the stairs to Reikiki's, she rushed up them until she reached the beautifully ornate timber door. The door wheezed opened and welcomed her.

Stepping in, Aliyah nostrils flared when she caught the scents circling within. Lorelei's being the more prominent one. Unfortunately she smelled fucking delicious.

Centering herself, she lifted her shoulders and walked toward the mingling aromas. In a lounge area she found Jadis, Dolph, Reikiki and Lorelei sitting around a coffee table talking. *Where is Dany,* she silently questioned. Aliyah reminded herself that she'd need to call him later and figure what the hell was up with him.

As if sensing her, Lorelei's head snapped up and a smile spread over her ivory face. Jumping up, she ran toward her, her long red hair flowing down her back. She was no longer in the short dress that she left Draven's place in. Instead she was wearing a fitted teal tracksuit.

Lorelei's arms snaked around Aliyah's back and she knew her eyes were as wide as saucers when she caught herself staring at the trio before her. She felt awkward as fuck.

Patting Lorelei on her back gingerly, she stepped out of the embrace to put some distance between them. Something flickered through those malachite eyes before she schooled herself and planted what looked like a fake smile on her face.

"It's nice to see you again, pretty head." She tipped her chin up and followed it with, "Who's the other man with Draven?"

Canting her neck, Aliyah peered over her shoulder to see Draven and Grunge watching them. Clearing her throat she replied, "That's Grunge. He's Dolph and Draven's good friend."

"You've got to be kidding me! Look at you, ya fucking knob!" Dolph's deep voice cut through. "God damn, brother, it's been too long."

Dolph sauntered toward his friend and embraced him in a hug. Aliyah found herself smiling at the pair of these big, burly shifters hugging. Sobering, she really hoped they'd still be close after Grunge dropped the pregnant Laney bomb.

Aliyah watched on to see Grunge step out of the embrace and place each hand on his friend's shoulders. He looked somewhat defeated and she sensed he was worried what this was going to do to their relationship.

Grunge's neck leaned back as he looked to the ceiling and released a heavy breath. Dolph's eyes twitched and she noted the foreboding shadow consume his features. He knew Grunge was about to tell him something that he wasn't going to like.

"What is it, Grunge? Fucking tell me."

Grunge's head snapped forward, the tendons in his neck tightening while his chartreuse irises bored into Dolph's jade rimmed coal pair.

"I need you to know that I love her ok."

"What are you talking about?" Dolph growled.

Draven nudged closer to the pair, gaining the attention of Dolph briefly before he looked back to Grunge.

"Laney," Grunge's whispered. "Laney, I love her."

Dolph shrugged Grunge's hands of his shoulders, his fists clenching beside his legs. He hissed, "You better spit it out brother before I lose my fucking shit. I know you've always crushed on my sister but something tells me you're about to pull the rug out from under my feet somehow."

Tension was rising in the small room and Aliyah hadn't noticed how close Lorelei was to her until she clasped her hand. Aliyah jolted and withdrew her hand, offering Lorelei a small smile then focused back on the shifters in front of her.

"Laney is pregnant and it's mine."

Aliyah didn't even see Dolph's fist connect with Grunge's face, he was so fast. She did however hear the growl reverberating from Dolph and the curses pouring from Grunge's mouth.

Draven stepped between them while Aliyah screamed and ran forward, stopping them in their tracks. Grunge was rubbing his jaw whilst Dolph was baring his teeth at him. He looked on the precipice of shifting.

"Both of you fucking stop this. Dolph, your sister is pregnant to one of your best friends. I'm sure there could be worse things, considering the mess we're all in. Don't let this fuck up decades of friendship, or however the fuck long you've both known each other. Get your fucking shit together. You're acting like children. And Grunge, hurry the fuck up and tell him where you think Laney is so we can fucking find her and bring her back to us because I don't think she has much time left."

Dolph sobered. "You know where she is?"

"I think so. I was given some coordinates that could lead to her," Grunge answered.

"Why the fuck didn't you lead with that you dumb shit? What are we waiting for? Let's go get my sister from the clutches of fucking Neferity's talons."

And like that, the whole pregnancy debacle was forgotten. Jadis and Reikiki took Lorelei out of the room, much to her dismay, while Aliyah stayed and listened closely to the plan they were hatching.

Thirty minutes later they were loaded up in Draven's fifty with their diamond daggers strapped to their flesh. Aliyah looked out the window and sent a silent prayer to the Goddess, praying they'd find Laney and bring her home safely.

Draven drove like a bat out of hell. Aliyah's mind tumbled with thoughts and she couldn't help but think that even though Laney was like a sister to Draven, she was also the first soul that he had to save. The first win against Melantha and a step toward his freedom from her and her evil fucking sharp nails.

No matter the cost, Aliyah promised herself they would bring Laney back to the light. Not only for herself and Draven, or even Dolph and Grunge, but for that little miracle growing inside her stomach.

Chapter Twenty-One

~ Draven ~

The majority of the drive was in broken silence during the trip to the coordinates that Grunge was given. Draven half expected both Grunge and Dolph to ignore each other, but that was not the case. *As I Lay Dying's song Gate keeper* pumped through the speakers on low while Draven maneuvered the car to its destination. He had no idea where they were headed.

Dolph and Grunge were in the backseat talking as if nothing had happened earlier. Thankfully Jadis and Lorelei had stayed back. Thank fuck. That new vamp was en-thralled with Aliyah and he didn't like it one bit.

Stealing his mind back on track and away from his jealousy, Draven thought how he knew his best friend wouldn't stay angry long, especially when he realised he was about to be an uncle. The asshole was ecstatic; although, he was still pissed that Grunge hadn't told him he was seeing Laney.

Draven drowned their voices out and focused on the grey road ahead and the trees passing along the sides. Spring was setting in but it was still cool out.

Stealing a side glance at Aliyah, he noticed her typing on her phone. She'd been awfully quiet since they left and he wondered what was on her mind. He couldn't seem to read her this last hour. It was as if she had switched off their connection, which she fucking promised not to. Honesty, he didn't think she had.

A cacophony formed within his mind. Draven had so much resting on his broad shoulders, and he prayed to the Goddess that he'd be able to pull Laney from that fucking bitch's clutches. Neferity. He abhorred that name.

Shifting down a gear, he approached a set of lights and stopped on the red signal. Tapping his fingers on the leather steering wheel, he looked up in the revision mirror to see both Dolph and Grunge watching him.

"What the fuck you douches looking at?" Draven spat.

"You look so pretty when you're deep in thought, Savage," Dolph chuckled.

"Fuck off, wanker," Draven retorted.

Grunge snickered, then said, "Next set of lights go left and follow it until you reach some old warehouses. That's where these coordinates lead."

Draven felt his eyes bulge out of their sockets. "She's at a fucking warehouse? You don't think that, well, I don't know, that it could be a fucking trap?"

"Of course I did. Fuck you're wound tighter than a nun's cunt, Savage. When was the last time you had your dick sucked?" Grunge jeered.

The light turned green and Draven dumped the clutch, leaving rubber burning in their wake. He then turned and slapped Grunge across his forehead before facing the road again.

"Don't fucking be a pig in front of Aliyah, you tool. You do realise she's the one sucking my dick, yeah?"

He glanced up to see Grunge rubbing his forehead with his hand and a scowl firmly in place. "You do need to get laid or something because you're acting like a pussy. You know damn right that I would never disrespect Aliyah, especially given how she helped me recently."

"Huh? What did Snow White do you for you," Dolph teased.

Draven blocked out their voices once more and looked toward Aliyah. She hadn't stopped typing, even when the three of her were talking about her like she wasn't even there. Something wasn't right.

Squeezing his hands around the steering wheel, he ascended on the next set of lights and turned left like Grunge had instructed then drove toward their target.

Draven removed one hand off the wheel to turn The Amity Affliction *Soak me in bleach* up then reached over to cup his hand over Aliyah's thigh.

Lowering his voice so they others wouldn't hear, he said, "What's up with you, baby? You've been quiet."

Aliyah switched her phone to sleep mode and laced her hand over his and sighed. "It's Dany. Have you noticed he hasn't been back to Reikiki's in a couple of days? It's like no one cares," she hushed out.

Draven pondered. He'd noticed that he hadn't been back, figuring he needed some space to accept the changes that were occurring.

"You're worried about him," he stated.

"Yeah I am. He's my best friend, Shrek. I have this unsettling feeling that he's not ok, and there isn't anything I can do to help him right now. I feel helpless."

Squeezing her thigh, he tried to reassure her. "He is a big boy, baby. Give him the benefit of the doubt. I'm assuming you've been texting at least?"

"Yeah we have. But he's being so fucking vague and it's worrying me."

"Maybe he's with someone?"

"Perhaps. Look what happened to me recently. What if that happens to him? What sort of best friend would I be if I wasn't there to help him?"

"Snowflake, baby, I think you're shouldering too much of the blame. You can't take away his heartache or suppress it. This is his burden. I'm sure when he's ready he'll let you be there for him. All you can do right now is exactly what you're doing. Keep checking in on him like you are, because he'll know where you are when he finally needs you."

"I know you're right, Shrek. It's just hard. He's never shut me off like this."

Draven was about to answer her when Grunge yelled out, "That's it over there Draven, veer off to the left."

Pulling the car off to that direction, his nerves jumped on edge and he had an eerie sense of déjà vu. The sky turned darker. So much so that it almost looked like it was night, and it was barely noon.

Aliyah undid her belt buckle. Draven immediately

braced her back in her seat.

"Something's wrong." Draven speculated.

"Yeah, brother, I can feel it too," Dolph agreed.

"Fuck," was all Grunge muttered.

Aliyah peeled his arm away from her chest and said, "You're not leaving me in the car. Stop with your caveman shit, Draven. "I'm coming."

Draven groaned, "Yeah, I know."

The four of them climbed out of the fifty and surveyed the area. Someone staggered behind him and he turned to see it was Dolph.

He looked ashen all of a sudden and his cool and calm demeanour was no more. Draven flicked him an *are you ok* look and Dolph nodded his head yes.

Draven wasn't convinced but he nodded back in acquiesce. Stepping forward, he pushed Aliyah just behind him and made his way toward what looked like an abandoned warehouse. Dolph and Grunge sidled up beside him. That's when he heard the growls.

"Fuck," he seethed. "Can anything ever be clear cut for us bastards?"

Grunge chuckled without humour, and said, "Nope. It's always gotta be fucking laced with silver and wolf's bane."

Four sets of red eyes emerged from behind the warehouse. Draven did a double take when he laid eyes on Laney. Her eyes were still vacillating between the red and her lime green, coal eyes and her stomach was slightly protruded, with a cub growing fiercely within.

Ripping his eyes away from the wolves, his mismatched irises landed on Dolph and Grunge. Both of them had equally pained looks marring their features.

The coolness of the diamond dagger suddenly felt warm against his back and he readied his stance. Just as he was about to pounce, two sets of blood orange rimmed eyes stepped out of the shadows. *Fuck.*

Dolph growled, causing Draven to snap his eyes toward him. His teeth were bared. No, his fucking canines were on full display but he wasn't shifting and those sharp cuspids seemed more like vampire fangs than wolves.

He sprinted toward Jill and John, Aliyah's adopted parents, and slammed into the pair of them, pulling them down with him. He didn't shift but Draven sure as shit heard the crack of ribs and the screams as he sunk his teeth into each one of their necks.

Aliyah cried out, "Don't kill them! Please, Dolph!"

Draven was momentarily stunned by what had transpired and stole a quick glance at Grunge. He seemed to share the same sentiment as him.

Wolves growled, snapping him back to the present. Then they pounced. Aliyah ran out in front of him, dagger in hand as the dark red wolf came at him. She slashed her dagger straight through its abdomen and it howled, dropping to the ground like a bag of shit.

He didn't have time to follow Aliyah when she took off toward Dolph and her parents because the wolf to the right made its move. Circling each other, the wolf lunged as Draven brought his blade out from his waistband.

Teeth grazed against his shoulder and he winced. Forfeiting the pain, he corrected himself and turned around to see the wolf pawing at the dirt. Draven rushed forward and slammed the dagger into the chest cavity where the heart would be.

The wolf howled out in pain and Draven stabbed it again. Slowly it returned to its human form, dead. Distracted by watching the life drain from its eyes, he hadn't heard another wolf sneaking up behind him.

Canines embed themselves deep into his right shoulder, causing Draven to bellow out in agony and anger. Dagger still in hand, he reached behind with his free hand and gripped the wolf by the mane then threw the body over his head. The wolf wailed out in pain when it slammed against the cold dirt.

Draven felt the blood flow freely down his arm and he was beyond pissed. Kneeling down, he pawed the wolf by the mane. He looked into the red eyes to make sure it wasn't Laney. When he was satisfied, he snapped the wolf's neck and waited for it to return to human form.

Draven stood up and dusted his knees off then ripped the bottom part of his shirt to tie around the bite mark. Just as he knotted the material around the wound, a guttural growl penetrated the air.

He jerked toward the sound and found John's neck still

in Dolph's grasp as he growled at Aliyah. His eyes firmly on her, Draven sprinted toward her side.

He looked at his best friend's face and couldn't help but see the feral glint in his eyes. Something he hadn't seen in very fucking long time.

Pushing Aliyah behind his back once more, he risked a step forward. "Dolph, buddy, it's me, Draven. You need to let that demon lackey go."

Shaking his head, Dolph's eyes flashed with uncertainty and he reared back dropping John to the ground. His hands flew up to his mouth and when his fingers tore away from his lips, his hands were bloodied.

"What—what the fuck is happening to me?" he stuttered.

"I don't know, brother, but you need to step away from those putrid souls."

Aliyah gripped his shirt from behind and looked around, breathing a sigh of relief when she clearly saw that both Jill and John weren't dead.

Dolph staggered away and closed in on Draven, his hands shaking. He tripped forward into his arms. "I think, shit, I think I'm going to vomit."

A loud cackle followed by a baritone chuckle pierced the dark sky. Draven clenched his jaw and fists knowing full well who they were.

Bracing himself, he turned to meet two sets of crimson irises, one of those pairs rimmed in black and amethyst speckles. That pair belonged to his mother, Efah. Inside Draven fumed. He was angry at himself that he didn't bring the gold laced diamond dagger to eradicate her nasty ass back to Purgatory, and for good.

"Must you all be so fucking predictable?" Efah clucked her tongue, breaking him from his thoughts as she surveyed the area.

It was the first moment that he realised he hadn't seen Grunge or Laney since this shit started. Inconspicuously, he assessed the area looking for the pair. He felt like someone punched him in the gut when he couldn't find them."

"Aliyah, it's so nice to see you again," Gorgon drawled, which fuelled Draven's anger further.

"You don't get to fucking talk to her, you vile piece of poison."

Gorgon smirked, pulling at the scar on his face before he added, "As always, Draven, a pleasure. And I will talk to my daughter however the fuck I see fit!"

"Not by fucking choice," Aliyah seethed. "What the fuck do you two pieces of carrion want from us? Because you sure as shit ain't here to talk about the weather."

Her face was tight, her stance rigid as she faced her father. Draven was fucking proud of her. Gorgon's smirk widened and he chuckled.

"It's simple. Neferity wants you. And that fucking totem. Where is that good for nothing bitch?" Gorgon growled.

"I can't wait for the Revelation to take place so I can plunge a dagger through your heart and send you to Purgatory. Believe me *son,* you won't ever leave. Aliyah will be ours and while your trapped in the devastation of your mind, guilt ridden that you couldn't save your precious Aliyah, that's where the real fun will begin," Efah raged.

Gorgon placed his hand on her shoulder and he watched his mother's eyes flick down to his embrace and then back to the three of them.

"I forgot how much of a cunt your mum is, D. But we need to go now. I'm serious," Dolph urged.

Draven offered a slight nod of his head and looked toward his mother. The dark tendrils were sweeping around her feet ready for her command, and he knew from experience they were odious little fucks.

He watched the demons with ire, figuring he could take them. However, given Efah was under Neferity's wing, he wasn't so sure if the Dark Goddess had gifted his mother with some nasty brandings.

The main reason that stopped his ass form going all Rambo on them was Grunge and Laney. Draven sensed the urgency in Dolph's voice and his gut told him to listen to it. He needed a decoy, and he knew exactly what would give them the leverage to flee.

Gorgon and Efah stood there, smiling. They thought they had everything worked out. Boy were they wrong. Tapping into his and Aliyah's telepathic link, he said, *I'm going to create a detour so to speak. Be ready, Snowflake.*

Draven caught the soft nod of her head from his peripheral and knew she'd heard him. Satisfied that Dolph would follow suit, he reached around to grip his dagger.

Withdrawing it faster than the speed of light, he threw it at Efah. The crack of her ribs and her shriek filling the air told him that he hit her exactly where he wanted. Where her heart should have been.

Gorgon screamed, "NO!"

Snapping him from the image unfolding before him was the footfall of the others slamming against the dirt floor. Following Aliyah and Dolph, he hightailed it to the fifty to find Laney passed out in Grunge's arms.

Chartreuse eyes pinned him, tears falling freely. Draven knew they were in dire straits. Once they were all piled in, he turned the key in the ignition and smashed his foot to the accelerator.

Aliyah, panting hard next to him in the passenger seat whispered, "They're really gone, aren't they?"

Dolph spoke before Draven could answer her. "I'm sorry, Liah. I—I don't know what happened. Fuck. I..." he trailed off.

Draven caught his melancholy riddled and conquered face in the rearview and a sense of déjà vu washed over him. The reflection in the mirror also revealed Efah and Gorgon on the floor, red slits facing the car as he raced further away and toward safety.

White knuckle grip on the wheel, he put the pedal to the metal and hoped to the Goddess of Light that he would be able to sway Laney back to the light. He desperately needed for her and the baby to be ok, and not to owe that rotting bag of carrion, Melantha, anymore of his flesh.

Chapter Twenty-Two

~ Aliyah ~

As Draven sped down the highway toward Reikiki's, Aliyah's mind was consuming her from the inside out. She tried to switch off from the mayhem coursing through her brain but it proved futile.

It was too much; this was all too much. Aliyah had entered this relationship in the beginning, unwilling. Now? Well now she was bound to her mate, to her Draven, but she didn't ask for all of this. The vampirism, the demon, the faery, even the fucking angel blood jettisoning through her veins.

Sucking her lip into her mouth, she chewed on the bottom one and allowed these dubious thoughts to drag her under. Heat swirled in her gut, and it wasn't the toe-curling heat she'd become accustomed to either.

It wasn't the first time Aliyah wished life was simpler. Like how it'd been before the knowledge that she was in fact an Otherworlder.

Taking a deep breath in through the nose and exhaling through the mouth, Aliyah attempted to smother the insecurity and uncertainty in its wake.

Closing her eyes, she began to center herself and tried to connect with the elements around her. Five Finger Death Punch's *Full Circle* blared through the speakers and she drummed her fingers on her thigh.

Black/red was all she saw behind her close eyelids, until the scene of Jill and John having their necks shredded open by Dolph's massive fangs. Their eyes hadn't changed one bit. Those blood orange rims ever vibrant like the first time she'd seen them. It was that exact moment she'd realised the trigger for those wavering feelings she'd just experienced.

Aliyah loathed John and Jill. But there was still that squidgy part in her heart that felt for them. Never mind that her apparent father was enticed by her beauty at such a young age, or the fact that alleged mother really abhorred her living form.

Her lids felt heavy and tears threatened to break free when she learned once again that her entire life up until a few months ago was a colossally fat fucking lie.

A memory slammed into her, one she hadn't remembered until it bared its ugly face.

The door creaked and Aliyah braced underneath her bright purple blanket and cuddled her teddy bear. She was scared of the dark and the footsteps sounding closer caused her to choke back a sob.

"Sshh, princess, its daddy. Scoot over for me. I want to lay with you."

Aliyah's dad snuck into her room every so often. When he did, he placed his arm around her and pulled her so her back was flush with his chest. She sighed in contentment. No one would hurt her while her daddy was here.

Her dad's hand laid splayed upon the tummy of her pink flannelette pj's like every other time he snuck into her room.

Aliyah's eyes drifted closed and she snuggled into her dad's embrace. It was then she felt something hard up against her backside.

Her eyes popped wide, and she whispered, "Daddy, there's something hard on my back."

He laughed quietly. "It's nothing, really. Would you like to feel for yourself?"

Aliyah stilled. An icky feeling planted itself in her belly but she didn't want to upset her daddy. So she nodded yes.

"Good girl," he cooed.

His arm moved her little one to rest on the hard thing. Aliyah jerked back and her dad brought it back down to

*touch the hard thing again, showing her what to do before
moving it back over her tummy.*

*He hissed, "That's it, princess, it won't hurt you.
Squeeze it a little harder for daddy."*

*Aliyah chewed on her lip and squeezed the long hard
thing like her daddy asked. It felt weird; it felt wrong; but
the way her dad chanted "yes, that's it, princess," over
and over caused her to continue to do as he'd asked.*

*The hand that was laying on her belly moved up under
her pajamas and her body shivered. He started massaging
her chest as he thrust his hips into her hand. Aliyah didn't
like that he was touching her chest. It didn't seem right.*

"Harder, squeeze it harder, princess."

*Aliyah did as instructed and then he groaned into her
hair as he pinched her little nipple and kissed her hair. Noticing her hand was wet, she tugged it away and her daddy
shushed her.*

*He took off his shirt and wiped her hand with it then
leaned down close to her face. She could scarcely make
out his dark eyes, but she sure noticed his smile.*

*His lips brushed hers and he said, "Thank you, prin-
cess. Sleep well. Daddy will see you in the morning."*

Then he was gone.

Aliyah jolted forward, causing the seatbelt to strangle
her as she came back to consciousness. Breathing fast,
she pat down her chest and looked around only to realise
she was still in the fifty.

Flinging her head over, she noted Laney, Dolph and
Grunge weren't in the back seat. "Where—where are we?"

Her eyes sought Draven's and she recognised the worrying stare marring his beautiful face. "What happened,
baby? It was like you weren't present here."

Aliyah racked her brain, the memory ingrained in her
mind. "It was... Fuck it was John. He made me touch him,
Draven, and he touched me. I—I just had a flashback. Oh
god I feel sick."

Bile swirled and her throat burned from the acidity
tunnelling up, readying to spew out of her mouth as she
envisioned all the nasty stuff she was certain happened
but could not yet remember. It made her violently fucking
ill. Heat forged behind Aliyah's retinas as hot tears leaked

down her face. She hadn't even noticed she'd been crying.

Shame railed into her first. Anger quickly followed when the tie between her fake parents and herself snapped in her mind.

Feeling the tug at the corner of her mouth, Aliyah knew she probably looked crazed to Draven. In her mind, she'd never been saner.

Nothing tethered her to those demon lackeys now. Emotions switched off and all she could feel was revenge sizzle beneath her flesh. John and Jillian would regret snuffing her innocence and crossing her by the time she was finished.

Clearing the fog from her mind, Aliyah turned to face Draven. The red in his ruby eye was more prominent and when she further assessed him, she noticed his jaw was clenched and his fists were so tight they were white.

"I'm going to fucking annihilate those pieces of shit!" he fumed.

Aliyah hushed him. "No you're not. I am. If I only have partial memories now, what else did those disgusting excuse for humans do to me? No, this one is for me. However, I promise you can watch."

She observed the anger bleed from his features, followed by something cruel, sadistic and utterly damnable monopolise his face. What struck Aliyah down to the core was the sense of pride that emitted from him.

"You know you're sexy when you're angry and decisive?"

Aliyah sensed the underlying intention in his words. "I'll keep that in mind. Before you ravage me, we need to get upstairs and figure out how to save Laney."

Cursing, Draven wretched open the door and Aliyah followed suit. They jogged up the stairs toward Reikiki's domain. The ornate timber door was open and awaiting their arrival. As soon as they stepped over the threshold, the door slammed and a painful scream bellowed out down the hall.

Aliyah locked eyes with Draven then they ran to find the source. Barging into one of the rooms, they found Laney tied down to a bed resisting against the binds.

Stepping closer, Aliyah could easily pinpoint the hysteria in the depths of those irises. Her lime green coal eyes were muddied with crimson red and she looked crazed beyond belief.

Aliyah stumbled back a step feeling the hostility and darkness pounding off Laney. That's when she noticed the orange blaze around the bed.

Tearing her gaze from Laney, she glanced around the room and noticed Jadis, Dolph, Grunge and Reikiki watching on with pained looks etched on their faces. For a splinter of a second she wondered where Lorelei was then figured it clearly wasn't important.

"What's happening to her?" Draven interjected her thoughts.

"She's resisting, vampire. What does it look like, you nincompoop?" Reikiki said, exasperated.

Aliyah watched Draven roll his eyes at Reikiki's comment before saying, "I can see this, Mad Warlock. I mean what is she resisting? The light, the dark?"

"Laney is fighting the darkness. I believe she can sense us. Unfortunately, Neferity has those sharpen talons of hers dug in deep," Jadis replied.

Aliyah canted her neck to the right and observed Laney's rapid breathing and how her eyes darted around the space. "I think she's resisting the light," she added.

Reikiki pulled at the beads in his silver hair and cocked his head to the right, mirroring Aliyah's pose. "Why do you say that?" he inquired.

Aliyah was quiet for a minute or so, calculating how to answer the question. "Neferity wants Grunge's totem, right? It's evident to me that she hasn't given it up yet. My gut feeling is if she gives into the light then she will be forced to listen to the morality and goodness within herself and not give the totem to Neferity."

"And what the fuck does that matter. That's a good thing," Dolph roared. "That means that we have one up on Neferity."

"No, not necessarily. When I tapped into Laney and Grunge's connection, when I saw Laney huddled on the ground holding her tummy, I sensed the trepidation pulsing off her. She owes Neferity a debt. For that debt to be repaid she needs to hand over the totem. But that's not why I think she's fighting the light. She's at an impasse. I believe without a doubt that Laney loves Grunge and doesn't want to betray him. That's why she hasn't given the totem to the Dark Goddess. However, from what I overheard if she doesn't forfeit the totem then Neferity will take the baby. None of that will matter if the Dark Goddess succeeds in turning Laney dark. She'll end up a shell like Jill and John."

"NOOO! Grunge hollered. "Neferity can't have our child. Just give her the damn totem if need be. Fuck I can't lose her and our kid. I just can't!"

"That would not be wise, wolf," Reikiki tutted, seemingly ignoring his outburst. "This totem is worth something to the Dark Goddess. Giving her such an instrument could prove disastrous. Laney will be safe here provided we can bring her back. Neferity can't enter my realm."

An ear shattering scream pierced the air and Aliyah's head snapped toward Laney. Her eyes were the normal shade and her body was sheened with sweat as she tugged at the binds.

They splintered and she raced toward them. She was thrown back before she reached them, like something had hit her. "What the fuck, Uncle," she hissed. "Let me the fuck out this instant!"

"You aren't going anywhere, niece. Not until you tell us what in Purgatory is going on."

Abjection slashed through her eyes, followed by fear. Whatever was going on in her head wasn't good. Schooling her features she planted a smile on her face.

"Ok, Uncle. You're right. If you let me out, then I'll tell you everything."

Laney was lying to the bone, Aliyah mused. Reikiki laughed.

"You think I'm that foolish? That I wouldn't know a decoy when I saw one? Please, Laney, I raised you!"

Laney growled darkly and her irises flashed to red once more. She looked terrifying, and Aliyah wondered what the hell the baby was dealing with if Laney couldn't decide which side of the fence she was sitting on. Surely the flummox of emotions wouldn't be good for the babe.

"Laney, honey, calm down," came Grunge's soothing

voice. "I'm here for you. We all are."

Laney's irises oscillated back and forth between the red and her natural colour at the sound of Grunge's voice, before the red slammed back in place.

"It's no use. She's a puppet and Neferity is pulling the strings," Jadis stated.

"I can't, no I won't believe that. My girl is still in there. She just needs more time."

"Alas, time isn't on our side," Reikiki relented.

Dread filled Aliyah to the core. Reikiki was right. They didn't have even a breath of time. Not only would Melantha be ready to claim her victory, Neferity wouldn't be far behind once she realised what they were attempting.

Lassitude invaded. The sense of failure sang fiercely within in her body. Melantha was about to have her cake and eat it too and there wasn't a single thing Aliyah could do. After all the contract was sealed and bound by blood.

Wobbling on her feet, her hand flew to the catch herself on the desk near the doorway. She vaguely heard Draven speak, telling the others that he would be back later, then his warm embrace balled her up in his burly arms and he walked out the room with Aliyah holding onto his neck for dear life.

Her eyelashes fluttered. The leaden feeling in her gut was almost too much to bear. The last thing she remembered was looking up into that one amethyst and ruby eye and seeing the anguish blemish his perfect features. Then all she saw was black.

Chapter Twenty-Three

~ Draven ~

Entering the lair, Draven peered down to gaze at Aliyah. After she passed out, he vamp sped to the fifty and got the fuck out of there. Obviously something was bothering her and he intended to find out what it was. Although, he couldn't shake how peaceful she actually looked right now, and if he was honest with himself he hadn't seen her unburden in a long fucking time. Perhaps ever.

Draven laid her down on top of the black satin sheets and pulled the cover over her. Leaning on the purple wall, he observed the rising and falling of her chest. Her dark hair fanned around her and looked like a raven halo encompassed her. She was the most beautiful thing he'd ever seen.

He had no inkling on the measure of time he stood there watching her sleep peacefully. The penny dropped and Draven came to see the world in which they were living. The forces they were up against were weighing heavily on Aliyah, as it was on him.

All he'd wanted to do was protect her, to keep her safe in a state of utopia. Instead, all Draven managed was to force her into a place of calamity.

Guilt coursed through his ancient body followed by anger. How could he put the one person he loved more than anything else in the clutches of danger and evil?

Wrath fermented inside Draven while he speculated at the possible scenarios laid out before him. What he came up with was his complete and utter selfishness.

Draven refused to see the peril he'd placed Aliyah in from the beginning. Blinded by lust, he avariciously took what he wanted when he wanted without thinking of the repercussions.

Could he let her go now he asked himself? The answer bottled through him, threatening to erupt and splinter him to pieces at the mere thought. The answer was plain and simple. No.

Shoving off the wall, Draven walked toward the one room he hadn't stepped foot inside since Aliyah frequented his life.

Unlocking his shameless, licentious fuck chamber, he left the door open and passed by all the benches, toys and other contraptions. He stalked toward the shelf at the back and pushed it aside to reveal a door that he kept hidden. Draven wondered how Aliyah had missed it when she inspected this part of the lair.

The old wooden door creaked upon entrance and Draven inhaled, smelling the old leather, timber and... blood. Pushing memories from his mind, he switched on the dimmable lights and hightailed it to the bar in the corner. He snatched the first bottle he saw filled with amber liquid from the shelf and turned on the Bluetooth surround sound and pressed play.

Draven didn't bother using a glass. He twisted the cap and brought the bottle to his mouth. The cold glass hit is lips at the same time the warmth of the whiskey washed onto his tongue and down his throat. He shuddered, but welcomed the sting.

With his hand around the neck of the bottle he moved toward the ancient leather lounge that was his father's once upon a time in this realm. Draven didn't want to think of his dad tonight. The pain was still a raw and gaping wound that continued to fester.

If his half-brother Emilio was right about one thing, it was that Draven was the cause of his father demise. It was his fault that Eilam was no longer reachable. In the name of both The Enchantment and Purgatory, he'd tried.

Blocking anymore unwanted reminiscent moments from his head, he leaned forward and placed his elbows on his knees and nursed the whiskey bottle between both hands.

Always a fuck up. That's all he would ever be. Continuously and recklessly putting the ones he loved most in harm's way. Draven was beginning to think he in fact was an abomination.

He embraced the burn as he took another heavy swig of his liquid courage, then he placed the bottle at his boots and reached behind his back to withdraw the replacement diamond dagger.

Lifting it up in front of him, Draven admired the brilliance of the cuts in the blade. They were deadly, yet none the less beautiful.

Holding the dagger in his right hand, he reached down to grab the bottle of whiskey and skulled some more. The burn was still there sliding down his throat just not as elaborate.

Draven went to take another sip and realised the bottle was empty. He threw it across the room and watched it shatter against the cobblestone wall. The low hanging lights shimmered upon the broken glass and he figured it was fitting given how he was feeling in the moment.

Reclining back in the lounge, Repriever's song *Grimm* blasted through the speakers.

Who do you blame
It's all the same
Pointing your finger won't open the cage
You're still stuck reliving the pain
Bury it deep
Bury it deep as you rip out the page

Draven thought the song was fitting given the circumstances. He brought the dagger down and sliced into his wrist. He pushed the dagger in with force, a lot more so than what he'd done to Aliyah when he traced the dagger over her skin recently.

He hissed as the magic properties in the dagger collided with his flesh while the pain emanated throughout his body. Yet somehow it provided him some reprieve from the ever-growing affliction and guilt.

Draven knew he was being a pussy and feeling sorry for himself, but in this moment he didn't give a fuck and welcomed that sliver of darkness.

Slashing another gash into his wrist, his head fell back on the cushion of the leather lounge and he breathed heavily, revelling in the pain bleeding out of his veins. The stab of agony from the dagger was almost blissful and he yearned for this moment to filter on infinitely. Of course it never lasted. Draven wasn't naïve. Hell, he'd done this enough times to appreciate that this was a Band-Aid on his immortally fucked up soul.

These lacerations would heal, the scars disappear, but the ones on his soul and his heart would never perish. They would be with him until the end of time, forever shackled with ghosts of his past.

Draven woke with a jolt. Finding his bearings he noticed he was still in the bar inside his fuck room. Aliyah's voice permeated the air. Her scent was drawing closer and closer to the room.

Draven rushed to his feet and quickly assessed his wrist. There was barely a scratch there now and he wondered how long he'd been out.

"Babe? Are you in here?" Aliyah called out.

"Shit."

Draven stumbled out of the bar and slammed the door closed. He pushed the tall shelf in place and sped to the door. Aliyah rounded the corner and ploughed into his hard chest.

He looked down, his eyes colliding with her stunning violet hues as she gasped in surprise.

"There you are." She assessed him first, then her eyebrows quirked as she tried to look over his shoulder into the chamber. That was when he smelled it. It was faint, like she was cloaking it, but her arousal was evident.

"I woke and you were gone. Are you ok? What happened?"

The devastation he'd just experienced slowly trickled out and was replaced with lascivious images of him and Aliyah doing every taboo thing imaginable. A thought weaselled itself inside and he briefly wondered how he could go from slicing his wrist to smothered with arousal and an iron hard dick.

He stamped that thought down and brought his lips to

Aliyah's tentatively. She moaned into his mouth then snaked her hands around his neck and deepened the kiss.

Draven threaded his hands through her long locks and pulled Aliyah flush against him as his tongue wrestled with hers.

Aliyah broke from the kiss and said breathlessly, "Please, I—I need you."

And he needed her too. Pulling her into the room, he ignored all the contraptions and headed toward the bed at the back of the room.

Draven placed her onto the bed and she braced herself up by her elbows, giggling. Draven's lips turned up at the sides as he prowled between her legs then yanked her jeans from her hips and off.

Aliyah made quick work of her shirt and demanded Draven do the same. Who was he to deny her? Ripping his shirt over his head, he threw it to the floor and toed out of his jeans awkwardly since he was still perched between her thighs.

There was no time for foreplay. He was too far gone, and by the heavy scent of her arousal drifting around, so was she.

"Clasp your hands on the bed posts above your head and don't fucking move unless I say so, do you understand?"

"Yes," Aliyah replied breathy.

Sitting back on his heels, he took a moment to admire her. Her cheeks were flushed, her violet hues glittering up at him, and those damn bow-like lips were slightly apart with her tongue darting in and out to moisten them. His eyes drifted lower over her big tits and nipple ring, then lower over her toned stomach until his eyes locked on her pretty dripping cunt. Draven groaned and his cock seemed to grow harder at the image.

A sliver of guilt surfaced but he pushed it down draconically. She was his forever and he wasn't going to allow anyone to take that away from him, not even himself.

Anchoring himself forward, he placed her legs over his thighs then settled his cock at her entrance. Without another word Draven drove into her fiercely. Aliyah keened out, egging him on, telling him how good he felt pistoning himself inside her tight channel.

His cock swelled beyond belief and he felt like her cunt was strangling him. Reaching up, he fastened his hand around her throat and pummelled her fast and hard.

Draven watched as her plump lips formed into the shape of an O while she moaned for more, and he wasn't about to deny her. Aliyah's walls squeezed around his length, telling him she was close. Removing the hand from around her throat, Draven maneuvered one of her legs up over his shoulder then leaned down and sunk his teeth into her thigh. That's all she needed. She screamed out her release, milking him in the process. But he wasn't done.

Draven rutted into her, all while her plasma washed down his throat and nourished him completely. The familiar tingle was racing down his spine and bunching in his balls, but he staved off and placed his wrist at her mouth.

Aliyah's fangs were already elongated from her arousal. When she embedded them deep into his radial artery, he couldn't stop the impending climax ricocheting through him.

Draven's vision blurred and he stilled, jettisoning deep inside of her while she garbled out her release around his wrist. When Aliyah finished feeding, Draven leaned forward, laying his forehead to hers.

"Promise me you won't leave me, Aliyah. I couldn't... I couldn't handle it."

Aliyah weaved her hand through his dreadlocks and drew his head back so she could look into his eyes. "Why would you ever say something so idiotic? I am yours, Draven, always."

Draven's cock was still hard when he pulled out of Aliyah gingerly. He turned on his side and pulled her to face him and said, "You deserve more than all of this, Snowflake. All I've brought to you is drama upon drama. I'm not good at this shit. All I do is ruin things."

Something flickered through her eyes and Draven thought it looked a hell of a lot like anger.

"Shut your whore mouth, Draven. You fucking saved me! Can you imagine what might have happened if you didn't find me before Gorgon? Before Neferity?"

Draven was silent for a few moments while he reflected

on what she'd purged. Was she right? Could Aliyah have been worse off if he hadn't sorted her out? A part of him would always feel as if it was his shortcoming by reaching out and thinking with his dick and nothing else.

He inhaled sharply, remembering the first time Aliyah's scent annihilated his every essence and brought him to his goddamn fucking knees. She was insatiable then, but after thrumming throughout his entire body and bloodstream, she was everything, his home.

"Yo, babe? You ok?"

Draven snapped out of his thoughts and cleared his mind. "Yeah, I'm ok." His hand reached up and he played with a loose strand of her ebony hair. "I sometimes wonder if I'd not sought you out that maybe you wouldn't be in this situation. But then I think about it and know you were destined for this and there is nothing I could have done to stop it." He sighed. "I just want you to be happy. Are you happy, Snowflake?"

Aliyah offered him a small smile as a tear tracked down her ivory face. "You make me happy. Yes, I see we are in a fucked up position, but you make my world a brighter place even with the darkness closing in around us. You are my home." She sobered. "Now stop talking shit would you? We have bigger fish to fry."

Draven smirked and drew her in close. His hand glided down her locks while they laid there in silence. Peace, that's what he felt. For this moment he wanted to relish it and capitulate to it.

He held her tightly then heard Aliyah's soft snoring surround him. She felt safe with him, and that's more than he deserved.

Draven was exhausted. Slowly his eyes began to drift shut and he knew he was about to join Aliyah in slumber. Or so he thought. His phone rang and he jolted awake. Maneuvering Aliyah out of his arms, he raced to his cell and answered, seeing Dolph's number flash on his screen.

"What's up, brother," he hushed.

"It's Laney. Get your ass here pronto. She's nearly back, D. Hurry!"

He hung up the phone and sprinted toward the bed. Shaking Aliyah, her eyes popped open and she groaned.

"Move your ass, sweet cheeks. We need to get to Rei-kiki's asap!"

Draven darted out of the room followed by Aliyah. Once they were both dressed, they fled the lair to pick up the fifty.

Draven sent a silent prayer to the Light Goddess, Kaltemis. *Please, please, Kaltemis, give me the strength to bring her back to us, please.* With that, he drove to Rei-kiki's like his life depended on it, and it did.

Chapter Twenty-Four

~ Draven ~

Arriving at Reikiki's, Aliyah and Draven jumped out of the car and dashed up the stairs and into the Mad Warlock's home.

A feral scream vibrated around them as soon as they ascended the apartment. Dashing toward the sound, Draven pumped his legs and felt the liquid fire course through them. His entire body was hot, and his mind was in shambles with the what if's this day was going to bring them.

Stepping through the room, Draven noted Jadis, Dolph, Reikiki and Lorelei gawking at Grunge. He was breaching the blazing orange protection spell surrounding Laney.

Lorelei's eyes snapped up over his shoulder when Aliyah had arrived. Draven observed something pass through those malachite irises and he was certain it was melancholy. Her eyes lingered for a moment before she tore them back to watch the spectacle before them.

Grunge kneeled down in front of Laney with his arms up in surrender, showing her that he wasn't going to hurt her. She was on her knees pressed up hard against the wall looking at him. Her eyes vacillated between the coal and red once more, and she looked like she was readying herself to pounce and annihilate Grunge.

"I know you're in there, baby. Please come back to me."

Draven stood there frozen whilst feeling the tension pulse through the room. It was that dense he could feel within in his bones. Laney growled and stepped forward.

"Don't you fucking see? Once I give her the totem she will leave me and the baby alone!"

Reikiki butt in, "You know as well as I do, Niece, Neferity will never relinquish her hold on you. You will be nothing more than a puppet for her. When she requires something else, she'll threaten you with something more. It has been the way she's always functioned. They don't call her the Dark Goddess for nothing."

Laney whimpered and Draven watched the fresh flood of tears fall from her lime green rimmed coal eyes.

Grunge rushed in and scooped her into his arms. She peered up at him while he wiped the tears from her cheeks. He smiled a sad smile down at her, his own eyes shimmering with tears when she placed her hand on his face. In that moment, Draven had no doubt that they felt like they were the only ones in the room. Nobody else existed.

"I'm so sorry, Grunge. I—I didn't mean to betray you. When Neferity threatened the baby I didn't know what to do. Please forgive me."

Grunge swiped a stray piece of hair out of her face then placed a hand on her stomach and said, "You were always forgiven, love."

Laney nestled into Grunge's chest and wept. Her cries felt like stabs to the heart and Draven was afflicted by the duality of emotions thrumming off the couple.

Warm arms circled him from behind. Draven knew it was Aliyah by her scent and touch. Immediately his body relaxed into hers and he released a heavy sigh. Maybe things were going to be ok. Did this mean that they'd won the first match against Melantha? Draven figured it was too easy. That demon always played dirty.

His ruminations were disrupted by a sickening cry. His head jolted upward and he realised it had come from Laney. Grunge's face turned ashen as he watched on helplessly while Laney convulsed on the floor.

"What the fuck," Draven hissed. Reluctantly he disengaged from Aliyah's hold and stalked toward the couple.

Laney's screams intensified. Her eyes opened and they were no longer her own. They were redder than the queen of hearts. Blood began trickling from Laney's tear ducts and nose, causing Draven's veins to turn to ice. He knew something was terribly wrong. He'd also known delivering Laney's soul to the light was too fucking good to be true.

Draven turned to face Reikiki. He started chanting the same phrase over and over again.

"Darkness seeks what darkness needs; no hope for the weak; shackled to the past darkness seeps; no light remains only darkness beneath."

What the fuck?

His eyes darted around the room, taking in Jadis, Dolph, and Lorelei's frightened faces before finally landing on Aliyah's.

"They don't call him the Mad Warlock for nothing and this is not fucking good at all. Jadis, can you feel any entities?"

She shook her head no, her eyes never leaving Laney and Grunge. *Fuck.* Turning back to the pair, Draven noted Grunge stacking pillows around her as his body wracked with sobs.

Laney's head lurched forward and she had stopped fitting. Eerie red eyes stabbed deep into his marrow the moment her lips kicked up at the side. "You'll never get her back. She's gone," came the distorted voice from Laney's mouth.

Draven heard a few gasps but his eyes stayed rooted on Laney. Another shrill cry left her mouth and her eyes glassed over, turning to her normal coal.

"Help me, Draven. Please!" That was all she managed to say before the red eyes snapped back into focus.

Was Melantha toying with their contract or was she truly fighting Neferity? This was something he needed to get to the bottom of, just not yet.

Laney's scream reverberated around the room, mingled with the sobs from the girls. Looking to Reikiki briefly, he noticed he'd stopped chanting. His eyes still had that tinge of madness, signalling he wasn't quite back yet.

Laney's pain was palpable; the agony mauled at his gut. *Fuck this,* he thought and stepped over the threshold of the protection spell. Aliyah cried out but he placed his hand up without looking at her to tell her that he was doing this.

Determination and melancholy bled through his veins. If this didn't work then they could lose Laney forever. Stricken, he glanced at Grunge.

"Hold her down. This is going to fucking hurt."

Confusion perforated his poignant stare but he did what he was told and tried to hold Laney down. The screaming was going straight through him. Draven gnashed his teeth together attempting to block out some it.

Grunge finally managed to hold her down. Blood continued to leak from her tear ducts and nostrils at a steady stream and he sensed she was getting worse.

Kneeling down, Draven's knees cracked as he leaned toward Laney and hovered his hand above her heart. He sensed the darkness clawing away at her and was tempted to jerk his hand back because he knew how sinister it was.

He sent another prayer to Kaltemis, realising he'd been doing that a lot lately. Placing his hand where her heart was, he ground his teeth harder on connection.

"Fuck me," he growled.

"What the fuck is going on?" Grunge demanded and Draven remembered that he hadn't seen him do this before.

Vaguely he heard Jadis and Dolph explaining but Draven didn't have time for pleasantries. He needed to bring Laney back to the light before it was too late. This was not something he was going to have on his conscience.

White hot pain sliced through his body and he tasted the vomit in his throat. Swallowing it back down, he placed his other hand over the top of the one resting on her heart and squeezed his eyes shut. If he thought the pain from Dany and Aliyah was heavy, this was downright calamitous.

Draven could sense Neferity's dark magic. Actually he could taste it, and it was fucking vile. He gagged, trying to keep the vomit at bay as his body wheezed in agony. The pain was unbearable. Draven only hoped he could hold on long enough to bring Laney back.

Pain erupted within in his whole being, making him tremble. This time he couldn't hold the vomit down. Leaning to the side he spewed up everything he'd eaten. The blood in his vomit didn't go unnoticed. However that was something he'd worry about later. He only hoped it was just what he was ingesting from Laney.

"It hurts, Draven, please."

His eyes opened to see Laney's coal eyes pleading with him. He knew then that he'd done it. He'd taken her pain away successfully. But deep down he knew he'd also consumed some of the darkness.

Gingerly, Draven removed his hands from Laney's chest and fell backward, hitting the wooden floor. Stars formed behind his eyes and all he wanted to do was sleep. He was beyond fucking exhausted. All he wanted was Aliyah lying next to him and his bed.

Speaking of his Snowflake, he must have passed out briefly because when he opened his eyes, he was still on the floor with his head lying in her lap. Draven's head rolled to the side to see Grunge and Laney huddling close together whispering, and he smiled. He actually fucking did it.

Draven was about to ask Aliyah to take him home when a malignant force bottled into him: Melantha. His eye lids felt like sandpaper against his eyeballs but he forced them open to see her stomping toward them. For a split second he wondered how she had entered Reikiki's apartment. There was only one answer: he allowed it.

"This is not fucking over," she screeched. "You fucking deceptive piece of shit! You cheated!"

Anger pulsated off Aliyah as he sat up. He rubbed her thigh to ease her frustrations, then said, "I didn't break any clauses in the contract. I won this soul fairly, and you fucking know it demon."

Melantha's black flecked, amber eyes blazed wildly within the host body. She was so furious her body was quaking.

"You may have one this one, vampire. I swear to the Dark Goddess the next soul will be mine. And you," she paused and chuckled for effect, "will be mine once more. I'll be seeing you around. Oh, and Aliyah, I look forward to tasting you." With that the black and red mist formed around her and she evaporated along with it.

Draven's head fell back into Aliyah's lap, feeling heavy, and there was an unsettling feeling sitting in the pit of his stomach. She seemed so sure about the next soul. That unnerved him some.

He was too tired to analyse what she said anymore. Draven's body felt leaden and he needed to sleep for fucking days. Regardless of feeling uncomfortable, his eyes closed once more, urging him to surrender to the sandman.

He was lightheaded and felt like his body was in another realm. He knew it was the delirious feeling because of ingesting so much pain and darkness.

There were butterflies flying and bunnies hopping around in a field in his mind and the sides of his face kicked up watching them. They were so pretty. Then something changed. Darkness shrouded the field and he sensed the damnable change immediately.

Blood oozed from all the bunny's orifices and he cringed, watching. Something was wrong. He just couldn't put his finger on it.

A deafening scream rang out and his eyes popped wide, looking for the source. His irises landed on Laney and he felt the sob wretch from within in his chest cavity and lodged itself in his throat.

There was blood everywhere and Draven knew he'd failed her. He looked up to Aliyah, watching the pained expression cross her face. His heart hurt even more.

Her violet hues drifted down to his and he could see the sadness pooling within them. She pushed one of his dreadlocks from his face then whispered, "It's not your fault, babe."

His heart fractured once more at her words. Then he plunged into darkness, losing all consciousness.

Chapter Twenty-Five

~ Aliyah ~

Looking down at Draven's clammy face in her lap, Aliyah knew he'd passed out from exhaustion. She couldn't get the excruciating look within his mismatched eyes out of her damn mind.

Laney was still screaming and holding onto her stomach. Aliyah knew it before anyone said it; she could smell the death in the air. The baby was gone. Her heart splintered into a million pieces, feeling Laney's anguish twist at her guts.

They'd succeeded at one thing and failed at the other. Although there was an inkling within her that this was no one's fault, Aliyah knew that's not how the rest of them would feel.

The orange blaze around the bed evaporated. Reikiki started fluffing around, his tunic flapping behind as he chanted something she was unable to decipher.

His hands reached out in the direction of Laney then closed his eyes and mumbled something under his breath. A yellow orange glow shot from his hands to her belly.

It seemed he had relieved some of the pain because she immediately relaxed. Although the pain was lessened, the tears still flowed abundantly at the loss of her child.

Jadis and Lorelei were no longer in the room and Aliyah was thankful for that small win. Dolph and Grunge's lips were moving but Aliyah didn't eavesdrop on their conversation. Instead she gazed around the room, noting how it was in shambles.

Stroking Draven's forehead, she peered down at him thinking she needed to get him home in one piece, and soon. Guilt gnawed at her insides. It wasn't only the desire to get him home and safe. No, she needed to escape this place because she felt like she was drowning in melancholy ridden water.

As if sensing Aliyah's thoughts, Dolph crouched down beside Draven's sprawled out legs. His coal eyes were bloodshot because he'd been crying. Aliyah wanted to comfort him but couldn't bring herself to say anything. What could she possibly say that would alleviate any of their pain? Nothing.

"Grunge and Laney are going to stay the night with Reikiki. Then they're going to head back to the pack. I'll round Jadis and Lorelei up and we will head home." His brow crinkled and he hesitated. "Have you, uh, um, have you seen Dany?"

Aliyah released a heavy sigh and shook her head no. "I haven't seen him but I have spoken to him. And before you ask, I have no idea where he is."

Dolph offered her a curt nod with his chin, stood up and walked to the door. He stopped before exiting and looked back. "Give me five then I'll grab D. And I get it, Liah. I know he's your best friend and you're trying to pro-tect him, but we all care about him too."

Aliyah didn't want to argue right now. She nodded her head as if accepting what he'd said and watched him turn on his heel and leave.

Laney's sobs had quietened. Aliyah tried not to listen in on Grunge's hush words to his mate. She placed her hand over Draven's heart and felt the steady rhythm under her palm. Instantly the tension eased in her gut.

Looking toward the door, she hoped Dolph hurried the fuck up because she wasn't coping. The insidious aura was still in the room and the darkness was latching on.

Dolph took that moment to strut in and haul Draven over his shoulder. She breathed a sigh of relief and all but ran out of the fucking room.

Within half an hour they were all back in their respect-ful lairs. The tension in her head had eased, but her heart was still galloping within her chest cavity like it was threatening to break out.

Aliyah left Draven asleep on the bed where Dolph had put him. His face looked drawn and his eyes almost hollowed out. He didn't look like himself. She wondered quietly if there were any adverse side effects to Draven using his gift often, and she told herself that she would ask him what Kaltemis had said when he awoke.

Aliyah stood in the middle of the sitting room before making the decision to head to the kitchen. The black appliances along with the dark granite benches winked at her when she stepped foot inside the room. Everything was so damn shiny and she wished their life was half as clean as this fucking kitchen.

Aliyah opened and closed the fridge door before deciding on wine. She pulled a wine glass from the cupboard then opened the walk-in pantry to grab a bottle of red.

After filling the glass, she pulled a stool out and sat down. Her mind began swimming with so many thoughts that she literally couldn't keep up. Aliyah sipped her wine and took a few deep breaths to centre herself. Once she felt grounded she let her mind wander again.

They'd won this match with Melantha, but there was still four more souls, well at least two more if Draven was able to deter the next soul from capitulating to the darkness.

Trying to take another sip, she saw her glass was empty. She reached for the bottle and refilled the glass before returning to her pondering. Amidst her ruminations, Aliyah realised that Neferity, Gorgon and Efah had been extremely quiet. That worried her. She was certain after their little debacle when they found Laney there would be more backlash from the Dark Goddess. Aliyah truly thought she was going to come after them full-fledged.

After all, Aliyah was supposed to be the key to this revelation prophecy shit. Yet all she could hear was crickets creaking. What were they waiting for?

Laughter rang outside the lair, startling her. Aliyah figured that Dolph and Jadis were heading out, which in turn made her think of Dany once again. Diving into her pocket she retrieved her phone to text him.

Aliyah began typing out a message when a knock sounded on the door. Her ears pricked up but she couldn't hear anything. She racked her brain on who it could be. There wasn't many people who knew where Draven lived.

Sculling the rest of her wine, she traversed to the front door. Aliyah knew who it was before she opened it. She could smell the strawberry scent even from this side.

She really didn't want to deal with Lorelei now, but she also didn't want her to keep knocking and possibly wake Draven.

Aliyah pulled the door wide and planted a smile on her face to greet Lorelei.

"Hello pretty head."

The smile was wiped off her face when Lorelei pounced on her and her lips found Aliyah's. Momentarily shocked, Aliyah opened up to her before pushing her away.

"What are you doing, Lorelei?" she panted.

Red crept up her neck and she bit her lip. "I—I missed you. I thought you were being standoffish because of Draven."

Aliyah felt her eyes go wide. "You think that I'm distancing myself because what? That I'm pretending to stay away from you so I don't upset Draven? Lorelei, I'm sorry for what I did to you and I enjoyed what happened between us, but it won't happen again. Draven is my soul and my heart." She sighed, knowing this was going to hurt Lorelei. "I am happy to be your friend. That's all I can offer you."

Aliyah watched a lone tear slide down Lorelei's face and she wanted to step in and comfort her. Conversely, she didn't want to send mixed signals either.

Lorelei swiped at her face and said, "I'll forever be chasing a love that I can never find. I just thought there was more between us. I'm sorry."

Aliyah's hands fidgeted beside her as she felt the insecurity pulsating off Lorelei. She wanted to comfort her and tell her that she was beautiful. She shook the need from her body, readying herself to reply.

"You don't love me, Lorelei. It's because I revived you. Draven explained to me how a fledgling vampire can cling to those hopes, and given your senses and emotions are already heighten..." Aliyah was about to continue when her phone started vibrating. Leaving Lorelei standing there she signalled she'd be a minute.

Retrieving her phone she saw it was Dany facetiming her. Swiping her finger across the screen to answer, Aliyah was prepared to give him a piece of her mind. She was stunned into silence when she saw what was happening on the screen. He must have accidently dialled her.

There was one man with red hair and a beard on his knees deep throating him and gagging loudly, struggling to take him to back of his throat while Dany was kissing and finger fucking a blonde haired woman.

Instantly her pussy throbbed at the scene in front of her. She knew she should exit the screen but she couldn't bring herself to do it.

Aliyah heard footsteps behind her and knew it was Lorelei. She looked over her shoulder and moaned. "Who the fuck is that?"

Aliyah's wetted her dry mouth with saliva and replied, "That's my best friend, Dany."

"He's hot. Why is he facetiming you?

"I don't think he realised he called."

"Accident or not that is fucking sordid. Why didn't you tell me how sexy he is?"

Aliyah turned her eyes from the screen to scald Lorelei. "Seriously?"

Lorelei shrugged her shoulders. "Sorry."

A scream reverberated through the phone and Aliyah's eyes snapped to the screen. Dany had his fangs embedded in her neck while his other hand forced the male's head down on his cock harder.

Aliyah suppressed the moan bubbling up and watched Dany face fuck the man while the red head stroked himself as he gagged.

Her sex drive had always been high, but since she turned into a vampire it'd increased tenfold. She shouldn't be watching this, yet she couldn't tear her eyes away.

Dany's body convulsed and she knew he'd climaxed when she watched the man's Adams apple bob as he swallowed Dany's load.

The man pulled back, leaving Dany's still erect cock

jutting upward. He started to watch Dany and the woman. Except Dany retracted his fangs and threw the woman to the floor in front of the red headed man. He quickly wrapped his dick in plastic then propped her ass up to slam into her. He growled as his hips pistoned. He placed his hand on her head and guided her to the redhead's angry looking cock.

As her lips wrapped around his length, Aliyah realised she'd never entertained the idea of Dany being bi. His man bun was dishevelled and she watched the sweat drip down his inked chest. He looked pissed off but still beautiful as ever.

Lorelei pushed up behind her and whimpered in her ear. With how aroused she was feeling right now, Aliyah was almost certain she'd go back on her word about Lorelei and herself.

She resisted the urge, even though Lorelei's nipples hardened into her back. Aliyah felt the slickness pooling beneath and was readying herself to end the call until the three of them all climaxed.

"Fuck," Aliyah hissed.

"You don't say," moaned Lorelei.

Dany's body stilled as he emptied out into the condom. His face was pointed up toward the ceiling with his eyes closed.

Lorelei whimpered again and Dany's eyes snapped open. His head jerked to the side and then he was looking at the both of them.

"Aliyah?" he panted.

Aliyah stuttered, "You, ah, accidently called me."

His face kicked up at the sides and he smirked. "Did you enjoy the show with your little hot friend there, Liah?"

His voice seemed different, yet laced with amusement. She was about to reply when the woman ripped her mouth from the man's crotch. That's when Aliyah saw it. Eyes as red as blood held her in place. She heard Lorelei's sharp intake but ignored her as her own mind ricocheted with questions.

No, no, no! What the fuck is he doing?

Before she had the chance to voice her concerns, the red headed man looked at the screen. His lips pulled back in a grin to reveal fangs, but that wasn't what frightened her. It was his eyes. They were blacker than the ace of spades.

Dany's face morphed and she knew it was concern written all over his face. "What's the matter, Liah? You look like you've seen a ghost."

The demon smiled eerily at the phone and she knew for certain that Dany had no idea he'd just ingested demon blood and had his cock milked by a vampire. That was her guess, but then again, she was new to this fucking world.

As calmly as she could, she said, "Dany, where are you?"

The demon's face broke out in a wider smile and she began laughing. Dany's eyes shot to the woman, and he growled, "What the fuck?"

"Where the fuck are you, Dany?"

The demon launched at him and the man started chuckling. Dany snap kicked her and his foot landed across her cheek bone. Bluish black fluid sprayed all over the room and she rolled into the corner of the room.

"Use that stupid tracking thing we downloaded on our phone years ago, Liah. I'm near St Louis cemetery no 2!"

Aliyah opened her mouth to reply but the words didn't leave before the red headed man stood and threw what looked like a dagger at the phone. The connection broke.

"Fuck!"

She felt absolutely revolted that she was actually turned on by the scene that had unfolded. She also knew it wasn't because of the participants but because of Dany, and that confused her.

Aliyah began scrolling through her phone for the app she'd made him download years ago. They'd never needed to use it, but right now she was grateful she'd made him download it just in case.

Once she found it, she signed in so she could access his location. Aliyah reminded herself she needed to logout when she returned home just in case someone got a hold of his phone.

The little location icon dinged and flashed where he was. Trepidation swirled in her guts, she needed to move her fucking ass.

Rushing from the kitchen she balked momentarily, staring at the bedroom door where Draven was asleep. Aliyah thought about letting him know where she was going but if she did that he'd want to come, and he needed to rest after the magic and energy he'd just consumed.

Shaking away the guilt, she ran for the door hearing footsteps behind her. Aliyah stopped abruptly and turned around. "You can't come, Lorelei. It's not safe."

"Like fuck I can't. The woman I lo..." she blushed then corrected herself, "I care about you, Liah, and I'm part vampire and witch, I can hold my own."

She didn't have time to argue. Dany could be in deep shit right now. "Please stay close to me. And for what it's worth, I care about you too. Do you know how to vamp speed yet?"

"Yeah kind of. Dolph explained how to center myself and focus so I'm confident I can do it."

"Good. Let's move." Aliyah only hoped they got there in time.

They hit the surface and a cool breeze kissed her skin. Aliyah grounded herself then opened up to the elements. Looking to Lorelei, she found her doing the same. She nodded her head, signalling she was ready and Aliyah took off at full speed.

In no time her legs felt like they were on fire and her hair slapped against her face. The wind was ferocious at the speed they were travelling.

Peering over her shoulder, she saw Lorelei wasn't far behind and that she was doing a good job at keeping up. *Good*, thought Aliyah. Five minutes later they arrived at the front of a small house.

Horripilation spread across her body. Her eyes darted around the street looking for any sign of the demon and red headed vampire. Aliyah drew in a deep breath through her nose and the scent of blood infiltrated her nares. It was Dany's. She knew that strong earthy, testosterone laced whiskey and marijuana scent anywhere.

Aliyah didn't think, she barged straight through the door to find Dany curled in a fetus position, naked, with four gashes on his ribcage. As if knowing, she drew the conclusion that it was the demon that'd hurt him. Aliyah remembered Melantha's nails were sharp as shit.

Aliyah ran toward Dany and dropped to her knees beside him. Her vision blurred when she took in the gash marks, and a selfish part of her wished Draven was here to steal the pain away from him.

Seeing a sheet alongside him, Aliyah draped it over him. For some reason she didn't want Lorelei to see him like this.

As if on cue, she heard Lorelei's feet crunching the shards of glass on the floor behind her before she appeared beside her. "Is he ok?" she hesitated.

"He will be. I need to get him home. Jadis will know what to do."

"Maybe I can try? Jadis has taught me a couple of spells."

"No," Aliyah thundered. "Dany isn't your guinea pig, Lorelei. It's not happening."

She didn't need to see Lorelei to know she'd flinched at her harsh words. Even though guilt seeped within Aliyah, she couldn't bring herself to apologise.

"I'm sorry. I just wanted to help."

Aliyah released a heavy breath. "I know. You're new to your magic and it's tentative. I can't risk him. Thank you though." She pushed out the last sentence to lessen her guilt.

It wasn't Lorelei's fault. Aliyah chastised herself internally. She really needed to cut her some slack. Becoming an Otherworlder was not easy. Hell, Aliyah knew that first hand.

She softened her tone and said, "I'm sorry, Lorelei. I know this isn't easy for you and it's scary. I'm just worried, sweets."

"I know. Let's go. Do you need a hand?"

"Nah, I'm good." Aliyah tucked the sheet under Dany and lifted him easily. She was grateful for the added strength that came with being a vampire.

Aliyah didn't need to instruct Lorelei what to do. Her long red hair flew manically in the breeze as she took off. Aliyah nestled Dany close to her chest and vamp sped all the way back toward the lair. For a fleeting moment, she laughed thinking about what she'd look like to anyone that saw her carrying Dany. Thankfully, at the speed she was running that was almost impossible.

Aliyah recognised the alcohol, gluttony and lust in the air when her feet hit the pavement in The Quarter. Deviating through the crowd, she zigzagged until she found the alleyway that led to the lairs.

Lorelei was waiting for her. They locked eyes and something passed through the pair of them. Uncertainty pooled to the surface but she quashed it and forced a small smile.

"Let's get him to Jadis."

Lorelei nodded, then turned and head down the secret passage that led to her space underground. The temperature dropped while they descended. Aliyah saw Jadis standing at her door waiting for them like she knew they were coming.

"What the hell happened to him?" Jadis rushed toward them.

"Long story. I think a demon slashed the side of his ribs and it's not healing as quick as it should."

Dolph appeared before her. His eyes bugged wide when he saw Dany. Before she knew what was happening, Dolph had him in his arms and they were following him into Jadis's lair.

Dolph screwed up his nose and laid him down on the lounge. "Fuck he stinks. He smells like fucking sex, demon and something rancid. What happened?"

"He ingested demon blood for one." Aliyah stopped herself and sent Lorelei a look that she hoped she'd interpret as keep her lips sealed. It wasn't her place to tell Dany's once lovers what he'd been doing. Lorelei nodded and offered her a small smile.

Jadis crouched down beside him and unwrapped the top part of the sheet, revealing the ugly lacerations. "Oh my Goddess," she whispered. "I can sense the dark magic. This isn't only claws of a demon, they were laced with something."

Jadis's forest greens sought Aliyah's violet pair. "You need to tell me what happened Aliyah," she demanded.

"It's not my place. However, I did see him ingest demon blood. Is that why he's not healing?"

Jadis's eyes flared and she knew that she was pissed with her. Aliyah didn't care. It would always be Dany before any of them, except Draven.

Jadis huffed and sent her one last disapproving stare before rushing out the room and into another on the left. Aliyah looked around the space and realised that she'd extended it once more.

Aliyah walked the short distance to the couch and crouched down close to Dany. His breathing was laboured and his face scrunched up as if he was in pain, which he undeniably was given the gashes along his ribs.

Pushing a stray strand of hair from his face, she sighed. All of this was too much for him. Finding out he was a vampire and wolf, then the fact his parents didn't die in a car accident and were in fact murdered. By her boyfriend's ex-fiancé who was supposed to be dead, none the less. If that wasn't a lot to work through, she didn't know what was.

The sweet smell of sage and lavender interrupted her ruminations. Aliyah looked up and found Jadis peering down at her and Dany with a pained look on her face.

"Hold his hand, Liah. This is going to hurt him."

Aliyah grimaced then reached for his hand. Her fingers laced with his warm ones and she squeezed, hoping he could feel she was with him.

Aliyah breathed deep and took in the smell of the sage and lavender. She realised there was another scent mingling with the others but she couldn't name it. The smoke from the herbs billowed around them. She watched Jadis crouch down and lay her hands on Dany's lacerations. She sent a worried look at Aliyah and began chanting.

Dany bellowed out in agony, his back bowing off the multi-coloured couch while his hand gripping hers with immeasurable strength. Tears sprung to Aliyah's eyes and she watched helplessly as Jadis did her thing.

Perspiration trickled down his screwed up brow and his face was the colour of a beetroot, it was that red. Seconds turned into minutes. Her ears thrummed from Dany's pained screams and her hand felt like it was about to splinter in his hold. She needed it all to stop.

Thankfully, Dany's cries stopped and his body melted

into the lounge once more. His breathing came in irregular bursts at first. They slowly evened out and Aliyah released the heavy breath she hadn't noticed she was holding. Jadis moved away and went to stand with Dolph and Lorelei.

Dany's eyelids slowly lifted. His umber, amethyst speckled orbs landed on hers and he mumbled, "Bitchface. I missed you."

Aliyah choked on a sob and slapped him lightly on his shoulder. "Don't fucking do that again, you hear me D-Bag?"

Dany chuckled then winced as he drew his hand down to his ribs. His eyes went wide like saucers as realisation settled into those troubled looking eyes.

He grimaced and tried to sit up but Aliyah pushed him back down. Slowly he took in his surroundings. His eyes lingered and a small smile played on his lips. Aliyah looked over her shoulder to find him gawking at Lorelei. She wasn't standing next to Dolph and Jadis after all.

Dany continued surveying his surroundings and she knew when he laid eyes on Jadis and Dolph because his pained expression hardened.

He went quiet. Aliyah watched the copious amount of emotions flash through his eyes before he growled, "Like fuck. Get me the fuck out of here."

Chapter Twenty-Six

~ Dany ~

Dany turned away from Jadis and Dolph and raked his hands through his hair. This was not fucking happening. His vision blurred and he allowed his mind to take him away.

Dany lost count of the how many days and nights he was absorbed by absolute drunkenness, debauchery and sinking his dick into any hole he so desired. That followed by feeding until he spat his seed into whoever was beneath him.

Stumbling down some dank smelling street in The Quarter, he staggered into a nearby bar and ordered himself a whiskey on the rocks.

He tried to focus his blurry vison on the dimly lit bar as he struggled to a booth in the corner of the room to wait for his drink. Closing one eye like Forest Whitaker, his vision improved some. He fell into the booth and looked around. At least the room wasn't spinning like it was when he first walked in.

The room was full of humans. Dany could sense some Otherworlders but he was too intoxicated to care who they could have been. How the fuck did I land myself in this fucked up position? Everything was fine before I realised I'm a part of this damnable world.

He missed Aliyah so fucking much. What fractured his heart into pieces was Jadis and Dolph. As much as they both claimed to love him and care for him, he felt like a third wheel. He never said anything to either of them, but now that Dolph was awake he saw the twinkle in Jadis's eye when he caught her looking at him. She sure as shit didn't gawk at him that way.

When they fucked, all the issues of their worlds splintered into a million pieces and it was only the three of them. Dany had secretly hoped it would be a forever kind of thing. Deep down he knew it was only an interim solution. At the end of the day, Jadis and Dolph had a history. A serpentine like, windy as fuck history that he sensed would always lead them back to one another no matter the cost.

There was a small selfish part within Dany that wished Dolph had never woken, because when he was deep inside of Jadis his world stopped and he could breathe. When he had her all to himself he swindled himself into believing there was hope of her loving him like she did Dolph. Such a foolish fucking thing to think because as soon as Dolph opened his eyes, those breaths shattered and dispersed into the air around them like nothing.

Dany didn't want to relive that heartache, so he catapulted his mind to better times with Jadis and Dolph. He could feel the electricity in his fingers as he focused on the magnetism between the three of them. It was undisputedly off the fucking Richter scale, and Dany felt his cock swell in his jeans, making it uncomfortable when his mind staggered down memory lane. Dany felt Dolph's hand wrapped around his cock while his was threaded around Dolph's, with Jadis rocking back and forward on his face. He groaned out loud and his hand moved under the table. He squeezed his dick in the hopes it would lessen the painful hard-on he was sporting. Fuck. If he concentrated hard enough he could still smell Jadis's sweet cunt and Dolph's...

A glass slammed down on the table, breaking him from his memories. Looking up, he was met with a blonde-haired woman with pretty eyes, a cheeky smile and tits pushed up so high they'd knock her out every time she walked, he was certain of it. His eyes traversed slowly down her body, cataloguing her assets before Dany reached her long legs. The blonde had legs for days. She looked beautiful, or maybe it was his whiskey googles. Either way she'd do.

He closed one eye and focused on the   blonde. "Wh—when do you finish, love?" Dany stuttered.

"In an hour, spunk. I have this ache down below. Think you could help me ease it?" She winked at him and he knew he had her.

"Find me, be—before your leave."

The blonde smirked and left him to his whiskey. Dany lifted the glass to his lips and closed his eyes. It was that moment he felt the seat dip with someone else's weight.

Draining the remainder of his drink, he opened his eyes to see a man with red hair and a beard sitting next to him. Dany inspected him through his drunken haze and noted the slight crooked nose, and that he was wearing a black fitted shirt that showcased all his tattoos and muscles. Dany thought he was attractive. He'd never gone the whole way with another man. But beggars couldn't be choosers and he was certain the blonde would be down for a threesome.

"You need another drink, man?" the red head asked.

Dany was quiet for a moment while pondering his answer. "Yeah, Jack on the rocks."

The redhead winked at him and pushed back from the table to saunter to the bar. Dany threaded his hands through his now loosened man bun and sighed. Am I really going to do this?

The little devil popped up on his shoulder and Dany knew he was plastered. Of course, you're going to fuck them both. Then you won't have to think about Jadis or Dolph any longer.

The man plopped down on the lounge and slid the glass over to Dany. He closed one eye to focus on the man and noted how dark his eyes were. They promised trouble, and that was fine by him.

Idle chit chat formed between the two of them then the redhead came in closer to Dany. His hand reached under the table and massaged his semi erection until it was punching the zipper of his jeans.

Dany sucked in a breath and hissed between clenched teeth while the man chuckled under his breath. "Wanna get out of here, big boy?"

"Yeah. Do you mind if I bring a plus one?"

The redhead withdrew his hand from Dany's crotch, his dark eyes never wavering from his. The sides of his lips curled up in a devilish smirk. "Why of course. The more the merrier."

The blonde woman found them five minutes later and he followed them to a rundown house not too far from the bar.

The moment the three of them stepped over the threshold it was on. Their clothes lay shredded and discarded all over the squeaky floorboards. They began kissing and touching every square inch of each other's bodies. It was beyond fucking scorching hot in the small room.

Growls and moans reverberated around the room while they were eating each other up. Dany hadn't realised how fucking starving he was until that moment.

The redhead disappeared from his sight and Dany sucked the blonde's face, kissing her like the air he needed to breathe. His fingers raced down to her pussy and he thrust three fingers into her soaking snatch. She moaned and started grinding her hips into his hand. Dany couldn't recall ever feeling this turned on. Or perhaps it was because of how intoxicated he was. Either way he wasn't whining like a little bitch about it.

He was finger fucking the woman while he kissed her and felt a pair of lips wrap around his shaft. Dany stilled momentarily and opened his eyes to see the red headed man's dark eyes watching him intently.

The thought of protesting bubbled up, then the man took him to the back of his throat. His eyes rolled to the back of his head and Dany lost all composure.

He continued his finger and mouth assault on the woman, but he needed more, wanted more. Ripping his mouth away from hers, his tongue traced the length of her jugular artery before piercing it with his fangs.

Metallic and iron brooked over his tongue. Her blood tasted... different. The metallic taste faded out into a sweet tone and then ended in an acrid taste. His face scrunched up briefly before he decided it didn't matter.

As he sucked her life force down, a trifling thought popped to the surface. He hadn't used his transotic of them. In the moment, he didn't give a flying fuck. Looking back now he really should have.

Dany's hand found the back of the man's head as he forced his cock down the back of his throat. The redhead gagged and Dany moaned. His balls bunched and electricity shot through him then he emptied out in the man's mouth.

The cool air kissed his still hard dick when the man moved away. Dany retracted his fangs and threw the woman to the ground in front of the redhead. Quickly he withdrew a condom and rolled it over his impressive length before slamming into her saturated core. At the same time, he guided her lips to the man's massive cock.

Their eyes met, and the intensity grew between him and the man. For a split second, it was like he was looking into Dolph's pair as he seesawed into Jadis. He shook the memory from his mind and focused on fucking her raw.

Those dark eyes promised a fuck load more to come. Dany was all too willing to oblige. He pummelled into her fast and hard, and a debauched part of him was ready to do the same to the man.

The redhead's lips kicked up at the sides. His mouth forming an O as the woman moaned around his cock. The blonde's cunt clutched down on Dany's cock, and by the look in the man's eyes, he was close too. Emotions and senses soared within him at the debauchery unfolding in front of him, which in turn sent him freefalling over the damn edge at the same time as both the woman and the man.

A whimper drew Dany's attention to his phone. He squinted, only to find Aliyah and some stunner gawking at the current fuck fest.

"Aliyah?" he panted.

"You, ah, accidently called me," she stuttered

Dany's face kicked up at the sides and he smirked. "Did you enjoy the show with your little hot friend there, Liah?"

He snapped out of his ruminations and rubbed his hand over where his heart was situated in his chest then looked up into Aliyah's violet eyes.

"I can't be here right now, Liah. I'll stay with Draven

and you in the spare room. Do you think he'll mind?"

Dany knew he sounded like a pussy but he couldn't be around Dolph and Jadis. It was too fucking much. He watched Aliyah open her mouth to respond. Instead of hearing her voice, Jadis's smooth sexy voice pierced the air.

"There's no need, baby. I made a space for you down here. I—I wasn't sure you'd feel comfortable here, seeing you've been gone for days."

Dany heard the poignancy drip from her words and he almost dropped to his knees to beg her for forgiveness and ask her to take him back. But he'd decided over the past few days that he wasn't going to be Jadis's consolation prize. As painful as it was he'd come to realise that it would always be Dolph when it came to her.

He wasn't going to be their third wheel no matter how much he cared for the pair of them. A current ran down the length of his neck and when he craned his head to the side, he noticed the redhead watching him. Shaking out the electric feeling in his body, he let out a deep breath and tightened his man bun while he pondered how to respond.

"Thank you. I appreciate that. Where is it?" His tone was clipped and he knew he sounded like an ornery child. Fuck that shit. He was entitled to those feelings.

"I'll show you," Jadis countered.

Without even looking to Jadis, Dany placed his hand up. "No Jadis. I can't be around you right now. I need space and time."

He was certain he felt her flinch from where he was sitting. Warmth radiated around his arm when Aliyah linked her arm with his. The tension immediately dissipated. It'd always been that way between them and the comfort and familiarity was welcomed. When it came to him and Aliyah, he knew you couldn't have one without the other.

"Come on D-Bag. I'll take you there now."

"I'm coming."

Dany looked over his shoulder and his eyes locked with the most brilliant malachite set he'd ever seen. He mentally kicked himself for not noticing how stunning she actually was in the flesh.

The red headed woman began to follow them out the door when Aliyah froze. Something had happened between these two, and by the way his dick started to harden in his jeans, he wanted to be right.

The air was thick between them. Dany could almost taste the lust floating around him. Aliyah canted her neck to look at the redhead and he watched her face light up at Aliyah's attention.

"It's ok, pretty head. My space is close to Dany's. I know you'll want some time with your friend." Her eyes travelled up and down his body while she basically fucked him with those malachite hues. Those damn orbs promised destruction in the most blissful of ways.

Aliyah's brow creased then smoothed out. She smiled back at the woman. Dany chewed on the inside of his cheek then smirked. He really shouldn't be thinking with his dick with all the shit that was fracturing around them, but he could barely contain his cock let alone control it.

Shaking his head from side to side, Dany was scalded himself when Aliyah all but dragged him out of the room. Silence stretched between them until they reached a door he didn't remember ever being there.

Dany heard another door open and close behind them and he automatically felt the loss of the redhead's energy. Aliyah turned the knob and Dany promised himself he was going to drill her about her affiliation with the sexy redhead, and where the fuck she came from. Purely out of curiosity, of course, because he wanted to fuck her twenty seven ways to Sunday.

How did that saying go again? The best way to get over someone is to get under someone else.

Chapter Twenty-Seven

~ Aliyah ~

Turning the handle, Aliyah crushed the small spark of the green eyed monster lurking at her back when it came to Lorelei and Dany. She didn't understand the feelings, but she also wasn't going to look into it more than necessary. Shoving the thoughts in her mind into a box in her head, she opened the door and walked in. She released Dany's arm and pivoted on her feet, drinking in the room. It was Dany to a T.

The walls were painted a dark jasper and the smooth slate tiles opened the room up into a spacious little sitting area. There was a charcoal coloured five piece leather lounge in the middle of the space with a small jarrah coffee table situated in front of it. Peering up, Aliyah noticed the flat screen television mounted on the wall and underneath was small entertainment unit that matched the coffee table.

Standing back, she observed Dany stalking over to the unit, clutching his ribs. Opening the draws and cupboards then slamming them, he huffed, "Looks like she thought of everything. My XBOX and PlayStation are here as well as my games.

His umber orbs met hers and she offered him a sad smile because she could see the conflict and sadness splashing through his retinas.

Breaking eye contact she continued to tour through Dany's new house. After all the shit went down, Dany had brought everything that he wanted from his house and stored it at Jadis's. Aliyah was thankful he left that worn-down lounge exactly where it was.

Shaking her meandering thoughts from her head, she walked into a room and noticed it was the main bedroom. A matte black chest of drawers sat in the far corner and in the center of the room was a massive king size bed dressed with black and red linen. Jadis really had thought of everything.

Leaving the room, Aliyah found a spare room with a queen-size bed and draws, a tidy little bathroom between the two rooms and a small kitchen with stainless steel appliances and dark aquamarine cupboards and white/grey speckled granite benchtops.

Absentmindedly, Aliyah wondered where the fuck Jadis hid all this money and where she found the time to decorate this space. Her ruminations ceased when she remembered her age and the fact she was indeed a witch. Aliyah assumed she also came from old money so that wouldn't be an issue either.

Stepping out of the kitchen, she was met with Dany sitting on the lounge with his hands in his dark messy hair. It was no longer in his man bun. It hung around his face, hiding it because his head was leaning forward.

Moseying her way toward him, she crouched down in front of him and brought her hands to his face to angle it up so she could see him.

His umber irises were more red than brown. She watched the tears track down his face. Aliyah's heart cracked.

Dany fell to the floor and sobbed, "It's too much, Liah. The fucking pain is destroying me. Why does it hurt so much?"

She drew him into her arms and stroked his hair. Biting back the tears threatening to escape, she answered, "Because you love them. Both of them."

"I don't want to anymore. Make it stop Liah, please."

Dany's head tilted up to look at her. His lips were puffy and his eyes pleaded with her. "Please," he whispered. His lips drew closer to hers.

Compulsion almost had her capitulating to his plea. At the last minute she pulled away and swiped the tears away from his eyes, watching his face morph into one of defeat.

"I love you, Dany, I do. But I can't do that for you and you know it. We tried that once, remember? I am your comfort, your best friend, and no matter what we've been through or go through I will always be here for you. Sinking your dick into me won't cure your heartache. And I can't do that to Draven."

Dany pushed away from her and pulled at the strands of his hair. "I don't know what's wrong with me, Liah. Fuck I can't believe I just tried that. Fuck!"

Aliyah hushed him. "It's ok, D. You're in pain and I fucking feel it as if it was my own. Look at me."

Dany hesitated then his head slowly came up. "I'm not going anywhere, ok. Ride or die, I will be by your side, ok?"

Dany nodded once and wiped the tears that were starting to dry on his face. A small smirk graced his perfect features and Aliyah sensed his cheekiness creeping in.

"Sooo, what's the go with you and the redhead?"

Aliyah groaned. "It's a long fucked up story."

"Good, because I could do with a distraction."

Aliyah shook her head and grinned. She delved into the depraved, yet sexy catastrophe that was Lorelei. She explained everything that had happened since he'd left Jadis and Dolph. Gorgon, Efah, the Dark Goddess entering her dreams; rescuing Laney and saving her soul from Melantha; her twist of fate with Lorelei and then her romp with her and Draven. She deliberately left out the jealousy she felt for him and Lorelei, figuring it was just her being overprotective.

When Aliyah finished reciting what'd transpired, she realised that Dany was playing with his tongue ring like crazy and was sporting a massive hard-on.

Quirking an eyebrow at him. "Really?"

Dany chuckled darkly. "You cannot blame me for this one, Liah. That is fucking hot, and Lorelei is easy on the eyes, I'm just saying! I can't believe Draven actually shared you, like what the fuck!"

She felt her lips tugging up at the sides. "It was pretty hot. But uh..." She pointed down to his crotch. "I think I'll let you sort that out. I need to check on Draven. He was depleted beyond measure when I left to find you."

Dany sobered. "Yeah, go Liah. I'm good."

Aliyah shot him a look.

"I promise. Go to your man before he comes in here banging on his damn chest like fucking King Kong."

Aliyah laughed and hopped up. After giving him a quick hug and demanding he call her if he needed anything, she found herself outside of his space and heading back to the lair.

"Aliyah!"

Closing her eyes, she let out a deep breath, opened them and turned to face Jadis.

"Is he ok?" she questioned.

Red splotches formed behind Aliyah's retinas. "Are you seriously fucking asking me that?" She threw her arms to the sky. "After everything that's happened and what you've put him through, you're asking me if he's ok being discarded by the people he chose to fall in love with?"

Jadis winced and Aliyah couldn't stop her mouth from running. "I knew you were going to hurt him. I only hoped I was going to be wrong." She shook her head in disappointment.

"He needs time, Jadis. Please give it to him so he can grieve the relationship he had with you and Dolph."

Jadis nodded and Aliyah knew it was with reluctance. She turned on her heels to check on Draven. Closing the steel door, she walked over to the bedroom and found Draven stirring. His head thrashed from side to side, words spilling from his mouth.

Aliyah rushed to his side and wrapped her arms around him. He stilled, then in a blink of an eye he was straddling her. Draven's eyes were open but something was off.

Trepidation solidified within her. She brushed his dreadlock out of his face with a shaky hand. "Babe?"

Draven growled and ground his hard length against her pussy. A moan bubbled up, but the fear didn't ease.

"Mine. Fucking mine!"

His fangs elongated and he locked onto her throat. Pain pierced through her neck before slowly lulling and transforming to pleasure.

Her hips rolled up to meet his hardness and she whimpered. Snapping out of her lust induce coma, she slapped him across the face. Draven didn't budge.

Aliyah summoned as much of her power as possible and threw him off her. He landed across the room, smashing a set of drawers to smithereens.

Draven shook his head and growled. When he looked up, his eyes still looked feral. Thankfully they'd softened, as well. "What the fuck, Snowflake?"

Aliyah scattered to the edge of the bed. "Draven?"

"Yeah, of course it's me. Why the fuck am I on the floor with wood sticking into my ass?"

Usually Aliyah would have laughed at a comment like that. This time she only studied him. "You don't remember?"

His forehead screwed up as he threw a piece of timber across the room before he zoned in on her neck. His face morphed into one filled with wrath.

"Who fucking fed from you?"

Aliyah reared back. "This is what I'm trying to fucking tell you! I just came back from saving Dany's ass to find you thrashing around on the bed. The next thing I know you're straddling me with your fangs in my neck!"

Draven paled. "I thought that was a dream? Fuck, I'm sorry baby."

"Your eyes were crazed, Draven. Fucking manic."

"But you're turned on," he said, looking confused. "I can smell you."

Aliyah felt the blush coat her skin. "Because you were grinding that monster up on me!"

His lips kicked up at the sides.

"Uh oh. What are you thinking?"

"Run."

"What?"

"I'll give you two minutes. Mask your scent so no one else can smell you. Oh, and Snowflake, run fast."

Aliyah's walls clenched and butterflies settled in her belly. "What are you talking about?"

Draven tutted. "You're running out of time. One minute and fifty seconds."

"Dra…"

"RUN!"

Aliyah jolted up and ran out the door and out of the lair. Passing Dany's and Lorelei's space, she headed for the surface. She hit the pavement and looked left then right and vamp sped toward Midnight Mayhem.

She wasn't sure what compelled her to seek this damnation of a place out, but as soon as she was close the darkness washed her over like a lover caressing her skin.

Aliyah moaned then darted to the side of the building. Pulling the steps down from the balcony above, she darted up the stairs until she reached the top of the building.

Heat nestled inside her core and she squeezed her legs tight together in attempt to calm the raging tingling down.

Aliyah looked around and saw scattered bricks and a decrepit attempt of a fence around the outskirts of the roof. Walking over she peered over in hopes of seeing Draven, instead all she witnessed were humans bustling around looking for their next sinful act.

A warm body came up behind her and she froze. The air crepitated around her with the familiar scent of sandalwood, whiskey and sex. It infiltrated her nostrils. Aliyah sighed and leaned into Draven.

He pressed his hard cock into her ass, wrapped his fist around her hair and snapped her neck back to meet his eyes. His red and amethyst irises shimmered back at her as his lips came to her ear.

"I can smell that traitorous cunt of yours, baby. And of all places to find you, it's on the top of the most depraved building in The Quarter."

Aliyah whimpered, "How did you find me?"

His tongue snaked out and traced down from her ear to her clavicle. Her eyes shuttered closed at the wetness coating her flesh.

"I'll always find you, Snowflake. You can't even escape in my dreams."

She pressed into his cock once more, causing him to growl.

"Poking the bear again I see."

Aliyah knew she should ask him if he was ok and if his strength was revitalised after how fucked up he was earlier, but surely he wouldn't be here if he wasn't and fuck it to Purgatory she needed him.

Draven cupped her pussy, hard. "Whose cunt is this?"

"You—yours," she moaned.

He chuckled low and dark. The deep timber of his laugh vibrated around her and sent an SOS straight to her core. She needed him inside of her like yesterday.

Everything fell away, all the burdens and troubles that were slowly eating her away on the inside. All that was left was this moment with Draven and her.

A loud tear permeated the air. The cool breeze kissed Aliyah's thighs and she felt her jeans fall away. They hit the cold concrete roof.

Her head was still held back by Draven's hand in her hair. It rested on his shoulder as his tongue lapped at her flesh. Her mouth dropped opened and she panted feeling him in every single cell of her body.

Her panties were pulled to the side and he pushed her lower back down with his free hand to jut her ass out. She felt the breath of his smile against her neck then he slammed his into her, with his canines finding her jugular artery.

Aliyah keened out as he pummelled into her, reckless and unrestrained. She could feel him in her damn stomach and she didn't think he'd ever been this fucking deep. Draven knocked the damn air out of her as he continued thrusting himself deep within her tight canal.

Aliyah felt dizzy. Her eyes closed as the stars burst behind her lids. With Draven's name on her lips, she clamped down around his length, screaming out.

Withdrawing his mouth from her neck, he chuckled. "Such a needy little cunt, Snowflake." Then he placed his wrist in front of her mouth urging her to take what she needed, and she did.

Her canines punched through her gums and her fangs found Draven's radial artery. Blood gushed over her tongue and her body turned to liquid while she drank down his life force.

Aliyah's body broke out in goosebumps as Draven continued to piston into her, moaning out her name. The darkness that wrapped around her earlier was suckling on their debauchery and she sensed something in the shadows. She was too drunk on Draven to give a fuck.

The stars behind her eyelids turned into flashes of red before turning to atramentous sludge. Her insides screamed for her to run and to pull away but the draw was too strong. Her knees buckled and she felt herself succumbing to the magnetic force.

Slowly the sludge transformed. Aliyah squinted her eyes and pulled harder on Draven's wrist as the figure began to resemble a body and face she'd seen before.

A ruthless smirk curled on the woman's face and Aliyah balked. Yet she couldn't retreat.

"I told you, Aliyah. I always get what I want." She laughed. "I just had to bide my time until you were so consumed with your bonded mate to take what I'm entitled to."

She quirked a perfect manicured, black eyebrow and tossed her long ebony hair over her shoulder. "Your walls are down, Aliyah, and you're fucking on top of a building that is run by one of my own. Can't you feel the darkness welcoming you home? Don't tell me you actually thought you *chose* this place? I guided you like I always do," she snickered.

"No!"

"Yes." The slender figure moved forward and Aliyah shrunk back. "Don't be coy, little one. It will all make sense soon. I bet you can feel every damnable thing seeping into your skin as you stand rooted in place. It was always a lure, Aliyah. I watched the first night you and Draven entered this realm. You were in your element."

Aliyah shook her head from side to side. She could vaguely feel Draven pumping into her and she could taste his vibrant blood on her tongue, but for some reason she couldn't pull back from what was about to happen. It was like she was stuck in some dream state.

A hand plunged forward and embedded itself into her chest cavity. Pain spiralled and the nausea thrashed inside. It lodged itself in her trachea. Silent screams froze inside her larynx and she tried to connect with Draven.

The woman's voice cackled and she leaned in to whisper in her ear, "You're too far gone. He can't save you this time." Her hand squeezed around what Aliyah knew was her heart and tears streamed down her face while she hollered out from the affliction.

Aliyah knew the exact moment the evil pervaded within and penetrated her very essence. Neferity's crimson irises smiled, leering. She had her exactly where she needed her.

"Why are you doing this to me," Aliyah stuttered.

Neferity cocked her head to the side like she was contemplating the question. "Once you are mine, you will know everything. Until then, enjoy the pain you have so diligently forced upon yourself."

Neferity offered her one last smirk before her essence dispelled in the air. Everything slammed back into Aliyah. Her senses overloaded as she felt Draven tense behind her.

Draven released her hair and Aliyah slumped forward, feeling his cum drip down her thighs. She wept loudly, violent sobs wrenching out of her. She knew she sounded dramatic but couldn't stop the onslaught.

Without a doubt, Aliyah knew there was a piece of her missing. Neferity had stolen something so precious and she feared she'd never get it back.

Wind whooshed around her and the cold air licked at the exposed parts of her body. She opened her eyes to see Draven kneeling down in front of her, with blood dripping down his chin and uncertainty swimming through his mesmerizing eyes.

Draven cupped her face and flinched. "What—what happened?" His tone was corrupted with pain and melancholy, except the emotion that shone through was guilt.

"She got to you, didn't she?"

Aliyah traced her index finger over his forehead then pushed his dreadlock out of his eyes and nodded yes.

Draven pried himself away from her with a scream that she was sure would wake the dead. Her heart beat frantically in her chest. She was slowly fracturing apart inside. How could she save and comfort Draven when a vital part of her was missing?

On his knees, Draven pulled at the beads in his dreadlocks before his traumatized eyes met hers. She wanted to comfort him but a part of her felt dead now and she despised the feeling.

"I was supposed to protect you, Snowflake. I failed you, just like I do everyone in my life."

Aliyah was about to console him when that dark feeling she felt earlier graced them with its presence.

"Of course you did, brother. That's what you do. Although it was more than a pleasure to watch you fuck her like you hate her. It felt like the old times," the voice quirked.

Aliyah searched the aphotic night sky for the voice. When her eyes landed on the entity she shivered. She watched his hand move south to wrap around his hard length. She couldn't see his face, but she felt like she knew him.

Draven vibrated behind her, and as the Otherworlder stepped forward, her world froze in place with what she saw before her.

Eyes as black as the ace of spade appeared first, followed by pallid skin covered in ink. After he came into focus, Aliyah noted the leering smirk fixated on his face before she realised where she'd seen him.

He chortled, his hand clutching his chest at the same time his dark eyes devoured her soul. "You remember me, princess. I'm honoured."

Turning her face from the stranger in disgust, she faced Draven. He looked wounded.

"You know him?"

"No, not personally." Aliyah canted her face away from Draven's disappointing stare.

"Tell him, Aliyah. Tell him how you were so fucking turned on you were ready to give yourself to that siren Lorelei. Tell him how you watched Dany fuck my mouth and that demon until you were almost ready to burst before you realised what we were. TELL HIM!"

Fat, wet tears slashed down her face and she readied herself for Draven's wrath. Instead, his eyes softened and he placed a kiss to her forehead then sat back on his heels. The softness in his eyes dissipated and was replaced by something that made Aliyah's skin crawl.

Draven stepped in front of her and pushed her behind him. "What the fuck do you want, Shredder?"

"You—you know him?"

The man's voice bounced off the night sky when he spoke and Aliyah shrunk back. Whoever he was, he was not someone she wanted to know.

"Tell her, Draven. Tell her how fucked up you are beneath that façade."

Draven growled, "What the fuck do you want from me, Cyrus!"

The memories of what Draven had told her about Cyrus paired with what she'd watched mere hours ago happen with Dany flooded into her mind.

"I will fucking kill you!" she screeched.

Cyrus leaned against the broken bricks with a smirk firmly in place. "Oh please do. I want to see those claws, *Snowflake.*"

Aliyah's whole world shifted on its axel, followed by Draven flying through the air toward Cyrus. "You can't fucking have her, Shredder. I won't let you!"

Draven's voice silenced in an instant, and Cyrus laughed. Aliyah watched, stunned while Draven fell to his knees bowing to the psycho standing in front of her.

"That's it, Slasher. Give into the bloodlust and come home."

She looked up at him in a daze. Her head was spinning.

"It's in motion, little one. The sooner you submit, the easier this will be."

Aliyah leaned over and braced herself on her hands and knees. She watched Cyrus stroking Draven's head, realising he must have somehow placed a compulsion of sorts on him because there was no way the Draven she knew would bow to this fool. It was surreal and odd to watch someone touching what was hers. Aliyah crawled on her hands and knees until she reached Draven and Cyrus.

Peering up into those black eyes, she watched the smile stretch across his pale skin. Cyrus's eyes devoured her from head to toe before he reached out to lift her chin up.

"Oh little one, I can't wait to feel those claws within my flesh. But for now," he laughed, "now you will sleep."

He trailed his hand down her cheek before rubbing his index finger along her bottom plump lip. Aliyah tried to fight his compulsion, to no avail. The calmness settled over her limbs as did every sinful thought she'd ever had. Slowly but surely she succumbed to whatever Purgatory she was about to ensue.

Darkness poured itself within her every cavity. As Aliyah drifted off to the land of perdition, she prayed she had more light than dark, because she was going to need it.

About the Author

Lena Moore

Lena lives in Melbourne, Australia with her husband and three sons. She spends most of her time being a stay-at-home mama, and when not chasing them and doing mama things, she writes, with her husband fully supporting her.

She has been writing since she was 13-years-old and focused mainly on poetry until her Instagram page prompted her to finish her book.

Lena is a metal head when it comes to music and has her qualification in counselling. She loves long romantic walks to the tattoo shop, yoga, reading and writing.

"I try and focus my writing on deep, dark and all things taboo, because, hey, we all have a little darkness lurking."

Thank you for reading *Deceived*. I really hope you have enjoyed Draven and Aliyah's story so far. There's a lot more to come. If you wouldn't mind, I ask you to please take the time and leave an honest review. Your reviews mean the world to indie authors like myself, and they matter.

www.ingramcontent.com/pod-product-compliance
Lightning Source LLC
Chambersburg PA
CBHW022028240626
47154CB00007B/2321